MEN WHO
LOVE MEN

Books by William J. Mann

Novels

THE MEN FROM THE BOYS

THE BIOGRAPH GIRL

WHERE THE BOYS ARE

ALL AMERICAN BOY

MEN WHO LOVE MEN

Nonfiction

WISECRACKER: The Life and Times of William Haines,
Hollywood's First Openly Gay Star

BEHIND THE SCREEN: How Gays and Lesbians Shaped
Hollywood 1910–1969

EDGE OF MIDNIGHT: The Life of John Schlesinger

KATE: The Woman Who Was Hepburn

GAY PRIDE: A Celebration of All Things Gay & Lesbian

MEN WHO LOVE MEN

WILLIAM J. MANN

KENSINGTON BOOKS
http://www.kensingtonbooks.com

KENSINGTON BOOKS are published by

Kensington Publishing Corp.
850 Third Avenue
New York, NY 10022

All Kensington titles, imprints, and distributed lines are available at special quantity discounts for bulk purchases for sales promotion, premiums, fund-raising, educational, or institutional use.

Special book excerpts or customized printings can also be created to fit specific needs. For details, write or phone the office of the Kensington Special Sales Manager: Attn. Special Sales Department. Kensington Publishing Corp., 850 Third Avenue, New York, NY 10022. Phone: 1-800-221-2647.

Kensington and the K logo Reg. U.S. Pat. & TM Off.

Library of Congress Card Catalogue Number: 2006939871
ISBN-13: 978-0-7582-1375-4
ISBN-10: 0-7582-1375-1

First Printing: April 2007
10 9 8 7 6 5 4 3 2 1

Printed in the United States of America

As ever, for Tim

I

TEA DANCE

Eye candy.

That's what these boys are. If my eyes were diabetic they'd be going into insulin shock right now. Look at that one. Tall, dark, copper-skinned, pecs flat and square on his chest. Or that one, with the buzzed head and the lightning bolt inked across his big round shoulders. Or that one over there, with the milk chocolate skin and the eight-pack chiseled into his abdomen. Hell, anybody can have a six-pack these days. Now you've got to have *eight*.

Eye candy. That's exactly what these boys are. I can imagine popping any one of them into my mouth, rolling them around on my tongue like saltwater taffy. Or hazelnut cream. Nothing nutritious about these boys, nothing at all, nothing that will do any lasting good for the heart or the soul. But how delicious any one of them would be at this moment, and how sweet they'd taste on the way down.

Once, I was eye candy myself. Once upon a time, I knew what it was like to be looked at. To be wanted. To be lusted after, pursued, fantasized over—the way I'm fantasizing about these boys now. Once, I was one of the beautiful boys, one of the A-list. Those days seem like a hazy dream to me now, but they were real. They happened. Right here at this very spot, too. And not really so long ago.

"Henry, that boy over there is looking at you."

Reluctantly, I move my eyes away from the milk chocolate abdominals on the man across the deck and focus on my friend Ann Marie, all big blond hair and mascara. She's returned from the bar with martinis for both of us. I take one, bring it to my lips, and taste the alcohol before I look at her again and ask which boy she means.

"That one, over there." Ann Marie gestures with her head, trying not to be obvious. "In the green tank top."

I see which one she means. He's not looking at me now, if he ever was. He's leaning against the railing, oblivious to me and anyone else.

Ann Marie draws in close. "I know you tend to go for more muscley types, Henry, but he's really cute."

Unsaid is that the muscley types don't go for me. Not anymore. And neither is this kid, despite Ann Marie's claims. I look back at him, framed by the startling backdrop of blue harbor, white sky, and scattered sailboats. He is exquisite. Blond hair hanging over his eyes like a schoolboy. Long lashes, perky nose, pouting lips. Lean, tight, with arms that are sinewy rather than pumped, the blessing of youthful muscle that needs no enhancement from a gym.

"He's cute, isn't he?" Ann Marie asks.

I simply close my eyes. "I'm on eye candy overload."

Ann Marie laughs as she takes a sip of her drink. "If he really *were* a piece of candy, what would he be?"

"A lollipop." I open my eyes and take a sip of my drink as I look around the deck. I'm feeling arch, a little brittle, a sensation the alcohol only intensifies. "Ah," I say, "how quickly changes the light."

Ann Marie grins. "Are you going poetic on me, Henry?"

"Summer's almost over," I say, doing my best to sound like Noel Coward. Not that I ever heard Noel Coward speak, but it's what I imagine he must have sounded like. Wry and world weary. "Look around you," I continue. "Once, this deck was filled with light. Now, the earth has turned. Winter isn't far ahead."

"You've been hanging around my brother too long," Ann Marie says. "You're starting to sound like him in one of his melodramatic-writer moments."

"Is there even time left to dance?" I ask, airily.

She looks at her watch. "I think so. Tea goes to seven, and it's only six-twenty." She's taking me literally, as Ann Marie often does. "But the dance floor is pretty crowded."

"It's always been crowded," I tell her. "It was just easier once to make room."

"Oh, Henry."

"That's a candy, too. Now, see that one over there?" I indicate a strapping blond number, shirtless, of course, smooth and shiny. "He's a Three Musketeers. Light. Fluffy. Easy to swallow. Done in a minute." I nod over at a thicker, meaner bald guy with an eagle tat blazing across his back. "Now he's a Snickers. A little harder to chew, but still, in the end, if you're not careful, he will melt all over you." I cast my eyes toward a short, blue-eyed muscle boy with dark hair and an intelligent face. "Beware that one. He's a Butterfinger. You'll never get him out of your mouth."

"He looks like Jeff."

I shrug. "You think?"

"And that one over there looks like Lloyd."

I follow her nod. Indeed, a handsome, green-eyed, goateed buzz cut talks intently with a group of women, a soft downy fuzz covering a perfect V-shaped torso. "Ah yes," I say. "A Hershey's Kiss. The most addictive candy of all."

"You're making me hungry."

I look at her over the rim of my martini. "I've been hungry for a year and a half."

Well, actually only a year and four months and a couple of weeks. Not that I'm counting. Not that I'm thinking about Joey, standing here on this glorious mid-August day, among this throng of delectable eye candy, listening to Kelly Clarkson whine that she even fell for that stupid love song, yeah, yeah, since u been gone. Oh, how Joey had loved Kelly. He followed her right from her humble beginnings and giddily cast his vote for her on the big night. I was a Justin man myself. Until then, I'd thought we were made for each other. We both had been devoted to Kurt Cobain in our youth. We both owned every album put out by every Seattle grunge band that had ever caused teenagers like us to pogo or headbang. Yet by the time our musical tastes had been co-opted by Kelly and Justin, any relationship between us was probably doomed.

"Just like that?" I asked on the night Joey broke up with me. "You're ending our relationship *just like that?*"

"Henry, I fell out of love with you. I don't know how else to explain it."

I was incoherent. "How does one fall *out* of love? Tell me that, *please,* Joey."

Joey was short for "Jomei," a Japanese name that means to spread light and awareness. But that night Joey was offering no such enlightenment. "I don't know how it happens," he told me. "It just did."

In that circus of illogic, I was grasping for some shred of rationality. "All right," I said, attempting to calm myself. "I will grant that maybe it's impossible to stay 'in love' forever—though I *was* hoping maybe it might endure past our ten-month anniversary at least."

"I'm sorry, Henry."

Forget calm. I blew up again. "What I'm trying to say is, this is *natural,* Joey! Don't you see? This is the way it *happens!* Being 'in love' eventually morphs into just 'loving' somebody. That's all this is. It's just a transition for us."

"I don't think so, Henry."

"Look," I said. "I'll accept that you're not 'in love' with me anymore. Fine. I'll deal with that. But you still love me. Right? You *do* still love me?"

Yes, I actually asked him that, and in a voice that sounded even more pathetic in person. I'm not proud of that fact. No more than I am of voting for Justin Guarini on *American Idol.* But I did both things. And in neither case did I get the answer I was hoping for.

Joey said nothing more. He just turned around. Walked out that door. Oh, I know I should've changed that stupid lock, I should've made him leave his key.

But it didn't matter. Not for one second did Joey ever come back to bother me.

"Are you humming something?" Ann Marie asks.

"No."

"You are, *too*," she says. "'I Will Survive.'"

I roll my eyes.

"And you *will*, Henry. You are a *survivor*. Hey, I know about surviving. More men have dumped me than have dumped you."

"Oh yeah? How many?"

"Five."

"Okay, so you beat me by one. Congratulations. You win this round. Rah, rah, let the balloons fall. Let me buy you another drink to mark the occasion."

She smirks. "I think if we play our cards right, we can get someone to buy them *for* us." Her eyebrows rise as she turns slightly, pretending not to notice that the Exquisite Lollipop is making his way through the crowd toward us.

I have to laugh. "You are *so* like your brother."

The kid saunters up, his fingers hooked in the pockets of his low-rise jeans. "Hey," he says, in a deeper-than-expected voice.

"Hey," says Ann Marie, fluttering, tossing back her blond locks. "I was wondering when you'd come over and introduce yourself."

"I'm Luke," he says, offering his hand.

"Well, hello, Luke, I'm Ann Marie," she says, grasping his hand and pumping it like a man, "and this is Henry, who I'm sure is the *real* reason you came over here."

His soft hazel eyes flicker over to me. "Hey," he says.

"Hey."

We shake hands, though I don't pump him like Ann Marie did.

"Where are you from?" Ann Marie asks.

"Well," Luke says—and I try to detect just what kind of accent he has but I can't, just something broad and flat—"last stop was Tucson, but I was thinking of trying a winter here."

"Really? In Provincetown?"

"Yeah."

"No way! *We* live here, too." Ann Marie seems absolutely tickled. "Don't mistake *us* for tourists!"

The boy is looking at me. "Year-rounders, huh?"

"Well," Ann Marie says, "I go back and forth to Boston. I work there during the week. But I'm here every weekend, because my son is here."

He seems surprised. Most people are. Ann Marie is in her mid-thirties. She might be as old as thirty-eight, I've never been sure. But she can pass for twenty-two. Good genes, she says. And, of course, good access to Botox in the city. She works for a dermatologist.

"How old is your son?" Luke asks.

"He's nine, almost ten. His name is J. R. Want to see a picture?"

I've seen this little ritual before. Whenever anyone inquires about her kid, Ann Marie immediately slips her purse off her shoulder, like she's doing now, and starts riffling inside to find her wallet. "Here he is," she says, flipping open to J. R.'s fifth-grade mug shot. All freckles and big blue bug eyes. Not so different from pictures I've seen of his Uncle Jeff from that age.

"Cute kid," Luke says, but I notice he's looking at me again. Could Ann Marie have been right? Is he really cruising me?

It seems unimaginable. I have, this summer, entered into what Jeff calls the "shoulder season" of gay life. It's a term he derived from living here in Provincetown, where the "shoulder season" consists of those few months at the end of summer when the weather is still pleasant enough to pull in some business. Guest-house managers, of which I am one, can still hope for a few knocks on our doors in the shoulder season of September and October. If it's not quite the thrumming vitality of summer, it's still something to keep us going for a while longer. Now, to apply Jeff's analogy, let us consider that the season ends for gay men sometime around the age of thirty—maybe thirty-one, if you're lucky. I myself, refusing to go gracefully, hung on for still another year after that. But now I'm thirty-three, and at long last the crow's feet and receding hairline have forced me to accept without further struggle my inevitable entry into the "shoulder season" of gay life. It's by no means retirement, but you can't expect the business you got at peak.

On the other hand, this young man standing in front of me has a long, long way to go before he hits his own personal September. Early twenties, I suspect. Twenty-three, tops. Now I don't normally go for twinkies. Ann Marie's right. I like the muscley ones, and unless a boy has been pumping iron since high school, it's unlikely he'll have the bulk and hardness that I find so fetching. But this boy, this Luke, is looking at me with those big hazel eyes of his and for some reason I can't quite look away. He *is* cruising me. The first to do so in quite a while. It is, quite unexpectedly, exhilarating.

"Do you want to dance?" he asks.

I don't know how to respond. I turn rather helplessly to Ann Marie.

"You boys go ahead," she says, pleased that I seem to be hooking up at last. "I should be getting home anyway. I've got to get J. R. his dinner. And later we're going to the drive-in movies in Wellfleet."

"You sure?" I ask her.

"Absolutely," she says, kissing me. "Nice to meet you, Luke. You boys have a good time!" She winks at him. He winks back.

My dick gets hard in my cutoff camouflage pants.

And so—we dance. We don't speak. We just shoulder our way onto the tiny dance floor and begin to shuffle our feet. It's about all one can do, it's so crowded out here. I notice the looks being shot Luke's way by other shoulder-season guys, especially when he reaches down and peels his shirt off. I try not to stare but I find myself mesmerized by his taut hard stomach. Little beads of sweat leave shimmering trails down the smooth brown flat plain. A ghost of his tan line peeks out from above his low-cut jeans, making me yearn—ache—to see the rest of it.

I catch him smiling at me. He reaches over, attempts to pull my T-shirt up, but I resist, shielding my torso with my arms. Once upon a time, my shirt would have come off as soon as I entered this place, and all other places like it. Once, I lost so many T-shirts in so many different clubs that I'd have to pack at least five extra ones whenever Jeff and I headed out to yet another party. But now my shirt stays on. Henry Weiner had such a short time at center stage, so few brilliant years, that I won't do anything that might tarnish his memory. The love handles jiggling under my shirt will not be exposed for the world to see. Let people keep their memories of Henry intact.

Or perhaps it's just me who remembers him at all.

Luke motions for me to follow him. I'm glad to leave the dance floor. I'm not at home there the way I once was. These days, I'm happier on the sidelines. For a moment, I lose sight of him, and I feel a tinge of panic. But then I spot him, pushing through the crowd with an agility I find impressive. The sea parts for boys like him, as I'm left to battle my way forward on my own.

Once outside in the sharp salty sea air, Luke turns abruptly to face me.

"So," I say awkwardly, "will you be looking for work here?"

He doesn't answer. He's suddenly in my face, his lips on mine, hot, wet, slippery. He kisses me. Oh, *man*, does he kiss me. But I don't kiss him back. I'm too stunned to do anything but stand here, allowing myself to be invaded by his tongue.

He pulls back, the suction of our lips actually popping when we break contact.

"Wow," I say.

He's looking at me again from under his long thick boylashes. Ecstasy? Maybe. Tina? Quite possibly. But then I dismiss the idea. Luke's eyes don't have the typical hardness of tweakers. "You want to get out of here?" he asks.

"I—I—well, it depends on where you want to go."

"Upstairs. To my room."

Thank God he has a room. I couldn't take him back to the guesthouse that I manage with Lloyd. Too many guests hanging around, plus Jeff would probably be there and he'd want to meet him, and then—well, let's just say it's never been a good idea to introduce my tricks to Jeff. They rarely remain my tricks when that happens. Besides, Ann Marie and J. R. would be out in the backyard grilling tofu burgers on the barbeque . . . no, it just wouldn't do.

So I let Luke take my hand and lead me out of Tea Dance and up the wooden steps to the bank of motel rooms that overlooks the pool. He fumbles for a key and lets us in. The room is dark, the drapes pulled. It's chilly, smelling of air-conditioning and cig-arettes. I don't get much of a chance to look around because sud-denly Luke is pushing me down on the bed. Literally. His hands on my chest, shoving me backward. I topple over, flopping down onto my back across the shiny bedspread. Then he's on top of me, kissing me again. This time I manage to kiss him back.

We pull at each other's clothes. His shirt is already off, so all I need concern myself with are his jeans. They slip off easily. He's not wearing any underwear, just a seven-inch boner that's already engorged and raging. After all, he's twenty-three.

He finally gets my shirt off. Looking down, he seems pleased enough by what he sees. He slaps my pecs with his palms and grins widely. Then he turns his attention to my shorts and briefs. My own dick is plump with excitement but not yet at full attention. After all, I'm *thirty*-three.

"Nice tat," Luke says, fingering the starburst around my navel.

"Thanks," I say, in a husky, unsure voice.

Luke drops down on top of me again. "Henry," he says, lips pressed against my ear. "I want to put sliced peaches on your chest and lick them off you."

Now, there is just no answer for a statement like that. I don't even try.

He's off me once more, jumping like a naked bunny in the half-light, popping open the small refrigerator against the far wall. I hear the snap of a Tupperware lid. Then, not expecting it, I feel the coldness of the peaches on my chest. I gasp. Luke pays no mind, rubbing the fruit into my skin with the balls of his palms. My nipples perk up immediately at his touch and the coldness of the peaches. My nipples are quite sensitive: it's like they're little dicks. Luke senses this, leaning down to lick them. I shudder in pleasure. Then his tongue travels up to the hollow spot under my Adam's apple, where some of the peach syrup has gathered. He laps at it like a kitten.

Is this really happening? We make eye contact, Luke and I. Such soul-filled eyes gaze at me from under those long lashes. I make a sound, close my eyes, and roll back my head. His tongue is incredibly nimble, darting down between my pecs, licking up the peaches, teasing my nipples. I can sense that my dick has finally responded fully. Next thing I know he's on it, giving me the best peaches and syrup blow job I've ever had.

I pull him up to me. I don't want to cum. Not yet. He lies on top of me, our torsos sticking together from the syrup.

"Damn," I say, and kiss him.

And then, in that moment, Henry Weiner comes back.

I flip Luke over, pinning his arms against the pillows with my hands. My mouth moves down to conquer his ears, his neck. It's

Luke's turn now to squirm in pleasure. I continue licking and kissing along his smooth torso, his skin so tight, so flat, so young. I make love to him with a passion that's been too long bottled up, that bursts out of me like champagne released on New Year's Eve. I move down his legs, making him tremble when I lick the inside of his thighs. I take first one foot then the other and massage them with my tongue.

No more thoughts—no more conscious ideas. I'm inside him now, the bed is squeaking, I'm pumping and pushing and he's moaning and crying and everything is tingly and sparkly and who the fuck knows what time it is.

Or where I am.

Or who this boy under me is.

Silence.

Blackness.

"Henry."

A voice from somewhere.

I open my eyes.

I'm collapsed on top of Luke, breathing deeply in and out.

"Henry, *dude*," he says under me. "That was fucking awesome."

I pull up slightly, looking down at him. Our skin still sticks together. Cum and peach syrup.

"Man," Luke says, "how'd you get so *good?*"

I smile. "Age has *some* advantages."

"Man, you were rockin'."

I slide off him. The boy sits up, reaching over to a side table to light a cigarette. I don't like cigarettes, but say nothing. It's his room.

"Actually," I tell him, "I was a professional."

Luke gives me a quizzical look, blowing smoke over his shoulder.

"I was an escort," I explain.

"Cool," he says. "For how long?"

"A year or so. Then for a while after that I was kind of a quasi-prostie, billing myself as a 'sacred sex' bodyworker."

Luke grins. "In other words, you rubbed their shoulders and then jacked them off."

I roll over flat onto my back, looking up at the ceiling. "Sometimes it was a lot more than that. It was all about reaching spiritual catharsis through physical sensation."

"Sounds hot," he says, nestling up beside me.

"It was."

"Well," he says, running his hand down over my slimy pecs and stomach, "you sure have the body for it."

For the first time since my orgasm I'm conscious of my body. I roll over onto my side, pull my legs up a bit. The kid just complimented me, but I don't think he meant it. He was just being kind.

"I *used* to have an awesome body," I tell him.

"You still do. Great pecs, great arms . . ."

"No, no, I used to be really in great shape. What's weird is that for most of my life I was just this scrawny kid . . ."

I stop. I don't want him to think I mean like him. He's nothing like I used to be. He's beautiful. Tight. Lean. I was—well—I was *scrawny*. No other word for it.

"I didn't have the ease with my body that you do," I tell him. "I didn't carry myself the same way. You're *hot*. I was just—scrawny."

He's not buying it, I can tell. Doesn't matter. I know it's true.

"Anyway," I say, "then I started working out and suddenly I had this body that guys were willing to pay to have sex with. It was—well, a really heady time."

"I imagine," he says, exhaling smoke.

"But nothing lasts forever. You try to keep up, you try to continue going to the gym with the same devotion. But things start happening. You get busy. You get pulled in a million directions." I pause. "You get old. You get tired. You get fat."

Luke barks out a laugh. "You are *not* using those words to describe yourself, are you, Henry?"

"I just mean that—I'm not in the shape I was five years ago. The bodyworking is finished. My other job got pretty demanding and that takes up most of my time now."

"You mean the guesthouse?"

"Yeah, it's really—" I stop, and look over at him closely. "I never told you I manage a guesthouse."

Luke grins, cuddling up next to me again. "I have a confession to make. I saw you there the other day. What's it called? Nirvana? Anyway, I was thinking of getting a room there, but you had no vacancy. But I thought you were hot, and so when I saw you today I had to make a move."

It's another statement for which there is no answer. At least none that I can think of at the moment. I just look at this boy, this beautiful boy, next to me. *He thinks I'm hot.* He smiles, reaches across the bed and stubs out his cigarette, and leans in to kiss me again. Ignoring the acrid taste of tobacco, I kiss him back.

"I gotta pee," Luke says, breaking gently free.

He stands and heads into the bathroom. In seconds, he's back in the doorway, tossing me a handtowel. I catch it. It's wet. "You might want to get that peach juice off yourself," he says.

I laugh. "Thanks."

Wiping my torso, I can hear his loud stream of piss hitting the porcelain.

"So what made you decide on spending the winter in Province-town?" I call into him.

"Just thought it was a good place to find myself, know what I mean?"

I just grunt in reply. People have lots of romantic notions about Provincetown off-season, but I've lived through some of those bleak winters, when everything closes up and most of the residents who are left are either drunks or twelve-steppers. Very few in-between. "Well," I say, wiping up the last of the cum and the syrup, "you ought to come out to the guesthouse. Maybe I can find you a room."

"Really? That would be awesome!"

"Sure, after Labor Day the crowds die down and then—"

My eyes catch the corner of a book sticking out from under the bed.

A book that seems familiar.

"And then what?" Luke calls.

"And then—well, maybe we can—get you something more per-manent than—" I can't resist. I reach down and pull the book out from under the bed. I look at the cover.

It's what I thought.

The Boys of Summer.

By Jeffrey O'Brien.

I slide the book back under the bed as Luke flushes and heads back into the room to flop down beside me again.

I turn and give him a tight smile.

"That would be great," he says. "To get a room at Nirvana . . . I could help out, do chores, that kind of shit."

"Well," I tell him, "I don't know for sure if we'll have any rooms . . . I'd have to check with the owner. I'm just the manager . . ."

"Mm, so handsome," Luke says, ignoring me as he kisses me, his mouth minty fresh. He must've gargled with Listerine in there. "You are such a stud muffin, Henry."

I pull back, gently. That damn book has made me even more defensive than I was before.

"So." I'm trying to get a hold on Luke's eyes, but he's averting them. "Enough about me. Tell me about you. What romantic notions have you heard about living here at the end of the earth?"

He shrugs. "Nothing really. I don't know anyone here."

I can feel my lips hardening, tightening. "Gets pretty isolating in February and March, you know."

"That's what I want."

I raise an eyebrow. "You *want* to be isolated from the rest of the world?"

"Well," Luke says, finally meeting my eyes, "I'm a writer. Or I want to be one. I think living here in the winter would help me concentrate."

His answer seems to suddenly make sense of a lot of things. I move back against the pillows, steadily inching away from him.

"A writer. Interesting." I pull my knees up to my chest. "And what is it that you write?"

"I'm working on a novel."

Suddenly I want to shower. I want to get away from this kid and stand under a scalding hot stream of water and wash all this stickiness off me, in a way no puny moistened hand towel could ever accomplish.

Luke, meanwhile, is busy rhapsodizing. "I've had this dream of coming to Provincetown and finishing my novel for over a year now," he's saying. "I just want to let my creativity flow. Release all the energy inside me. I just want to hunker down somewhere and write to my heart's content."

"You'll need some kind of job," I say, aware of the new hardness in my voice. "Unless you're independently wealthy."

He laughs. "No, I'm not. I figure I could get something. Maybe trade a room at your guesthouse for—"

"You know, I may have spoken too soon about that," I tell him, cutting him off.

He seems not to notice my change in attitude. "Well, then, some other guesthouse. Or I'll just get a little cheap apartment somewhere . . ."

I laugh. My voice has moved past hard to brittle. "Cheap little apartment? Shows how much you know about this place. You can't just roll into Provincetown anymore and get a job and a place to live. There are very few year-round affordable rental properties." I try to smile to tone down my obvious cynicism. "I don't mean to discourage you, but that's the reality."

Luke returns my smile, and for some reason, I don't like it. His is the arrogant smile of youth, a cocky *I-can-do-anything* grin. "I'll find a way," he tells me.

I imagine he will. All he has to do is lift that shirt up again the way he did on the dance floor and he'll get anything he wants.

"I really want the experience of living here," Luke is saying, filled with passion. "I've wanted to ever since—"

I narrow my eyes at him. "Ever since you read *The Boys of Summer*?"

He looks surprised. Now it's my turn for a little confession. "I saw the book under your bed."

Luke smiles again, and again I don't like it. "Have you read it?" he asks.

I nod.

"Do you think it's a good portrait of this place?" he asks me.

"Well, the author lives here."

"I know."

Our eyes hold. Of *course* he knows. Of course. That's why he's here. That's why *I'm* here, covered in slimy peach juice. That's why Luke cruised me at Tea in the first place.

So he could meet Jeff.

Story of my life. How many guys have approached me on the dance floor and asked me if I'd introduce them to my friend Jeff, who they find "just so fucking hot"? And ever since Jeff wrote the most popular gay novel of three summers ago, it's gotten worse.

Everybody's always trying to meet him. He's written two more books since—he's like a fucking book-writing machine—but *Boys of Summer* is still the one everyone talks about.

The afternoon's events are now much clearer in my mind. Luke is a fan of Jeff's. He probably came by the guesthouse looking for him. Jeff's readers often do, wanting him to sign their books. It's common knowledge that Jeff's lover Lloyd Griffith owns Nirvana Guesthouse in Provincetown. Jeff's talked about the place in several interviews. Even if somehow Luke *didn't* know, as soon as he got here anyone could have told him, and also explained that Jeff and Lloyd live in the house adjacent to Nirvana. And that, working as manager and living above the guesthouse in a little apartment, is none other than yours truly, Henry Weiner—the "stud muffin" Luke so conveniently found so hot and handsome.

Goddamn it. How could I have been so gullible? The kid's game plan is obvious to me now: cruise me, eat peaches off my chest, and presto. An invitation to meet Jeff O'Brien. Story of my fucking life.

"I suppose," I say, drawing out a very long breath, "you'd like to meet Jeff."

"Sure. Do you know him?"

I hold eye contact with him. If he's playing games, he's very good. There's no deceit in his eyes. There's just a reflection of my own.

"Yes," I say. "Jeff is my best friend."

"Really? Well, sure, I'd love to meet him." He snuggles up to me, nuzzling me with the tip of his nose. "Maybe we can hang out again sometime, Henry."

I should get out of here now. He wants Jeff, not me. Just like Joey wanted the blond goy instead of me. Just like, before Joey, *Daniel* had wanted someone else, and before Daniel, *Shane* had told me it was over, and before Shane, *Lloyd* had looked me in the eye and told me he could never love anyone the way he loves Jeff. *Jeff*—who it always seems to come back to.

Jeff—my best friend. Who's had a lover now for more than sixteen years, not to mention numerous part-time boyfriends all along the way—while I, thirty-three and in the shoulder season of my life, have never managed to hold onto a relationship for even a year. There are times I ask myself: is this it? Will I never have a boyfriend? I know guys who never have, who at forty, fifty—*sixty!*—look back and sigh, lamenting that they never found Mr. Right. It terrifies me. Am I one of those people destined never to find a lover? Time keeps ticking, and I'm still alone.

"Well?"

I blink. Who is this boy sitting in front of me, peering up at me again from under those damn long lashes?

I thought you were hot, and so when I saw you today I had to make a move.

I want so much to believe him. I want so much to believe he's telling me the truth.

"Well what?" I ask.

"Can we hang out again sometime?"

"Yeah," I say. "I guess so."

"Excellent."

Why don't I just tell him it's over? I should just thank him for the hot sex and then get the hell out of here. Why am I keeping this charade going on any further?

But then I look over at Luke lighting another cigarette. He glances back at me again with those eyes.

"Here," Luke says, tossing me one of his clean T-shirts. "I dribbled peach juice all over yours."

I pull his shirt on over my head.

"We might have time for one more dance downstairs," he says.

"No, thanks," I respond. "I've got to get back to the guest-house. I'm supposed to meet somebody there."

"Okay." He blows smoke over his shoulder. "But can I call you sometime?"

"Sure." I give him my number, which he punches into his cell. Then I make my way outside, back into the daylight.

Luke follows. After he closes the door behind us and we're heading back down the stairs, I realize I never grabbed my slimy T-shirt off the floor.

I wonder if it's one more that I'm going to lose.

2

ABOVE THE NIRVANA
GUESTHOUSE

Back home, I pop open the refrigerator door and stare inside, contemplating dinner. There's one thing, at least, that I can be grateful for.

There will be no more green peppers in the tuna fish.

I don't like green peppers. Or peppers of any color for that matter. Why anyone would want to put green peppers in tuna salad is beyond my comprehension. But Joey did, and when Joey made my lunch I always had to pick them out or swallow them whole with my milk.

Now that I'm alone, I make my own meals. Every single one of them. And most of the time, I eat them alone, too.

I remove a bowl of tuna salad—pepper free—and start picking at it with a spoon. Alice in Chains' *Dirt* is playing on my stereo. A paean to isolation, in my opinion, and therefore rather fitting for my mood.

Outside, below my window, I hear a gaggle of boys heading back to their guesthouses after Tea Dance. Cautiously, I peer down at them. They're a little drunk—or tweaked—or maybe just high on life, laughing in that way only gay boys can laugh when they're together in their little posses. Testosterone-driven girlishness, if such a thing is possible. Their laughter is high-pitched, grating and giddy, but aggressive and sensual, too, their eyes bouncing off passersby like rubber balls. One of the boys, a shirtless dark

Latino with a goatee and abs for days, catches sight of me eating my tuna fish at the window. I look away quickly, letting the curtain fall back in front of me.

I lied to Luke. No one was waiting here for me to meet. No one but my bowl of tuna salad—which will serve as my dinner this Saturday night, when most everyone else in Provincetown is heading out to fabulous meals at fabulous restaurants looking absolutely fabulous. As for me, I'm happy to be able to call it an early night— one of the benefits of tricking in the afternoon. I'm able to curl up on the couch and watch *Leave it to Beaver* and *Bewitched* on TV Land.

The problem with such early evening hibernation, however, is the sun. If only it would get dark, I could pretend it was just a Tuesday night in March, a night when you can go to bed early and alone without feeling you're missing out on the party. But here it is, the hands on the clock already passing eight, and the sky remains defiantly bright. I can't escape the fact that the night is young, very young. But not for me.

There was a time, and not so long ago, that I'd be out there with those boys, laughing in that same high-pitched way, ogling passersby and gearing up for adventures to come. But ever since Joey left, I just haven't had the drive, the spunk, to get out there and play the game. Neither have I had the body. Already I'm thinking about that half-eaten carton of Chunky Monkey ice cream in the freezer, the tuna salad quickly losing whatever minimal appeal it may have had. That's how I'll spend my night, eating ice cream and mouthing along as Endora casts campy spells on *Bewitched*.

Alone.

All my friends tell me I'm so young and that being alone for a while after a breakup isn't fatal. It might even be a good thing, they say. But they don't understand that just when you think you'll never have to be alone again, and then suddenly you are, no amount of reason can blunt the shock of seeing one toothbrush in the bathroom.

But it's the middle of the night that's the worst part. Those moments when I wake up at four a.m. and wonder in the stillness what it is that's wrong. And then it hits me.

Joey's gone.

Fuck, they're *all* gone. Joey and Daniel and Shane—and though Lloyd might be right downstairs, he's gone, too.

Every time I have fallen in love, I've been convinced it would last forever. That this would be the man with whom I'd buy a house, make out a will, take my last breath. We'd die just minutes apart, holding hands in the same bed. How romantic would that be? And of course, we'd be buried side by side. HERE LIES HENRY WEINER AND HIS HUSBAND, THEIR HEARTS UNITED TOGETHER FOREVER.

Forever. It's a fascinating concept. What's forever for me, of course, would only be a heartbeat for the Galapagos land tortoise, which the Discovery Channel has taught me can live up to two hundred years. Given the number of boyfriends I've already had in my thirty-three years upon this planet, I must say I'm glad humans don't have the lifespans of tortoises. There's no way I could keep getting my hopes up for another sixteen decades only to watch them get dashed over and over and over again.

And yet, for a very brief time, I wasn't alone.

Why has my short time with Joey become so imbued with the rosy romantic glow of nostalgia? I remember with such longing the day we met at Tea Dance, the euphoria after the first time we made love, the sense of future and forever in the air. When things started getting serious between Joey and me, I moved into his apartment on Commercial Street. I needed some space away from the guesthouse. I'm the manager here, after all, Lloyd's right-hand man—and Joey knew that for a while, a brief and crazy time, I'd fancied myself in love with Lloyd. Obviously it wouldn't do to go on living here, so instead, I moved in into Joey's cramped little two-room apartment over a seafood restaurant in the center of town.

Yet no matter its limitations, I adored living at Joey's place. The harbor, sunkissed and blue, was always sparkling outside our window, and I found I actually *liked* picking up Joey's socks and underwear from the floor and depositing them in the hamper. I *liked* doing things for him. His laundry. His ironing and vacuuming.

But there was one thing Joey didn't like about me. My dog. Back then, I had a little pug named Clara. She was so ugly she was adorable. She belonged first to my friend Brent, and I took her in after Brent died. But Joey didn't like dogs, and didn't want a dog running around his apartment, so I gave Clara away to a couple of lesbians who promised her a good home. It's a decision I've never stopped feeling guilty about. I chose Joey over Clara. A boy I'd known for only a little over a month instead of my faithful companion of several years. I'm sure the lesbians made good on their promise to provide well for her, but a day hasn't gone by when I don't regret giving up Clara.

And what made it worse, of course, was that soon Joey was gone too. I'll never forget the night it ended. I was making dinner. Joey entered sullenly, his jacket over his shoulder, tie askew, briefcase in hand. He'd been hired by a real estate company in town, and should have been a dazzling success. The market in Provincetown was at its hottest during that time, and Joey had big dreams. Yet so far he hadn't even sold a single condo. Everyone else around him was raking in the cash, but Joey kept coming up short.

Looking at him that night, I could see it had been a particularly disappointing day. I waited for the kiss, for the little nuzzle of his nose on my cheek to which I'd grown accustomed. But nothing came. Joey went straight to the bathroom to take a shower.

In the living room, I set up two folding TV trays and lit a candle. Joey came in, towel drying his hair, the smell of Ivory soap lingering around his body. His straight black Asian hair, electrified, fell into his eyes. He flipped on the television.

"Just for the news, okay?" he asked, seeming to want to keep conversation at a minimum. I nodded.

We talked little during dinner. Afterward, Joey washed the dishes. Usually if I cooked, he cleaned up. This time, I helped, scraping the plates.

Then we settled down to watch *Jeopardy*. It was just like any night. After the show was over, I expected that we'd have sex, and then maybe head out to the Wave bar to see who was around. Maybe we'd have a cocktail. Or maybe two, given Joey's mood. But before the game show ended, Joey suddenly flicked off the set with the remote control. The abrupt silence in the room choked me. My toes curled up in my sneakers.

"I can't go on," he said, and I knew instantly what he meant. He didn't mean his job, he didn't mean this place, he didn't mean anything but me—he couldn't go on with *me*. It was as if, the whole time we'd been together, I'd just been waiting for this moment. It always came. It was inevitable.

Still, I tried to reason my way out of it. "Shouldn't this be something we decide together?" I asked. In my first reaction to Joey's decision, I was calm, rational, mature.

But all Joey did was shake his head and tell me he had fallen out of love with me, the cruelest phrase in the universe.

"So," I said, my rationality beginning to crumble, "you want me just to pack my things and go?"

"You can stay here if you want," he said, his eyes closed against me. "For tonight."

He headed off to bed. I watched him walk down the hall. Then I placed myself stubbornly in front of the television set, snapping it back to life, refusing to turn it off until the early hours of the morning. It was as if by keeping the night going I could keep the relationship from ending. When I finally gave up and joined Joey in the bedroom, his eyes were closed, but his breathing didn't have the usual rhythm of sleep.

Crawling into bed next to him, as I'd done so many times before, I knew I'd never fall asleep that night. I just lay there, feeling his warmth and watching the changing moonlight on the ceiling. I dreaded the sun, because then it would be over. All of this—our time together—over. When the first slivers of orange slipped between the Venetian blinds, making horrible stripes across the bed, I wanted to run outside, like a cartoon I'd once seen, and push the sun back down behind the horizon like a basketball.

Without a word, Joey got up. I reached over and pressed his pillow against my face, savoring his smell. I thought maybe that I'd just get up as usual, grind the coffee beans, bring in the paper, pour our juices. I'd pretend he never said what he did. Let him *throw* me out! But instead I rose, scuffed over to the closet, and gathered a few shirts and a pair of pants.

Joey cried only once. I stood in front of him, slowly removing his keys from my key ring. One by one I handed them to him. The apartment key, the downstairs door key, the laundry room key. When he had them all, he began to sob. I walked out.

For a moment, I was afraid I'd handed him my car key, but then I found it, still safely on the ring. The ignition started my tears again, and I drove back here, to Nirvana, and let myself in. I expected Lloyd, but I found Jeff, and I made sure I'd dried my eyes when he saw me. Still, I never could fool Jeff.

"What's wrong, Henry?" he asked.

I told him it was over with Joey. His face wrinkled in compassion for me.

"Are most of your things still back there?" Jeff asked.

"My whole *life* is still back there," I told him.

He scolded me for being melodramatic. But still he wrapped his arms around me, and I was grateful for them.

And so I moved back in above the guesthouse. When I found one of Clara's toys under the refrigerator, I sobbed for two days.

I should have known I'd end up back here.

It's where I always end up.

Back with Jeff and Lloyd.

When I lived in Boston, some of the guys in the clubs would call me "Henry O'Brien," because they didn't know my real last name and because, after all, I was just an appendage to the popular Jeff O'Brien, traipsing along behind him on the dance floor, always to be spotted somewhere hovering in his backlight. Here in Provincetown, some of the townies even today know me only as "Henry, Lloyd's manager," because, after all, that's who I am here, the manager of Lloyd Griffith's popular guesthouse.

Without Joey, Henry Weiner exists only in reference to Jeff or Lloyd.

The siren song of the Chunky Monkey in the freezer finally wins out. Without even thinking about it, I'm lured over to the refrigerator, and it's with the first spoonful into my mouth that Jeff catches me. He barges into my apartment without knocking.

"What are you, *Kramer?*" I ask, annoyed. "What if I was in here with a trick?"

"From the looks of it, your only tricks tonight are named Ben and Jerry." Jeff's all smiles, as if he has good news. "I thought you were trying to lose weight."

I toss the ice cream into the sink. It was getting crystallized anyway. "For your information, bucko," I tell Jeff, still a little pissed, "I already tricked today. A very hot boy I met at Tea Dance. Ask your sister. She saw him."

"Yeah, yeah, she told me. Good for you. But come downstairs, okay? Lloyd and I have been waiting for you to get back. We have something to tell you."

I look over at him. What is it about Jeff O'Brien? He's forty now, maybe even forty-one—he's always been cagey about his age—but people still sometimes think he's younger than I am. That's because, unlike mine, Jeff's hair hasn't started to recede. Nor does any fleshy excess mar Jeff's middle. He maintains the same strict gym routine we both kept during our days on the circuit. Of course, Jeff has always known a few shortcuts to looking good. He buys his T-shirts one size too small and has his jeans taken up in the seat to make his butt look more perky. And I suspect an occasional injection of Botox from Ann Marie's dermatologist boss might explain why Jeff's forehead is still as smooth as a nineteen-year-old's. He argues that he keeps up appearances simply because a hot author pic sells books. Who am I to question success? Certainly I'm no expert at it.

I think again about Luke, and the copy of Jeff's book under his bed. I decide against telling him.

"What's the big news?" I ask.

Jeff winks at me. "We'll tell you when you come down."

He's back out the door. I can hear his steps on the staircase, fast and happy. He's probably signed another book contract. Good for him. The bounty never ends for Jeff O'Brien.

I turn to the sink to rinse the ice cream down the drain when my cell phone rings. The caller ID shows a wireless number with an area code I don't recognize. Normally I just let calls I don't recognize go to voice-mail—but for some reason I answer this one.

"Henry?" comes the voice at the other end.

"Yeah."

"Hey, it's Luke."

"No way," I say, smiling despite myself, my words ahead of my brain. "I was just thinking of—"

Bad. Very bad. Never admit right off that you were thinking of somebody. I learned that much from Jeff. Play aloof. Make them do the work.

Luke seems pleased. "Of me? Really? You were thinking of me?"

"Well," I explain, "of my shirt. I left my shirt in your room."

He laughs. "Isn't the fact that you're wearing mine an even exchange?"

"It's not really a big deal—"

"We can make the switch tomorrow." I can hear Luke blowing smoke from his cigarette. "I was thinking maybe we could hang out."

So you can meet Jeff. "Well," I say, regaining my stride, "tomorrow's kind of busy for me . . ."

"I really enjoyed meeting you, Henry. Can I call you in the morning?"

"Like I said, tomorrow is kind of busy . . ."

"But can I just call and see if things lighten up for you? I'd really like to see you again, Henry. Maybe we can just, you know, get together for a little while?"

This is one pushy kid. I should just say no, end it right here. But instead I say, "Yeah, okay. Call me tomorrow afternoon."

"Awesome. Talk to you tomorrow, Henry." And he hangs up.

I smirk. By tomorrow Luke will have met someone else, probably some hot boy closer to his own age, either on the dance floor at the A House or on the steps of Spiritus Pizza, and he'll have forgotten all about me.

Unless, of course, he still wants to meet Jeff badly enough.

"*Henry!*" Jeff hollers up the stairs. "Are you *coming?*"

I head down. "I had a call," I tell him as I enter the guesthouse's common area. "This may be hard for you to accept, Jeff, but I *do* have a life of my own. Sometimes your beck and call has to wait."

Jeff just smirks. "Oh, Lloyd, our boy is feeling rebellious tonight."

"We do appreciate you coming down, Henry," Lloyd says from the bar. He comes around from behind, carrying a bottle of champagne and three glasses.

"Well," I say, "I guess this really *is* a celebration. What's the big news?"

"Don't rush things," Jeff says, settling himself onto the couch and propping his feet up on the coffee table. "We need the proper mood."

Lloyd sets the bottle and the glasses down and softens the light. I sit in a chair opposite Jeff, wondering what this is all about. It's more than just a book deal. It concerns Lloyd, too. I watch him move across the room to the front desk, where he turns off the ringer on the phone. Lloyd might not be as put together as Jeff, but he still looks damn good for his fourth decade as well. Buzzed head, a sexy soul patch of hair below his lower lip, a tattoo of a dragonfly on his well-rounded shoulder. He's wearing a white ribbed tank top and low-rise jeans, and for a moment my mind flickers back to sex with him, as those green eyes hovered above me, those lips softly touching mine . . .

"Okay," Lloyd says, breaking my reverie as he plops down on the couch next to Jeff, putting his arm around his lover's shoulders. "You want to tell him or should I?"

"Tell me what?" I ask, sitting forward, finding myself getting anxious, despite the happy grins and the bottle of champagne waiting to be opened.

Jeff holds my eyes. "We're getting married," he says.

I look from him over to Lloyd.

"The middle of next month," Lloyd adds.

"I know it's not far away," Jeff says, "but we want it to coincide with the anniversary of the day we met."

"So we can keep the same anniversary," Lloyd says.

"And Henry," Jeff says. "We want you to be our best man."

The words haven't fully penetrated my mind. "Married," I say.

"Yeah, one hundred percent legal," Jeff exults. "After sixteen years I'm finally gonna make an honest man out of him."

They giggle like schoolgirls.

"Married," I say again.

"Well, what do you think?" Lloyd asks.

"Well," I say, unsure of my thoughts, "I didn't think marriage was something you'd be interested in." Years of political pontificating from Jeff and Lloyd come flooding back to me, their endless rant against the status quo. "I mean, marriage is a failed heterosexual institution, isn't it? You've both called it that."

"Sure it is," Jeff says, "but maybe we homos can improve on the formula." He's beaming like a jack o'lantern.

"But," I say, feeling the need to somehow challenge them, "you both have always rejected the whole marriage thing. I mean, when have you guys ever been monogamous?"

"Why does monogamy have to go part and parcel with marriage?" Lloyd asks. "That's part of how we can improve on the formula. After all, haven't Jeff and I shown, after sixteen years, that you can have a lasting commitment without being monogamous?"

"Oh, come on," I say, surprised at how antagonistic I'm feeling. But I can't help myself. "You guys haven't been together for sixteen years. Not really. You've had your share of ups and downs. There have been big chunks of time when you've been apart, when you haven't known how to define yourselves. I know. I was *there*."

"That's why we want you as our best man, Henry," Lloyd says simply. "We've been through a lot together. You know us better than anyone."

The smile has faded from Jeff's face. I can tell he's annoyed that I'm not jumping for joy. Indeed, I'm surprised myself. Why am I being such a *putz*? Why am I not thrilled? Why am I not throwing my arms around the two of them, congratulating them? Jeff and Lloyd are my best friends!

"Henry," Jeff says, talking to me patiently, as if he were addressing a child, "what marriage offers Lloyd and me is a public acknowledgement of our relationship. After all, I had to show up for three—count 'em—*three* of my brother's weddings, even though each one of them was a disaster and everyone knew it from the start. Now he can show up for mine—which, by the way, has lasted longer than all three of his put together."

I make a face. "So *that's* why you're getting married? To get even with your family? To force some kind of acknowledgement from them?"

Jeff holds my gaze. "That's one reason, yes. That's the reason anyone gets married. So that the world can see and recognize and affirm their relationship. Finally the state is giving gay people that same opportunity."

"Henry," Lloyd asks, "are you not happy for us?"

"Well, of course I'm happy for you," I manage to say. "Don't get me wrong."

"It sure doesn't seem that way," Jeff says, clearly peeved. "Maybe we ought to skip the champagne."

"No, we're not skipping the champagne," Lloyd says. "I'm going to pop the cork as soon as Henry gives us his answer."

I frown. "My answer to what?"

"Maybe you didn't hear me." Lloyd smiles kindly and finds my eyes. "We're asking you to be our best man."

Once, years ago, during one of those in-between, questioning periods for Jeff and Lloyd, I had allowed myself to imagine Lloyd asking me a very different question. I had imagined him asking *me* to marry him, or at least to join him in a committed relationship. Of course, it was folly, and deep down, I knew it. Jeff was always the one Lloyd loved. But still I allowed myself, however briefly, to dream. And now, instead of asking me to marry him, Lloyd was asking me to be his best man.

I gaze into his eyes, then look over at Jeff, who's looking back at me.

"You are hopelessly enmeshed with those two," Joey once told me. "You *want* Lloyd and you want to *be* Jeff."

I shrugged him off, but an earlier boyfriend, Shane, had once made a very similar statement. "Henry," Shane had said, handing me back my keys in a manner not so different from the way I'd later hand Joey his, "you won't be able to really love anyone until you learn to love yourself."

I had sighed. "Please, Shane. Can we end this without psychoanalysis?"

"No, we can't," Shane insisted, in the way only Shane could insist. "The problem is that you are always defining yourself against either Jeff or Lloyd, and in your estimation, you always come up short."

Shane was smart. Of all my boyfriends, he probably knew me best. He saw through everything. He'd met me, in fact, on the dance floor with Jeff, and saw up close and personal my early infatuation with him. That I once worshipped Jeff and everything about him was obvious. Just by asking me to dance one night, Jeff O'Brien had changed my life. I'd been a skinny computer geek in my early twenties who'd always watched Jeff from afar, and when one night he'd looked over and extended his hand to me, I couldn't believe my luck. Jeff O'Brien—he of the blue eyes and six-pack and bubble butt—was asking me to dance.

And though we never had sex, Jeff dubbed me his "sister" and took me under his wing. Henry Weiner only really came alive under Jeff O'Brien's tutelage. Jeff got me to the gym. He taught me how to dress. He allowed me to tag along with him in the days when the gay party circuit was at its height. Off we'd fly to San Francisco and Palm Springs and Chicago and Atlanta and Montreal, and in Jeff's afterglow, I was transformed. He became, in the words of Shane, my own personal deity. Despite the fact that my grandfather had been a rabbi, I'd never believed in God—until Jeff came along.

It was a pretty heady time, I admit. How thrilling, how completely new, was the experience of being looked at, of being able to take off my shirt at Gay Pride and get barked at by hot boys. I got so buff, in fact, I discovered there were guys who were willing to pay good money just to touch—and maybe lick a little—so, for a time, I was an escort. Jeff called me the Happy Hooker. But I didn't stay happy for long. Despite all the attention, I felt lonely. Instead of making me feel more special, hustling eventually made me feel pretty worthless. Enter Lloyd Griffith.

It was, of course, inevitable that I'd meet Lloyd through Jeff, and in the gaze of those soft green eyes, a different sort of fascination emerged. Lloyd had spent many years as a psychologist, though when I met him he was transitioning to his new career running his Provincetown guesthouse. Still, Lloyd knew very well how to zero in on one's core issues. He helped me to see that my whole life was ego—not just in my need to be physically admired, but in my constant search for external affirmation. By going within—which we did, in long, intimate meditation sessions at sunrise in the stillness of Beech Forest—I was able to find some internal peace and satisfaction. Then, after a sacred sex workshop, we had incredibly passionate sex, and that pushed me over the edge of bliss. In no time at all, I was head over heels in love with Dr. Lloyd Griffith.

Of course, the feelings for Lloyd went exactly nowhere, and I was soon back to doing what I do best: being alone. I stopped going to the gym. Ice cream became a substitute for all the sex I'd been having. There were brief flickers of hope—named Daniel, named Joey—but always I ended up back in my little apartment above Nirvana watching *Good Times* on TV Land. When I started responding to ideas with shouts of "Dy-no-mite!" Jeff issued a moratorium on seventies TV shows for a month. I cheated. I was back to J.J. and Maude and Fred Sanford in a week and a half.

And despite all I'd learned from Lloyd about ego, I can't deny that I've come to miss some of that old external affirmation. Sure, I still try to meditate, and sometimes I still practice little rituals like saying, "I love you, you are good" to my reflection in the mirror. But there's something about a guy coming up to you on the dance floor, running his finger down your torso, tasting your sweat and telling you, "You oughta bottle this stuff," that just makes your day.

Yes, I know all this dependence on my ego to feel good about myself once ensured my downfall. But here's the thing: I spent too many years on the sidelines to go happily into retirement. My time at the ball just wasn't long enough. I had, what? Three years? Four at the most. Jeff might be able to sit in on a Saturday night baking brownies and watching old Bette Davis movies with Lloyd and a bunch of lesbian friends—but he had a good *fifteen years* out there! I'm not ready to fade away like that.

Is that the reason I'm being so resistant to the idea of Jeff and Lloyd getting married? Because the idea of settled domesticity unnerves me? Because I don't want that to be me, curled up on a couch eating brownies, getting fatter, becoming more and more forgotten by the boys on the dance floor?

No, that's not it. I'd be only too happy to go that route if it was Lloyd next to me.

Or anyone, for that matter.

I'd give anything to have what they have, to not be alone.

Marriage. What a strange concept. I grew up never thinking marriage was an option for me. For my sisters, yes. For other people around me. But not for little gay Henry Weiner. In some ways, never having to think about marriage made things easier. You didn't have to worry about not finding the absolutely right person because, after all, there was nothing that legally kept you together.

Now, as I watch all those happy faces on television—all those happy gay faces running down to apply for marriage licenses across the Commonwealth of Massachusetts—it just underscores how alone I really am. Am I for gay marriage? Maybe—if I could find someone who wanted to marry me.

See, here's the thing. When the state Supreme Court ruled that the state had to allow gay couples to marry, I just never thought Jeff and Lloyd would be among the throng who scampered down to Town Hall. They've never been the type for convention of any kind. They make great shows of rejecting old, failed paradigms—like monogamy, they say. But here they are, sitting across from me like two little high school lovebirds. Be happy for us, their faces are pleading.

Be our best man.

Best man.

What a strange turn of a phrase.

How can one feel *best* when one doesn't even feel all that *good*?

"Well?" Lloyd is asking.

I take a deep breath.

"Of course," I say.

Lloyd is up off the couch in an instant, his arms encircling me. Jeff doesn't move quite as fast, but he comes over, too, tousling my hair. "Thanks, buddy," he says. "You'll look grand in a tux."

"Tux?" I look up at him as Lloyd moves off to uncork the champagne. "It's going to be that formal?"

"Sure thing. All the trimmings. It'll be the event of the season."

I smirk. So that's part of the motivation, too. Since Jeff's become a success, he likes to put on a good show. I can only imagine *who* he's getting for entertainment.

"We're bringing in Connie Francis," he tells me, as if reading my mind. "You know, 'Where the Boys Are.' I met her in New York a few weeks ago and we got to be friends. I'd like to get Kimberley Locke, too—you know, this year's second runner-up on *Idol.* I met her at the Abbey in West Hollywood last month."

"Cat," Lloyd says, using Jeff's nickname, "let's not make this into a three-ring circus." He's pouring the bubbly into three glasses.

"Hey, it's our wedding. A once-in-a-lifetime event. Let's do it up!"

Lloyd hands me a glass of champagne. "I just can't imagine the two of you, married," I say. "Legally and everything. Until death do us part and all that traditional mumbo jumbo."

"Happens to the best of us," Jeff says.

The best of us.

But not the best man.

I figure I ought to offer a toast. "To the two of you," I say, not sure where I'm going with this. "To . . . what moments lie ahead." Not very romantic, I suppose, but the best I can muster.

We clink glasses. We drink.

The loneliest sip of champagne I've ever had.

3

ON THE PIER

Even though the sun has failed to make an appearance today, hiding stubbornly behind a dreary gray haze like a sulky child, Luke wears no shirt, just a backpack slung over one shoulder. A breeze is blowing in off the water, making me shiver, but the boy seems oblivious to it, striding ever closer to where I'm sitting, parading that flat little belly of his, the lines of his damn obliques running down into his loose-fitting cutoff cargo shorts.

Why the hell am I doing this? Why did I agree to meet him when he called? The kid only wants to meet Jeff. Why am I allowing myself to be suckered?

"Hey, handsome," Luke says, sitting beside me on the bench.

Maybe because of the way his dark blond hair falls in his eyes. Maybe because of the way his lips curl at the corners. Maybe because he called me handsome.

"Hey," I reply.

"Where's the sun, dude? I can't see hiking all the way out to the beach without any sun." He rustles out a pack of cigarettes from his backpack and shakes out a cancer stick. "Want one?"

"No, thanks, I don't want to die a gruesome death."

"Yeah, I know I should quit," Luke says, lighting up. "Picked up the habit at a young age, and it's hard to get out of the mindset."

"It's called nicotine addiction." I frown. "And just what is a 'young age' for you? *Twelve?*"

"Close to it." Luke exhales smoke away from my face. "I was probably thirteen when I started."

"So how old are you now?"

"Twenty-two."

Well, what do you know? Seems I'd given him credit for an extra year that he'd never lived. Actually, to look at him, it's pretty tough to guess his age. He's definitely got a baby face, and in some ways twenty-two seems too old for him. But in other ways, he seems a bit overripe, a tomato left on the vine a little too long.

"You must have *some* bad habits," Luke says, squinting those hazel eyes at me.

"Ice cream." I pat my belly. "As this squishiness demonstrates."

"Dude, you're *not* that squishy. You need to get over your body hang-ups."

"Thanks for the advice."

In my head, I'm keeping a countdown. It's been nearly two minutes since Luke sat down, and no mention yet of Jeff.

"So, Henry," the kid says, "you want to get some food later? Maybe you can show me where to eat cheaply in this town."

I lift my eyebrows. "Not too many cheap options here. At least not if you want to avoid clogged arteries and high blood pressure."

Listen to me. I sound like my mother. When did I get so old?

"I'm thinking of becoming a vegetarian," Luke says. "But I figure if I'm going to turn my body into a temple, I gotta quit these things first." He takes one last, long drag on his cigarette and flicks the butt into the water below. "But that will take some effort."

"Well, if I can quit the ice cream, you can quit the nicotine."

"Is that a wager?"

"Oh, I didn't mean—"

"It's a deal." Luke is smiling. "We can check in every day to make sure we're not cheating."

I let out a sigh. Overhead a seagull swoops down low, arcing over our heads. I decide to move the conversation away from addictive behaviors.

"Where did you say you were from, Luke?" I ask.

"I've lived all over the country."

I look at him closely. "But in what particular part of it were you born?"

"Long Island, New York."

Now it's me who makes a face. "Lung Gyland?" I ask, using the local vernacular. "You sure don't sound like you're from Lung Gyland."

He smirks. "I told you. I've lived a lot of places. Besides, not everyone from Long Island sounds like Joey Buttafuoco."

I can't help but smile a little. "I guess."

"My stepdad was a lawyer," Luke tells me, "so I had a pretty upscale, middle-class childhood. At least for the later part. The beginning of my life is a whole other story." He pulls his legs up onto the bench to sit cross-legged next to me. Our knees touch. It distracts me from asking a follow-up question and allows him to keep control of the conversation. "So how about you?" Luke asks. "Where were you born?"

I'm very conscious of his knee touching mine. "West Springfield," I say. "Western Massachusetts."

He cocks an eye at me. "You sure don't sound like you come from Massachusetts."

"Not everyone from Massachusetts sounds like Teddy Kennedy."

Luke laughs. "And you used to be a hustler?"

I feel my face redden. "Look, it was for a very short period. Before my job at the guesthouse, I worked at an insurance company."

"So after you punched out, you walked the streets of Boston?"

"No," I say, surprised at how embarrassed I am remembering that part of my life. It's never embarrassed me before; in fact, I've always been rather proud of it in an odd sort of way—that I'd actually been hot enough to get *paid* for sex. But now, for whatever reasons, I don't want to talk about it with Luke. "I had a profile online," I tell him, trying to find a quick way to end the discussion. "It wasn't a big deal." Even though it was.

"I've thought about hustling myself," Luke says, looking down his smooth chest and fingering his navel. "But then I figured, if I'm gonna be a famous writer, I don't want any skeletons in my past."

Okay, here it is: the moment when the conversation begins to lead us inexorably to Jeff. I let out a long breath, bracing for it. "And that's why you moved here," I say. "To be a writer."

"Yeah." Luke's so natural about it, so confident—as if his dreams will just inevitably come true. "I took a writing class at Nassau Community College and my teacher thought I was a natural-born writer." He widens his eyes as he looks at me. "I'm not trying to brag, Henry. I'm just telling you the facts. I wrote this short story that not only my teacher but the entire class thought could become a novel."

"So what's it about?"

"I'll tell you over a plate of fried clams." Luke is standing all of a sudden, adjusting his backpack on his shoulder. "Okay?"

"I'm not really hungry—"

"I am. I haven't had lunch. And I have a craving for a cigarette—so unless I get some food, I'm gonna smoke. And you agreed to help me quit."

"I never—"

"Come on, Henry."

He motions me up.

"Well," I say, giving in, "we can go over to Mojo's. It's quick, it's cheap, and the food is pretty good, considering it's a take-out stand. We can sit at the tables in back."

"Perfect."

I follow Luke back down the pier. It's mostly straight tourists out here, women with large butts encased in loud floral print shorts, dragging along husbands who look as if they'd rather be anywhere else. A horde of screaming kids suddenly runs toward us, diverting only at the last possible moment from a collision with my gut. This isn't the Provincetown of the popular gay imagination. The pier is the flip side of town—where few queers ever venture, except to board the ferry back to Boston. Why I picked this place to meet Luke, I don't know. It just seemed the best choice—far away from the center of gay P-town. Why that should be important I still haven't figured out.

In truth, there is no part of Provincetown that is less than beautiful. Even here—even among the tacky T-shirt shops and seashell emporiums—there is a certain exquisiteness to the place. Here, at the end of the earth, even the most ordinary buildings are infused with Provincetown's particular glow, a result of the sun reflecting off the water all around us. When I first started coming here years ago, Provincetown was just a playground, a place I came with Jeff to take Ecstasy and trick with sexy boys—or attempt to, anyway. I'd dance until two a.m. fuck until five (if I was lucky) and then sleep until noon.

But now Provincetown is home, and my rhythm here is different. I cast my eyes ahead of me, past the colorful kites and Himalayan blankets being hawked in the square. Not far beyond stands the large white nineteenth-century Town Hall, and up on the hill behind it looms the 252-foot Pilgrim Monument. I'm giving Luke a picture postcard view of Provincetown. It's still sometimes hard to believe that this is my home.

We live here clinging to the last dangling finger of the outstretched arm of Cape Cod, making our lives on a sandy spit that spirals off into the cold Atlantic. No one just "passes through" Provincetown. Only one road leads here, and it ends here, in crumbling asphalt swept over by drifting sand dunes. Here, Thoreau said, you can put all America behind you. The whole world, in fact.

A home at the end of the earth. I remember wondering if it were possible—for anyone other than sea crabs and mussels, that is, or the witless piping plovers forever being chased by the surf. But humans? It's *cold* here, and wet, with the bitter winds that blow through here every winter reminding us we sit on just a few square miles of sand in the middle of the sea.

Summers are bliss here. The living—as the song says—is easy. But the winter is a whole other story. New England winters are legendarily tough, but try it out here, with everything boarded up, with the most of the population having headed south to Fort Lauderdale or Miami. Luke has no idea what awaits him. I know I didn't. Night comes quickly in December, and January, and seemingly even more so in February, despite every logic of the season. "No one passes through Provincetown," I kept repeating to myself that first winter. The headlights of cars never sliced through my living room. Wayward travelers never stopped me at the gas station to ask where they'd made a wrong turn. Days would go by in my little apartment and I'd see not a single person, or a light in any neighboring window. In those first years, we closed the guesthouse in February and March. Jeff was off on a book tour; Lloyd in a spiritual retreat in upstate New York. I sat out blizzard after blizzard by myself.

At first, I was claustrophobic from the isolation, but that changed. I discovered there was something rather magical about the sea in winter. The way the waves crashed against the hard sand, fierce and brittle, the unrelenting pound of the surf that eats away, bit by bit, year by year, a little more of the land. Looking out at the ocean my first winter in Provincetown, I realized the locals had been right: to say one has lived in Provincetown without experiencing the winter is like saying one has lived in New England without ever once seeing an autumn.

"You'll get used to it here," one old timer told me, wearing shorts in a blizzard. "The rules are just a little different."

Those who live in Provincetown do so purposely. Even without a plan, there is nonetheless purpose. "I just got fed up," a woman told me last week at the post office, the single point of intersection for many of us. "One day I just quit my job, packed my car, and drove as far as the road went."

Washashores, the locals call them. I suppose that's what I am, too, surrounded by writers and painters and people who make little carvings out of driftwood and shells.

But can it be home? Provincetown is a place people come *to,* not come *from.* No, that's wrong: there are still families who've been here for generations, descendants of the fishermen of the last century, who cling defensively to their vanishing culture. But the summer population edges fifty thousand; year-round there's barely three. The old fishing family homesteads are being bought up for exorbitant prices by affluent, mostly gay second-homers who envision Provincetown as the perfect place to retire. They will make it home then, these aging babyboomers, but for now, there's still no fast food, no giant supermarket, no parking garage, no cinema multiplex, no Kinkos, no Staples, no Home Depot.

Ah, paradise, one might think. And certainly I have no desire to see golden arches looming over Commercial Street. But Luke's in for a rude awakening when he runs out of printer paper on a late Sunday afternoon. Or tries following a recipe that calls for bok choy in February.

But if home is just convenience, then any strip mall in suburbia could be home. And I suppose it is, to somebody. I'm just glad it's not me. I've come to subversively enjoy the fact that shopkeepers in Provincetown open only when they want to, despite the hours posted on the door. I like that the women in the post office wear outrageous wigs, and that drag queens cash you out at the A&P. Home is a place where you can stand face to face with what's real in the world, like at the top of a dune, or on a stretch of unspoiled beach.

That's what comes with making a home at the end of the earth. The rules are different. You don't meet people passing through because there aren't any. This is the crossroads of nowhere. This is the end of the road. The people you meet are the people who are *here*. Some who have dropped out, who have fallen through the cracks. Some who have said the hell with it, and some who have found heaven in a half-mile stretch of sand.

Luke will have to find his own rhythm, discover the town's secrets for himself. A clerk at the scrimshaw shop once showed me the little shady corner of the town cemetery where on particularly busy days in July he could retreat with his thoughts and his journal. A guy at the Provincetown AIDS Support Group invited me to experience the bleak beauty of Long Point in November. Now I have my own secrets, my own special places.

Working here, living here, I'm not always able to drop what I'm doing when old friends pop in and expect a weekend of revelry. It's been a very long time since I've slept in until noon. I like the sunrise in Provincetown far too much, an event I experienced in the old days only when I staggered home from a trick's house at dawn. I follow a different rhythm now, but I realize it is the multitude of dances that makes Provincetown so unique. I was once in the same place Luke is in now, wide-eyed as he discovers the magic. And it pleases me to no end that there are still crowds on the steps of Spiritus Pizza at two a.m., still boys sleeping in until noon before stumbling out to Herring Cove beach. I might grumble when the line at the post office extends out the door or when buying a quart of milk at the Grand Union takes an hour and a half, but I'm glad when the boys of summer return. I love the drag queens sashaying down the street, the circuit boys in their spandex, the leather dads and the bear cubs. Each to their own rhythm, their own magic. This is their town as much as mine.

There are those who rue the "commercialization" of Provincetown, who gripe that the place has become too geared to nightclubbing and resort tourism. And yet I remember, soon after arriving here, picking up *Time and the Town* by Mary Heaton Vorse, published in 1942. Vorse had made Provincetown her home since the days of Eugene O'Neill some three decades earlier, and she was lamenting, "A few people have been allowed to damage the beauty of Provincetown. The rowdy nightclubs, the wholesale selling of worthless knick-knacks, make it possible . . . to brand the place a 'honky-tonk.' Those few who cater to some unwholesome element for a little money rob themselves as well as the whole town."

Yet Provincetown survived Vorse's fears, going on to several more "golden ages" after the one she described. Elsewhere, she seemed more optimistic, writing: "The one certainty is that Provincetown is in history's path as it has always been." Every season someone new will discover Provincetown and find his or her own rhythm in the place. And so it will go on.

For the boy walking ahead of me—indeed, for all first-timers like him—Provincetown retains its power to bewitch. Here, anything goes. Here one can spot, as Luke and I do now, the fabulous Ellie, a seventy-two-year-young transvestite pulling a sound system in a red wagon down Commercial Street while she croons "My Way" by Frank Sinatra. Watching her, Luke is beaming, pointing her out to me as if I've never seen her before—as if Ellie is as new and as fresh as he is. And in that moment, in Luke's smile, she is. We all are.

At Mojo's we order fried clams and Diet Cokes and settle in at one of the picnic tables.

"So your novel," I say.

"Do you really want to hear?"

I smile. "Sure, why not?"

"Well, it's about this kid, who was homeless, who gets adopted by this really great family but then . . ."

Luke's words trail off. He just sits there staring straight ahead.

"But then what?" I ask.

Still he doesn't say anything. A little voice inside me tells me not to follow Luke's gaze, not to turn my head and see what he's seeing. But of course I look anyway.

It's Jeff, scrutinizing Mojo's menu a few feet away.

I can't help but laugh. "Ah," I say, "if it isn't your literary idol."

"Jeffrey O'Brien," Luke says softly.

"In the flesh," I say. "What d'ya think?"

"I thought he'd be taller," Luke says.

I laugh out loud. That one little comment makes my day.

My laughter has drawn Jeff's attention. He looks over at us.

"Henry," he says, heading our way. Already I see him checking out Luke. God, do I know that look. It's the look of a kid in a shopping cart as his mother pushes him down the toy aisle. *I want that*, his eyes say. But as soon as he's passed his object of desire, he's forgotten it and moved on to another.

"Jeff," I say, accepting the inevitable, "this is Luke. Luke, Jeff."

"Jeff O'Brien," Jeff echoes, shaking the kid's hand.

"I know," Luke breathes in awe.

"He's got your book under his bed," I tell Jeff.

"Actually," Luke says, unzipping his backpack, "I have it right here."

Out comes not one book, but three—two in paper, one hardcover.

Jeff beams. "You've got the whole Jeffrey O'Brien collection right there. All three of my books."

Luke spreads them out on the picnic table in front of us, careful to move the fried clams far away first, so they don't stain his treasures. There's the well-read, much-creased copy of *The Boys of Summer* that I saw under Luke's bed, plus its sequel, *More Boys, More Summer*. The hardcover is Jeff's latest, a more "literary" attempt—one without the prerequisite shirtless boy on the front. *Finding Home*, it's called.

"I especially loved this one," Luke says, tapping the cover of *Finding Home*. "I thought it was just . . . I don't know. Just brilliant."

Jeff sits down on the other side of the picnic table, facing us. "The critics weren't so sure," he says, eyes glued on Luke.

"That's because they pigeon-holed you. They weren't ready to let you try something different."

They couldn't be playing their parts any better if Jeff had written the goddamn script. I lean my head on my hand, watching this little drama unfold.

"Well, that's what we like to believe," Jeff says, in that slightly deeper-than-usual voice he uses around fans. "I'm glad *you* liked it, though."

"Oh, man, I *loved* it."

I wonder. *Finding Home* has none of the signs of being well read. Unlike *The Boys of Summer*, its pages aren't dog-eared. Its binding isn't even cracked.

Luke is still gushing. "And I loved the interview you gave to *The Advocate* about it. You know, where you revealed that you, like the protagonist, were also an old movie and TV fan."

Jeff twinkles on cue. "You mean the interview where I came out of the closet as a secret geek."

The boy's smile threatens to close his eyes with his cheeks. "You are so *not* a geek. *I'm* a geek."

"Well, if so," Jeff says, "geeks are a lot cuter these days than they used to be."

I feel my stomach roil, and it's not the fried clams.

Luke is clearly smitten. He's rummaging in his backpack again, and produces something I can't at first identify. It's flat, and wrapped in plastic.

"Take a look at this," he's telling Jeff.

It looks like a small movie poster. Slipped into a plastic bag and backed by a piece of a cardboard, it showcases a woman I don't recognize. Jeff takes it from Luke's hands and gazes at it with a kind of wonder.

"Holy shit," he says. "A lobby card from *Becky Sharp*!"

"Yeah," Luke replies, in the same breathless tone of awe.

"Excuse me," I say, "I hate to interrupt, but who the fuck is *Becky Sharp*?"

Jeff glares at me. "*Becky Sharp* just so happens to be the very first feature film made in Technicolor."

"Yeah," Luke adds, though he doesn't look at me, keeping his eyes squarely on Jeff. "And in 1935, starring the amazing Miriam Hopkins."

"Miriam who?" I ask.

"You wouldn't understand," Jeff tells me. "Miriam Hopkins is very big for true film fans, one of the forgotten greats."

"Well, in fact," Luke says, reaching into his bag again, "look what else I have." He pulls out a videotape in a battered cardboard slipcover. "I've got one of Miriam's last appearances—on the TV show *The Outer Limits.*"

Jeff takes the videotape and inspects it. "*The Outer Limits*! That was a great show. Sometimes even better than *The Twilight Zone.*"

"I agree," says Luke. "Do you know both Geraldine Brooks and Sally Kellerman appeared on it?"

I laugh. "Are they favorites of true film fans, too?"

Luke eyes me. "For true fans, Henry, the people on the screen can sometimes seem like your best friends."

"But why," Jeff asks, lifting his eyebrows at Luke, "are you carrying these around in your backpack? You don't want that lobby card to get damaged."

"I know," the boy answers. "But I just don't feel comfortable leaving it back in my hotel room. If the maid found it . . ."

Jeff hands the precious relics back to Luke. "You're staying at an inn?"

Luke nods. "Until I can find a permanent place."

I notice the smile creep across Jeff's face. "You're planning to move here?"

"Yes, so I can . . ." Luke's voice trails off.

"So you can what?" Jeff asks.

"Oh, please," I say to Luke, impatient with this little charade, "just *tell* him."

"So I can write." The boy blushes. "Like I have any business saying that to *you.*"

Jeff beams. No one on the entire planet is more susceptible to flattery than Jeff O'Brien. It's impossible to lay it on too thick with him. He just laps it up like a pig eating slops.

"A writer, huh?" Jeff smiles. "Well, Provincetown can be a wonderful muse . . ."

"So I've heard." Luke carefully returns Becky Sharp to his backpack. "And your novels are a big reason why I'm here."

"I'm flattered," Jeff says.

"No, really, I mean it." Luke returns his eyes to Jeff with a passion that exceeds anything I saw yesterday while we were having sex. "Your work has had such an influence on me. Your words . . . they've changed my life."

That's when I stand up, grip the sides of the table, and puke all over both of them. Diet Coke and bits of fried clams rain down on their heads.

Okay, so I imagine that part. But for the moment, anyway, the fantasy allows my stomach to stop lurching.

"That's awfully sweet of you," Jeff's saying. There's a moment of eye-holding silence that leaves me feeling utterly invisible. Finally Jeff asks, smiling warmly at Luke, "Would you like me to sign your books?"

"*Would* you?"

"Sure," Jeff says.

What a guy. So magnanimous.

Luke produces a pen from his backpack. Is there anything he *doesn't* keep in there? Jeff opens the first book to its title page, pausing to think before he writes. Then, suddenly, without warning, he reaches down and pulls his T-shirt up over his head, revealing his defined pecs and abs. "Damn," he says, "it's so hot out today."

"It is so *not* hot out today," I say, unable to keep quiet.

But I'm ignored. Luke is mesmerized as a shirtless Jeff O'Brien signs his books. What our esteemed author writes, I don't know, and in truth, I don't care to know. But Luke reads each inscription in turn, cooing appreciatively, and replacing each book in his backpack. When they're done with their little playlet, they just sit there, two naked torsos grinning stupidly across the table at each other. The sexual energy between them is so strong it could power a small city.

My mind goes back to a night some five, six years before.

"But I thought he *loved* me," the boy from Montreal was saying. What was his name again? Jean-Pierre? Jean-Michel? Something like that. There have been many boys from many different places, beautiful boys who fell in love with Jeff and were crushed to discover his affection for them barely lasted through the week. And most of those boys turned to Henry Weiner for counseling and consolation.

Will it be the same with Luke? Once Jeff is done with him, will he come running back to me? Will I let him?

But as I watch them, I feel the situation is a little different this time. Jeff, for all his smooth skin and still tight abs, is no longer the young buck that he was. He's not out there in the scene in the way he used to be, partly because he doesn't have the stamina to stay up all night the way he used to but also because he's no longer quite the focus the way he was in years past. Back in the day, all eyes in the room would turn to look when Jeff O'Brien walked in. But now, as well preserved as he might be, Jeff has discovered the playing field can never be truly level for him again—not when he's facing off against a new class of twentysomethings.

Like Luke.

And that's the other reason this time is different. Luke is no wide eyed kid still green in the ways of gay life, like so many of Jeff's previous boys have been. Jean-Michel—and Raphael and Eduardo and Anthony—were all refreshingly free of guile. But looking at Luke, I see very clearly that he's been around the rodeo a couple of times. After all, he'd known to search me out and to sleep with me, all part of his nefarious plan to meet Jeff.

And how well that had worked out, all within a day. I wonder if Luke had spotted Jeff on his way into town? Was that why he'd insisted we leave the pier? Had he know somehow we'd run into Jeff? Even if he hadn't maneuvered their meeting, the kid had known exactly what to do once his prey showed up. Out came the flattery in generous helpings, topped by that well-timed appearance of Supergirl in her carefully wrapped plastic bag. Luke was good. No question about that. *Shrewd.* Unlike Jeff's other boys, this time both sides had their own games to play.

"You know what?" Jeff is asking, breaking the charged silence that pulses between him and Luke. "You ought to stop by my house when you have the time. I'll show you my entire collection of movie posters." He lowers his voice into a sexy whisper. "I've got one from *The Birth of a Nation.*"

"No way!" Luke gushes. "From 1915?"

Jeff nods. "Not quite near-mint, but pretty fine."

"When can I come by and see it?"

"What are you doing right now?"

"Nothing," Luke says. Then, as if remembering there's another human being seated next to him, he turns to me. "Except that Henry and I were—"

"Go ahead," I tell him. "Who am I to keep you from *The Birth of a Nation?*"

"You'll come too?" Luke asks.

I make a face. "I've already seen Jeff's movie posters."

"You sure you guys weren't doing anything?" Jeff asks me, standing up, apparently forgetting about the lunch he'd been about to order for himself. Or maybe he's just decided he's hungry for something other than a grilled chicken sandwich. It seems he might prefer his chicken raw.

"Not to worry," I assure him. "Luke and I weren't doing a thing. I've actually got to head into town. I'm meeting a friend."

"Well, come on over around seven," Jeff tells me, motioning to Luke to follow him. "Elliot and Oscar are in town, and they're coming for dinner."

"I'll try to make it," I say, staying seated as Luke zips up his bag and hurries around to follow Jeff. "But I can't promise."

"Who're you meeting in town?" Jeff asks.

"Oh . . . no one you know."

Luke stops suddenly and looks over his shoulder at me. "Want to hang out again tomorrow, Henry?"

"I'm going out of town," I tell him.

"Well, I'll call you."

I give him a little salute. "Say hello to Mary Pickford and Douglas Fairbanks for me. I think Jeff has them, too."

"Really? Awesome!"

And then Luke is gone, trotting out after Jeff onto Commercial Street.

I take one last sip of my Diet Coke through my straw, making that sucking sound against the bottom of the paper cup. I pick a few crumbs off the plate in front of me, placing them in my mouth, one by one. A gull lands on a post not far from me, folding in its wings against its body. It stares resolutely at me. I look away.

"If you ask me," comes a voice to my right, "that guy is a shmuck."

I glance over. At the next table is a guy I recognize from the gym. A real hottie, in fact, with dark eyes and a closely shaven head, and very round biceps that stand out against his tank top like small grapefruits. I don't know his name, but apparently he witnessed the entire scene between Jeff, Luke, and me.

"Excuse me?" I ask. "What guy?"

"That Jeff O'Brien." The hottie nods toward the street. "You came in here with that kid, and he took off with him."

"Oh," I say, embarrassed. "It's not like that."

"Whatever." The guy takes a bite of his hamburger. "I shouldn't say anything. It's none of my business."

"No, really, Luke and I—there's nothing between us. And Jeff's just taking him back to show him his movie posters."

The hottie practically spits out his burger. "What, were his etchings in storage?"

I smirk. "It's really okay."

He wipes his mouth with his napkin and stands, reaching across his table toward mine and extending his hand. "I'm Gale," he says.

"Henry," I say, shaking his hand.

"Seen you at the gym," Gale says, sitting back down.

"Seen you too."

Had I ever. This guy has a fucking amazing body. He must do two hundred chin ups and then, for good measure—or maybe just to show off—he flips himself over the bar a few times. And when he does a leg press, I sometimes have to force myself to look away, so hot are those bulging calves.

Yet for such a well-muscled body, it's a delicate one, too, in a way. Gale can't be more than five-seven, and his waist is tiny. Twenty-eight, probably. Maybe even twenty-*seven*. His features are soft and pretty, almost like a girl's. Not really my type—but there's no denying this guy is hotness personified.

I don't know why I feel I need to defend Jeff, but I do. "Jeff is just a natural-born flirt," I tell Gale. "I'm totally used to it. And that kid . . . well, I knew all along it was Jeff he wanted to meet."

Gale shrugs. "I still think it was rude. But it's none of my business."

"Jeff's my best friend," I go on. "He seems shallow, but he's not. Please don't think badly of him. Inside, he's a sweetheart, and he'd do anything for somebody he cares about. Really."

"Okay," Gale says, smiling. "I believe you."

"Good." I laugh. "I can't have people thinking badly of him. I'm going to be the best man at his wedding."

"At his wedding? And meanwhile he's taking this twinkie back to his place?"

"It's . . . a long story."

"No, it's not," Gale says, shaking his head. "Non-monogamy rules the gay world."

"Not *my* gay world," I tell him.

He arches an eyebrow at me. "Really? Is that true, Henry? Are you really one of those rare believers in monogamy?"

I laugh awkwardly. Why am I talking so much? I don't even know this guy. But I continue, just the same. Talking, in fact, suddenly feels good. "Well, I believe in it for me, anyway," I explain. "If other guys can make open relationships work, then good for them. I just never could."

And never *would*, I suddenly think, if it were *me* marrying Lloyd. If Lloyd was *my* lover, there's no way I'd be bringing some twinkie in off the street for a quickie.

"Well, Henry, I'm glad to hear it," Gale is saying. He stands up, carries his tray to the trash, and slides the remains of his lunch into the barrel. Then he turns and walks back over to me. He stands in front of the picnic table where I'm sitting. "In fact," he says, "hearing that makes me want to ask you out to dinner. How about it?"

I stare up at him, momentarily unable to speak. "Yeah, sure," I say finally.

"When?" Gale asks.

"Anytime," I reply, still looking up into his big round brown eyes.

"Well, tomorrow's no good," Gale says.

"No?" I ask.

He grins knowingly. "You told the kid you were going out of town."

I can't resist smiling myself. "Well, I think my plans might change."

Gale's grin broadens. "When will you know for certain?"

"Right now." I stand, realizing I'm a couple of heads taller than he is. But height hardly matters—not when I'm caught in the gaze of those soft brown eyes. "What time do you want to meet," I ask, "and where?"

"How about seven-thirty at Café Heaven?"

"Good deal," I say. We shake. Gale's hand is small in my own, but his grip is firm and masculine.

"See you tomorrow night then," he says, heading out.

"Yeah, see you tomorrow night," I echo.

I watch him hop on his bike and ride away. Those amazing calves flex as he pumps the pedals, and his butt looks pretty damn good, too, as it lifts off the seat.

I carry my own tray to the trash. My eyes find those of the gull, who's still sitting there staring at me.

"You can go now," I whisper. "Everything's done here."

The bird spreads its wings and flaps away.

I smile to myself, and head home.

4

MY ROOM

When do we stop dreaming?

Do we still dream at sixty? At seventy? At eighty? Do we still hope to find what we haven't yet found? Do we never give up?

I get into bed and stare at the ceiling, thinking about Gale.

My future husband.

I laugh to myself and shift the pillows behind my head.

Outside, it's started to rain. I can hear the steady tap-tap-tapping against the skylights. Inevitably my thoughts drift back to a year and a half ago. Few things in life were ever sweeter than falling asleep next to Joey on a rainy night. He'd always nod off before I did, breathing softly in my ear. I'd just lie there, inhaling the fragrance of his air, listening to the rain on the roof. Sometimes I'd hold off from falling asleep, just wanting to savor the moment, as if I knew it was too good to last.

Why does it always come back to Joey? Or Daniel? Or Lloyd? Why do I grieve my former lovers so, even after I make a date with a hot little jock? Why is being alone so goddamn *hard*?

Two months after Joey dumped me, the phone rang, and somehow I knew it was him. "I'm leaving Provincetown," he said to me. "I can't seem to make it here." He was moving to New York. Did I want to meet him for coffee before he left?

I felt the blood quicken in my veins. "Yes," I said, hoping.

I cleaned my apartment, just in case. I told myself it was entirely possible that Joey might want to come back here. Maybe for one last quickie. Maybe after we fell into each other's arms over coffee and decided how foolish we'd been to ever break up.

We met at a coffee joint in the West End. Joey was wearing clothes I didn't remember. A yellow polo shirt, a pair of khakis I'd never seen, and red tennis shoes that clashed with his shirt. In two months, I wondered, had he bought a whole new wardrobe? Had he discarded everything that I had known, chucked every last bit of our life together?

We ordered our coffees. Standing at the counter, we made small talk. "How's the guesthouse?" he asked. I told him fine. I asked about his mother. "She's fine," he told me. "How are Jeff and Lloyd?" They were fine, too, I told him.

I wanted to scream. *For God's sake, Joey, how can we be standing here talking like mere acquaintances on the street when I've licked lint out of your navel?*

But we kept our faces composed and our voices level. I asked him why he decided on New York.

"I'm seeing someone there," he told me.

It was then that our coffees arrived. The girl behind the counter attempted to fit a lid onto mine, but as she did so, she spilled a little, burning her hand. She put it quickly to her mouth, and Joey asked her if she was all right. "I'll live," she said.

That's when it hit me. *I'm seeing someone.*

"I didn't know," I told him as we walked out to the benches, my legs threatening to turn to jelly. "Did you meet him here?"

"Yes," Joey said, "at Tea Dance."

Where *we* had met, too. Where most boyfriends are met in Provincetown. I searched Joey's eyes for something, for *anything*. Had he forgotten?

What is the process in which emotions become memories? At what point does the feeling recede, the passion dissolve, and the details become merely data stored by the brain? For me, it has yet to occur, but Joey seemed to be moving along just fine.

Still, unlike the night we broke up, I remained composed. "I wish you all the luck," I told him. "What I want is for you to be happy."

"Thank you, Henry."

I felt absurd for having taken so long fixing my hair before I came over here. I was an idiot for trying on four shirts before deciding on the one I was wearing. Suddenly I wished I hadn't shaved, and that the apartment I was planning to return to wasn't quite so spic and span.

"I didn't go looking for a new relationship," Joey said suddenly, defending himself even without any accusation from me. "It just happened. And it feels right."

I smiled at him, sipping my coffee, burning my tongue. I don't remember what else we said. Nonsense stuff, really. About the real-estate market, about mutual funds and mutual friends. When we'd run out of even those topics, Joey stood, extending his hand and saying good-bye. But I wasn't quite ready to separate from him forever. I stood as well, and told him I was going his way, so we might as well walk together. His presence was comforting to me after so long apart, if slightly unreal—and unsettling, too, because Joey was different, with his new clothes and his new lover. But it was preferable to being apart from him, for this time I sensed it would be forever. We walked a few blocks, and again Joey put out his hand to me to say good-bye. "I'll walk a little further," I said. So we walked on in silence, the only sound the squeak of his new sneakers. Still, it was something.

"Why don't we part here?" Joey said finally, firmly, as we approached the center of town. I knew I could go no further with him, so I nodded. We hugged, at his initiation. No last cry of yearning bubbled up to escape from my lips, just a simple, "Thanks." I felt, fleetingly, the warmth of his body once again, a body I knew every inch of, even parts Joey himself had never seen.

He continued down Commercial Street, while I hurried up to Bradford so I could peer down from the next block and catch a glimpse of him crossing the street, a flash of yellow and red in a crowd of people. That's the last time I saw him. For all our time together, that's the image that stays in my mind.

I didn't go looking for a new relationship. It just happened. And it feels right.

So why hasn't it just happened for me? I *have* been looking.

Over and over again. Lloyd thinks that's why I haven't found a lover since Joey. I've been looking too hard. It's when you're *not* looking, he says, that you find it.

And I wasn't looking when I met Gale. He approached *me*.

Maybe this is it. Finally.

But so had Luke approached me, and I hadn't been looking then, either. And look how that turned out.

I try not to project anything about Gale. I try to beat back the urge to fantasize, to hope. That's what always does me in. I start hoping, wishing, praying—and then it falls apart.

I wonder, for just the briefest of moments, what happened between Jeff and Luke. I skipped the dinner with Eliot and Oscar, even though they're friends from way back and I haven't seen them in a year. I just wasn't in the mood to be chatty tonight—or to see Jeff's rosy post-coitus glow. Instead, I slipped into my apartment and kept the lights turned off so no one could see that I was home. With the blinds closed I watched *All in the Family*, the episode where Archie gets locked in the basement. Buoyed by my meeting with Gale, I was able to laugh—and my laughter almost allowed me to resist the urge for a dish of ice cream. Resistance, of course, proved futile, so while the end credits ran, I snuck downstairs to the guesthouse kitchen and absconded with an unopened pint of Cherry Garcia. I ate two thirds of it straight from the carton watching reruns of *The Match Game*. Gotta love that Charles Nelson Reilly.

So I remain in the dark about what actually transpired between Jeff and Luke. But I can surmise this much: Jeff's not the sort to let tricks hang around too long after sex, so I imagine the kid was sent on his way about thirty minutes after both had shot their loads, with maybe a couple of movie posters rolled up in his backpack as consolation prizes. If Luke had been hoping to weasel his way into Jeff's life in order to jumpstart his own writing career, no doubt he was keenly disappointed. I know Jeff all too well.

Jeff. Jeffrey Michael O'Brien. I lie here wide awake shaking my head as I think about him. Even as he plans his goddamn wedding, he's rolling around in bed with boys he picks up off the street.

Well, at least I had Luke first.

"Damn," I say, sitting up in bed.

I can't sleep. I punch my pillow, resettle myself on my side. But the silence of the room overwhelms me. The rain has stopped. Gone is the steady, reassuring beat against the glass of the sky-lights. I find myself thinking, as I do quite often lately when I can't fall asleep, about Joey's new boyfriend. Except that he's not so new, at least not anymore. Surely by now they've settled into a routine, with their own set of little code words and habits, like Joey and I used to have. Does Joey still call hair in the shower drain "goopers"? And has the boyfriend figured out the best way to make sure Joey starts his day in a good mood is to get up before him and make sure there are no goopers in the drain?

The new boyfriend is blond. And a goy. I know, because Jeff saw the two of them in New York at Gay Pride. Until then, I'd been insistent that I didn't want to know what the boyfriend looked like. But of course, on another level, I was *desperate* to know. So after feigning disinterest for about a minute and a half, I begged Jeff to tell me.

"Tall, blond, pretty hunky," he reported.

"God damn it," I muttered.

"Body's definitely better than the face," Jeff assessed. "Kind of a heavy brow, a little Herman Munsterish."

"Oh, that's much better."

"But awesome pecs and bis though."

I was no longer listening. All that mattered was that Joey's new boyfriend had a monster face. I now refer to him as Herman. I have no idea what his real name is, and I don't care to know. Herman suits him just fine.

My arm is going stiff lying on my side.

"Fuck."

I sit up again, letting out a long sigh. I know now it's impossible to fall asleep without chemical assistance. I throw off the sheet and place my feet against the hardwood floor. Even before I make it to the bathroom I remember that I've used up all my sleeping pills. Insomnia has been a rather frequent visitor to my room these past several months.

"Damn," I say, flicking on the light and looking at myself in the mirror.

What I notice first are the bags around my eyes. When did they become so prominent? When did I start looking so old? Then my gaze drops down to the tiretube of flesh jiggling above the waistband of my Calvin Klein boxer briefs. What the hell was Gale *thinking* when he asked me out? If he'd seen me like this—the real me—he'd never have gotten such an absurd idea. Like I'm going to want to take my shirt off in front of Mr. Four-Percent-Body-Fat!

I decide to try some of that Sleepytime tea Lloyd keeps downstairs for guests. No caffeine but plenty of chamomile. It's not Ambien, but it's something.

I creak open the door and start down the stairs to Nirvana's common room. I don't want to wake any guests; the last thing I want right now is to make small talk with a couple of horny middle-aged guys from Pittsburgh or a large baby dyke from Ottawa. We've got a full house tonight, and each and every one of them was wide eyed and eager to start exploring Provincetown when I checked them in this afternoon. They all got my very best Chamber-of-Commerce spiel, recommending restaurants and explaining shuttle schedules. But now, at half past twelve in the morning, I'm not in the mood to play tour guide.

I'm in luck. The common room is empty. I hurry over to the bar, where in just six hours I'll be putting out blueberry muffins and croissants (reheated from yesterday's batch, no way I'm getting up an hour early now to whip up some new ones). I fumble around in the darkness, not wanting to switch on a light, searching for the little baskets where we keep tea bags and sugar packets.

"And what are you lurking about for at this time of night, Mr. Weiner?"

I jump, even though I know the voice.

"Lloyd," I say, not bothering to look up. "I can't sleep. I need some of that tea. Or better yet, if you have some Ambien lying around . . ."

"No need for all those toxic chemicals," Lloyd tells me. He easily finds the basket with the tea and motions me to follow him into the small kitchen area. It's thankfully separated off from the common room by a solid oak door. Once inside, Lloyd flicks on the overhead light. I blink, my eyes adjusting, while he drops a tea bag into a mug filled with water and pops it into the microwave. "So, tell me, Henry," Lloyd says, while the tea spins slowly inside, brewing, "what's keeping you awake and prowling the halls?"

"Oh, nothing much," I say. "Except my entire life."

Lloyd smiles. The microwave beeps. He carefully removes the mug of tea and sets it down in front of me. "Honey?" he asks. I shake my head no—too many calories. He tells me to wait a couple of minutes before drinking. "It's hot."

I look over at him. Nothing in the world feels better than being taken care of by Lloyd Griffith. He always knows just what to say, what to offer, how to be. Once, I really believed we were right for each other. Maybe I still believe that. Jeff doesn't appreciate Lloyd the way I do. Jeff's always too busy, always rushing off somewhere, to just sit and *be*, the way Lloyd prefers. Jeff never pauses long enough to listen to Lloyd's soothing, wise words and truly take them in. He's never admitted as much, but I think Lloyd agrees with me about the whole monogamy thing—that if Jeff didn't insist on remaining a tramp, he'd reel him in, and they'd have a lovely, one-on-one, monogamous relationship.

He could have had it with me—but the one blind spot in Lloyd's wisdom is his love for Jeff. What he puts up with from that man! Today, while Lloyd was probably here at the guesthouse, Jeff was back in their bed fucking Luke's hot little butt. As much as Jeff is my friend, I really don't see what keeps Lloyd so attached to him. They're day and night, black and white. And now they're getting married.

"Your entire life," Lloyd says, sitting down at the table opposite me. "That's a lot of territory."

"Not really," I tell him, holding my hands against the sides of the hot cup. "My life is pretty small, in fact. There's the guesthouse, you, Jeff, Ann Marie, J. R., visits to my parents a few times a year . . . that about sums up my life."

"Oh, we're reducing Henry Weiner to exteriors again, are we?"

I manage a small smile. "I just mean . . ."

"You mean, you're lonely."

How is it that Lloyd knows so much? How is it that in just one phrase he can sum it all up for me? Yes, I'm lonely. And I'm tired of it. Way past tired of it.

"I got asked out today," I tell him. "And I just started thinking about things."

"About Joey."

I smile, more easily this time. "Yeah, he was one of those things."

"Who asked you out?"

"This guy I've seen at the gym. Do you know him? A real cute, humpy little guy named Gale?"

"Oh, yes," Lloyd says, nodding. "*Very* cute. I've met him, but don't really know him."

"Well, anyway, I saw him at Mojo's and—" I decide against telling him the exact situation that prompted our meeting. I'm not sure if Lloyd knows that Jeff tricked with Luke. "And he asked me out to dinner tomorrow night." I make a face and finally take a sip of my tea. "Actually, tonight."

"Good for you," Lloyd says.

I find his soft green eyes. Is there any jealousy there? Any hint of a pang? Any suggestion that somewhere, deep down, Lloyd might wish things had turned out differently, that he was marrying me instead of Jeff?

No. I see nothing there. I can't even pretend I do.

"Henry," Lloyd says, "I've said it before and it bears saying again. The universe has a plan for you. You've just got to trust."

"Oh, I trust the universe just fine," I tell him. "I just happen to think its plan for me is to be alone, and I think it sucks."

Lloyd laughs. "I don't think that's the plan for you."

"How do you know? Come on, Lloyd. I'm thirty-fucking-*three*."

"Good God," he says. "Decrepit."

"And I've never had a boyfriend last past the one-year mark. Meanwhile, I've been hung up on Joey for longer than we were even *together!*"

"That's because your ego was wounded, Henry. He *left* you. It fits into your core belief that you aren't worthy of being loved."

It's Lloyd's psychology background coming out. There's truth

to his analysis, I'm sure, but it still sucks. It's not like I can ratio-
nalize my way out of feeling bad about being dumped.

"If you truly believe you aren't good enough to be loved,"
Lloyd's telling me, "then you'll always fail at relationships. If you
can change that deeply held belief—"

"I know, I know. I should get back into therapy."

Lloyd shrugs. "Couldn't hurt."

"Or maybe I should just drive out to West Springfield next
weekend and tell Mom and Dad 'fuck you' for screwing up my
sense of self-worth."

"I'd try therapy first," Lloyd says, smirking.

"Do you know my parents were married at twenty? Both of
them the same age. I can't say it's been a happy marriage, but it's
lasted. Forty-one years, in fact." I take another sip of tea. If this
stuff is supposed to be making me sleepy, it's doing a very poor
job of it. "But it's easier for straight people. You get married, you
have kids, you accept what comes. Gay people are always on the
lookout for the next best thing."

"That won't be so easy to do now that we can get married, too,"
Lloyd reminds me.

I scoff. "What would it matter to you guys? You're nonmonogamous. You can have your wedding cake and still eat all
the boys you want to."

Lloyd says nothing, just drops his eyes to the table. He begins
fidgeting with the tea bags in the basket. "The point is, Henry,"
he says, not looking up at me, "you need to get over your victim
energy. Joey didn't dump you. Neither did Daniel or Shane." He
moves his eyes back up to meet mine. "And neither did *I* reject
you. What we all did was simply get out of your way so you could
live the life you were supposed to."

I sigh. "So I could meet Gale, maybe."

Lloyd nods. "Maybe. Or someone else."

"I'm just so tired of waiting."

He reaches over and places his hand on top of mine. "I know."

We sit in silence a couple of moments.

"That tea working?" Lloyd asks.

"Fuck no."

He sighs. "Okay. I've got some Ambien back at the house."

"Sweet."

"You need to get some sleep," he says, standing up. "I've got a new houseboy starting in the morning, and you'll need to show him around."

"Where'd you find this one?" I ask.

"I didn't find him. Jeff did."

My ears perk up.

"Some kid who came by to see his movie posters. Hope this one lasts." He gives me a smile. "I'll be right back with your wonder drug."

I sit staring at the door after he's gone.

I can't believe it.

Jeff finagled Luke a job here.

Or maybe Luke was the one who did the finagling.

Either way, I have a feeling that our new houseboy is indeed going to last.

And my life is going to be hell.

5

THE BACKYARD OF NIRVANA GUESTHOUSE

It's such a beautiful morning I decide to serve the muffins and coffee outside. I set up a table under a locust tree, hauling out the coffee urn and arranging the blueberry muffins on a platter. The guests begin dragging themselves down the stairs around seven. First comes the baby dyke, Michelle, with another woman I hadn't met at check-in. Tall, fresh-faced, freckled—I wonder if maybe she's a trick. Do baby dykes trick? They mumble a greeting to me, then consume three cups of coffee each in rapid succession, popping a couple of muffins into their mouths along the way. They giggle a lot under their breath, then head out front to pedal away on their bikes.

Next to rise are the lecherous pair from Pittsburgh, genial bears who seem to have been on twenty-four-hour cruise control ever since arriving in Provincetown yesterday. For this type of tourist, the beaches and bike trails and nature walks hold no interest. It's all about sex, as if P-town was just one big bath house, from the bars to the taffy shops to the Pilgrim Monument. The hairier of the two guys is named Bert, and he keeps winking at me, almost as if he has an eye twitch. It's unnerving to say the least. I'm certainly not going to wink back, but even if I smile to be polite, he'll see it as an encouragement. So I just try to stay as far away from them as possible.

I'm saved by the timely arrival of Ann Marie, dressed in smart white shorts and a gauzy pink blouse—her work attire. Her son J. R. follows a few steps behind her.

"Is there coffee out here?" she asks. "Jeff didn't make any this morning, and I need a cup desperately before I get on Cape Scare."

Cape Scare: Ann Marie's pet name for Cape Air, the little eight-seater puddle jumper she takes every Monday morning and every Friday afternoon back and forth to Boston. You'd think by now she'd be used to it, but she's still terrified every time that little plane takes off down the runway, circling over Hatches Harbor. I love Cape Air flights myself. Nowhere else can you get such a sublime view of the outer sandy spiral of Cape Cod and the blue waters lapping at its shores. Occasionally you can even spot a whale.

"Help yourself, doll," I say, gesturing to the urn. I turn to J. R. "You're up early. You and Uncle Jeff heading out to Long Point today?"

The kid just shakes his head sullenly. He's been sullen a lot lately, come to think of it.

Ann Marie takes a sip of coffee and savors it, her whole body seeming to relax as the hot liquid pours through her body. "J. R. wants to come with me to Boston," she tells me. "But I just can't have him staying at the apartment all alone all week while I'm at work."

Ann Marie has taken over Jeff's old apartment in the South End. I look from her to J. R. "It's summer, buddy," I say. "Why would you want to be in the city when you could be here?"

"I'm bored here," he says.

I laugh. "A lot of kids in the city might be glad to change places with you."

He's not buying it. He just sighs, scrunching his hands deep down into the pockets of his baggy black jeans. He wears a black Green Day T-shirt and black Converse sneakers to complete the outfit. J. R. was once such a happy kid, always laughing, pulling pranks. But lately he's seemed more like a moody teenager than a nine-year-old boy. I used to be able to make him crack up by slipping on a plastic nose and glasses whenever he'd stroll by the front desk. Now, whenever I've tried it, he's completely ignored me, making me feel like an utter fool. Who can figure out kids?

"Sweetie," Ann Marie is saying, stooping down so that her eyes are level with his, "you know how much I miss you during the week. Don't you think I wish I could just stay here and have a summer vacation like you? You know I hate leaving you during the week, but I have to work."

Before she moved here to Provincetown, Ann Marie had been worried that J. R. was missing out on having a father figure in his life. Since he loved Jeff and Lloyd so much, the move made sense. J. R. got two dads, but, in the bargain, a part-time mom. Maybe that's the reason for his current discontent.

"I thought you liked living here, dude," I say to him. "The beach and the bike trails and the Jet Skis."

He shrugs. "Whatever."

"And now you're a star basketball player at school—"

"Basketball sucks," he says, and walks off.

I look over at Ann Marie. "Whoa. When did he decide that?"

"I don't know. But he says he doesn't want to play again next year." She finishes her coffee. "He'll get over it. It's just a phase. Tell Jeff to take him out on the boat or something." She looks at her watch. "Oh my God, I've got to get to the airport. But tell me one thing, Henry."

"What's that?"

She grins. "How in the world did you get Lloyd to hire your trick from Tea Dance?"

"So you've heard."

"I was there when he hired him!"

I scowl. "Well, the true credit goes to your brother. Who had his own nefarious reasons, I'm sure."

Ann Marie laughs. "Let the drama begin." She kisses me quickly on the cheek. "Here he comes now."

As she rushes off, calling after J. R. for one last hug, I spot our new houseboy trudging up the walk. He's still shirtless, still with his backpack over his shoulder. He spots me and waves.

"Henry!" Luke calls.

I nod. So now I'm Luke's boss. Two days ago he was my trick. Luke West—that's the name he gave to Lloyd. I wonder if it's real: sounds like a porn name to me. No matter, though: he's off limits to me now—a little rule Lloyd and I faithfully follow when it comes to our houseboys. Of course, the rules don't apply for Jeff. Rules never do. Jeff sleeps with whomever he goddamn pleases.

"So did you hear I got a job here?" Luke asks breathlessly, after planting a sloppy kiss on my cheek.

"Of course I heard," I say, not bothering to hide my annoyance. "I'm the manager here."

"So I report to you?" Luke is actually batting his eyelashes. "I've never had such a hunky boss before."

"Cut it out," I tell him. "I have a strict rule about not fraternizing with the houseboys."

Luke pouts. "You mean, no more fooling around?"

I doubt very much that he would have fooled around with me again anyway, now that Mr. Jeff O'Brien had inserted himself between us. So it gives me some pleasure, some face-saving satisfaction, to declare unequivocally that sex between us was in the past. It's my decision. Not his.

"No more fooling around," I say with authority, unaware that hairy Bert from Pittsburgh has overheard me, and is sidling up behind me.

"Oh, come on," he says, "just a little fooling around?"

Luke laughs. "Nope," he tells our guest, "Henry's cutting me off." He extends his hand. "Good morning, I'm Luke. I'm your new houseboy."

Bert shakes his hand. "Well, and a fine houseboy you are." His eyes move up and down Luke's lithe frame.

They look like they could pose for a before-and-after chart on evolution: Bert the hulking, hairy Neanderthal and Luke the lean, smooth Cro-Magnon man. Or boy. My own eyes seem riveted again to his tight belly, the way the lines of his internal obliques drop dramatically down into his shorts. Why am I so fixated on him? Ann Marie was right the day we met him: Luke is not my type. I like bigger guys, with more muscle, more experience. Not twinks like Luke. So why can't I stop looking at him as he chats up Bert?

Because Jeff got him. That's why.

Palm Springs, White Party, 1999. A boy named Nathan, not so different from Luke. Smooth, lean, with full red lips and long eyelashes. I'd met Nathan first, in line to buy water, and by the time we'd made it back out to the dance floor we were liplocked. Sure, it was our good friend Evelyn who provided the chemical rush between us, but no amount of ecstasy could cushion what happened next. Nathan took one look at Jeff, and before long he was moving between us, kissing me for five minutes and Jeff for ten. Then me for three and Jeff for fifteen. Then he stopped coming back over to me at all. That night, back at our hotel, I slept out by the pool so that Jeff and Nathan could go at it in privacy in our shared room.

Luke is walking around with the pot of coffee asking the guests if they want refills. "Jesus Christ," I grumble, moving over to him. I grab his elbow. "Houseboys aren't *waiters*," I tell him. "Your job is to get inside and make the beds and clean the bathrooms."

"Well," he purrs, "how would I know if you don't teach me, boss?"

"Come on in," I say, "and I'll give you the rundown."

"Mmm. That sounds sexy."

"Rundown, not rubdown."

Luke makes a face. "But I haven't had any breakfast yet. Can't I at least have a little bite?"

I sigh. "Okay. But we've got a lot to do today. We've got three new rooms checking in this afternoon."

Luke saunters over to the table of sweets. I watch him as he looks over the choices and considers what to have. "It's all carbs," he says finally. "Muffins and bagels and croissants . . ."

"Like you have to worry," I growl.

Luke looks back at me. "So did you keep your promise?"

"My promise?"

"No ice cream? Remember, we're checking up on each other." He beams over at me. "I haven't had a cigarette since yesterday afternoon."

"Oh," I say in a small voice. "Good for you."

"And you?" Luke asks. "No ice cream, right?"

"Right," I lie.

"Excellent!" He returns his attention to the table. "We ought to at least put out some peanut butter," he says. "You know, for protein." He ends up choosing a blueberry muffin and pouring himself a glass of orange juice.

"Look, Luke," I say, "don't think this is going to be a regular routine." I fold my arms across my chest. "Houseboys eat on their own *before* they start work. You can grab a muffin in the kitchen before you do your rounds."

He's ignoring me. "You know, maybe if we just boiled some eggs—"

Out of the corner of my eye, I spy the neighbor's calico cat suddenly leap onto the table from the fence that divides our two properties.

"Hey!" I clap my hands. "Get off, you damn cat!"

The cat darts away under the wild rosebushes, upsetting a few cups in the process.

"Goddamn animal," I mutter, still clapping my hands to make sure it returns to its own yard. "It's always trying to get at the cream whenever I serve breakfast outside."

"Poor little thing, it was just thirsty," Luke says.

I look over at him. Luke's eyes are on the rosebushes, trying to see if he can spy the cat.

"That cat is a *pain in the ass,*" I tell him, enunciating it clearly so he understands. "It's always scaring birds away from the bird-feeder, and guests like to watch the birds."

"Cats have a right to do their thing, too," Luke says.

"Not in my yard."

Luke's silent as he takes a bite of his blueberry muffin. "Do you know I had an uncle who looked like the Penguin?" he finally asks.

I'm a bit taken aback by the non sequitur. I turn and look at him. "Your uncle looked like a penguin?"

"No. He looked like *the* Penguin." He finishes his muffin and to my chagrin he reaches down and takes another from the table. "Like from *Batman.*"

"Oh, I see."

"Yeah. Short and round with skinny eyes and a long nose. And Uncle Louie was just as vicious as the Penguin, too. Now, don't be fooled by that funny Penguin on the old *Batman* TV show or Danny DeVito's shameless mugging in *Batman Returns.* As written in the comic books, the Penguin was a cruel, vicious criminal, and I should know. I had to live with him for a while."

I just look at the kid, not sure where the hell he's going with this.

"Once," Luke says, his eyes a world away, "I saw Uncle Louie kill a stray cat who'd turned over the garbage can. I can remember sitting on my swing set, watching as Uncle Louie's rifle poked out through a hole in the window screen. Then he pulled the trigger, and kablooey! That poor old mangy cat blew apart. I had to clean up the mess, and with each scrape of fur and blood off the concrete I cried my little heart out."

He pops the last of the muffin into his mouth, chewing thoughtfully.

"My mother had a cat," he continues. "She called it Puss. She loved Puss and so I did, too. There's not a cat alive that doesn't remind me of Puss, even though Puss was a big fluffy Siamese. Even the straggliest strays that came knocking around our garbage cans reminded me of Puss. Uncle Louie hated those strays. They'd cry up on the fence, mangy in heat, and eat from our garbage, knocking it all over the place. There'd be times Uncle Louie would go out and open the lid of a trash can to find a hissing cat inside, and he'd curse so loud that the old lady next door would scream over at him to shut up. Then he'd shout back at her, and soon the whole street was shouting.

"But after Uncle Louie killed that first cat, I decided never to let it happen again. Down at the Safeway I bought two cans of tuna. I opened them with a metal can opener out on the back porch, and the stink that came out was soon wafting through the night air. You know how canned tuna fish in oil smells. Hoo-*wee*! Well, half a dozen strays came by to sniff it out. And don't you know they slurped it all down when I plopped it onto the concrete, all runny and oily."

Luke looks over at me with his soft hazel eyes, more intense now than I've ever seen them before.

"So I repeated this every night," he continues, "and soon all the cats got into the habit. Dinner was served on the back step precisely at seven—far away from our trash barrels. Of course, no more knocking over garbage cans meant there'd be no more dead cats scraped off the sidewalk with my shovel." He laughs, throwing back the last of his orange juice and wiping his mouth with a napkin. "Problem was, more and more cats seemed to find out about my little restaurant, and so I had to buy three cans, then four, then *five* cans a day to keep them all fed. That meant I had to find ways to make money to buy them all."

I can't resist asking. "How'd you make the money?"

He winks. "I found ways. Hey, I had to. It was either that or the Penguin would slaughter all the cats in Gotham City."

Who *is* this kid? I just stare at him, wondering what he might say next.

"So," he asks, "are we going to get to work?"

I make an attempt to answer, but before I can formulate the words there's another voice interrupting us.

"Is Henry already slave-driving you?"

I look around. Jeff has sauntered over from his house, wearing floral-patterned boardshorts and a white T-shirt that hugs his pecs perfectly. I see him wink at Luke.

"No," Luke tells him, "we've just been gabbing like girlfriends." He smiles at me. "Henry was just about to show me the ropes."

"The ropes, huh?" Jeff smirks. "Henry, since when are you into bondage?"

I ignore him, turning my eyes back to Luke. "Start bringing some of the dirty dishes inside," I say. "Pile them in the sink for now. I'll be in momentarily."

"Yes, sir!" Luke says cheerfully, loading up a tray of cups and glasses. Jeff pours himself some coffee. As the boy heads inside, his tight little ass shows a hint of crack above his shorts. Both Jeff and I watch him closely.

"You sure know how to pick 'em," Jeff says to me over his coffee cup.

"*You* hired him, I didn't."

"No, no, no, *Lloyd* hired him." Jeff smiles, eminently pleased with himself. "I merely suggested it."

"Have you forgotten, Jeff," I say, drawing close, "that Lloyd and I have a rule? No sex with the staff. I know you're technically not staff here at Nirvana, but I still don't think it was kosher to fuck Luke and then hire him—"

"I didn't fuck Luke." Jeff scowls at me. "Are you thinking we had sex?"

"Oh, come on, Jeff."

"I *swear*, Henry. We did *not* have sex. Not so much as a kiss."

Here's one thing I can say about Jeff. He doesn't lie to me. Even if he tried, I could tell. We've been through so much together that I'd be able to see it in his eyes. I look at him now and see he's being completely honest.

"Not that I wouldn't have *liked* to," Jeff admits, "and not that I think he would have objected." He smiles smugly for a moment, but then his expression changes. It becomes more serious, more contemplative. "But it's weird, Henry . . ."

"What's weird?"

Jeff shrugs and takes another sip of coffee. "Ever since Lloyd and I started planning for our wedding, I haven't wanted to—no, that's wrong, sometimes I've *wanted* to—but it just hasn't felt *right* to sleep with anybody else."

"What? Am I hearing correctly?"

He sticks his tongue out at me. "Yes, Henry, I'm saying I'm holding back. For now, anyway."

"Jeff O'Brien? Monogamous?" I can't quite believe what I'm hearing.

"For now." He looks over at the guesthouse. "I haven't even discussed it with Lloyd. It's not carved in cement. It's just how I'm feeling right now at this moment." He smiles. "It's a pretty awesome feeling, you know. The man I love loving me enough to want to commit to me for all time."

I hold his gaze. I remember a rainy night in Boston, back when Jeff and Lloyd were living apart. It must have been about seven, eight years ago. It was one of their rough patches, and I could see how much Jeff missed him. He'd taken out his photograph album and was leafing through it, pointing out to me pictures of Lloyd back in the days when they'd first met. A young, bushy-haired twentysomething in lycra bicycle shorts. I remember how Jeff traced the contours of the image with his finger. He wasn't good at confessing his feelings back then—he's only marginally better now—but the heartache was plain on his face.

"So many times," Jeff told me then, "Lloyd has felt this restlessness inside him . . . and each time, when he goes off to clear his head, I think this is it. This time he's not coming back."

But he always did. Lloyd's old restlessness—the impulse that led him to me, in fact—has been quiet these past several years. Running this guesthouse, he's blossomed, and Jeff's concurrent success has meant the two of them, finally, are happy and content together.

At least, they *seem* happy and content. For, in truth, I often wonder about their contentment. They've been together now, off and on, for more than a decade, and it's clear they aren't the passionate lovers of their youth. If they were, they wouldn't require all those boys climbing up their stairs, sometimes with just Jeff, sometimes with just Lloyd, oftentimes with both at the same time. It's the boys who keep the sexual spark alive between them, I believe. If they gave up the boys, what might happen? I often wonder if it's the boys who actually keep them together.

I look at Jeff, sipping his coffee, lost in thought. How had he put it? *The man I love loving me enough to want to commit to me for all time.* I must admit it *is* a pretty awesome scenario. What I wouldn't give for such a thing—and there were times Jeff himself could never have imagined such a future. Once again my mind goes back to those lonely days in Boston, when we sat together poring over his photo albums. But now Lloyd was planning on announcing to the world that he belonged to Jeff and Jeff belonged to him. Quite awesome indeed.

And now Jeff is feeling—*monogamous?* If the boys disappear, what then? I wonder. Is it possible to still get hot over a body you've slept beside for sixteen years? Is it possible to ever really have only one person in your life—only one person who fulfills all of your hopes, all of your desires, all of your needs? Does such a One exist?

I want to believe there is. I want so much to believe in the One. I could have loved Joey—or Daniel—or Lloyd—for all time. I know that. I could have loved them emotionally and spiritually and yes, physically—from the day we met until the day we died. I know that. I feel it in my heart.

Part of me, deep down, believes that there must be something wrong between Jeff and Lloyd. That they don't really love each other—at least, they don't love each other *enough*. Because if they did, there would be no need for the boys. Twenty-two or forty-two, they'd still be boned at the simple sight of each other. There would be no need for anyone else. If Lloyd had only given me a chance, I could have shown . . .

No. I put an end to my thoughts. I can't allow myself to think that way. It's not right. Jeff and Lloyd are my best friends. I won't picture myself in Jeff's place, standing next to Lloyd saying "I do."

Besides, it's no fun going down that road. All I do is get depressed all over again, and I'm tired of being depressed. Lloyd says, in fact, that getting weary of one's depression is a good sign that one is coming out of it.

"Jeff," I say, drawing close to him, "I think it's pretty natural that you don't want to trick while you're planning for the wedding. It's actually quite sweet. In fact, you ought to talk about it with Lloyd. Maybe he feels the same way."

"Well," he says, "I just don't want to scare him off." He chuckles. "Like suddenly I'm demanding monogamy and becoming this shrew of a wife."

"Somehow, I can't imagine *you* ever demanding monogamy. And I don't think he'll see it that way, either." I smirk. "Of course, this new attitude of yours does ruin the gift I was planning to get you for your wedding."

He lifts an eyebrow. "How so?"

"I was going to hire Matthew Rush to surprise you on your honeymoon."

Matthew Rush is Jeff's favorite porn star. "Hey," Jeff says, laughing, "*after* the ceremony, anything goes." He winks at me. "Unfortunately, however, Matthew's not for hire. Believe me, I've checked."

"Well, I'm impressed you didn't sleep with Luke," I tell him finally. "The way he was throwing himself at you."

"At *me*? Henry, he slept with *you*."

"Only so he could meet you." I cut him off before he objects. "Oh, come on. Carrying around all your books? The whole 'I want to be a writer' thing. He's totally obsessed with you. It's obvious."

Jeff shrugs. "Better lock my underwear drawer."

"You should take this seriously, Jeff. I'll be honest. I don't trust him. Even when I first met him, he seemed to be a schemer. That brain of his is always plotting his next move. I'm keeping my eye on him."

"Henry?"

I spin around. And there's Luke, standing right behind me. How much has he heard?

"Should I start cleaning the rooms?" he asks. He apparently heard nothing, or he's playing innocent. "I'd like to get started so that I can spend the afternoon writing." He casts a look over at his idol. "I know you write best in the morning, Jeff, and so do I— but I guess from here on, I've got to make do with the time I have."

Jeff smiles.

"It's like you said when you were being interviewed on *This Way Out,*" Luke continues. "You said, 'If one is serious about writing, every excuse to avoid it will fail. You'll find time to write on your lunch hour, or during the time you usually spent watching television. Or you'll get up at four in the morning. If you're serious, you'll always find the time.'"

Jeff's smile fades, just a little. "I think those may have been my *exact* words."

"I live by them," Luke tells him. "Hey, there's that cat again."

I clap my hands to scare it away. "Damn thing. Cats are so sneaky."

Jeff looks at me coldly. "You know, you really need to work on your catphobia."

"I love cats," Luke chirps. "You *have* one, right, Jeff? Mr. Tompkins? You talked about him in an interview in *Bay Windows.*"

Jeff looks a little uneasy that Luke knows all this information about him. "Yes, I have a cat. He's been with Lloyd and me for a long time."

"I love cats," Luke repeats. "You know, it's hard in gay culture to come out as a cat-lover."

"Yes," Jeff agrees cautiously. "that's what I said in the interview . . ."

"It's like it's just not cool for a gay man to be into cats—the way lesbians are, anyway, or the way most gay guys are into their dogs."

Jeff is starting to smile. "Well, you know the faggot-canine connection is a long and honorable one. You see it on every street in every gay ghetto."

"I know!" Luke says. "You have to have a dog so you can strike up a conversation!"

"Well," Jeff says, "it's easier to chat up a hunky blonde walking down Commercial Street if he's got a golden retriever with him. 'Hey, nice dog,' you say, when what you really mean is 'Hey, nice abs.'"

"I know!" Luke says. "But when you ask gay men if they like *cats*, they invariably look at you a little funny, as if you'd just asked them if they liked drinks with little parasols in them or the music of Holly Near."

Jeff laughs. Damn. The kid is winning him over again.

"Cats are considered girly," Luke continues. "Dogs are manly—except poodles, but they don't count."

"Yeah, if you have a poodle, you're an old queen," Jeff says.

"I know a very hot guy in town who has a poodle," I say petulantly.

"You know," Luke says, ignoring me, "maybe that's why so many gay men claim to be allergic to cats."

"Have you noticed that, too?" Jeff asks. "There's *got* to be a correlation. None of my straight friends—or my lesbian friends—are allergic to cats. But gay men start sniveling as soon as you tell them there's a cat in the house. When one trick I brought home suggested I put my cat outside for the, um, *duration*, I tossed him out instead."

"And do you know what's so cool about cats?" Luke asks. "They could care *less* about what you do with some guy. Cats want no part of it. If cats could roll their eyes in disinterest at two guys in bed, they would. *Dogs*, on the other hand, will jump up onto the bed, tongues wagging, saliva dripping, as if they want to make it a three-way."

"Dogs are loyal," I protest. "Dogs are devoted. Dogs are loving. Dogs are fun."

"Dogs are wet," Luke says. "Dogs are loud. Dogs remind me of needy fag hags who'll do anything to keep their gay boys happy. Or some co-dependent boyfriend who doesn't even let us go to the bathroom alone."

Jeff gets a big kick out of that. Luke sure knows how to score points.

"It's so wrong how cat-hating is accepted in this culture," Luke says.

"My point in the interview *exactly,*" Jeff says. But he no longer seems unnerved by how much Luke remembers about it.

"In cartoons, dogs are always the heroes and cats are the villains. The whole point of a Sylvester cartoon was to watch Tweety Bird drop an anvil on the poor cat's head. And everybody on TV had a dog— from the Waltons to the Bradys to the girls on *The Facts of Life.* But only *witches* had cats."

"To me," Jeff says, "cats should be the gay men's pet of choice. No dirty clean-up. No running home in the middle of tea dance to take it out for a leak. Cats are what we as gay men aspire to be. Cool. Slightly mysterious, completely autonomous, perfectly groomed."

"So why hasn't it happened?" I ask.

"It's obvious, Henry," Luke tells me. "A cat would never, ever, consent to being put on a leash."

Jeff loves it. He drops an arm around my shoulder and leans in as if to share a secret. "You see, buddy, cats are tops, and most gay men are loath to advertise their bottomness walking down the street. With a dog, they can pretend to be master. But just let some faggot try to saddle up a cat and take him out for a trot. He'll quickly learn you can't use a cat to get the double takes or the chance to score."

"I can't wait to meet your cat," Luke says. "Where was he yesterday?"

"Mr. Tompkins is an old guy. He likes to hide out. Come on over, and I'll introduce you—"

"Excuse me," I interrupt. "But Luke has work to do."

"Oops," Luke says. "Of course." He smiles at me. "So will you show me where the laundry is?"

I let out a sigh. "Yeah. Come on. Follow me." I turn to Jeff as I start to walk away. "By the way, your sister wants you to do something with J. R. today. Maybe take him out on the boat. The kid seems depressed."

Jeff shrugs. "I just saw him and suggested we go jetskiing. But he said he just wanted to listen to his new CD. On a beautiful day like today!" He makes a face. "Kids. Who can figure them out?"

I head up the path toward the house after another kid I can't quite figure out. Inside, I yank open the cellar door and pull the string for the overhead light. I gesture to Luke to follow me down into the musty darkness. Lloyd wants to remodel the basement into a game room, but that's still another year or two down the road in his business plan.

"Okay," I'm telling Luke as we reach the bottom, "I've already tossed some of the sheets down here. All the rooms are going to need fresh linens and towels for—"

I feel a hand grab my crotch.

"Henry," Luke purrs, his lips at my ear.

I pull forcefully away. "I meant what I said, Luke," I tell him. "No more of that."

"No one will know," he says, his eyes burning in the near-darkness.

"Do you want this job, Luke?" I draw close to him, meeting his eyes directly. "Or do you want to fuck it up? If you fuck it up, you've lost your best chance to stay close to Jeff."

He backs off.

"Just as I thought. You wouldn't want to screw anything up between you and Jeff." I pause, rubbing my chin as I observe him. "What I'm not sure is, do you just want him because you find him hot, or is there more? Is it even just hero worship? Or do you think he can turn you into the next literary wunderkind?"

Luke says nothing, just stares at me.

"Let me tell you something, buddy boy." I draw in very close, just an inch from his face. "Jeff and Lloyd are getting married, and they don't need some sexy little number like you waltzing in and coming between them. And if you're thinking Jeff will introduce you to his agent or send your manuscript to his publisher, you've got another surprise coming to you. Do you know how often Jeff gets approached to do that? Do you know how many wannabe writers with stars in their eyes try to foist their manuscripts on him? I can assure you he's not going there with you, just like he won't go there with anyone."

I wait to see what he might say, but Luke remains silent.

"So," I say, "what will it be then, Luke? If there's not going to be any sex—with me *or* with Jeff—and if there's not going to be any book deal at the end of this little houseboy stint, do you want to quit now? I'm just laying it all out for you, so you know your options. What will it be?"

He regards me steely-eyed for several seconds. The seconds stretch into a minute, in fact, before he finally speaks.

"Where's the laundry detergent?" he asks.

I don't move from my position. I just keep staring at him.

"The laundry detergent, Henry," he says calmly. "How can I do my job without any laundry detergent?"

I hold his gaze for one second longer. "Behind you on the shelf," I say.

"Thank you."

Luke moves off to retrieve it. I head toward the stairs.

"I'll toss down the rest of the linens," I say. "And after you've got them loaded, I'll show you where we keep the supplies for cleaning the bathrooms."

"Yes, sir," Luke replies as he stoops to gather the sheets on the floor into his tight, sinewy arms.

I turn away and head upstairs.

I was right. My job has just become hell.

6

MY BED

That night, I have a dream.

I'm back in my parents' home, in West Springfield, Massachusetts. I'm fifteen. I'm getting ready to go out with my best friend Jack, the boy who introduced me to grunge music and, not incidentally, the first person who ever told me he was gay. Jack's two years older than I am; he stayed back in school at least one grade. So he's got his driver's license, and in my dream, I'm once again riding around with him, reliving a night that seemed to sum up everything I was at the time.

And maybe still am.

Jack is driving—fast—in his mother's car. It's a Chevy Nova. I'm sitting next to Jack in the front seat. He smells of boys perfume—stinking up the car, but I kind of like it.

"We're gonna get carded," I tell Jack. "I just know it."

Jack wiggles his wrist at me. "Stop worrying. We'll get in."

"But what if we get caught? What will my mother say?"

I *know* what my mother will say. "A *gay bar*?? My underage son was found in a—*gay bar*????"

The words carry a lot of weight. Jack's been wanting to go to the bar for months, ever since he admitted to me that he was gay. I was too scared to admit to him that I was, too, so I compromised and said I was "curious." It was a word used a lot in those days. Saying you were curious was better than admitting right out that you were gay, like Jack did. It also kept Jack from trying to have sex with me, the idea of which was both exhilarating and terrifying.

I like Jack. I may even be a little bit in love with him. But it's not so much *him* I'm in love with. It's the *idea* of him. Did I know this then, at fifteen? Or is it knowledge that came later, and only because I am dreaming do I seem to know it as a boy? No matter. Looking over at Jack as he drives the car, I am besotted with the image of him, the scent of him. Jack is everything I want to be but am not. Confident. Cool. Clear in mind and heart. And so I dress like Jack (lots of chains and cutoff flannel and Doc Martens boots). I wear my hair like him (spiky and uneven). I talk like him (learning words like *scumbag* and *bodacious*.)

But most importantly, I listen to the same music that Jack does, becoming fanatically converted to the belief that the only music worth listening to was coming out of Seattle. It's a grittier, more American version of punk that Jack calls "grunge." The pictures on the cassette covers of the various bands certainly seem grungy enough: guys with unshaven faces who look as if they haven't bathed in days. Within no time I've bought up all the old albums of The Melvins and The Wipers that I can find, and I developed a dreamy crush on Mark Arm, lead singer of an obscure (to everyone else but Jack and me) band named Green River.

Tonight, a Springfield bar known for its large gay clientele is showcasing a local band that Jack is certain to make it big. "They sound just like The Melvins," he tells me.

Of course, neither of us has ever been to a gay bar. So this is an opportunity we simply can't miss.

"Do you think I'll meet anybody?" Jack asks.

"If you do," I tell him, "just don't leave me alone."

"What are you so afraid about Henry?"

I shoot him a look. "I *mean* it, Jack. Please don't leave me alone!"

I snap down the passenger-side visor and check for nose hairs.

Jack is smirking. "What're you gonna do when I move to New York?"

"You're not going to move to New York. Your father won't let you."

"Yes, I am. Soon as I save up enough money. What—you think I want to work at Stop N Save all my life?"

Ever since his mother died during our freshman year of high school, Jack has been possessed with this idea of going to New York and becoming an actor. He figures he can drop out of school and make his way in New York—but he's still just a kid. I don't know where he gets off having such big ideas.

"My mother said I was better looking than any of the guys on her soap operas," he tells me, for the three-hundredth time. "She said I could make it." He looks over at me. "Springfield's got nothing for me. I want to be an actor."

"I *know* you want to be an actor, Jack," I tell him. "Just keep your eyes on the road."

He just snorts. I'm getting angry at a nose hair, trying to stuff it up my nostril with my pinky.

"My brother knows a guy who works at a theater on a Broadway. He's going to introduce me to him. He can help me get some parts."

"I don't know why you want to move away," I say. "Springfield's not so bad."

"Are you kidding? Springfield sucks. I'm moving to New York."

"Why do you have to go to New York? There are theaters here. Besides, Springfield's on the move. I read it in a magazine. The economy is good. Springfield's going to become a Major City. Capital M. Capital C."

"Where'd you hear *that?*"

"I dunno," I tell him. "Somewhere."

I squint at the city's skyline, glowing green against the purple sky as we approach. Even at night, one could make out the noble necks of the cranes, like sleeping giraffes. "They're building a lot of new skyscrapers, you know."

Jack snorts again.

We don't say much else until we arrive. The Gay Bar is a lonely block of concrete tucked between two giant warehouses. Cars are parked all the way up and down the street. There's a beat in the air: almost undetectable at first, no music, just a steady pounding, a bass vibration coming from inside the club.

"I hope I don't hate this place," I say, as we get out of the car and head toward the door. Jack isn't listening.

We pay our covers. By the grace of God, the doorman doesn't ask to see our IDs. Inside, strobe lights flash across the empty stage. Jack doesn't like it. Grunge is supposed to be straightforward. No laser shows, no frills. "You can tell this place is usually a disco," he gripes.

We hate disco. We hate glam rock. We might only be in high school, but we know what's cool. We know the future.

"Don't leave me alone," I tell Jack again, never far from his shoulder as we move through the crowd.

The lights on the dance floor pulse on and off, with moments of total darkness alternating between red, gold, and green light. Each time a new color flashes on, Jack's face looks different. We find a place close to the stage and position ourselves there. We don't even try to order a drink. No use pushing our luck.

I look around at the people in the bar. Mostly older men, but a few younger guys are starting to arrive now, drawn certainly by the band. A boy who can't be too much older than us stands a few feet away, his eyes flickering now and then our way as he checks us out. Thin and blond, he's dressed like us, in a flannel sleeveless shirt and torn jeans, a wallet chain looped low along his hip.

"He's sexy," Jack whispers to me.

"Not really," I say. I'm not sure why I'm denying the obvious. The guy is a bit wispy, but nonetheless very cute. Maybe I don't like admitting that he's cute because I think he's looking more at Jack than he is at me.

Then the band comes on. They hardly meet Jack's description of sounding like The Melvins. In fact, they suck—a bunch of pretentious local wannabe grunge artists trying too hard. And when you try too hard in grunge, you've automatically lost.

But Jack seems not to notice, or to care. He's hopping and jumping and shaking his head. When the lead singer attempts to stage dive into what passes for—in Springfield—as a mosh pit, he pretty much just lands on his knees on the filthy floor. Still, Jack is pogoing away, and before long the wispy boy next to us has eased his way closer. I watch as the two of them start banging heads, pretending they're in Seattle listening to Green River instead of in

Springfield listening to a bunch of guys who probably work at Burger King during the day. Jack actually looks orgasmic— or in the throes of agony.

I don't even try to keep up. I slip away to the men's room, where some old guy with a big walrus moustache seems way too interested in how I'm peeing into the urinal. I quickly zip up and leave.

I don't belong here. My first time in a gay bar—and all I'd really rather be doing is sitting in my room with Jack, shoulder to shoulder, our headphones clamped over our ears, listening to our music. That's all I need. I don't need to have sex with Jack—or with any other guy for that matter. Just shoulder to shoulder is enough for me.

I realize that I'm alone. I try to spot Jack in the crowd but he seems to have vanished. So has the wispy little boy.

"Hey," a voice says behind me.

I turn. It's the older guy from the bathroom.

"Hey," I say, not wanting to look at him.

"You doing okay?"

I shrug. "Just looking for my friend."

"He take off and leave you?"

"No, I'm sure he's around here somewhere."

"If you can't find him," Walrus Moustache says, "I'll be happy to give you a ride home."

"Thanks, but I'll be fine."

"I'm not trying to be a dirty old man," the guy says. But that's exactly what he is to my mind. He must be at least thirty years old.

I move off, scanning the crowd for Jack. Then I spot him, kissing the wispy boy in the corner. I watch them for a while, growing both aroused and uneasy. Jack doesn't even seem concerned about where I am. Finally they move off, through the crowd, toward the front door. I follow.

"Jack!"

He turns to face me. "I'll be back inside later," he says, his arm draped around the other guy's shoulders. "We're just going to the car."

"You're not going to leave without me?" I shout.

He doesn't answer. Under the harsh glow of the streetlight, the other guy no longer looks quite our age. He's got to be at least in college. He might be as old as twenty-five. I wonder if he knows Jack is only sixteen.

I head back into the bar. Walrus Moustache is waiting for me.

"Your friend making out in the car?" he asks.

I shrug. "I don't know what they're doing out there."

The guy smiles. "You feeling lonesome?"

He's creeping me out. I just fold my arms across my chest.

He leans in closer. "You're not having fun, are you?"

"No," I whisper.

"I meant it," he says. "I'll give you a ride home if you want."

I look over into his eyes. His breath smells like beer. There's foam on his moustache.

And I start to cry.

Did it really happen? Did I really cry that night in the bar all those years ago?

I'm certainly crying in my sleep as I wake myself up from the dream.

How many years has it been since I thought of that night?

Jack was my first crush, though I can't say it was ever really sexual. I didn't want Jack; at least not Jack the boy who drove his mother's car and talked about running away to New York. I wanted my own version of Jack—a Jack who didn't want to leave, who wanted to stay with me, who would never have left me alone in a bar while he made out with some guy in a car.

Jack and I never did have sex. By the time I'd gotten over myself and jettisoned the "curious" label, embracing instead an unequivocal identity of "gay," Jack was long gone from my life. He'd done exactly what he said he'd do. He dropped out of school, quit the Stop N Save, hightailed it out of Springfield and moved to New York. Whether he became an actor, I don't know. We didn't keep in touch. Jack disappeared from my life, if not my dreams.

At night, in my bed at my parents' house, I would try to imagine a future for myself, the kind that Jack had found so easy to visualize for himself. It wasn't New York that I dreamed about. It wasn't fame and glamour and success. I'd lie there in my bed, imagining myself sleeping beside a man who I loved and who loved me back. My fantasies—which sometimes postponed sleep for several hours—were rarely sexual. Instead, they consisted of simple things—cooking together or watching TV or listening to music. And in these fantasies, the man of my dreams was always named Jack.

He didn't have Jack's face, or his voice, or any of his history— but still my imaginary lover bore the name of my friend who had vanished from my life not long after that night at the bar. That night, my friend Jack had found himself, come to some core truth about who he was in the backseat of his mother's Chevy Nova. Was it that experience that gave him the strength to do what he did—to get out of town and follow his dream?

There was nothing for me to do but watch from a distance. Furious with Jack, I finally accepted Walrus Moustache's offer of a ride home. I remember opening the door of his electric-blue Trans Am, crinkling up my nose at the smell of cigarettes. Looking back, I think I was both fearing and hoping for the same thing that Jack had found—that the guy would suggest we make out in the backseat. I understood then that that was what Jack had come to the bar for—not for the music. I wanted the same reward, even if it had to come from a man as old as this one was.

Lying here now in my bed, the leftover tears of my dream still rolling down my cheeks, I try to picture the man's face. Surely I'm older now than he was then. It's the moustache that stands out most clearly in my mind. I remember little else about him other than his car—and, of course, his words. Words that have often come back to me as the years went on.

"Where do you live?" he asks, starting the ignition, and I'm back in my dream.

"West Springfield," I tell him.

He nods, and we drive in silence. He makes no move. He's no gay basher, no dirty old man. He's giving me a ride home, just as he'd promised.

When we get to my street, I ask him to let me off a few houses down from my own. My mother would certainly question why I was coming home in a strange car. The guy nods. He understands.

"That was your first time in a gay bar, wasn't it?" he asks, turning to look at me.

I nod.

He smiles under that heavy moustache. "It's going to get better," he tells me. "You'll have nights much better than this one."

"Thanks," I say to him.

"Thanks," I whisper again in the dark, half asleep and half awake.

I scrunch up my pillows the way I used to do as a boy. In my arms they come alive—the body of the man I love. It's been a long time since I've thought of that man as "Jack." More recently he's been Joey, or Daniel, or Lloyd. But tonight the invisible man beside me is once again Jack, the childhood hero of my fantasies, the one, true lover I must never stop believing is out there for me, who will someday take me in his arms and tell me that he loves me—on a night much better than this one.

7

COMMERCIAL STREET

I take one last surreptitious look at my reflection in the café's window before I head inside.

I look okay. The evening, thankfully, has turned out to be a little breezy, so I was able to wear an unbuttoned short-sleeve collar shirt over my tee. It hides the love handles. I've spiked my hair a little bit with gel, and the tan I got at the beach this afternoon is working. At least I hope it's working. It's hard to be sure about anything anymore. Every year it gets harder to keep up. Damn, I hate getting older.

I take a deep breath and enter.

Gale isn't here yet. I hold up two fingers to the waiter and he gestures toward the table by the window. I sit, staring back out onto Commercial Street, watching the street theater.

It's the colorful parade of characters up and down this narrow street along the harbor that makes Provincetown so popular as a resort town. Across the way some woman in a long diaphanous dress is playing a giant harp. From my left a tall man in leather chaps comes striding into view, flabby hairy butt hanging out for all to see. A girl walking with her boyfriend hurries behind him to snap a picture. Suddenly from the right comes Varla Jean Merman, riding by on her bike, a big, long-legged, redheaded drag queen in a blue polka-dotted dress, waving and honking her horn as she zooms off stage left. Then a shirtless, tattooed man with a live boa constrictor wrapped around his shoulders appears, sauntering over to the café window to study the menu posted outside. Instinctively I shrink back a little in my seat.

That's when I see him. Gale is heading down the street, in a green A & F tank and faded jeans that reveal an impressive bulge. God, he's sexy. I take a sip of water and notice my hand is shaking.

"Hey," Gale says, coming inside and spotting me.

"Hey," I say, and he kisses me, quick, on the lips. I'm surprised by it. But also pleased.

Gale sits down at the table. "Waiting long?"

"Just a few minutes. Watching the world go by."

"It's an amazing street," he says. "When I first visited here two years ago, I thought I was on another planet."

"Where are you from?" I ask.

"Michigan. A small town in the middle of the state." He raises his left hand to me and points with his right to the middle of his palm. "Right here."

I don't get the gesture at first, then it hits me. "Ah," I say. "Michigan is shaped like a hand."

"Well, like a mitten actually, with a separate thumb." He's looking at the menu. "What are you going to have?"

"I think just a cheeseburger."

Gale lifts his thickly-lashed eyes over his menu. "But isn't *Weiner* a Jewish name?"

I smile. "Yes, but I'm far from kosher. There's really very little that's Jewish about me except for my last name."

"Oh, I don't think one can be something other than mainstream heterosexual, white, and Christian, and not have it inform one's identity."

I smile. He's deep. I just give him a shrug.

The waiter has arrived. I order my cheeseburger, medium-rare, with fries. Then I change my mind and ask for a salad instead of the fries. The waiter nods knowingly. He must get a lot of gay men conscious about carbs and fried foods.

Gale, on the other hand, orders a hummus plate, with a side of greens topped with tahini sauce. "I'm a vegetarian," he informs me. Immediately I feel like a big fat sloppy politically incorrect carnivore.

"Hey," I say, suddenly remembering something. "Didn't I see you eating a hamburger yesterday?"

"It was a veggie burger," Gale tells me. "They make good ones, and good ones are very hard to find."

"How long have you been a vegetarian?"

"Since a summer I spent working on a dairy farm and saw how they mistreated the cows and the chickens." He shudders.

I so wish I'd ordered pasta. I manage a small smile and take a sip of my water, trying to think of something to say. "So what do you do?" I try the oldest conversation-starter in the book.

"Nothing at the moment. I was working as a house painter for a while, now I'm just looking around for odd jobs."

I nod. What do you say to that? Evidently Gale knows what I do, because he doesn't ask. We sit without speaking for a few awkward seconds.

"My father was Jewish," Gale says, making his own attempt to jump-start the conversation. "But that doesn't count, right?"

I shake my head. "It comes through the mother. But I guess if your father was really into Judaism—"

"My father left us when I was three. But still, I always knew I was part Jewish, that I didn't really fit in with what was supposed to be the rest of the world."

I nod. "I know what you mean. I felt similarly."

"My mother took us kids to Rhode Island and then got remarried to some swamp Yankee. And then after that divorce, she married again to a high Episcopalian, so I guess I'm just a mutt when it comes to religion."

I smile. Good, we're talking.

"The only time I ever went to the synagogue as a kid," I tell Gale, "was when my grandfather or some friend of the family's died. I hated putting on those skull caps. I felt like an idiot."

"So you weren't bar mitzvahed?"

"Nope. My parents were pretty ambivalent about all of that. We had a Christmas tree every year. I believed in Santa Claus. But still they always reminded me that we weren't Christian, and that as Jews we were God's chosen people."

Gale smiles. "I think that's what every religion believes."

"I suppose so."

"The root of all evil, too," he adds. "The belief that we're right, and everybody else is wrong. God is on our side. It's the core of the fighting in Israel and Palestine. It's what fuels Islamic terrorism. It's the corrosive force that's destroying American politics."

I'm not sure what to say. Five minutes, and we're already into a heavy conversation. I'm not good in heavy conversations, certainly not heavy political conversations. Now if this were *Jeff* sitting here instead of me, he'd be fully engaged and passionate, able to reply to Gale with an equally astute and powerful comment. Very quickly they'd be engaged in a lively, blood-pumping dialogue—one that, no doubt, would lead to some very hot sex after dinner. "Passionate conversations," Jeff has often said, "are the best foreplay."

But I'm not Jeff. "Yeah," is all I manage to say. "Things are bad in the world." Even before I finish the sentence, I know it's lame. And so more silence descends over our table.

"So," Gale says, searching for yet another topic, "how long have you lived in P'town?"

"About five years full time. Ever since Lloyd asked me to come work as manager of Nirvana."

"And you just chucked your previous life good-bye?"

"I was pretty unhappy in my job." I fill him in on all the boring details. Leaving the insurance company, moving here, working as a massage therapist. I leave out the escorting part. No need to scare him off further. He already thinks I'm an animal-hating dim bulb. Why add whore into the mix? So I finish up with some positive spin. "Since moving here," I tell him, "I've really come to love the place. I feel a real spiritual connection. I can't imagine living anywhere else."

"Even in the off season? This will be my first winter coming up."

"Well, it can get pretty desolate, but that's okay. I just think back to my old life of drudgery getting up at five-thirty in the morning and taking the T to work, all knotted up in my suit and tie. Now when I wake up, the first thing I do is take a walk along the beach, thinking about all the schmucks back in Boston schlepping to work."

Gale smiles. "You walk on the beach even in winter?"

"Sure. Winter's the best time." I don't tell him that lately I've turned into a big fat lazy dog, sleeping in the extra fifteen minutes instead of taking my walk along the beach. Better to paint a more romantic picture, especially since I'd seemed so lame moments before. "The wind howling," I say, "the salty air really fresh and alive . . ."

"I hope I make it through the winter," Gale says. "I'm a little worried about the isolation, but after the past year, I'm looking forward to a little peace and quiet."

That's the cue for me to ask about him, to inquire just what made this past year so intense that he's looking forward to some isolation. But something in me can't frame the words. I look over at him taking a sip of his water. Gale is so unbelievably handsome, more so than I'd realized. His brown eyes are so vital, so alive. The lines of his face are extraordinary. His lips are full and red. Suddenly I feel my cock fill up with blood. I have this vision of kissing him, and I feel my face burn.

Fortunately, at that moment, the waiter brings our salads. We eat for a few minutes in silence. Then Gale says, "I really liked that you said you believed in monogamy."

"Well, for myself anyway."

He smiles. "Well, that's all we *can* believe in, isn't it? What's right for ourselves. As soon as we start imposing our beliefs on others, we wind up like—"

"Like the rest of the world," I finish, "engaged in all their petty warfare over religion and their brand of truth."

A wide grin stretches over Gale's face. I've scored a point. Maybe the first one all evening.

"Precisely," he says. "All we can own is our particular truth. And for me, I want to explore being one-hundred-percent faithful to someone. And I don't mean just sexually. I mean emotionally, intellectually, spiritually . . ."

I pop a cucumber into my mouth, really craving some French fries and ketchup. "*All* of that?"

"All of it." Gale's eyes are even more passionate now than they were when he was talking politics. "I want to really find my soulmate. To reserve all my passion, every last drop of it, for him and him only."

"But intellectually?" I ask. "Spiritually? You mean you wouldn't be able to have a deep conversation with a friend?"

"That's what I mean," Gale says. "I know it sounds extreme, but I want to see if it's possible to really find one person who will satisfy every need."

I make a face. "Well, don't you think that's a bit unrealistic?"

He looks at me with some surprise. "But why? You believe that one person should be able to satisfy every *sexual* need, right?"

"Well, I, yes, but—"

"So why not in other areas of our lives too? Why should sex—which I don't even think is the most important expression of intimacy between two people—be the one thing we reserve as special?"

Again I'm at a loss as to what to say. Thankfully I'm rescued once more by our waiter, who clears off our salad plates and replaces them with our entrees. I look down at my hamburger bleeding on my plate. I wish I'd at least ordered it well-done.

"Bon appetit," Gale says, dipping his pita bread into his hummus.

I take a bite. Gale's words actually make some kind of sense—but it's warped sense. Does a true monogamous relationship really mean we forego all other close friendships? Certainly I know couples that have done so— usually to their regret when they break up later on, when they find they've alienated all their friends and have no support system left. As much as I might long for a sexually monogamous relationship, I can't see cutting off intimate talks and feelings and expressions with good friends. I can't imagine losing Jeff and Lloyd just because I find a boyfriend.

But Gale raises a good point: why should we single out sex? I agree with him that sex isn't the most important piece of intimacy between two people. Commitment and consideration and trust and understanding and companionship—those are the things that ultimately matter more than rolling around between the sheets. So why is it *sex* that we make exclusive and not those other things—emotional things, intellectual things, spiritual things?

I can almost hear Lloyd's voice answering for me: "Because it's *sex* that most people have hang-ups with."

"Good?"

I look up from my plate. Gale is smiling over at me, but I wonder if there's accusation in his voice as I chew my ground-up dead
cow. I nod and wipe my chin with my napkin.

Thankfully our conversation gets lighter as dinner progresses.
We talk about what shows we've seen so far this summer. We both
love Varla Jean and Ryan Landry's Showgirls, but split over the
new lesbian comic at the Post Office Café. I liked her, but Gale
isn't so sure. We agree to see her again together and make a decision.

Heading out of the restaurant onto Commercial Street, I'm
surprised when Gale takes my hand. I don't resist. We walk for a
while in silence, the sun having nearly set but still casting a soft
pink light across the white clapboard shops. I smell the salty air
that blows in from the harbor.

"Do you want to get an ice-cream cone?" Gale asks.

"Sure," I say automatically, then think better of it. "No, actually,
I'm trying to cut back."

"Why? You look great."

I pat my belly with my free hand as reply.

"You gay boys and your body image," Gale says, laughing.

"Hey, you act as if you're not one of us. You can't fool me. I've
seen you at the gym." I smile. "Flipping over the bar. Showing off
those calves of yours. You spend a lot of time keeping yourself
looking good."

He shrugs. "I try."

"And succeed." I lean into him. "You have an awesome body."

"I'm glad you think so," he says quietly.

"Why you're still single, I'm not sure."

Gale sighs. "I'm picky. As you may have gathered."

"I like a man with standards."

Something in what I've just said seems to inspire Gale. He suddenly stops walking and kisses me full on the lips. A hard kiss, lots
of tongue, right there on the street.

"Wow," I say when we finally pull apart.

"Want to go back to my place?" Gale asks.

"Yes," I reply instantly.

Gale lives in the West End, in a small studio apartment carved
into the attic of a nineteenth-century fisherman's house. It's dark

and musty, furnished with only a mattress on the floor, a beat-up old couch, and tables made of milk crates and plywood. Books are everywhere, on the floor and on the mattress. An ancient refrigerator crouches next to an equally old gas stove.

"Sorry for the mess," Gale says.

"It's not a problem." My lust is driving me now. I just want to get his jeans off and my mouth on that full ass and those shapely calves.

"I've got to pee first," he says. I nod. I watch him as he heads into the small, closet-sized bathroom. "Pee shy," he says, closing the door behind him.

I sit on the mattress and examine some of the books on the floor. *The Male Couple. Gay Men and Sex. Exploring Same-Sex Relationships.* Almost every title is about being gay or being in a relationship.

Gale has come out of the bathroom and is standing over me.

"In case you're wondering," he says, "I haven't been out as a gay man for very long."

I nod, a little grin playing with my lips. "So now that you've read all the texts, you're looking for some real-life experience."

"I suppose so." He sits beside me on the mattress. Our thighs touch. "Henry, maybe I shouldn't have asked you up here."

"Why not?"

"Because . . ." He looks at me with those big brown eyes of his. "Have you been in many relationships, Henry?"

"I've had my share."

"Were you monogamous?"

"Yes. For as long as they lasted, anyway, which was never all that long."

"Which one was the most significant?"

I'm about to say Joey, but something stops me. Lloyd was perhaps more significant, but that wasn't ever really a relationship. So instead I surprise myself by saying, "Shane."

"And why was he the most significant?"

I consider the question. Certainly I was never in love with Shane in the way I was in love with Joey. There was no great pang at the end of our relationship. I accepted it and moved on. There was never any great yearning for Shane the way there was for

Lloyd. But here's what was different: I was friends with Shane before we became a couple, so all in all, I knew him longer than any of the others. And Shane was the only one of my boyfriends who was more in love with me than I was with him.

"Shane forced me to confront things about myself," I tell Gale, realizing this myself perhaps for the first time. "He always knew when I was bullshitting, either him or myself. I think after my relationship with Shane, I knew myself better."

"So until then you weren't quite sure who you were?"

I smile. "Well, I had a few glimpses. But it was hard, you know. We were talking about being Jewish earlier. I never had any sense of myself as a Jew growing up, but I also knew I wasn't Christian. So it left me kind of confused. Who the hell *am* I? And then when I came out as gay, I didn't fit into that world, either. I felt really marginalized because I was skinny and nerdy and nobody talked to me at gay bars. I thought bars were the only place you could meet other gay people. So once again, I didn't quite know where I belonged."

Gale is nodding. "That's how I felt growing up. I wasn't like my brothers and sisters. I was the odd one out. And then, in the gay world, I still felt like an outsider."

I smile. I like this guy. I'm really starting to like him a lot, even with all his vegetarianism and extreme views on relationships. He's not so different than I am really—he wants to fit in, to be loved, to find the One.

"Maybe," I say, "maybe here, in this place of outsiders at the end of the world, you won't feel that way anymore."

Gale smiles over at me. Such an adorable smile. Dimples even.

We kiss again. This time I take the lead, kissing him softly, then with more urgency. My hands explore his smooth, rock-hard arms before moving up to his face. I cup his surprisingly soft cheeks in my palms as I continue to kiss him. My cock is so hard it's straining against my underwear.

We sit that way, kissing deeply, for several minutes. There's something about a long, deep kiss that's intoxicating. You're no longer breathing air, just pheromones. Time shuts down. You're not just one person anymore, but a new creature with four arms, four legs, and one heart.

Inevitably we ease back onto the mattress, barely breaking our liplock. We kiss side by side for a while, then I gently move on top of him. Between us is wedged the rock-hard pole in my pants, and I expect to feel Gale's own hard-on. When I don't, I worry he might not be as turned on as I am, and I think maybe I'm moving too fast.

I break free of our kiss and look down at him.

"You okay?" I whisper.

He nods, closing his eyes and moving his face up to kiss me again.

We resume our passion. I let my hands explore his body through his clothes. I feel his tight hard round pecs and the hard ripple of his abs. Gently I tug at his shirt, peeling it up and over his head. The sight is spectacular. Every muscle of his torso is defined in perfect relief. Running my fingers along the contours of his abs I marvel at his silky smooth skin. Not one hair anywhere.

"Henry," he says.

My finger is running along the waistband of his jeans.

"Henry," he says again.

I'm about to make the leap of unbuttoning his jeans. I look up at him.

"Can we just kiss for now?" he asks.

I'm disappointed, especially with how hard my cock is in my pants, but I also understand. He wants more than just a one-night stand. He wants more than just a quick fuck. He wants to find a relationship that is more organic than most, one that grows naturally and emotionally, that isn't rooted only in the loins. I manage a small smile and lay down beside him.

We don't kiss again, however. Gale just lies there looking up at the ceiling.

"I'm not like most gay men," he says finally.

"Neither am I," I tell him.

He turns and faces me. "I like you, Henry. A lot. But I think I want to say good night now."

"Okay." I reach over and kiss him quickly on the lips. "It's cool."

He watches as I stand, adjusting the weight in my underwear.

"Sorry about that," he says.

I laugh a little. "Don't be. It's just a promise of things to come."
Gale smiles but says nothing.

He walks me to the door and we kiss again briefly as we part.
"I'll call you," he says, and suddenly I'm convinced that he won't.

At the bottom of his stairs, I turn to wave good-bye, but he's
gone back inside.

I try not to feel shitty. It was a good date. We had some good
conversation. And some very good kissing. Gale's sweet, he's
sexy—and he said he liked me. A lot.

But he also asked me to leave. Maybe, in fact, that's a good
sign. Maybe it's a sign he wants to get serious. Maybe for once
someone will really want to get serious with me, commit to me, be
mine forever.

Except Gale's vision of forever was a little scary. I can't forget
that.

"Or his eyes," I murmur to myself, remembering those liquid
brown orbs that made my heart melt. I can't forget those eyes—
or that torso, or that ass, or those calves . . .

"Damn," I say, realizing my lust hasn't subsided.

I look up and realize where I am—approaching the Boatslip,
where by this time of night, out in back, under the pier, a certain
type of activity is surely taking place . . .

In all my years in Provincetown, I've never been to the dick
dock. Jeff has; of *course* he has, what hasn't Jeff done? He's described it to me. His tales of sex in the dark always seemed sleazy
and unappealing to me—all these guys lurking, occasionally
pairing off to suck and fuck while the others gather around to
watch . . .

I find myself stopped on the street, staring out beyond the
Boatslip.

I can't, I tell myself.

But inexplicably I'm drawn down the alley toward the beach,
my eyes straining to see under the pier. There's movement, several dark shapes in the shadows, though I can't make out any features. *Probably all trolls,* I tell myself. *Who else would—*

I stop, chiding myself for being judgmental. One man's troll is
another man's Prince Charming, Lloyd has often said.

When the moon slips out from behind a cloud, I spy my first

glimpse of recognizable humanity under the pier. Not a troll, really, but an older guy, probably late forties, early fifties, kind of thick and squat with a moustache. Hardly my type, so I figure I ought to back away. What was I even thinking?

But then I notice someone else in the shadows.

Someone much slighter, much younger.

It's Luke. I'm sure of it.

Who cares? Let him have his fun. I'd told him there'd be no sex for him at the guesthouse, so he has every right to seek it elsewhere.

Still, I am overcome with curiosity—and maybe more—to see just what happens to him under the pier.

I approach cautiously, staying outside, peering through the wooden diagonal slats that are nailed between the posts, ostensibly to keep people from entering. But slats have a way of breaking and never being repaired. I watch as one slightly inebriated man in nylon shorts steps through an opening and disappears into the shadows under the pier. I do not follow. I remain outside looking in, hoping my eyes will grow accustomed enough to the dim light to make out what's going on not four feet away from me.

If Luke is in there, he's been swallowed into the moving mass of bodies. It's far too dark to make anyone out clearly. Only those who come close to the edge, like the man with the moustache, are ever even partially visible. I keep looking—*hoping*, in fact, in some twisted, perverted part of my mind—to spot Luke impaled on some big cock. Fuck the little twerp. Fuck him good.

Suddenly I feel a hand on my crotch. I look down. From the other side of the wooden slats the guy with the moustache has approached and is now grabbing my cock. It's like an electric jolt.

"No," I whisper and try to pull away, but I don't resist very hard. He keeps rubbing my bulge, making me feel lightheaded. From seemingly some place far away I hear the sound of my zipper being pulled down. Then I feel fingers slipping inside my underwear, freeing my raging, imprisoned cock. Without warning comes the sensation of warm lips and tongue, licking and sucking me. I simply surrender and let go. I lean back, looking up at the moon. It's not long before I come, shooting the first dollop into the man's mouth. Then he stands aside, allowing me to watch as I shoot two, three, four and then five times in the moonlight.

Hastily I begin to zip up.

"Very hot," the man whispers. "Just make sure you bake me some extra special muffins in the morning."

I look through the slats at him but he's already moving away.

Jesus Christ. I've just let *Bert*—the horny bear from Pittsburgh—blow me! I let a guest suck my cock! Lloyd will be furious!

I stagger backward through the sand, then hurry back up to the street, ashamed and humiliated. When I see faces I know, I look away, afraid my activities at the dick dock are plain on my face.

I can't believe I just did that. *Why?* Why—after all my years of avoiding the place? Why—after all my earnest insistence that it's true love that I want to find, that I'm not just looking for a trick but for one special someone? Why would I do a disgusting thing like this after spending the evening talking heart-to-heart with someone who could finally relate to my desire for uplifting love and commitment?

I have never felt so ashamed of myself. Back in my apartment, I shower with the hottest water I can possibly stand. I dread facing Bert in the morning. If I'd been *under* the pier and not out in the moonlight, he might not have even recognized me. But now he'll tell his friend that he had me and—

Oh Christ.

He might tell *Luke*, who will then have something to hold over me.

"Fuck, fuck, and more fuck," I say, scrubbing my genitals.

Worst of all, now I'm certain about something else. Don't ask me how I know, I just do.

Gale is never going to call me as he said he would.

8

HERRING COVE BEACH

How cool would it be to be nine years old right now, able to act out and get away with being moody and surly just because you're a kid?

If I had my way, I'd be acting just as surly as J. R., Jeff's nephew, who's trudging through the sand behind us and sulking because we wouldn't let him stay home alone. He's taking his revenge by tuning us all out, the headphones to his iPod securely plugged into his ears. Whenever we ask him anything, he just grunts.

Which is actually what I would be doing, too, if I had my way.

"How about here?" Jeff asks, gesturing around him, stopping about a yard from the shore.

Lloyd shakes his head. "It's too far from the parking lot. My mother uses a *cane*, remember?"

Jeff frowns. "Well, if we keep too close to the lot we'll have the whole fucking world watching as we say our vows."

We're scouting wedding locations. To say I don't want to be here would be a major understatement. I woke up in a foul mood, the memory of last night lingering, and the day has just gone downhill from there. When Lloyd and Jeff asked me to accompany them to the beach, I tried to say no, but both were quick to remind me ("guilt-trip me" is a better phrase) that I'm their best man. "You *have* to come," Jeff insisted. "We'll need your input. I have a feeling Lloyd and I won't be seeing eye to eye on things."

That's for sure. Their first bone of contention was over the officiator. Jeff wanted a Catholic priest from Dignity, the gay Catholic group ("That way my mother will understand that this wedding is the *real deal*") while Lloyd wanted his friend Naomi to perform a New Age, drumbeating ceremony complete with Buddhist chanting. Lloyd also wanted to hold the wedding in the back garden of Nirvana, but Jeff was willing to give in on Naomi if they could get married on the beach.

So here we are, schlepping through the sand, stepping around a couple of teenage girls in striped bikinis spread out on a large blanket soaking up the rays. It's not even ten o'clock yet, and the temperature is already inching close to ninety. As they say around here, it's gonna be a scorchah.

I haven't told Lloyd yet about Bert. It was weird: Bert came downstairs alone this morning, his friend nowhere to be seen. It gave him a perfect opportunity to bring up our encounter, but he didn't. He just winked as usual—and there was nothing in the wink, no added lasciviousness based on what happened last night. Maybe he's being cool. Or maybe he was so drunk he's forgotten? Whatever his story, I was glad for his discretion.

Then Luke came climbing up the stairs from the little room in the basement Lloyd is letting him use. He acted as if no harsh words had passed between us. "Morning, Henry," he chirped. "Still keeping off the ice cream?"

"So far," I replied, disappointed on some level that he had apparently decided to play nice with me. I'd rather our hostilities be out in the open.

To my added dismay, he's proven a quick learner. Without needing any further instruction from me, Luke seemed to understand as if by osmosis when to gather up the plates from breakfast and when to stack them in the dishwasher. Then he was upstairs, stripping the beds from guests who were checking out.

"He's working out well, don't you think?" Lloyd asked me early this morning. I just grunted in reply. In truth, I was hoping Luke would turn out to be a loser and that Lloyd would can his ass.

So I'm feeling every bit as grumpy as J. R. as we trudge across the beach. "I'd rather be home too," I whisper to him as Jeff and Lloyd continue pacing back and forth across the sand.

He lifts an eye to me but says nothing.

"Henry? J. R.?" It's Jeff, arms akimbo. "Would you please show some interest here?"

"How come *I* have to show interest?" J. R. says, finally speaking. "I'm not your best man."

Jeff approaches us. "No, you're our ring bearer." He folds his arms across his chest and looks down at the kid. "So you need to see where you have to walk when you bring us our rings."

J. R. holds Jeff's gaze steady. "I'm not being no ring bearer," he says.

"What?" Jeff's eyes seem as if they'll pop out of his head. "We talked about this!"

"No, you and my *mom* talked about this."

Jeff's expression turns angry. "Stop acting like a brat, Jeffy."

He knows J. R. hates it when he calls him by his childhood name. In response, the boy simply turns up his iPod and stalks off. Jeff starts to follow, but Lloyd restrains him.

I'm not surprised by the kid's reaction. He let us all know in no uncertain terms about a year ago that henceforth he would be known as J. R. His first name is actually Jeffrey, named for his uncle and his grandfather. When J. R. was little—which is when I first met him— everybody called him "Jeffy," but he eventually came to consider "Jeffy" too juvenile. I think there was more to it than that, too. I think he wanted to declare a little independence from his sometimes overbearing uncle and father figure.

There's no question Jeff adores the boy—*dotes* on him, truth be told, and always has. When I first met Jeff, he was always running to Ann Marie's house to catch his nephew's first words or first steps or first bologna sandwich on video. One time Jeff roped me into dressing up with him as a couple of clowns and surprising the boy on his fifth birthday. Poor kid, he was terrified—and who wouldn't be with two grown men in pancaked faces and putty noses barging in and singing "Happy Birthday" off key?

Now, after every trip he takes to promote his books, Jeff returns with books, toys, or computer games for J. R. For the past six years, he and Lloyd have taken the boy to Disney World every November right after Thanksgiving. Once I joined them, and on my desk I still have the picture of J. R. on Jeff's shoulders in front of Cinderella's Castle. What makes it so dear to my heart is that the ice cream cone the boy is holding is dripping down into Jeff's hair.

It's always been apparent that J. R. adores his uncles—and especially Jeff—with equal enthusiasm. Jeff and Lloyd have been the only fathers he's ever known, since his real dad is in prison, doing time for theft. J. R. hasn't seen the jerk since he was two. And it's just as well. He's grown up among an extended family of uncles and aunts, myself included, who have indulged and sometimes spoiled him. When Jeff's mother once suggested it was too bad that her grandson wasn't being raised in a conventional mother-father family, J. R. had one line of response to her: "I think it's pretty cool. Nobody else in my class gets so many Christmas presents."

But Jeff can be a strict father figure, too. With Ann Marie gone during the week, Jeff has assumed the daily parenting role. He makes sure that J. R. does his homework. He cheers him on at school ballgames. He monitors his television and Internet time. It's that last one where he can be a bit of a nag. "Why don't you read *books*?" Jeff has argued. "When I was your age, I was reading all the time. I was always at the library."

"Then you were a geek," J. R. always retorts, enjoying a chance to needle his uncle.

Jeff will pretend mock outrage. "I was *nothing* of the sort," he says—but, of course, his movie posters and comic books stored in his basement gives the lie to that claim.

When J. R.'s increasing moodiness began to become apparent not long ago, Lloyd said it was natural. "He's trying to establish his own identity," he explained. Echoing Ann Marie, he insisted, "It's just a phase."

Now we stand watching him walk to the water's edge. His small form is dwarfed by the magnitude of the sea. Suddenly his retreat into his silence, his dramatic change in personality, doesn't feel like just a phase.

Lloyd lets out a long sigh. "He's feeling we didn't respect him enough by going through Ann Marie," he says. "He's feeling we should have asked him directly to be our ring bearer, and you know what? He's right."

Jeff isn't quite so understanding. "He's just being a brat."

"Maybe so," Lloyd agrees, "but his brattiness has some logic. At least to him. Instead of getting angry, let's just go ask him now, the way we should have in the beginning."

So we move over to him. Without any breeze, the waves are small and infrequent. J. R. is staring at his feet, seeming to dare the sea to reach his sneakers.

"J. R.," Jeff says, not entirely conciliatory, "I'm sorry we didn't ask you upfront."

The boy doesn't look up. Who knows if he can even hear Jeff over the music on his iPod.

"So we're asking you now," Jeff continues. "Will you be our ringbearer?"

Slowly J. R. lowers his earphones. He turns around and faces us.

"No," he says.

"*What?*" Jeff shouts, instantly getting angry again.

"Why not, J. R.?" Lloyd asks, far more calmly. He stoops down to face the boy. "We'd really like you to be a part of the ceremony."

"I don't want to," J. R. says. "It's too gay."

"Well, of course it's gay," Jeff says. "It's a *same-sex wedding.*"

"I mean it's lame," J. R. says.

"Look," his uncle says, seething now, "you know I hate it when you use the word 'gay' to mean 'lame.'"

"You know I hate it when you call me Jeffy."

"Oh, for Christ—"

"Jeff." Lloyd glares up at him, stopping him from saying anything more. He turns back to the boy. "Look, J. R., I'm disappointed. You're my family. I want you to be a part of this special day. But if you're not cool with it, then fine. I hope you'll at least come."

He just shrugs and replaces his headphones, signaling an end to the conversation.

Lloyd motions for us to leave the boy alone. We walk back up the sand a few feet. J. R. remains there looking out over the sea.

"That kid is getting too spoiled," Jeff whispers hard.

"He's nine years old," Lloyd argues. "Cut him some slack."

Jeff just sighs.

"He'll come around," I offer.

Jeff runs his hands through his hair. "I love that kid like he's my own son. But it's hard." He looks over at J. R., then back at Lloyd and me. "I never knew how fucking *hard* parenting could be. I want to avoid all the mistakes my parents made with me, but damn. I'm starting to see everything they did in a far more sympathetic light."

As much as I feel for J. R., I didn't come out here for a child psychology session. I have work to do back at the guesthouse, and I'm getting impatient. "Can we finish up here?" I ask. "Let's just decide where—"

"And what's up *your* ass, Henry?" Jeff's folding his arms across his chest, looking at me now. "Why are *you* so cranky?"

"I'm not cranky."

"Yes, you are, Henry," Lloyd says, moving in. "And since we seem to be processing emotions this morning, let's hear what's up with you."

I try to laugh. "You guys, I'm fine. I just have things to do . . ."

"Your date last night sucked, huh?" Jeff asks.

"No." I steel myself. "It was fine."

Jeff is shaking his head. "Whenever anyone describes something by saying it was fine, it's code for, 'It sucked.'"

Lloyd smiles. "Come on, Henry. Out with it."

"There is *nothing* to come out with."

"All right," Jeff says. "So when are you seeing this guy again?"

"I don't know. Soon." I can feel the defensiveness rising in my throat. "He said he'd call."

Jeff makes a wicked face. "Oh, no, the dreaded 'I'll call you' kiss-off," he says, smirking.

I stick my tongue out at him.

"Henry," Lloyd says, "something *is* bothering you."

I sigh. Why is it that Lloyd can cut right to the quick with me?

Why is it that around him I can't keep up any pretense? I turn to face him. "Okay," I manage to say. "Something weird happened."

"With Gale?"

"No, afterward." I don't want to look over at Jeff, whose eyes I can feel boring into me. "I went . . . oh man . . . I went to the dick dock."

Jeff bursts out into laughter. Lloyd shoots him a look. I figure I'd better finish my confession before I chicken out.

"And some guy there . . . I didn't know who it was until afterward. I . . . I think it was a guest."

"Oh," Lloyd says.

"Don't be pissed at me, Lloyd," I plead, trying to tune out Jeff's hysterics. "I really didn't know until after he—"

"Got up off his knees?" Jeff asks, cracking himself up.

"Yes!" I shout. "Exactly! Until he got up off his knees!"

"Who was it?" Lloyd asks.

"Bert."

"Which one is Bert?" Jeff wants to know. "Is he hot?"

"Some would say so," I tell him, defensive again. "But I'm sure he wouldn't fit *your* high standards, Mr. Jeff Almighty."

Lloyd is shaking his head. "No, it wasn't Bert," he says conclusively. "Bert and I sat up talking together from midnight until two a.m. He didn't go out last night."

"Are you sure?" I ask.

"Positive." Lloyd shrugs. "You got blown by someone else. What makes you think it was a guest?"

"Because he said . . ." Once again I refuse to look at Jeff. "Because he said he hoped I made him some especially good muffins this morning."

Jeff shrieks in laughter, doubling over, barely able to stand.

Lloyd is having a hard time holding back his own smile. At least he's not angry. "It's not a big deal, Henry. You didn't know."

"I can't believe you went to the dick dock, buddy," Jeff says, his grin a mile wide. "So Gale didn't put out, huh?"

"Will you shut up, please?" I nod my head in J. R.'s direction.

"He can't hear us," Jeff says. "And if he can, it sure won't be the first time he's heard about the dick dock."

"I think," Lloyd says, sage that he is, "what's really bothering you, Henry, has nothing to do with getting a blow job by some stranger."

At that moment the sun edges just a little higher in the sky, and its light reflects in Lloyd's green eyes. Suddenly I want to cry looking at him. I just want to sit down on the sand, curl up into a ball, and cry.

But I don't. Of course not. I'm sick to death of Henry Weiner's self-pity party, so I just jut out my chin and let loose with everything that's been building up inside me.

"You want to know what's wrong?" I say, louder than I intended. "Okay, I'll tell you what's wrong. Here I am, traipsing out with you guys to pick your perfect little wedding spot, listening to you bicker about where and when and who, and meanwhile I'm reduced to getting blow jobs on the beach from some big old bear because I can't find even one guy who I like who might like me back."

Lloyd starts to respond, but it's Jeff who moves forward. He's not laughing anymore. He takes my hands in his and finds my eyes with his own.

"Buddy," he says.

This is why I love Jeff. This is why, despite all his bullshit, all his narcissism, all his teasing, I love him with all my soul. It's not the same kind of love I feel for Lloyd, but in some ways it goes even deeper than that. Jeff knew me when I was a scared, skinny outcast. He helped me become someone else—someone stronger, someone wiser. There are times, like now, when I forget that side of myself, that strong, confident person Jeff helped me become. But Jeff never forgets that version of Henry Weiner, and he's always here to remind me of him when I need it. He doesn't even need to say anything. He just holds my hands, looks into my eyes, and says, "Buddy." I get emotional, biting back the tears.

Now Lloyd is at my side, putting his arm around my shoulder. "You will find someone, Henry," he says. "Remember what we've said about trust."

I look into his eyes, then back to Jeff's. These are my two best friends in the world. The emotional sustenance I have with them is quite unlike anything most people ever experience, even with lovers of many years. I know I'm fortunate. So why do I feel so un-fulfilled?

"You know," I say, my voice thick with emotion, "Gale brought up an interesting point."

"What's that?" Lloyd asks.

"He wants a monogamous relationship."

Jeff lifts his eyebrows. "Well, then, you've struck gold."

"Not exactly." I smile. "He said having this kind of emotional con-nection with friends—the kind we're having right now—would be cheating on my lover if I had one."

"That's fucked," Jeff says.

"Maybe, maybe not." I look from him to Lloyd. "Why should we single out sex as the only thing we need to keep exclusive in rela-tionships? It's not even the most important thing."

"Well," Lloyd says, "the argument could be turned around to say why keep *anything* exclusive? Why not be as open as possible, sharing everything with the entire world?"

I laugh. "Then there would be nothing special in a one-on-one relationship, no point in even having one." I give them each a smile. "Look, you guys. Be honest. You've been nonmonogamous for most of your time together. Sexually and often emotionally, too. But you've always held back one small but significant part of yourselves, a part that you've kept reserved only for each other." I find Lloyd's eyes. "I know. I've experienced that."

"Henry," Lloyd says kindly.

"It's cool. It really is. Because I *want* what you have. Maybe I'd shape it a little differently, but the love you guys have for each other . . ." My words trail off, as the doubts I've had about the depth of their love resurface. But such doubts feel absurd right now, or at least beside the point. "Here's what I want. I want to find someone who will love me enough to want to marry me, the way you guys are getting married. And sometimes I think . . ."

Again my words trail off. Jeff, still holding my hands, pumps me to finish. "Think what, buddy?"

I face him. "I think that maybe the closeness I have with the two of you prevents me from finding that one special someone."

Jeff lets my hands go. I notice the look that passes between him and Lloyd.

I know what they're thinking. "Javitz felt the same way, didn't he?"

They both nod. Javitz was their best friend before I came along, an older mentor who they both loved and cared for as he died from AIDS. They've told me how Javitz sometimes expressed feelings very similar to the ones I'm describing now. He'd say that as close as the three of them were, their friendship just couldn't completely substitute for a satisfying one-on-one lover—a lifelong dream Javitz never managed to find.

I can see Javitz's experience helps them to understand my struggle a little better. "I don't want to die without having found the One," I say softly.

"Henry," Lloyd says, "you're only thirty-three and in splendid health. You're not like Javitz, staring down the corridor of his mortality. Yes, we could all go at any minute. We could walk back out into the parking lot and get struck down by the shuttle bus. But you need to trust that you have the luxury of *time*, Henry. Why is it so hard for you to trust?"

I shrug. "I don't know, but it is. Like Gale's comment that he'd call me. You were right to laugh, Jeff. It's the most-often-repeated lie in the world."

"I *wasn't* right to laugh, buddy," Jeff says. "He'll call you."

"Do you *want* him to call you, Henry?" Lloyd asks.

"Of course I do. He's hot. And smart. His ideas about relationships seem extreme, but I'm willing to work with that."

Lloyd gives me a wan smile. "Well, if he had his way, the three of us wouldn't be having these little powwows on the beach anymore."

"I wouldn't let a lover come between us," I vow.

But even as I say the words, I wonder. Would I? If I found a man that I loved, who loved me back, who made me laugh and made me happy and wanted to marry me—would I turn away from Jeff and Lloyd if he asked me to do so?

"What about Luke?"

I'm startled out my thoughts by Jeff's question. "What *about* him?" I reply. I can feel my defensiveness rising again.

"Do you have feelings for him? You guys tricked and now—"

"It was a trick, that's all."

"But you're pretty hostile about him now," Jeff continues.

Lloyd is looking at me strangely. "Why are you hostile? I thought he was working out well."

I wasn't planning to go into this with Lloyd, at least not yet. But there's no way to avoid it now that Jeff has brought it up.

"I—I just have some suspicions about him," I say, already certain that Lloyd is going to call me paranoid and insist it's all about my difficulties with trust. But I forge on anyway. "I think Luke is kind of a schemer."

Lloyd smiles. "I think you're still intrigued by him."

"I am *not!*"

"Come on, Henry. It's obvious the way you watch him."

"I watch him because he's after something." I look over at Jeff. "Like Eve Harrington in *All About Eve.*"

Jeff flutters his eyelashes comically. "And are you casting *me* as Margo Channing?"

Lloyd smiles. "Well, it *is* obvious that Luke's hot for you, Jeff. That much is clear."

"It *is?*" Jeff asks, in a tone I find sickeningly disingenuous.

"Yes, my love," Lloyd says indulgently. "It's your choice in how you respond, but remember he *is* an employee."

I watch Jeff's eyes. I remember his conflicts over having sex with other guys as he and Lloyd plan their wedding. Not that he doesn't *want* to have sex with them—the drive is there—he just doesn't feel it's right. How long will he be able to resist Luke's charms?

Now, see, for me, if I were waiting to exchange vows with Lloyd, the drive for other guys would not even be there in the first place. There would be no conflict. If I were planning to marry the man of my dreams—my soul mate—then I wouldn't even be *looking* at another guy. No one but Mr. Right would even be on my radar screen. No conflict. None at all. All my love, every last bit of it, would be directed at the man I was about to—

A little voice suddenly says "Bullshit" in the back of my mind.

I'm stunned. I actually rock back a bit on my heels.

Bullshit.

How much have I been kidding myself? How much of my romantic notions are just that—rosy, idealistic dreams? Maybe, in fact, Jeff and Lloyd are as real as it gets, and what they have between them is the best I can hope for. Maybe true love—the way I've romanticized it—doesn't exist. Maybe it's simply about two people finding each other and making the best of it, the way Jeff and Lloyd seem to be doing. Because, in truth, part of me doesn't believe they are really, truly happy. Part of me thinks they're just glad not to be alone as they move into their fourth decade.

I look at them now—back to bickering about where people should stand, how many people to invite—and I wonder if maybe long ago they gave up the kind of romantic preconditions that I cling to so fiercely. If that's the case—if they are, in fact, *settling*— how can I believe that they are really, truly in love with each other?

But then I spot Lloyd making Jeff laugh—something he says, a lift of his eyebrows, a shrug of his shoulders. They speak in shorthand: one word, one gesture can conjure up a dozen years' worth of images and emotions. Instantly the tension between them shivers and breaks. Jeff reaches over and wraps his arms around Lloyd's neck, pulling him close. They share a kiss, the sun glinting from between their profiles. I have to look away.

What the hell do I know about love?

"Uncle Henry."

I look around. J. R. has walked back up from the water and is standing behind me.

"What's up?" I ask the boy.

"Do you think me and you could walk back now?"

"Well, I don't know if Jeff and Lloyd are finished here yet," I tell him. But then I glance back at the two of them, shoulder to shoulder now, hands linked, strolling away from us toward the water.

I shout after them, announcing that J. R. and I are heading back. They lift their free arms to wave at us without even bothering to turn around. They're probably glad to be rid of us.

"Come on," I say to J. R., dropping my arm around his thin shoulders. "Let's go home."

We move off down the sand.

"You okay, buddy?" I ask the boy.

"Yup."

"You sure?"

The boy just nods, adjusting the volume on his iPod.

"If anything is bugging you," I say, loud enough so that he can hear, "you know you can talk to me. You can talk to Uncle Lloyd or Uncle Jeff, too, of course, but in case, for whatever reason, you don't want to, you can talk to me. I promise to be cool."

J. R. barely nods.

I sigh. What I wouldn't give for an older, wiser uncle to drop his arm around my shoulder and offer to help me with my problems. I wouldn't be so tightlipped as J. R. I'd tell him exactly what was troubling me.

That is, if I could figure it all out myself—which, at the moment, seems impossible to do.

I make a conscious effort to leave all my doubts and confusions behind me on the beach, to refuse to carry them back with me to the guesthouse. Forget about Jeff and Lloyd. Forget about Mr. Right. Forget about what's real and what's not and what falling in love really means.

But there's one question I just can't seem to leave behind.

Who the hell blew me at the dick dock last night?

9

MY BED

Another night of strange dreams. Once more, I'm back in West Springfield. I'm wearing the orange-and-white polyester uniform of my first job—at Roy Rogers Hamburgers and Fried Chicken. On my head sits a little orange hat. In my hands I hold a bag of lettuce. I'm refilling the salad bar, much against my wishes.

"I'm supposed to be on cash register tonight," I complain.

"No way, Henry. *I'm* on cash register tonight."

The bane of my job at Roy Rogers—indeed the bane of my entire existence—is my older sister Susan. She's worked at Roy Rogers for two years now, every since she graduated high school. She acts as if it's the most important job in the world, but I know better. She's just pissed because I'm going on to college, and she decided against, preferring to stay here in West Springfield. Twenty-one and stuck in a low-paying, fast-food job. She knows I'm just here until graduation, which thankfully is not far away, and it just *burns her up*.

"You *have* to put out the salad bar, Henry," Susan is telling me. "I did it yesterday and I am *not* going to do it again."

My sister's acne-enflamed face fills my entire frame of vision. There is nothing else: just Susan, bearing down on me, threatening to smother me.

I hold firm. "I'm *not* going to do it."

"Oh, yes, you will!"

"No!"

Customers are listening to this. Four of them, to be exact: two women with a little boy in a booth and an elderly man up at the counter. They've all turned to watch the two Weiner kids fight.

"So help me, Jesus, Henry—" Susan snarls.

"Who are *you* to invoke Jesus, you Jewish frog face?"

She hauls off and smacks me across the cheek. I suppose I deserve it.

Paula, our manager, appears from the kitchen. She's a heavy-set, hard-eyed black woman with dyed red hair pulled back tightly in a hairnet. She glares at the two of us. "You both come on back in here," she says.

"Hey," says the old man at the counter. "Can I get some service here?"

"Just a moment, sir," Paula says, trying to smile. Her lips are tight and coated with cold scarlet lip gloss.

"I was supposed to be on cash register tonight," I argue.

"He was not!" Susan shouts.

Paula is staring at me. "Henry, you will put out the salad bar because I say so," she says, her voice hard but calm. "And don't you *ever* use such language in front of customers again."

"What kind of language did I use?" I ask. "Which term are you suggesting is offensive—Jewish or frog face?"

Paula narrows her eyes at me. "Henry, are you looking to get your ass fired?"

Susan smirks.

"And Susan," Paula says, turning to her, "you wipe that grin off your mouth or I'll do it for you."

She just might. I take great pleasure in watching my sister's face fill up with fear.

"Now do you hear me, both of you?"

"Yes, Paula," I tell her. "I'm sorry we got you all worked up."

No, I'm not. In fact, it felt good to call Susan a frog-face. A week ago, I wouldn't have had the nerve.

But so much is different in my life since a week ago.

I stood up for myself, I think as I dole out the lettuce into the plastic bowls. Okay, so I'm doing the salad anyway. But at least I stood up for myself.

"Why do you and your sister fight so?" my mother has asked, many times.

Here my dream shifts again, to our kitchen table, my mother seated across from me.

"You two act as if you hate each some times."

There's pain in her eyes, and bewilderment, over the way her children act toward each other. I feel guilty, not for how I feel about Susan, but for how it makes my mother feel.

"I don't hate her," I say.

I don't. Not really. But I think Susan hates me. Maybe because I'm the only boy, and I get to go to college. Hey, it was her decision *not* to go—even if, in fact, my parents didn't work very hard to change her mind. Still, being the only boy is special, and Susan knows that. I'm the one everyone expects to follow my father in the insurance business. I'm the one they expect to carry on the name.

If only they knew I had no plans of doing either.

Especially not after what happened last week. I smile to myself, the cat who swallowed the canary, as I drop the tomatoes one by one into their plastic bowl.

When we were kids, Susan had been my best friend. She was cool, because she was older, and so she could buy me stuff, like teen magazines. Handing me *Teen Beat,* she thought I wanted to check out pictures of Catherine Bach from *The Dukes of Hazzard,* but rather it was Duran Duran and Culture Club that had me more ensnared.

Back in those days, this place where I work wasn't a Roy Rogers but a local, family-owned diner called Higgie's. My parents would take Susan and me to Higgie's for grilled cheese sandwiches and cups of chicken noodle soup. Afterward, I'd always order a dish of strawberry ice cream and stir it until it had the consistency of soup. The memory makes me happy.

I stir in my bed, the smell of grease and charred beef filling my nostrils. It's the way my clothes would smell at home, when I'd come off my shift at Roy Rogers. My bedsheets began to smell the same way, because often I was too tired to shower and just fell right into bed. It seems my whole *life* began to smell like Roy Rogers: the deep, pungent odor of boiling vegetable oil. Even when I'd open my underwear drawers I'd get a whiff of grease, as if deep-fried mozzarella sticks were hidden under in my Hanes.

But back in my dream, I'm liking the smell. I'm liking most everything about my life. I'm whistling, in fact, as I put out the salad bar: nothing real, just a made-up tune. I'm imagining the day, when I'm a famous musician, when I'll tell the story of how I worked here, the way Chris Cornell of Soundgarden talks about working in a fish market as a teenager, wiping up fish guts.

"How's that salad coming?" Paula barks, snapping me out of my reverie. "The dinner crowd will be here soon."

"Almost ready," I call back. The lettuce and tomatoes are all done. Now I'm chopping some onions, making my eyes tear up.

"I'm going to be leaving soon," Paula says. "I don't want any trouble tonight. You and Susan better get along."

"Oh, we will, Paula, I promise."

It's at this precise moment that I wake up. What was I dreaming about? Higgie's? Strawberry ice cream? Roy Rogers and mean old Paula? I rub my eyes. People and places I haven't thought about in *years*.

Even dreaming about my sister is unusual. As adults, Susan and I enjoy a far better relationship than we did as teenagers. She's got a couple of adorable twin girls who I wish I could see more frequently—yet the truth is, with all that consumes my own life, I rarely think about her or them. So why tonight?

I roll over, drifting back to sleep. It's only as the dream begins again that I understand where it's taking me.

My high school English classroom. In front of me sit my friends, Dale and Howard. Across the aisle from me sits Linda Santangelo, who's had a crush on me since freshman year, but who became the very first person I told, just a few months ago, that I was gay. Since then Dale has revealed the same thing about himself, though Howard clings to the label of "curious"—a term I now find hopelessly self-delusional and self-loathing, despite the fact I'd used it myself not so long ago with Jack.

Jack, of course, has attained a certain heroic veneer among us, having ditched school and taken off for New York. Occasionally we'll wonder if Jack will ever be in touch with us, if we'll ever learn what became of him. I expect one of these days to see his name in the credits of a movie or television show.

But Jack is not the subject of my dream. Not tonight. Instead, my eyes move up from my desk to the front of the classroom to my teacher. Mr. Kelly. Mr. Patrick Kelly—a round, genial-faced Irishman with perpetually ruddy cheeks who was generally held in high esteem by the student population. I say "generally" because, while Mr. Kelly often clapped students on the back if they were members of the football team or the National Honor Society, he tended to ignore those kids, like me, who weren't so easily categorized. Those of us who wanted to be artists or musicians, or were simply rebelling against the lockstep of high school life. We were the ones trudging into school wearing our black T-shirts and Doc Martens, and we weren't so sure about this supposedly student-friendly Mr. Kelly. Underneath that crooked Irish grin of his there was something we just didn't trust. None of us could quite put our fingers on it, but something was there, lurking. Maybe it was in the way he made us start each class by reciting the Pledge of Allegiance. Maybe it was in the way he smirked, rolled his eyes and turned his head when one of the jocks called somebody a fag in class.

I didn't get called a fag, but I could have.

I'm slipping out of gym class now, counting on the astonishing obtuseness of the gym teachers, heading up the stairs to the library. I pull off a copy of the local alternative arts weekly from the newspaper rack and settle into a chair, hoping no one asks why I am here and not out on the soccer field. I flip through the newspaper to the personals. And there, in the pine-scented, hushed library, I read all about GWMs, GBMs, BiMs, GMMs—all looking for other men *with whom to have sex.* My mind can barely wrap around the thought. Some of the men here were into sadomasochism. Others just wanted cuddling, or long walks and candlelight dinners. Over and over, I read those personals, imagining myself answering every one—as the shouts of my classmates out on the soccer field seemed ever farther away.

My dream moves along, to a cool evening night with the moon riding high in the sky. His name is Doug. A freshman in college. Nineteen, two years older than I. I think that's why I chose his ad: the nearness in age reassured my trembling libido. Somehow I'd worked up the courage to send my home number, pleading: "Please, be discreet." In my dream, my mother once again answers the phone, and I feel once more the chill when she says: "Henry, it's for you. I don't know who it is."

We meet at the Holyoke mall. Doug's hair is big and curly, a white-boy Afro, and there are spaces between his teeth. But I find him beautiful because he's male—a male who wants to have sex with me. We stand facing each other in front of Spencer's Gifts, shuffling our feet and saying little. When he suggests we go for a ride, I'm all for it.

We park and he takes out a joint. "Want some?"

I nod, taking the joint from him.

"You've been with a guy before, right?" he asks.

"Sure," I tell him, inhaling, suppressing a cough, as if to say: *What a silly thing to ask.*

I will always remember two things as being the most thrilling about that night: holding Doug's hand as we walked through the woods, and kissing him. "I'm kissing *another guy,*" I keep saying to myself.

The sex is basic: we lie in the grass and perform 69 on each other. I guess what they say is true: gay men *do* know how to suck cock instinctively. It comes pretty naturally for me. At the very least, Doug seems convinced that it really wasn't my first time.

After we both come, we lie there looking up at the moon. Doug speaks, breaking the silence. "It's so beautiful here," he says, "being with you, with the moon up above."

In my sleep, I stir. My erection is spearheading my underwear.

For all my dreams of romance, that night I wasn't interested in lying there and looking at the moon. I just wanted to get home. We hadn't been caught—not yet, anyway. To stay there any longer would be pushing our luck.

In the days to come, however, that night with Doug would take on an incredible glow, a powerful patina of love and self-expression.

I whistled my way through work, inexplicably cheery to my friends at school. And here's the really important part: I wrote it all down.

"I will not read your journals," Mr. Kelly promises, standing in the front of the classroom. "You have my word on that. But I *will* collect them at the end of the semester, just to make sure you've kept them."

Our journals were a requirement in our English class. We were instructed to record our interpretations of life around us during our senior year. Now, after Doug, life around me seemed to suddenly blossom into unexpected beauty, and I wrote it all down. I wrote about how long I had wondered what making love to another man would be like, and I mused over whether in fact I wanted to continue on this particular journey, if being gay was really who I was.

I concluded, gloriously, that it was.

And even as I wrote, I knew Mr. Kelly would read it. *Good*, I thought. I *want* him to know. I trusted in his warped sense of honor that he would not ever reveal to me that he had actually read my passage, that I would in fact be safe from whatever retribution he might normally inflict on faggots. Perhaps it was a naive trust, but it proved accurate.

He looms over my desk, handing me back my journal with the hardest expression on his face. I perceive the look as anger—his eyes clamped onto mine, his lips tight and white. For several seconds he will not release my journal into my hands, but I don't waver in holding his gaze. For as long as he stands there I look him straight in the eye. I do not back down. Finally he lets go, giving up on his attempt to seer off my face with the power of his eyes.

I had stood up to him. And won.

"I need a bacon double cheeseburger, Freddie," Susan calls into the kitchen. "Plain. No pickles, no mustard, no anything."

My dream has returned me to Roy Rogers. The smell of grease once again consumes me. I'm through with the salad bar, and now I'm wrapping burgers. I watch as Freddie the cook plops another patty onto the grill.

"Do you know who's here?" Susan asks me. "Your teacher."

"What teacher?"

"Mr. Kelly." Susan seems eminently pleased with herself. "I always liked him. He was always nice to me. But I can tell by how you talk about him that you hate him."

"So?"

"So," she says, grinning evilly, "he's the one that ordered the special bacon double cheeseburger. And I'm going to make *you* bring it out to him."

"You bring it out to him!"

She smirks. "I'm on cash register. You have to do it."

Freddie flips the burger onto a roll and slides it over to me to wrap.

I look down on it.

I remember that scene in *Roots* where Leslie Uggams spits into Sandy Duncan's water.

Of course I don't do it. I just wrap the burger and place it on a tray.

"Excuse me," I say to Susan.

I'm pleased she's given me this opportunity.

"Hello, Mr. Kelly."

He looks up at me from the booth with some surprise. His wife and three kids are already chowing down their food. I make sure I give him a big shit-eating smile as I hand him his burger.

"Enjoy," I tell him, knowing he won't.

A man like him would never eat something a faggot had touched.

I head back into the kitchen. "What do you have against him?" Susan asks as I return behind the counter. "All the cool kids always liked him."

"Apparently, Susan," I tell her, "I'm not cool."

She doesn't know what to make of this new Henry, who seems so pleased with himself, who seems unable to be rattled about anything. In my mind, I know I have just a couple more months. Then summer will be over, and I'll be off to college. U-Mass isn't far away, just an hour up Route 91. But there I will, in fact, be a world away from all this. And my life will begin.

In my sleep, I grab hold of my pillows. That young Henry

Weiner had so many dreams. So many plans and hopes and expectations.

He was strong. He was confident.

I'm glad I'm dreaming about him.

I need to remember him, now and then.

10

FRONT DESK, NIRVANA GUESTHOUSE

Four days. That's how long it's been.

And I was right. Gale hasn't called.

I've seen him twice at the gym. Both times there's been a big smile and friendly greeting. But no kiss, and no mention of a second date. He just flips that fucking hot little torso round and round on the bar and I pretend not to notice as I struggle through ten reps on the incline press.

"He doesn't like me," I say to Lloyd, turning the computer on. It makes a small *ping*. "That much is obvious."

Lloyd sighs. "Look how you automatically draw negative conclusions," he says as he arranges black-eyed Susans in a vase, backed by tall sprigs of purple sage.

"Oh, come on," I argue. "Four days. And no mention, nothing."

"You could call *him*," Lloyd says, keeping his eyes on the flowers.

I shake my head. "He was very clear. *I'll call you.*"

"That's an excuse, Henry," Lloyd says, setting the vase on the counter. "If you want to see him again, call him."

"I agree," comes a voice from the basement stairs. In seconds Luke is in view, lugging a basket of freshly laundered linens. "He's probably thinking the same thing, that *you* don't like *him*."

The brat is naked from the waist up again. Doesn't he own any shirts? I've objected to the way he flits around here, his shorts hanging off his ass, but Lloyd has overruled me. The guests love Luke, he's explained. Especially the men.

At his job, Luke has become a pro. I continue to resent the fact that he's so fucking good. Every day he's here bright and early. He's smiling and wide awake, when I'm sleepy and cranky. Whistling while he works, he changes all the bedding in under an hour. Then he sweeps and dusts and polishes without needing to be asked. Goddamn him. If he were screwing up, I could fire him. But Lloyd thinks he's the best houseboy we've ever had.

I don't respond to Luke's advice about my love life, hoping he'll disappear upstairs, but he stops as he passes me, setting the laundry basket down on the counter.

"There was a guy I really liked once myself," he says, "but I couldn't figure if he liked me, and so I never let him know. Turns out he was waiting for me, too."

Lloyd approaches the counter. "How'd you find that out?" he asks, as I shoot him a look as if to say, *Don't engage him.*

But it's too late. Luke runs with it. "Oh, man, it's quite a story," he says. "If you want to know the truth, he was my *stepbrother*." The kid catches Lloyd's wide eyed reaction. "Now don't freak out. There was no blood relation. But we had to share a room, and well, you know, when your teenage hormones are hopping around and all . . ."

"Did the two of you actually do the deed?" Lloyd asks.

Luke grins. "Once. It was so hot. I had two stepsisters, too, and they were in the room next to ours, so we had to be really quiet."

I don't want to admit that the story is turning me on, so I try to veer it off course a bit. "So tell me, Luke," I say. "Is West the name you were born with, or was it your stepfather's name?"

His eyes move over to mine. He knows I'm testing him. Who's to say what this kid's real name is? Like so many guesthouses, we're paying him under the table; there's been no reason to check him out. I hold his gaze as he seems, momentarily, to consider how to answer me. What will it be, Luke? I wonder. The truth, or some version of it? What will serve your schemes best?

"Well, in fact," he says, "my stepfather had an entirely different name. I suppose calling him my stepfather isn't quite accurate."

"Oh no?" I ask.

Luke smiles. "I guess it was more like foster father. He and his wife took me in to live with them. You see, I had been living in a homeless shelter."

I see the look of compassion cross Lloyd's face. "Really? I didn't know . . . Where were your real parents?"

The kid makes a sad face. God, he's good. "My mother was dead, my father had taken off."

He seems genuinely forlorn for a moment, remembering his past.

"I should admit something to you guys," he says. "West is a name I made up on my way to New York. That's where my stepdad—well, the guy I call my stepdad anyway—found me and brought me home to live with his family."

"This would be on Long Island," I say, trying to see if I can catch him in an inconsistency.

"That's right," Luke says. "Oh, man, what a difference that was. Sleeping in my own bed with real sheets and pillows. Living on the street had been hell. But I have to say it was better than living with my Uncle Louie in the backwoods of New Jersey. I remember the night I left, heading up the New Jersey Turnpike. I was hitch-hiking and some guy in a Ford Bronco picked me up. I told him just to take me as far as he was going. We hadn't even gone a mile before he slid his gnarled hand onto my knee."

I look over at Lloyd. He doesn't look back. He's standing behind the front desk watching Luke as if he's mesmerized.

"The Bronco reeked of cigarettes," Luke continues, "though the guy hadn't smoked at all since picking me up. Still, I remember how the ashtray was overflowing with ashes and butts, and there were several lighters strewn about on the floor. Next thing I know the gnarled hand on my knee is giving me a little squeeze. For a second I wasn't sure what to do, then somehow I just knew. I looked over at the guy and made eye contact. He grinned. Some of his teeth were brown. I grinned back."

"Man," Lloyd says, "you were taking a big risk."

"I suppose, but it didn't seem scary or anything. I was acting almost on instinct." Luke's quite into his story, and despite my misgivings, I can't deny he's hooked me. He leans his head on the laundry basket as he goes on. "So the guy pulls over at the next rest stop. He didn't say anything. I just unzipped my jeans and let him slobber yellow nicotine all over my cock. I came, he swallowed. That was it. But I had an idea."

"What was that?" Lloyd asks.

"Zipping up, I told him that I had no money. Otherwise, I said, I'd be taking the bus, not risking my life hitchhiking like this. I told him that I knew there were psychos out there—men who got off on slicing young boys like me to pieces, but what choice did I have? I had no money, and I had to get away from my uncle and find a new life for myself in New York."

"Rather shrewd, but still risky," Lloyd says.

Luke nods. "But it paid off. 'Here,' the guy says, wiping his chin with the back of his hand and taking his wallet out of his pants with the other. He thrust three twenties over at me. 'How old are you anyway?' he asked. For all he knew I was underage and maybe planning on turning him in."

"How old *were* you, Luke?" I'm determined to file away all this information for later, hoping to catch him in a lie.

"Nineteen," he tells me. "I remember that the guy called me 'practically jailbait' and told me to get off the street, that I'd discover that not all the guys who'd pick me would be softies like him." Luke lets out a laugh. "But you know what? They were. Every single one of them. Another guy, who picked me up near Trenton, was a bit rougher, wanting me to blow him. Still, he coughed up a twenty. But the last guy, who took me all the way into Manhattan, gave me fifty bucks just out of the goodness of his heart. No sex. Nothing. I remember he had a rainbow sticker on his back windshield."

"Quite the adventure," Lloyd says. "I'm glad you made it through."

"So you see, Henry," Luke says, turning to me, "when you told me you had escorted, I could relate."

I immediately become defensive of my old life. "There is a big difference between escorting and hustling," I insist.

"Oh?" Luke asks, apparently sincerely. "What is it?"

I have no quick answer. Lloyd takes advantage of my indecision to bring the story back to its original purpose. "So the step-brother?"

Luke laughs. "Oh, right! It was really pretty hot, because he was gorgeous. All the girls were in love with him. Really pinup material. We kept our feelings for each other private for a long time, but finally one night, sleeping just a few feet away from each other in just our underpants, we started going at it. It was so nice kissing him. I wanted to be just like him, you know—and I vowed right then and there that someday I would be. But afterward we both felt guilty and never said anything about it, even though I wanted so much to make love to him again."

"So how did you find out he felt the same way?" Lloyd asks.

Luke smiles. "It took a while. It was right before I came up here, in fact. I was part of this writing group that gave a reading of our work at this bookstore in Manhattan. I hadn't seen Mike in a couple of years, but he must have seen my name on the flyers. So he came, and I read this piece about unfulfilled love, and afterward he asked if it was about him and me. I said yes, and he admitted he felt the same. But it was too late. He had gotten married and had a kid and was committed to being a born-again Christian."

"No way," Lloyd says.

Luke nods. "Very sad. Oh, well." He shrugs, lifting the laundry basket again. "Back to work. But take a lesson, Henry."

We watch him as he heads up the stairs, his shorts sliding down his butt.

"Did you believe a word of that?" I ask Lloyd after the kid is gone.

"Why shouldn't I?"

I sigh. "He's just admitted to being a hustler. He's hustling us the same way he did those drivers, except money isn't really his object anymore."

"And what *is* his object, Henry?" Lloyd asks. "Jeff?"

"I'm not sure. But Jeff's a part of it."

Lloyd shakes his head. "Even if he's telling tall tales, I think he's harmless."

"You just think he has a cute ass," I grumble.

"There's no arguing about that," Lloyd says, winking at me.

I turn back to the computer, going over the day's reservations. I don't know why I remain so hostile toward Luke. Maybe I'm still just peeved over his transparent ploy to meet Jeff through me. I suppose I should just let that go. But I can't help being suspicious of him. I simply don't trust the kid.

I try to busy myself behind the desk, totaling up credit card receipts. It's been a good summer moneywise. Maybe Lloyd will even give me a raise. Maybe then I can think about buying my own place. I'm tired of living above the guesthouse, tired of renting, of not having any roots. But whenever I've imagined buying a house, it's always been with a lover. To buy a place on my own seems almost a concession to the idea of being single forever.

"Excuse me."

I look up. Lloyd has left the room, and a man has come in, a backpack slung over his shoulder. He's got a beefy frame and sports a close-cropped beard. He looks vaguely familiar, but I can't place him.

"May I help you?" I ask.

"Hi, Henry," the man says.

"Hi." I'm still not sure who he is, but obviously he knows me.

The man smiles. "Wondering if you have a room. Maybe the same one I had a few days ago?"

Then I remember. It's Bert's friend.

"Oh," I say. "I thought you guys had gone back to Pittsburgh."

"We did." The man grins, his blue eyes twinkling. "But during my stay here, I fell in love with P-town. I went back home only long enough to quit my job, put my things in storage, and come back."

"Wow," I say. "You mean, you're going to *live* here?"

"That's my goal. Call it a midlife crisis. But I've never felt more clarity about anything in my life."

He's got to be pushing fifty. He was probably very handsome once, before he lost most of his hair and began suffering from middle-age spread.

"What do you plan to do to make a living here?" I ask.

"I'm a carpenter," he says. "I hope to find some work. I thought I'd check in here, then head out and look for a job and a permanent space."

"Jobs are easy to find, except they don't pay," I caution him. "As for housing, well, unless you have a ton of money, there's not much."

He smiles. "Thanks for the words of encouragement."

"I just thought you ought to know."

"I do. So is the room available?"

"Yes," I tell him. "What is your name again?"

"Martin Jackman."

I type his name into the computer. "Yep, here you are. Will you be using the same credit card?"

"Yes."

"Okay. So how many nights?"

"Three."

I raise my eyebrows at him over the computer. "Optimistic, are we?"

"Yes," Martin Jackman says. "We are."

I hand him the key to the room and he bounds up the stairs.

Once, I took a chance like he did. I quit my job and moved here, too. But I came with a job waiting, and Jeff and Lloyd in place as my support. Still, it was a risk. I think about what my life might have been like had I stayed in that boring, lifeless job back in Boston. Yes, I'd still be trapped in a frantic unrewarding lifestyle— but I've come to realize that Provincetown is not an easy place to live if you're single. In the summer there are lots of guys passing through, but I want more than just a one-night stand. And year round, the pool from which to fish is very, very small.

There I go, thinking about finding Mr. Right again. I had promised myself to cut it out. Get a grip, Weiner. Stop feeling sorry for yourself. So what if Gale hasn't called? So what if I end up alone in my old age?

So what if I give up all of my dreams?

I need some air. I make my way around the front desk and out into the yard, where I find Jeff deadheading the roses that grow along the fence. He gives me a little salute.

"Not writing this morning?" I ask.

"Too beautiful to stay inside," he tells me.

I nod, plopping down on a bench to watch him work.

The sun brings out the muscles in his back in stark relief. Every time he wields the clippers I can see the movement of his delts and traps. How does Jeff stay so lean? He's more than half a decade older than I am. It's not fair.

"You want to talk about anything, buddy?" Jeff asks, not turning around from the roses.

"No," I say. "I just needed some air."

"Okay."

I decide to ask him something. "Hey, Jeff. Be honest with me."

"Never anything but."

"Yeah, whatever. But tell me the truth. Have you slept with Luke yet?"

"Nope. Don't intend to."

"Well, he's watching you." My eyes flicker upward, to the bay window directly over my head. Since coming outside, I've noticed Luke's arms emerge once or twice, shaking out rugs and blankets. From that room he has a perfect view of his shirtless idol.

Jeff is nonchalant. "I'm aware of it," he says, keeping his attention on his roses.

"Still don't feel fucking his hot li'l ass would be right?"

"Still feel that way, yes."

I smile. "Okay. Just checking."

For some reason, I take comfort in the fact that they haven't hooked up. It's petty, I know. But that's me: Petty Henry.

"Hey Jeff," I say again.

"Yes, buddy?"

"Remember what you told me about getting hair in your ears?"

He gives me a bemused look over his shoulder. "No. Remind me."

"You told me when you first noticed hair growing in your ears that you freaked out."

He sighs. "Oh yes. One of the curses of getting older."

"That's what you said." I smirk. "Well, it's happened to me now, too."

Jeff laughs. "Welcome to middle age, buddy."

"Every morning now I have to add that to my grooming routine. Pluck, pluck, pluck. If not, I'd look like Eddie Munster." I pause. "Or my father."

"It's a never-ending battle."

"How often do you pluck?"

Jeff sets down his shears and comes over to sit beside me on the bench. Up close his ears look as smooth as a baby's.

"Laser hair removal," he says simply. "Cost a fucking fortune but it was worth it. No more plucking."

I smile. "So that explains it. And the fact that the lines around your eyes are gone . . . ?"

"Good moisturizer."

"Fuck you. Ann Marie gets you free Botox."

"Me?" He blinks innocently. "Botox?"

I give him a severe look. "And the lean waist? Liposuction?"

Jeff laughs. "Buddy, that's two hundred crunches a day at the gym."

"Be honest," I urge him.

He laughs harder. "Henry, what's this all about?"

"This," I tell him, reaching down into the pocket of my cargo shorts and withdrawing a photograph. I found it this morning in a drawer. It was the one I used for escort ads online and in the local gay paper. It shows me standing against a brick wall, head back, chest thrust forward. My abs are perfectly sculpted, reflecting the light. Neither my waist nor my age had yet exceeded thirty.

"Hey, it's Hank," Jeff says, taking the picture from me.

Hank was my escort name. I thought it was studlier than Henry. Hank rapped on the doors of hotel rooms and was admitted by clients who immediately fell on their knees in front of him. What a heady couple of years that was. All my life I'd been a skinny geek, and suddenly I was this lean, ripped muscle god who guys paid to lick and service. What the hell happened to that guy? How did he turn into an old man with hair in his ears, skinny and fat at the same time? My arms have shrunk, my waist has filled out.

"It sucks," I say to Jeff.

He smiles, still looking at the photograph. "There was a time I really agreed with you," he says. "I hated getting older. It's not easy anywhere, but in gay life it's particularly difficult." He moves his eyes over to me. "But that's when I was still going out, still doing the circuit, jumping from P-town to Montreal to Miami to Palm Springs. There was always another party, and always another set of boys just entering the scene. I felt like I had to keep up with them." He smiles, looking off toward the horizon. "But thankfully, there comes a point when all that no longer matters quite so much . . ."

I scoff. "I'd believe you, Jeff, if you weren't going in for laser hair removal and Botox."

He laughs. "Oh, I didn't say I was totally over it. If I can still get away with it, why not?" He puts his arm around me. "But lately . . ." His voice trails off. "Maybe it's the wedding again. Sometimes I think it's enough just to have looked this way once." He holds up the photo, and we both gaze at it. "That was you once, Henry. Maybe it's enough just to remember our youth, and not keep trying to relive it."

I take the photo back from him. "Well, I'm not yet ready to throw in the towel," I say. "You had a lot more years out there than I did, Jeff. I didn't get my fill. I want to get back in shape. I want to look good again. I want to get back out there." I smile. "Give me the name of the laser doctor."

"I will, but first let me ask you a question, Henry." He studies me with those piercing blue eyes of his. "*Why* do you want to get back out there?"

"Because I didn't get my fair share."

Jeff laughs. "And how do we determine what is fair?"

"Oh, come on, Jeff. You know what I'm talking about. It sucks to be thirty-three. No longer the young and fresh and nubile boys of summer—but not yet ready to go gracefully offstage like you middle-agers."

He glowers comically. "Watch it, Henry."

"You know what I'm talking about, Jeff. You wrote about it in *The Boys of Summer*. It's set when you were thirty-three."

"When the protagonist is thirty-three," he corrects me.

"Whatever. It just sucks trying to keep up, because it's impossible to keep up when new young bodies are always waiting in the wings."

Jeff folds his arms across his chest. "So how do you try to keep up?"

I shrug. "I don't know. I try to be aware of new trends, new fashions." I smile. "Like camouflage shorts. I realized the boys were wearing camouflage shorts instead of the cutoff denim shorts, so I switched."

Jeff shakes his head. "They're on their way out. I hear corduroy is the next big thing."

"Really?"

He gives me an exasperated face. "*Who the hell knows!* I was being sarcastic! The point is, Henry, you can't keep up with trends. They're impossible to keep track of."

I pout. "I don't want to look like some dated old fossil. Remember that guy Kenneth we'd see on the dance floor? He was older even than you."

He gives me an eyebrow. "I told you to watch it, Henry."

I smirk. "The *point is*, Jeff," I say, mimicking him, "we all thought Kenneth such a tragic figure. He'd be out there dancing in his love beads and freedom rings and spandex bike shorts and we thought, 'Poor guy. He's stuck in 1989.'" I lean in close to make my point. "*I do not want to be Kenneth.*"

"I thought you liked Kenneth. Didn't he hire Hank?"

"Yes." I sigh. "Kenneth was very sweet. But that doesn't make him any less sad. Or any less a cautionary tale for the rest of us."

"Then what are you out there buying camouflage shorts for?"

"Hey, at least I'm not still wearing spandex bike shorts. I'm trying to move with the times."

"I don't think that's always the best strategy, actually," Jeff says. "So what ever happened to Kenneth?"

"Who knows? He's probably still wearing those spandex shorts dancing in some club in Worcester."

"And if it makes him happy, so what?"

I look at Jeff with some frustration. "You are *not* taking me seriously."

"Because you can't possibly *be* serious, Henry." He scowls. "You've said it yourself. If you try to keep up with the kiddies, you'll fail. Because you're *not* a kid."

"But I don't want to be an old fossil, either."

He sighs dramatically. "You're *thirty-three*, Henry. You've got a few more years before fossildom hits. Trust me."

"*You've* managed pretty well," I tell him. "Lots of guys your age have let themselves go, but you still get twinkies like Luke looking at you."

He grins. Flattery always puts Jeff in a more generous frame of mind. "Henry, tell me again why all this is so important to you. And don't give me any song and dance about how you didn't get your fair share."

I'm quiet, thinking.

"Well?" Jeff asks. "Why are you so obsessed with trying to stay young?"

I turn my face to look at him. "So I can meet Mr. Right," I say definitively.

Jeff smiles wryly. "And you think Mr. Right will only accept you without ear hair and love handles?"

I shrug. "I think it'll be easier to attract his attention, anyway."

"I think if he's really Mr. Right, he's going to be looking for other things."

"Oh, please, Jeff. I could take that coming from Lloyd. But you . . ." I look him deep in the eyes. "Do you really think you could give it all up, Jeff? The other men? The way you feel now . . . is it forever? Could you really concentrate only on Lloyd?"

"Well, I already do. Lloyd has always been my primary focus."

"What I mean is, could you give up all the outside sex for good? Could you, *really*?"

He squints his eyes at me. "Are you including three-ways that Lloyd and I do together?"

"Yes. Could you accept a sex life that consisted of just you and Lloyd?"

He thinks for a moment. "Probably not," he admits.

I smile. "At least you're honest."

Jeff eyes me critically. "Could you accept an emotional life that was just you and Mr. Right, whoever he might be?"

I don't have an answer. And, as it turns out, I'm saved from having to provide one, because Luke has come outside, sauntering toward us, his eyes locked, of course, on Jeff.

"I've finished the beds upstairs, Henry," he announces, not looking at me. "Anything else for this morning?"

"We've got a new guest," I tell him. "He just checked into Room 5. He'll need towels."

"He's got 'em." Luke turns his eyes finally to me. "It's Martin."

There's a strange look on Luke's face. "Yeah, I know," I say, wondering why there's a flicker of a smile now playing on the boy's lips.

"How's the novel coming?" Jeff asks.

That's all Luke needs. He returns his gaze to Jeff, launching into a fevered description of his writing, how every day, as soon as he finishes his chores, he holes up in his basement room and lets the words flow. "I don't stop," he says. "I always keep in mind what you advised me. My pen rarely leaves the paper. I just write write write and worry about grammar and punctuation and all that stuff later."

Jeff grins. "Writing is a forward motion. Rewriting is a backward motion. And when you try to go forward and backward at the same time—"

"You go nowhere," Luke finishes.

Clearly they've had some little heart-to-hearts on the nature of the writer's craft. I wonder where these little chats have taken place, and how closely together the two of them have sat, and how difficult it's been for Jeff to restrain himself from flipping Luke over and fucking him hard.

Jeff stands now. "Well," he says, "when slave-driver Henry gives you the green light, you get back to writing." He stretches—just to show off his abs, I bet. "As for me, I've got some more pruning to do around back. When are you going to show me a draft?"

I can't believe what I'm hearing. Jeff has always steadfastly refused to read other people's work, believing if he said yes to one he'd be obliged to say yes to everyone, and soon would be inundated with amateur manuscripts. I had warned Luke it would never happen, and here Jeff now is, making the offer right in front of me. Luke makes sure to swing his gaze past me before he responds to Jeff.

"Really, Jeff?" he asks. "Do you really mean it? You'd read my work?"

Jeff smiles benevolently. "Sure, buddy. Give me your ten best pages."

"Oh, man, thank you, Jeff! I will!"

Jeff winks and disappears around the corner of the house.

"He's so generous," Luke says, still looking after him.

I grunt. "My warning still holds," I tell him. "If you try scheming with Jeff, you'll quickly find you've met your match."

Luke turns his eyes to me. "Henry, can't we be friends again?"

"To be honest, Luke, I'm not sure we ever were."

He approaches me. Still sitting on the bench, my face is level with his torso.

"Henry," Luke purrs, "I still think you're way hot."

My tongue darts out and I begin lapping up the beads of sweat on his stomach before I realize it's just a fantasy. I close my eyes so I can't see his skin.

"Really I do, Henry," Luke says.

"I told you," I say, eyes still closed. "No sex with employees. It's a house rule."

"But getting blown by guests is allowed?"

I open my eyes fast. "What are you talking about?"

Luke sits beside me on the bench. "Martin."

I stare at him. "What do you mean, *Martin*?"

"I was there the night at the dick dock when he sucked your cock."

"Oh, fuck." So it was Martin. And Luke had watched the whole thing.

"Don't worry," he says. "I won't say anything to Lloyd."

"Lloyd already knows." Goddamn it. The kid thinks he has something on me. I've got to dismiss that notion right away. "It's no big deal. Who cares?"

"I thought it was pretty hot to watch," Luke says, surely loving my discomfort. "You and Martin make a very hot pair."

I think he's being sarcastic, but I'm not sure. I can't tell when the kid is being authentic, if ever. But surely Martin isn't his type . . .

"I like hot daddies," he says, as if reading my mind. "Martin's quite handsome. I love his salt-and-pepper beard. And he has amazing eyes."

"I don't want you gossiping about guests," I warn him.

Luke places a hand over his heart. "Oh, never, Henry. Trust me."

"That's just it," I say, standing. "I don't." I start to walk away, then turn back. "Okay, you're done for the morning. Run off and start your writing writing writing."

"Thanks, boss," Luke says.

I head back inside. All of this is just fucking *great*. Now I have to face Martin. And not only is he staying here again, but he's moved to town! He'll talk, and soon everyone will know that I was under the dock.

Without even thinking about it, I pick up the phone and punch in Gale's number, which I've memorized.

"Hey, this is Gale," says his voice-mail. "Leave me a—"

I hang up. I'm glad he didn't answer. At least I was smart enough to call from the guesthouse's private number, so I wouldn't leave a record on his caller ID.

I think what's made my mood all the worse this morning is the conversation I had with my mother last night. Usually I don't think much about my parents. They're off in Western Massachusetts living their lives. I visit when I can, which is never enough for them—especially my mother. My parents, my sisters, my nieces are all part of my *old* life, the life I lived before I was gay, or at least before I was open about it. My family exists in my mind in a sort of netherworld—before Jeff, before Lloyd, before the guesthouse, before Henry Weiner came into his own. Yet as much as I seem to have moved beyond my old life, it's still there, always hovering in the background, and calls from my mother are usually the conduit by which all of my old memories and experiences and self-impressions come rushing back into my consciousness.

As usual, Mom was going on and on about when I was coming home next. I explained that I couldn't leave the guesthouse during high season, that she and my father would have to wait until after Labor Day for a visit. In response came those little noises from her throat that have always been intended to elicit guilt, little murmurs and clicks of her tongue which, when I was younger, had the power to completely overrule my reason. Whatever was on my agenda would be scuttled, and I'd be speeding down the Mass Pike toward West Springfield within the day.

But no more. Mom's come to realize that the hold she had over me for so many years isn't so strong anymore. So she's trying a new tack. "Henry," she said, just as we were getting ready to hang up. "Are you happy?"

What a question to ask your son. Oh, sure, it seems like a kind, caring, considerate question. A mother worrying about her little boy's welfare. But she already knows the answer. She must. How could she not? And by asking it, she only makes me realize it all the more.

No, Mom, I am not.

Except I said, "Of course I am. I'm just busy, that's all."

I close the door to my private office and sit down at my desk. Staring up at me is Joey's face. A photograph of him posing on our deck wearing only a pink Speedo is taped to my in-box. It's been there since our three-week anniversary. In all this time, even through all the heartache, it's never come down.

Maybe it's time it did.

I consider tearing the photograph up, but I don't. I just slip it into my top drawer. But its removal from my sight is a step long overdue.

I feel better for having done it, as I've just proven that I'm an adult.

I think again about Gale. Should I call him back and leave a message this time? Lloyd's words are in my head: *If you want to see him again, call him.*

But wouldn't he have called me if he were really interested? Why risk calling him and asking him out only to have him wiggle out, hem and haw, and finally tell me no? "I'll call you," he said.

Biggest lie in the book.

Once he'd gotten a good look at me, once he started to get to know the real Henry, he pulled back. Just like Joey did, and all the others. Just like Luke, when he saw he had a shot at Jeff.

It's *me*. What other conclusion can I draw? I just don't measure up. I'm boring. I'm fat in some places, too skinny in others. I'm—

A knock at my door causes me to jump.

"Henry?" comes a voice.

It's Martin.

I open the door. He stands there in a white tank top and khaki shorts. I notice that some of his chest hair is gray.

"I'm sorry to bother you," he says. "But is there any chance I can use one of the bikes out back? I haven't yet had a chance to buy my own . . ."

"Yeah, sure," I say. "Use any of them except the blue one. That's mine."

"Thanks." He grins. "Henry, about the other night—"

"It's cool. We didn't know . . . Just forget it."

He nods. "Well, I was wondering . . ." His face flushes. "Well, what I'm trying to say is . . ."

Again his words fade away. "What is it?" I ask.

He steels himself, suddenly determined. "Henry, would you have dinner with me some night?"

I'm stunned. I don't know how to respond. Oh man, this guy—this older man, this *bear*—wants me to have dinner with him!

His face seems frozen, his bright blue eyes waiting for my answer.

"Oh, Martin," I say, "thanks, but we have a policy . . ."

I watch as the muscles in his face droop, his steel-blue eyes lose their luster.

"It's not that I wouldn't like to," I lie, "but you're a guest and—"

"I see. It's fine. Really. I was just—" He makes himself laugh. "But hey, thanks for the use of the bike."

He's out the door before I have a chance to say anything else.

I return to my office.

I sit there for several minutes, feeling horrible.

Finally I pull open my top drawer, and tape the photo of Joey back up on my in-box where I can see it.

II

TEA DANCE

"So tell me I'm not a shit," I beg Ann Marie.

She's handing me a cosmo that's she's just brought back from the bar. "You're not a shit," she replies obediently.

I take a sip of my drink. "Yes, I am. Here I am, feeling sorry for myself that Gale never called me back and then I turn Martin down when he asks me for a date."

It's the Saturday of Labor Day weekend. The last great hurrah of the summer. The Boatslip's deck is jampacked with guys—another tasty sampler of nuts, mints, and crèmes. The music is thumping, the sun is shining, but I'm feeling as sour as a carton of yogurt left in the backseat of a car for a week.

Pesky thing, a conscience.

"Martin's a guest," Ann Marie reminds me. "And you have a policy about guests . . ."

I frown. "If I were a *nice* guy, I would have told him I'd have dinner with him after he checked out." I take another sip of my cosmo. "But I'm not a nice guy."

"Henry," Ann Marie says, "why are you beating yourself up over this? He's not your type. He's a lot older than you are."

"Not that much older when you think about it." And believe me, I've been thinking about it. "Martin is forty-five. I looked at his driver's license when he registered."

"So that's twelve years older than you are!"

I smirk. "Which is pretty much the same difference between Luke and me, except in the other direction. So how come I jumped at that? Why does scoring a younger guy always seem like such a goddamn prize?"

"There's no crime in liking younger guys," Ann Marie says.

I look at her plaintively. "That's just it. I *don't* like younger guys. Not as a rule, anyway. If a guy's hot, he's hot, no matter what the age."

It's true. I'm not one of these chicken hawks who automatically salivate over the sight of cheeks that have never sprouted whiskers. I like *men,* not boys—men with some muscle, some experience.

Then why is it that my tricks are always younger than I am? Why do I never cruise an older guy? Why is that the guys I look at, who command my attention, are always my juniors? Gale must be at least five years younger than I am. Joey was *seven* years younger. And if Lloyd is right that I'm still hung up on Luke, I suspect it's his very youth that fascinates me—so attractive, so confident, so unlike what I was at his age.

Maybe, in fact, that's what fuels the prevailing youth obsession among so many gay men. Even when I was in tip-top shape, I could immediately lose the attention of some potential trick if a skinny little twinkie walked into the bar. Many nights I'd feel frustrated and angry when some guy, after flirting with me, suddenly hurried away to follow after some chicken, preferring his scrawny little arms over my well-rounded biceps—and all because they were a decade younger.

"I think," I say to Ann Marie, "that gay men are always trying to capture the youth they didn't have. And I'm including me in this."

She eyes me over the plastic cup of her cosmo. "Are you going all philosophical on me again, Henry?"

"I mean it. I think we feel that if we can get a young guy, it will prove we're still players. That we aren't over the hill yet. But even more than that—" I lower my voice and draw closer to her, as if I don't want anyone to overhear. "Lots of young guys are living lives of far greater freedom and self-confidence than we ever did, and I think we feel that if we can capture one of them, we can maybe taste a little of that for ourselves. We can imagine we're still young and as open to possibility as they are."

"So answer me this, Henry," she says, looking eerily like her brother. "What's the cutoff age for Mr. Right? Thirty? Thirty-five? Forty?"

I smile. "I'd like to think there was no cutoff age, but I guess my rejection of Martin proved there is." I knock back the last of my cosmo. "And I'm not proud of it."

"I don't think it's anything that requires either pride or shame," Ann Marie says, finishing her drink as well. "I think we have a picture in our minds of Mr. Right and it's just hard to accept anything else."

"So what does your Mr. Right look like?"

She smiles. "Big. Football player build. Long hair. Maybe a beard. A leather jacket on his back and a Harley Davidson between his legs."

I give her a wry grin. "I'm assuming you mean a motorcycle."

"Oh, that too."

We laugh.

"And you, Henry? What does Mr. Right look like for you?"

I consider the question. My boyfriends have been quite the varied lot. Joey was a short, slim, tight-bodied Asian boy. Daniel was a tall, freckled, slightly stocky Irish boy. And then there's Shane, who I suddenly remember is arriving in town today.

I smile without even realizing it. "Shane," I say out loud.

Ann Marie laughs. "Your Mr. Right looks like *Shane?*"

"No," I reply automatically. "I just remembered that Shane might be here. He's coming down this weekend."

Two nights ago, as I was happily blanketed down on the couch for the evening watching *The Golden Girls,* I heard a muffled little *ping* from my computer. Glancing over at the screen, I saw I had a new e-mail. Never able to resist, even when it usually turns out just to be spam, I threw off the blanket and walked over to my desk. A smile stretched across my face when I saw it was from Shane—my ex three times removed, before Joey and before Daniel. He's the only one I've managed to stay in any kind of contact with, though it had been months, maybe even a year, since

I'd last heard from him. "I'll be in P-town over Labor Day week-end," he wrote. "Lunch? Dinner? Drink? Or . . . ?"

"Yes, to any or all," I quickly replied. "Will be great to see you. Xxoo."

I was surprised at how much Shane's e-mail cheered me. I was never in love with him the way I was the others. In fact, Jeff could never understand what had brought the two of us together in the first place, since Shane was far from my physical type. Shane took perverse pride in the fact that he hadn't set foot in a gym since his junior year of high school. Tall and thin, he was apt to dress in drag whenever the spirit moved him, which was about every other month. Hardly the picture of the boyish Joey, whose only drag was Abercrombie & Fitch.

But here's where Shane was truly different from the others: *Shane was in love with me.* Head over stiletto heels, in fact. I can't say that about anyone else in my life. Shane was there for me through some pretty tough times, especially when I was dealing with my convoluted feelings for Lloyd. So I decided, after months of friendship, to give a relationship with him a shot. But while we did our best, it just wasn't meant to be. Our time together didn't end so much as simply fade away. I moved to Provincetown, Shane started coming down less and less, and finally, mutually and ami-cably, we decided to part.

But as I read and reread Shane's e-mail, I found myself en-snared by the memory of him: the way his eyes would light up when I walked into the room, the way he would curl my hair around his fingers, the way he always knew just what to say to make me laugh, to make me feel good about myself.

Impulsively I typed out a second e-mail to Shane. "You can stay with me if you need a place," I tell him, knowing full well he usu-ally bunks in with a friend in the West End. "I promise not to hog the sheets. Xxxxxxoooooo."

He never replied.

"He must be here someplace," I say, standing on my toes and scanning around at the crowd. "He never misses Tea Dance."

"You know, Henry," Ann Marie says, "I wouldn't be so quick to dismiss Shane as the picture of your Mr. Right."

"Oh, please," I say, still searching. "He was hardly my physical type."

"I know. But who says Mr. Right has to be?"

I make a face at her. "So you'd accept some guy without a Harley Davidson?"

"Maybe that's why I'm still single ever since dumping the loser who, biologically at least, is J. R.'s dad."

"And here I was thinking that was a virgin birth."

She smirks. "The truth is, I've been waiting for somebody who's just not going to come riding down the street. That's the cold hard fact of my life."

We're both quiet. I want to encourage her, to tell her not to give up. But I can't. Not when I'm feeling the same way myself.

"You want another drink?" Ann Marie asks.

I nod. She heads back off toward the bar.

I look around at all the guys here at Tea Dance. There's a good mix of ages, everything from early twenties to sixties. Everybody seems to be having a grand old time, but I make a point to look at the eyes. Very few are focused on the person with whom they're speaking. Instead, eyes are everywhere, glancing over the tops of heads, peering around shoulders. Everyone is looking for something else, something new, something fresh.

Isn't that why I'm here? Isn't that why, after three days of moping around, depressed over Gale, feeling guilty about Martin, I allowed Ann Marie to convince me to come? In the back of my mind, beyond all my doubt and pessimism, isn't there always the hope, forever springing eternal, that I might meet Mr. Right? That this will be the day? That if I sat at home, losing myself in another afternoon of TV Land reruns, I might be missing out on finding true love at last?

Make no mistake: I gave up a lot to be here today. It's a *Facts of Life* marathon that I'm missing. TV Land has started adding the great eighties sitcoms to its roster. The shows of my youth. I was eager to reacquaint myself with Blair, Jo, and Tootie, but instead I allowed myself to be dragged over here. I'm consoled by the fact that later this week comes *Family Ties*, *Growing Pains*, and *Gimme a Break*. But still, part of me wishes I were back in my apartment, safe on my couch, eating a carton of Häagen Daz and admiring a young George Clooney as Mrs. Garrett's handyman.

"That guy's looking at you," Ann Marie whispers, nudging me as she returns with our drinks.

"Please," I tell her. "Don't start that again. Look how it ended up last time."

"But he *is*, Henry."

I glance in the direction she's indicating as I take a sip of my cosmo. The guy is about my age, blond, handsome, muscular, wearing green cargo shorts and a gray T-shirt emblazoned with the words MUSSEL BEACH across the back, advertising Provincetown's gym.

"And he even *looks* like your version of Mr. Right," Ann Marie says. "Muscles for days."

"You know," I say, "I think he *is* looking at me."

"You see, Henry?" Ann Marie's leaning close to my ear. "Not everyone looks only at young guys."

I laugh. "So now you're calling me old?"

"Oh, Henry."

I smile at her. "So what about you, sweetie? The Mr. Right you describe ain't gonna be found at Tea Dance."

She nods. "That's for sure. But it doesn't matter. I am *so* over men. I'd like to get up on the bar here and shout out to all these queens to quit while they're ahead. Stop looking! He's not out there! Mr. Right is a fantasy like Santa Claus and the Easter Bunny!"

"Gee, thanks for making me feel better."

She smirks. "J. R. is the all Mr. Right I need."

I notice the blond taking another look over his shoulder at me. It frightens me a bit. He's too close to my ideal physical type for me to allow myself to hope. I try to concentrate on Ann Marie, to refuse to join this wandering army of eyes.

"You know," I say to her, anxious to change the subject, "I'm starting to share your worries about J. R."

Her face takes on a pained expression. "What have you noticed?"

"He's been so sullen and quiet, sitting on his bed, rarely removing his headphones. Jeff's tried to get him moving, tempting him with activities he usually jumps for, like swimming in the Wellfleet ponds or off-roading through the dunes. But each time J. R. just grunts, shaking his head no. I ask him what's wrong, but he won't say."

Ann Marie sighs. "He won't confide in me either. I'm starting to worry all this isn't just a phase."

"Well, he was pissed that Jeff and Lloyd didn't ask him directly to be their ring bearer, but instead went through you."

Ann Marie shakes her head. "That's just a cover for something deeper."

"Well, you know, it's tough to be a kid in Provincetown," I tell her. "Sure, it's great in summer, but what happens when stuff starts shutting down? The closest mall is an hour away. The one movie theater in town shows mostly arty independent stuff and not the big blockbusters. A kid can probably feel a little trapped."

She's nodding. "But it's more than all that, Henry. Did I tell you what happened at J. R.'s last basketball game a few months ago?"

"No."

Ann Marie looks off over the water. She's emotional as she remembers the day. "His team was playing an away game someplace down Cape—Harwich or Mashpee or something like that. I was sitting in the bleachers watching as J. R. and his teammates filed into the gymnasium, and all of a sudden a couple of kids on the other team held up a sign that read PROVINCETOWN FAGS. We tried to boo them down and some teachers threw them out, but still, all through the game the Provincetown players kept getting taunted with fag this, fag that."

I'm stunned. "You mean, just because Provincetown has a large gay population, the kids from its schools get called faggot?"

Ann Marie nods. "And it really bothered J. R. You know how he idolizes his uncles—including you, Henry." Her eyes are moist. "I think seeing the kind of hatred that's out there really stung him. You know, J. R. grew up thinking gay was natural, just part of the diversity of the world. Now he's discovering the world doesn't always see it that way, and it hurts him. He won't talk about it, but I know the experience that day at the game traumatized him. He's been really quiet ever since."

"Is that why he doesn't want to play basketball again next year?"

"I think it probably is."

"Oh, man. Have you shared any of this with Jeff?"

She shakes her head. "You know my brother. He'd go ballistic. He'd be down at that school, screaming for the coach to be fired."

"Maybe he should be."

"Maybe." Ann Marie doesn't seem to want to finish her drink. She sets it on a table nearby. "But I think to cause a scene at this point would make the situation even worse for J. R. It would draw attention to it. Right now J. R. just wants some time to himself."

I think about how pervasive homophobia really is, how long its reach. Even cool little straight boys can get hit with it sometimes.

"You know," Ann Marie says, her earlier light-hearted mood now completely gone, "I should really get going. I'm taking J. R. for lobster at Clem and Ursie's tonight. It was the only offer that seemed to entice him out of his room."

"I'll go with you," I tell her.

She manages a smile. "Oh, no, you don't. You have that blond number to attend to."

I make a face. "Do you know how *tired* of the whole scene I am right now? I couldn't *bear* meeting someone new."

"Henry, stop lying to yourself. What if he's Mr. Right?"

"I thought you said he doesn't exist."

"He doesn't. But deep down I want you to prove me wrong." She gives me a kiss on the cheek. "And if not him, maybe you can find Shane. You know, of all your boyfriends, I liked Shane the best."

I smile. "I think maybe I did, too."

I watch her go. At least Ann Marie has J. R. to go home to. I don't even have a dog. In that instant I miss Clara more than I've ever missed her before.

I take a deep breath and turn to face the blond guy in the gray T-shirt.

Sure enough, he's looking.

What if he's Mr. Right?

I decide to approach. He's with two friends, who seem oblivious to our cruising each other.

"Hey," I say to Blond Guy.

"Hey," he says in reply.

I grip Blond Guy's hand firmly.

"Couldn't help but notice you over there," Blond Guy says. "Your friend leave?"

"Yes. She has a son. Dinner time."

"Cool." He seems both surprised and delighted that I actually came over. His smile is pushing his cheeks up into his eyes. "My name's Evan."

"I'm Henry," I tell him.

"Good to meet you, Henry."

We're still shaking hands, and now I'm smiling just as broadly as he is.

"Oh," Evan says, finally breaking eye contact with me, "this is Curt." He indicates the dark-haired, taller guy standing beside him. I let go of Evan's hand to shake with Curt. "And this is . . ."

Evan gestures toward the third guy, a young twink with reddish spiky hair whose name he seems to have forgotten. I quickly grasp that the twink is another new acquaintance.

"Andy," the twink reminds him.

"Andy," Evan echoes. I shake with Andy, who smiles but quickly returns his gaze to Curt.

So that's what this is. Evan was feeling shut out by the fact that his friend had found a potential trick, but he hadn't, so he aggressively sought one for himself. I can't help but wonder: is he really attracted to me—or did he just settle on anyone in close proximity?

No matter. He seems genuinely pleased now that I've approached, and I must admit Evan is even more handsome up close than he was from a few feet away. Rare that such a thing happens. Usually it's the other way around.

We exchange the usual small talk. Where he's from (New York), what he does (manages an art gallery in SoHo). In fact, the more we talk, the more we seem to have in common: we're both Jewish, brought up without strong connections to our roots; we're both into grunge music, both owning original EPs of Soundgarden's *Screaming Life*; we're both former insurance company drones who made last-minute escapes before corporate dementia overtook us; and we're both originally from western Massachusetts. Evan grew up just fifteen minutes north of me on Interstate 91 in the town of Holyoke. "No way!" we both say in unison, and we laugh. We're also nearly the exact same age, just off by a couple of weeks. I feel as if I've found a long-lost twin.

"You have a great body," Evan says, looking me up and down and clapping me on both shoulders.

I'm all set to protest, to point out my love handles, but I resist the urge. Instead, I simply clap Evan's shoulders in a similar way and return the compliment. "Are you a trainer at the gym?" I ask.

"Me? A trainer?" He laughs. "Oh, you mean the T-shirt. No, I just bought it on my last visit. Thanks for thinking so, though." He shakes his head, patting his belly. "Actually, I need to get back to the gym. It's been a while. I've gotten out of shape."

"Out of shape?" I make a face in disbelief. "We should all be so lucky if that's out of shape."

"Dude," he tells me, "*you're* the lucky one."

It's in that moment that I realize how distorted we all are about our bodies. Here's this guy with great shoulders and biceps, thinking he's "out of shape." And for all my fretting about the tire tube around my waist, I am sure for some guys I represent a physical goal they've given up all hope of ever achieving.

Immediately I like Evan even more. He's not like Gale, with his perfectly sculpted body, every ounce of fat worked off by those goddamned twists around the pole. He's not like Luke either, cocky with youth. Instead, he's like me, just making his way the best he can.

"So," Evan says, "you want to come back for a drink and a dip in the hot tub?"

I smile. "What guesthouse are you guys staying at?"

"Oh, Curt and I share a place here," Evan says, glancing over at his friend, whose conversation with the other guy—Andy—now appears very intense. "It's not far from here."

"Sure," I say. "Why not?"

Evan smiles at my agreement, then leans forward to whisper

something into Curt's ear. Curt nods, putting his arm around Andy's shoulders and guiding him toward the exit. Evan does the same to me.

All the way down Commercial Street, Evan and I stay about four feet behind Curt and Andy. Evan's arm remains firmly around my shoulder. I snake mine around his waist.

"God, I love this place," Evan is saying, inhaling deeply the tangy salt air. "When I get here, I just *breathe*. It feels like I never take a breath in New York. Here I breathe in the air and breathe out all my stress." He whistles in appreciation. "The smell of the sea in the air gets me high."

"That's why I moved here," I tell him. "Why I left behind my corporate job and made a new life for myself."

"And you're one hundred percent happier, I bet."

I smile, but I don't answer. Of course I'm happier than when I was schlepping through that soulless job. But given my recent angst, I can't wholeheartedly commit to being *happy*. I'm not so different from J. R., feeling cut off from the world at times. J. R. can't find a good movie in the off-season, or a store that sells the latest Xbox. I can't find a boyfriend.

But Evan's arm around my shoulder feels good. It may be Labor Day and winter may be looming right around the corner, but right now I feel good. I look over at Evan and he kisses me. He might be rolling—the kiss seems possibly fueled by ecstasy— but it might also simply be a rush of heartfelt emotion, suggesting Evan likes me as much as I'm starting to like him. Could it be possible? Dare I let myself imagine?

For once, this guy is definitely my type. Finally—a mature, well-muscled, handsome man. I like how solid Evan feels. I move my hand up from his waist to feel his back. Hard, sinewy muscles. I begin to get an erection.

"Do you know what I love best about Provincetown?" Evan is asking, as we round the bend that Commercial Street makes at Perry's Liquors. "I love the *love*. Do you know what I mean?"

"I think so, but say more."

"I don't want to sound syrupy," he says. "But I mean it. From the moment I get here from New York, I feel like I *belong* here. That this is my real home. That I never want to leave again."

I smile again. This is one sweet man. Not many guys would allow themselves to come across as so emotional, so soft, this quickly. Evan's the kind of part-time resident I always think about when some year-rounder stands up at Town Meeting and laments the houses bought by out-of-towners that sit dark all winter. Sure, I understand the need for more housing for those who make Provincetown their full-time home, but to castigate the seasonal people as leeches or selfish rich boys just isn't fair. Most of them, I suspect, are like Evan, who deeply love this place, who cherish every moment they can spend here, and wish they could spend more.

Evan shares my love of this place. That much is clear. He sees beyond the standard images of Provincetown that are shared by most gay men—the gaudy parade of street theater under a blazing hot sky, Cher on a motor scooter, shirtless gay men holding hands, dykes on bikes roaring through town. He's found the other face of Provincetown, the way I have and, for him, this is *home*, not merely a vacation destination. The hardy band of tough-skinned, warm-hearted folk who populate this village year round can no more claim ownership of Provincetown than the person who has just stepped off the ferry for the first time. No one can claim Provincetown as more theirs than anyone else's. It belongs to all. That's the beauty of the place, the enchantment.

Last summer, one of our guests, a young gay man who had never before set foot in Provincetown, was particularly sad as he checked out. "I feel as if I've been waiting to come here all my life," he said to me.

He knew nothing about local politics—about the history of conflict over the late-night gatherings at Spiritus, for example—only that those assemblages of hundreds of gay men and women was an incredibly affirming experience for him. He didn't know that some in town didn't really want him here, that instead they wanted to redirect the town's tourism to focus on straight families. All this young man knew was that he couldn't wait to return here again next year to walk among people like himself.

So many things he didn't know about Provincetown. He'd probably never heard that a pirate ship had been found in the harbor, or that a rare species of tree frog populated its woods, or that Divine once worked here slinging hash. He may have had some inkling that Provincetown was a famous art colony, but I doubt that he could have told a Hensche from a Hoffmann—as if I could.

Yet, despite all this, the town was *his*. This young man, like so many others, felt the mystical lure of the place where the land meets the sea, where the road ends. Four days were all he spent here, in the middle of the Fourth of July crush, but when he left he shed tears at our front desk. "This is the warmest, happiest place on the planet," he said to me just before he boarded a Cape Air flight and flew out over Hatches Harbor back to his home in the Midwest. I believe this firmly: Provincetown belongs to him as much as it does to me.

Evan's making that whistle of appreciation again. "God, smell that air," he says. "I wish I could bottle it and take it back with me to New York."

Overhead there's a slight rumble of thunder.

"The forecast said we might get some rain," I report.

Evan peers over at me and offers a goofy, boyish grin. "You know what else I love?"

I smile back at him. "There's more?"

"Fuck, yes."

I nuzzle his nose with my own. "Tell me."

"To run barefoot along the beach when it's raining."

I think I'm already a little bit in love with Evan as we turn down a daisy-lined path toward his house. It's a small attachment to a larger residence that may have once been a garage.

Once inside, Curt mixes us martinis while Evan opens the spa out on the deck. I'm not really in the mood for an orgy, but given that Evan has paid no attention to Andy and Curt has paid no attention to me, I suspect the dip in the hot tub will only be foreplay. Afterward, we two couples will each head off separately—though, as I look around the place, I see only one door that might lead to a bedroom.

Still, I disrobe without thinking too much, enjoying the floating sensations courtesy of the alcohol. I'm struck at once by how beautiful Evan is—hard, square pecs, defined abdominals, all covered in soft blond fuzz.

The water in the spa is hot—over one hundred degrees—and I need a few seconds to adjust before I crouch down onto a seat. The water rises to my shoulders. One by one the others get in. Evan makes a beeline to me. We clink our plastic martini glasses and begin to kiss. Out of the corner of my eye I notice Curt and Andy are now liplocked as well.

"You are so sexy, Henry," Evan whispers in my ear. "Don't disappear from my life after all this is over. Promise?"

At that moment, the axis of the earth shifts. Everything around me—the water, the other guys, the sky above—disappears. Suddenly I'm sucked feet first into a time tunnel, and I'm zipping along faster than the speed of light, my head rolling back and forth, barely able to catch my breath. When I open my eyes and take a look around, I see Evan sitting in a rocking chair on the front porch of a beautifully restored Victorian house, gazing out over the ocean. And wonder of wonders—I'm sitting next to him. A bottle of champagne rests on a table in front of us. Evan reaches over and takes my hand. We're celebrating our tenth anniversary. At our feet is our dog, another pug, who we've named Clara II.

"Dude?"

I blink. Evan is looking at me over the rim of his martini glass. "You seemed to zone out there for a moment."

"Sorry," I say.

I reach over and kiss him. His tongue fills my mouth.

Just then it starts to rain. I feel a light tickle of drops on my forehead.

"After we make love," I whisper to Evan, "let's walk barefoot on the beach in the rain."

He smiles—but it's a smile that's interrupted by Curt, who floats over to ask Evan quietly, "Honey, did you close the skylights? I don't want the rain getting in."

I freeze.

"Yeah," Evan replies. "I closed them before we left for Tea."

Curt nods and returns to Andy.

Honey.

Curt just called Evan *honey.*

Of course. How *stupid* of me not to figure it out! Evan and Curt are lovers. They're not just two friends who own a house together. They're lovers who own a one-bedroom condo and who've been through this little scene many times before. They're in a god-damned open relationship, and spice up their sex life with a steady infusion of new blood.

Just like another couple I know.

Part of me wants to stand up, get out of the hot tub, put my clothes back on and go home. But Evan is kissing me again, and his hand is on my dick. I'm raging hard. I can't back out now.

I allow myself to be led out of the hot tub and wrapped in a thick terrycloth towel. I follow Evan into the bedroom. Curt and Andy are hot on our heels.

Evan didn't lie to me. He told me he owned the house with Curt. He used the revealing pronoun "we," but still I heard only what I wanted to hear.

On the bureau opposite the bed is a photograph of Evan and Curt in tuxedos.

"Your wedding?" I ask Evan.

"No," he tells me. "Last year's HRC dinner. Our wedding picture is over there." He points. On a table is another picture. They're in flower-print boardshorts wearing leis around their necks.

"We had our commitment ceremony on the volcano in Maui," Curt says, coming up behind me.

"Really? Maui?" Andy asks. "How cool."

Yes, I think. *How fucking cool.*

I lay down on the bed. Evan places his body—still warm from the tub—on top of mine. We kiss, but I'm losing my erection. The image of Evan and me on that front porch with Clara II is fading away, replaced by that picture of Evan and Curt on that god-damned volcano.

Evan is a great kisser, though, so I surrender to the sex. He gives an incredible blow job. But Curt and Andy are right there next to us on the same bed, and at one point Curt reaches in to kiss Evan, and Andy places his sloppy wet lips over mine. My erection goes up and down. Curt eventually fucks Andy while Evan and I watch. Everyone comes but me.

There's a moment of stillness as we all lie on the bed just breathing. I'm the one to stir first. I get up off the bed and bring back a hand cloth.

"You're a doll," Curt says, accepting the cloth to clean up the mess that's dripping from his—and everyone else's—torso.

Except mine.

"Henry," Evan says, pulling me to him, "don't you want to come?"

"No," I tell him truthfully. "I'm kind of beat."

He kisses me. "Should we take that walk now?"

"What walk?" Curt asks, flopping horizontally across the bed, his head coming to rest on Andy's stomach.

"On the beach," Evan tells him.

"But it's pouring," Curt retorts.

Evan winks at me. I manage a small smile.

"Look," I tell them, "I have work to do back at the guesthouse. This was fun."

"Will we see you later?" Evan asks.

There's that pronoun "we" again. How different his question sounds from his earlier plea not to disappear from his life. But in truth, both requests were saying the same thing: *You'll fuck with the two of us again, won't you?*

"Well," I say, "you know how to reach me."

Evan sits up. "It's the Nirvana guesthouse, right?" he asks, jotting the name down on a pad next to his bed. I wonder how many names and numbers have been jotted down on that pad.

"That's the one," I say, pulling on my jeans.

"We'll do that walk another time," Evan promises.

I give them all a little salute as I leave. My throat is suddenly too tight to speak.

Heading outside, I try not to think, to block any unwanted thoughts or feelings from intruding into my mind. I shudder. The rain is coming down heavy, and it's cold. Much too cold for a barefoot walk on the beach, I tell myself.

I stuff my hands down into my pockets and hurry home.

12

NIRVANA GUESTHOUSE

I'm standing behind the front desk watching Luke vacuum in the nude.

Okay, so he's not totally nude. He's wearing a neon-pink thong. He'd been sunbathing on the roof during his break, and decided not to pull his shorts back on when he resumed his work. When I tried to object, Lloyd overruled me, insisting, "It's good for business. Do you know how many guests we've gotten because they've heard we have a hot houseboy?"

I'm disgusted at the way Lloyd makes sure he gets an eyeful of Luke's ass cheeks as he passes through the room.

Okay, so I can't deny that Luke in his pink thong is a pretty sight to behold. For a moment I remember his tongue on my chest, licking up the syrupy peaches. *I could have had him again,* I tell myself. *If not for my own wounded pride, I could have had that sweet supple body in my bed for a second round . . . and maybe a third and a fourth . . .*

"Henry," he says, catching me staring.

"What?" I ask, my face burning.

"How have you been doing on the ice cream?"

I roll my eyes. "Look, I'm not keeping track, and neither should you."

"I've had only three cigarettes in six days," he says, beaming, ignoring my churlishness. "Aren't you proud of me?"

I grunt, pretending to busy myself at the front desk computer. That's when I notice I've got an e-mail. Shane has finally responded.

"I'm here in town," he writes. "Call me on my cell. Maybe we can have breakfast tomorrow."

My heart sinks. Apparently I'm Shane's last priority if he's waiting to see me on the very last day of the long weekend. I'd hoped we'd have some time to catch up.

"Sounds good," I type back. "But if you're not doing anything today, call me. You have my cell."

I hit SEND.

I've been depressed and grouchy all day, trying to put the memory of Evan and Curt out of my mind. How could I have been so stupid? It should have been plain as day that they were lovers, but I saw only what I wanted to see. That's always been one of my chief problems.

Standing motionless in the shower this morning, letting the water just cascade over my head and down my body, I had a realization. The worst thing about dating isn't getting rejected. It's allowing yourself to hope. Hope is the absolutely *worst* thing you can do when you're dating. Oh, I know hope is supposed to be this great sustaining human emotion. Everybody always says, "Don't lose hope." Fuck that. Hope *sucks*. It's because I hope so hard that the disappointment is always so great.

I mean, I'd known Evan for only an hour. Sixty fucking minutes. And in that short span of time, I allowed myself to imagine a whole life for us together. How stupid. How ridiculous. It's about time I simply accepted the fact that there is no one out there waiting for me. Ann Marie is right. Mr. Right doesn't exist.

I can hear Lloyd chiding me about my pessimism. "You create your own reality by what you believe," he's said. "The energy you put out there is what comes back to you." Yeah, right. Blah blah blah.

All I know for sure right now is this: if I'd held on to my skepticism walking with Evan back to his house—if I'd kept my dreams bottled up, refusing to permit even a little bit of hope to bubble up—I wouldn't be feeling so shitty today.

"Uncle Henry?"

I look up from the computer screen. J. R. stands in front of the desk, his blue eyes peering out at me through hair hanging over his forehead.

"Hey, kiddo," I say.

"Can I talk to you?"

"Sure." I lean forward on the counter. "What's up?"

He looks around to make sure no one will hear him. Luke is off at the far end of the room, and the whirr of the vacuum cleaner prevents him from overhearing.

"Do you think . . ." The boy's voice trails off. He's clearly having a hard time with something.

"Go ahead, J. R.," I tell him. "You know you can talk to me."

I've always had a good relationship with the kid. Jeff and Lloyd have been his primary father figures, of course, but I could always make J. R. laugh with my spot-on impersonations of some of his teachers, who I'd see at town meetings. He especially loved my take on Mrs. Randall, the principal, who has an eye twitch. I'd stand behind the desk here twitching my eye and talking through my nose, and J. R. would be rolling on the floor laughing. And he long ago discovered that I keep a stash of Almond Joys and Three Musketeers in my top desk drawer. He always gets a big laugh when I attempt to inventory my stock and find one or two missing.

So I'm hopeful I might be able to connect with him where the others haven't. "Go ahead," I tell him. "Talk to me. Nobody's around."

He speaks fast, as if he wants to get the words out before deciding against it. "Will the newspaper be at Uncle Jeff and Uncle Lloyd's wedding?" he asks. "Will there be pictures of it in the paper?"

I nod, though I don't quite understand the point of his question. "I think it's probably likely," I say.

The boy makes a face. "That's what I thought," he says glumly.

"I don't understand, kiddo," I say. "What's the big deal?"

"Do you think they'll have a picture of everybody who's there?"

Ann Marie's words at Tea Dance come back to me, and I start to understand J. R.'s dilemma. "You mean," I ask, "do you think they'll publish a picture that includes you?"

He nods.

"I can't say for certain," I tell him, "but I suspect that the picture will just be of Jeff and Lloyd."

He sighs. It's the answer he seems to have been hoping for, but still, I haven't completely allayed all of his fears.

"What is it, buddy?" I ask quietly. "Are there kids in school who might give you a hard time?"

He shakes his head. "Not really. It's just . . ." Again his words fade away.

"Just what, kiddo?"

But before he has a chance to answer, Jeff comes bounding through the front door. Shirtless, of course, his abs even more pronounced after his morning workout. I notice how quickly Luke stands at attention, switching off the vacuum cleaner to wish his hero a cheery good morning.

"How's the writing coming?" Jeff asks our nearly naked houseboy.

"Great," Luke replies. "I almost have that chunk ready for you to read."

"Excellent," Jeff says, giving him a thumb up. He spots J. R. at the desk and hurries over. "Hey, buddy!"

"Hey," J. R. says without enthusiasm. I notice the way he drops his eyes to the floor.

"You know what?" Jeff's beaming as he squats down to J. R.'s level. "I've got the whole day free and was thinking about taking the boat over to Long Point. Want to come?"

"No thanks," J. R. says.

I see the hurt on Jeff's face. "You got other plans?" he asks.

J. R. nods. "I'm going Boogie-boarding with my friends."

"Oh." Jeff stands up. "Okay."

He says nothing else as J. R. heads out the door.

My heart breaks for my friend Jeff. I wish I hadn't been a witness to that. Worse, I wish Luke hadn't been a witness to it. Several seconds of awkwardness linger in the room as Jeff stands there just looking at the door.

"Jeff," I say quietly, not wanting Luke to hear. "J. R.'s going through some stuff . . ."

"Clearly." He forces a smile onto his face. "Who can figure out kids? God knows I had my moods when I was his age."

"You still do," I say, and his smile changes from forced to genuine.

"Why don't *you* come with me to Long Point, buddy?" Jeff asks. "It's been awhile since we did anything together, just you and me. Unless"—his eyes twinkle—"you have a date . . ."

"Please," I say. "I'm through dating."

He smirks. "Word around town is that you went home with a real hottie from Tea yesterday."

I can't believe how fast stories spread in this town. "What—do you have spies posted along Commercial Street?"

Jeff winks. "It's a small town, Henry. So out with it. Who was he?"

"It's not worth talking about."

Jeff leers. "From what I hear, he was more than worth a description."

"Oh, sure," I say. "Gorgeous. But married."

"And the problem with that is—?"

I scowl at him. "The problem with that is, I was clueless. It turned out to be a four-way with the husband and *his* trick." I sigh. "I thought I was going home with Mr. Right."

Jeff leans his chin his hands, his elbows on the counter. "And what makes him fill that particular bill?"

"Oh, nothing except perfection. Evan is sensitive. Romantic. He loves living here. He has a real sense for the place, and about what really matters in life. We have so much in common." I pause for dramatic effect. "Except that he had already found *his* Mr. Right."

"Maybe he's hoping for another one," Jeff says. "Mr. Right bookends."

I glare at him. "I am *not* going to be one half of a pair of bookends."

"Just an idea," he quips.

"I need to face it," I say. "All the good ones are taken."

"Don't give up hope, Henry."

I grunt. "Hope, shmope. If I never hope again, I'll be a lot happier."

Jeff grins. "Whatever works, buddy." He slaps the counter, getting ready to head out. "Okay, I'll be back around three and we'll head down to the boat. Pack a bottle of vodka. We'll make martinis and watch the sunset from Long Point."

I glance over at Luke, who's worked his way closer to us, dusting tables and making sure we get a good view of his buns. But what's even more noticeable is the unmistakable envy on his face as he listens to Jeff describe the excursion he'll be taking with me. In that, I take no small satisfaction.

After Jeff heads out, Luke approaches the counter. "I've never been to Long Point," he says in a small voice.

"Well, don't get any ideas about showing up there this afternoon," I tell him. "Jeff needs some time away. It's going to be just the two of us."

He flutters his eyelashes and places a hand on his bare chest. "I wouldn't *think* of intruding," he says. Then he smiles. "Tell me, Henry. Are you in love with Jeff?"

"Don't be absurd. He's my best friend."

"Doesn't mean you can't be in love with him."

I narrow my eyes at him. "Don't be projecting your own feelings onto me, Luke."

"If I seem smitten with Jeff," Luke muses, "it's probably because he reminds me of the first man I ever loved. Did I ever tell you about him, Henry?"

"Yes, you did. Your stepbrother."

"Oh, no, no, no. Mike was just a boy. I'm talking about a *man*. A real man." He smiles over at me. "You mean I've never told you about Darryl?"

"No," I say, holding his gaze. "But I suspect you're about to."

"Darryl died," he says dreamily. "Yes, it was AIDS. The meds just seemed not to work for him. I was still just a kid, living in New York, trying to make a go of my life, and I met Darryl at a book reading." He smirks. "A book reading by Jeffrey O'Brien, as a matter of fact."

"How perfect," I say.

"Yes, it was," Luke agrees, missing—or ignoring—my sarcasm. "There I sat, at the Barnes & Noble in Chelsea, bumping knees with this guy next to me. Though truth be told, Darryl was the one who was doing most of the bumping." He giggles. "I was too intent on listening to Jeff read. But afterward, there Darryl was, waiting by the door and watching me. It was only then that I got a good look at him. He was older than I was, of course, by some fifteen years, but there was something about his spirit that I—"

Luke stops talking abruptly, distracted by the sound of footsteps coming down the stairs. We both look over. It's Lloyd. I turn back to Luke and observe a broad smile stretching across his face, revealing his dimples.

"What perfect timing!" Luke exults. "Lloyd! You're the expert on spirituality around here! What does an old soul mean?"

Lloyd meets Luke's smile with one of his own. "Well, it describes someone who's lived many lives, who's accumulated a lot of wisdom and experience in the course of those many lifetimes."

"Luke's telling me about the first man he ever loved," I report dryly.

"Oh?" Lloyd asks. "And this guy was an old soul?"

"Oh, no," Luke says. "He was a very *young* soul. *I* was the old soul, Darryl said, even though, in years, he was a lot older than I was."

"Interesting," Lloyd says.

"They met at a reading of Jeff's," I add. "That's even *more* interesting."

"What's funny," Luke says, "is that Darryl wasn't even a fan of Jeff's. We got to talking afterward and I asked him if he thought Jeff was hot. 'He's not really my type,' Darryl said. I replied, 'What? Jeff is *everybody's* type.' Darryl shook his head. 'Not mine,' he insisted. In fact, he'd never heard of Jeff before that night. He just happened to be in the bookstore when they announced the reading and so he decided to stay."

Luke looks at us to gauge our reaction. I'm determinedly not giving him one, but Lloyd is smiling, so Luke goes on.

"'You mean,' I asked, 'you haven't read any of Jeff's books?' Again Darryl shook his head no. I was aghast. 'Well,' I asked, 'what did you think of what he read tonight?' It was from *Finding Home*, which is, of course, Jeff's masterpiece. 'Wasn't it awesome?'

I asked Darryl. He just shrugged. Can you believe it? He just shrugged! 'I wasn't so impressed,' he said. 'I guess I prefer work that has more literary merit. This guy Jeff O'Brien seems more of a commercial, popular writer.'"

At this point, Luke puts his hands on his hips dramatically.

"'And what,' I asked Darryl solemnly, 'is wrong with being popular?'" The kid lets out a hoot. "And do you know what Darryl's reply was?"

"He took out an M80 and blew away the entire store," I say deadpan.

Luke scowls. "He might as well have. His answer had the same impact on me a machine gun would have. He said, 'I've never been popular myself, so I wouldn't know.'"

Luke looks deeply into our eyes, first Lloyd's, then mine.

"It was at that moment," he tells us, "that I fell in love with Darryl."

"Why then?" Lloyd asks. Silently I curse him for keeping Luke engaged, for not letting the story end there.

"Because I saw his *soul*," Luke says earnestly. "Our spirits just met in that one moment."

Lloyd makes a face in sympathy, but I want to barf. Around Jeff, Luke talks *his* language—all about the craft of writing and being dedicated to his novel. Around Lloyd, he uses words like *soul* and *spirit* because he knows Lloyd will respond to them. In both cases, he's simply sucking up, trying to win his listener over—but I see through his games. I refuse to pay attention to Luke any longer. I return to the computer to see if Shane has written me back yet. He hasn't, but I pretend to be reading something on the screen.

"We were only together a short while," Luke is saying, with Lloyd still listening raptly. "Darryl got sick very soon thereafter. But in that short period of time I truly fell in love with him. He was such a young soul, Darryl was. He wasn't ready to leave this life. He kept saying he would come back, that I'd meet him again, and since I was an old soul, I'd be able to recognize him."

"Have you?" Lloyd asks.

"Sometimes. In the stars over Provincetown. In the way the water laps at the shore . . ."

I have to clamp a hand over my mouth to prevent a groan from escaping my lips, but from the look on Lloyd's face, I can tell he buys the kid's tale one-hundred percent.

"You had a loved one die of AIDS, too, didn't you, Lloyd?" Luke asks. "So you know what I went through."

Lloyd nods. "Yes, I do know." Their eyes hold.

"You know, I've been wondering about something," I say, delighted to shatter their little moment. "When I first met you, Luke, you said you were from Tucson. I'd forgotten it, but Ann Marie reminded me of it the other day. But later you claimed to be from Long Island."

He looks over at me. For a second—no more than that—he considers me with some caution. Then he smiles.

"I never said I was *from* Tucson," he says. "I just said that was my last stop before setting out on the road to come here."

"I'm just having a hard time keeping your chronology straight."

"I don't see why. It's very simple. After leaving my stepfamily, I found my real father. He was a trucker. I moved with him to Tucson for a while, where he ran a truckstop. Then I decided to head back East."

I'm not letting him off easily. "Was that before or after meeting Darryl?"

"Henry," Lloyd says, interrupting. "What's with the third degree?"

"Just curious," I say.

"*After*," Luke replies simply. He sighs, and returns to his dusting. "I guess I've talked enough. Henry's going to dock my pay if I don't get this room all spiffed up."

Lloyd and I both watch him scamper away with his dust mop.

"You're not being fair to him," Lloyd tells me when the kid is gone.

I frown. "You're smitten with him."

"I think he's a lost soul who needs our compassion."

I laugh. "It wasn't his soul you were ogling earlier."

Lloyd crosses his arms over his chest. "What do you have against him? Suspicion doesn't become you, Henry. You're better than that."

"Better than what? Of being able to see things clearly?"

Lloyd just shakes his head. "Henry, your discontent about your love life is making you hard. You're letting bitterness change your character, and I'll be honest with you. I don't like it. This is not the Henry Weiner I've called my friend."

He turns and walks out of the room.

For one long moment, I stand there not thinking.

Lloyd's words sting. There are precious few people whose opinions I value as highly as Lloyd Griffith's. I don't know if his words are accurate, but they hurt nonetheless. Have I really become a bitter old queen?

I need air. I need to get outside. I need to breathe the way Evan described it, breathe the pure air in, breathe the stress out. I put the computer to sleep and head out the front door.

The air is warm and fragrant. The screen door slams behind me, startling a couple of finches who are perched on the eaves. The birds flutter into the sky, resettling on the branch of an old elm tree. I move my eyes from them to the path that winds its way to the street, lined with butterfly bushes. Flitting around the purple branches are monarch butterflies, lively little specks of orange. I watch the butterflies as if mesmerized. My pace slows, and I inhale deeply, once, twice, three times. I take a seat on the bench and watch the world go by.

Everyone seems to be in pairs. First a man and a woman, mid-forties, hand in hand. Then two women pushing a stroller, their wide-eyed toddler a symbol of their union. Then two young guys, their whole lives ahead of them, who stop to kiss not three feet away from me.

I understand that the desire to mate is instinctual. Cats and dogs, those finches in the tree—they suffer from it too. Yet if only it were that simple. What drives me is not just adrenaline or hormones. I am not merely hungry or horny. I am incomplete. Sitting here, I realize it's the only description that truly explains my state of mind. I am *incomplete*. Not whole.

I feel as if I lack one arm and one leg, that I have only one eye, and I am impatient for the missing parts to be delivered. When I was a boy, my sister had a book of paper dolls that fascinated me. On the last page was the figure of a bald woman, clad only in a flesh-toned one-piece bathing suit; ahead of it were sheets of transparent plastic, complete with hair, clothes and shoes. Only by layering the plastic sheets onto the figure would the woman spring to life, become complete. This is what I am waiting for: for someone to layer the rest of my life onto these bare bones.

You should be complete by yourself. Lloyd's words. He's said them many times. *You'll never find someone if you aren't truly happy with yourself first.*

"Fuck that," I whisper. I've heard it all before, and I don't buy it. We are meant to be coupled. The human instinct to mate goes beyond a simple urge to reproduce. As gay people prove, it's not just about procreation. We seek our own completion with another person. It's a feeling far more intense than any hunger pang I've ever known, and as I get older, it only grows more acute. The sands in my own personal hourglass are running low. A glance out on the street confirms it: what I see now are not pairs of happy lovers, but a single man, maybe fifty-five, walking by himself. He moves slowly down the street, not looking at those who pass him by. His shoulders are hunched, his head lowered. His feet take tiny steps, his knees barely bending.

"Buddy."

The word is whispered into my ear, so soft that it seems at first like the flutter of wings from those monarch butterflies. But then I realize Jeff has quietly sat down beside me. So lost in thought have I been that I didn't even hear him approach.

"Hey," I whisper back.

"You seemed very far away."

I nod. "I was. Do you see that man there?"

"Which one?"

"That one. The one by himself. Does he seem sad to you?"

Jeff considers him. "Yes, I think he does seem rather sad."

"That's me, Jeff."

"Henry, that man is approaching sixty."

I shrug. "How many are like him? How many middle-aged men, single and alone, move into old age without ever finding Mr. Right?"

Jeff folds his arms across his chest. "Maybe he *did* find him, and maybe he died. Maybe *that's* why he's sad."

I shake my head. "It's a different kind of sadness. Look at him.

It's obvious. It's not the grief of losing a loved one. It's the sadness of never having had one in the first place."

Jeff looks at me kindly. "Henry, why is this so hard for you?"

I feel the blood rush into my face. "Because I am so goddamned tired of being alone!" I sit back on the bench and close my eyes. "But I'll tell you what I'm even more tired of, and it's the goddamned dating game. It sucks, Jeff. It's horrible. Heartless. Soul killing."

"You know what Lloyd would say."

I sigh. "Of course I know what Lloyd would say. I've been sitting here trying to convince myself that if only I could love *myself* more, maybe I'd be happier. But I'm not that strong, Jeff. I just can't start loving myself so much that being alone will be okay. I'm just not that strong."

"Sure you are, buddy."

"I'm *not*." I stand up, feeling too edgy to remain seated all of a sudden. I pace up and down along the walk. "And I think very few people are. In college, I remember reading this German philosopher. I can't remember his name. But he said that humans are incomplete as individuals, and that we seek another person for completion in order to become a whole person. Together they bring to each other a kind of fullness. It's mutual give and take, and this binds them together. This is what I'm craving!"

Jeff stands, placing his hands on my shoulders, stopping me in my tracks. "I'm aware of all that, buddy, and it's quite real. For years, when Lloyd and I struggled with our own relationship, I wrestled with the very same feelings you're having. I felt incomplete. Now, being with Lloyd, I feel whole. I can't deny that."

"And now you're getting married." The words crack in my throat.

He nods. "Yes. Now we're getting married. But we might never have gotten to this point. We might have fractured so badly during those difficult years that finding our way back into each other's lives would have proven impossible. And do you know how we avoided that fate?"

He leans in so close to me that the tips of our noses touch.

"I'll tell you." He smiles, and his eyes, being so close to my own, seem to fuse together. "Since we're talking philosophers, Henry, let's consider Plato, because he's the only one I've really read. Now, in his *Symposium*, quoting Socrates, Plato tells us that the only true path to love is to be the *lover*. That's key. For years, my struggle with Lloyd was due to the fact that I wanted not to be the lover but instead the *beloved*—the one who was loved. I wanted to be the center, the object of desire. It was all about my needs, not Lloyd's, a very selfish worldview. I wasn't willing to love Lloyd just for who he was. I wanted him with me on my terms." He smiles. "You remember that time?"

I nod. It was during the period when Lloyd needed to go off and find himself, a time of personal and career transition for him, and Jeff just couldn't understand what was happening. He was left feeling anxious and angry, resenting Lloyd for buying the guesthouse and not moving back in with him in Boston. I remember that time all too well, for it was me to whom Jeff turned most often to share his unhappiness.

"But I changed," he tells me now. "I'm not quite sure how I found the strength to do it, but your friendship certainly helped, Henry. You believed in me then the way I believe in you now."

"I did?" I ask.

"Yes, you did. You were always there, boosting me up. And eventually I came around to understanding that Lloyd's wanderlust—the very thing that I saw as tearing us apart—was actually part of the reason I loved him. I saw that our relationship wasn't just about me, and that by giving up the need to be the beloved all the time and allowing myself sometimes to be the *lover*, loving Lloyd without expectation, I could find a fulfillment that had always eluded me in the past."

"But at least you had someone to practice all this with," I argue. "I have no one."

"I wish you'd stop saying that," he says. "You have us."

"It's not the same."

"I know it isn't. But damn it, Henry. You're wrong when you say you have no one."

I look into his eyes.

"I think you still see yourself only as the beloved," Jeff says.

"You are waiting for someone to love you on your terms. You have this picture in your head, and if a guy doesn't fit it, you just go on waiting."

I laugh bitterly. "I had that conversation with your sister yesterday, and I'm not settling for less than what makes me happy."

"I'm not suggesting you do. This isn't about lowering your standards. It's about a mindset." He smiles. "We're not good at waiting for what we want anymore."

"I'd wait as long as I needed to if I had a guarantee the waiting would be worth it."

"Let me tell you a story," Jeff says.

I sigh. "Is this going to be one of your writer's treatises? The kind you try out on people before writing them down?"

"Maybe." He grins. "What's my favorite movie of all time?"

"*The Wizard of Oz.*"

His grin gets larger. "You do know me well, Henry. Okay. So you remember when we were kids how we'd have to wait a whole year for *The Wizard of Oz* to air on TV? It came just once a year, like Santa Claus."

I shrug. "I never really watched it."

Jeff gives me a look. "You are one strange duck, Henry. What gay kid didn't live to see *The Wizard of Oz?* All year long I'd carry vivid memories of it—those flying monkeys and good witches in their silver balls. Come to think of it, they were like the rare porcelain figures my father had brought home from Japan, figures that fascinated me because of their odd and delicate beauty, and with which only on very special occasions would I be permitted to play."

I roll my eyes. "Oh, this is *so* going to end up in some book."

"Just listen. It was that rarity of exhibition that made *Oz* such a special experience. When its annual showing was over for yet another year, I was faced with the enormity of the interim ahead. *A whole year!* So much changes in the life of a child in the course of a year. A new grade, new friends, a whole new way of seeing the world. All of that—and I wouldn't see *Oz* again until it was over. A *year's* wait." He smirks. "Which, of course, was plenty of time to make it seem brand new once again."

"Okay, and your point *is?*"

"I'm *getting* to it, Henry. God, we really have lost all sense of patience!" He shakes his head. "Today, *Oz* can be had for $19.95. Or less, if you just rent. Any old day or any old night. No waiting. Get it right now. Blockbuster stands ready, ruby slippers and all."

"I still don't get your point."

"Henry, instant gratification is all well and good. I love being able to download songs on iTunes. But all this accessibility and convenience seems to symbolize something that we've lost."

"And what's that?" I ask, indulging him.

"It's something that changed in my adolescence, when the whole world was changing along with me. I remember the giddy simplicity of a Pac-Man game in a pizza joint, of pinball machines and the Good Humor man. I remember the odd futuristic look television antennas gave to our roofs. I remember playing a favorite record over and over until the needle wore down. I remember the NBC peacock—when the words 'in living color' signaled some great event was about to occur."

"Gosh, you really *are* old," I tease him.

"Then listen to your elders, Henry," Jeff says, and he almost sounds serious. "We can teach you a few things."

"Okay, okay, I'm listening."

"Today every whim can be immediately gratified," Jeff continues. "Today stores and books and TV shows are designed to grab you, wow you, give you everything you ever wanted in one fell swoop. Technology has made waiting unnecessary." He leans in to look at me. "So maybe we've forgotten little qualities like patience. That all good things come to he who waits."

"Thank you, Confucius."

"Hey, we used to take out personal ads in newspapers to meet guys. Now we've got Manhunt and MySpace and instant messages."

I suddenly think of Doug, and the crazy excitement of waiting to see if he'd call me after I responded to his ad.

Jeff's lost in his reverie. "Remember that old ketchup commercial that used Carly Simon's song? *Anticipation . . . is keeping me waiting.*" He smiles as he sings the line, dragging out the syllables. "I miss waiting for good things, Henry. Anticipation makes us appreciate them even more. I would hold onto that final scene of

The Wizard of Oz because I knew it was precious. I knew I wouldn't see it again for a whole year. Until then, it would live only in my memories."

I wait to see if he's finished. He's not.

"You know, today I own *Oz* on DVD. The extras are fun, but the movie . . . There it is at a switch of a button. Where's the excitement in that?" Jeff makes a face. "Watching it, I know where all the commercials are supposed to be—but aren't. I kind of miss those little blurbs for Dolly Madison cupcakes, when I'd run to the bathroom or grab another bottle of Coke from the fridge. Now I can just hit pause and take a phone call, or rewind back, or fast forward through the Lion's boring 'King of the Forest' scene. Watching my own copy of *The Wizard of Oz* just isn't the same as watching it on network television when I was a kid back in the 1970s. The world has moved on since then, and there's no need to wait. Not for anything. Not even for *Oz*."

He looks over at me.

"Damn," he says, more to himself than to me, "that's going to be one fine essay."

"Jeff," I tell him, "I get your point. The waiting will make finding Mr. Right even more special. But that doesn't mean I'm not fucking *tired* of waiting. You can't deny that when you were a kid, you grew very impatient waiting for *Oz* to be back on."

"But you're missing *another* point, Henry." He goes nose-to-nose with me. "The waiting isn't just about making the experience more special. It's also there to get you *ready* for it." He shrugs. "Are you ready, Henry? Really?"

I start to rise to my own defense, to insist that of *course* I'm ready—when my cell phone rings. I try to ignore it, but there it is between us, clipped to my belt and screeching for attention.

"Do you want to get that?" Jeff asks.

I look down at the caller ID. It's a local number but not one I recognize at first.

"No," I tell Jeff, not wanting to interrupt our conversation. But even as I say the word I realize who's calling. "Oh, fuck," I say. "It's Gale."

"Get it if you want," Jeff says.

I bring the phone to my ear. "Hello!"

"Henry, it's Gale."

"Hey."

"I've been meaning to call. Do you have plans tonight?"

My eyes find Jeff's.

"Go ahead," Jeff whispers kindly.

I feel rotten backing out of my plans with Jeff. But I tell Gale, "No, I don't have any plans."

I look at Jeff with pleading eyes. *Forgive me?* He just smiles and nods.

"Great," Gale is saying. "I'd love to cook you dinner at my place. Want to come by at seven?"

"Sure."

"Terrific. See you then."

I snap the phone shut.

"Jeff, I'm sorry."

"It's okay, buddy."

I'm stunned that he called. I can feel a smile pushing at the edges of my cheeks. "Maybe 'I'll call you' isn't always a lie," I say.

Jeff puts his arm around my shoulder and starts leading me back to the house. I still feel bad about canceling our plans. Jeff's down about J. R., and here I am, selfish Henry, bailing on him for some guy . . .

"Stop fretting," Jeff tells me.

"How do you know I'm fretting?"

"We're sisters, Henry, and sisters know such things." He looks over at me as we reach the front steps. "I'm fine. Really I am."

"J. R. adores you," I tell him. "This is just a phase."

"I know that." He cocks his head at me. "Can the same be said of you, Henry? Is all this angst you're going through just a phase as well?"

I give him a little smile. "Maybe Gale's call is a sign that things are changing. The anticipation is over, and it's time for a little gratification."

Jeff frowns, as if that wasn't the response he was hoping to hear from me. He just shrugs, and we head inside.

Well, if Jeff isn't convinced that the long wait is over, neither am I. Not by a long shot. In fact, I refuse to hope. Hope has been my downfall. I am determined to get through my date tonight with Gale without letting even the tiniest sliver of hope wedge it-self into my brain.

Somehow, however, I know I won't be very successful at that.

13

AN APARTMENT IN THE
WEST END

"Have another piece?"

Gale has made the most luscious key lime pie I've ever eaten. Just the right among of tang and just the right amount of sweet, kind of a metaphor for how I prefer my men. I've already had one slice of this scrumptious pie, which came on top of an incredibly fabulous meal of rosemary-infused roasted vegetables sprinkled with baby peas. So I beg off from having any more dessert, insisting that my appetite has been fully sated.

Actually, I lie.

My stomach might be satisfied, but other urges are still waiting to be fed. All throughout the meal, Gale has been jumping up and down from his place at the table to serve me more helpings or to refill my wine glass. Each time, his well-rounded thighs, encased in form-fitting blue jeans, have come perilously close to my face. At one point, as he bent over to retrieve a napkin that had fallen, his shapely round butt was positioned not six inches from my lips. It was all I could do to restrain myself from wrestling him down to the floor right there and then.

"More wine?" Gale asks.

I nod. I've got a nice little buzz. Might as well keep it going.

Gale tips the bottle and fills my glass of rosé back to the brim. We clink glasses and sip.

Funny how fast one's mood can change. How depressed I was

this morning. Now, sitting across from Gale, I find myself laugh-ing easily, riding my chair on its two back legs, playfully catapult-ing peas at him with my spoon.

"Henry," Gale tells me, "I like you. I really do."

I smirk. "So how come you waited so long to call me?"

He takes another sip of his wine. "You could've called me."

"You said *you* would call."

Gale shrugs. "I wanted to, several times. But I . . ."

I look over at him. He's looking past me, out the window. For a moment only the sound of crickets fills the room.

"But you what?" I prod.

He closes his eyes once, then opens them again, looking di-rectly at me. "It's been a long time since I let myself like anyone."

I nod. "I understand. I've been burned in love myself."

"I'm cautious." Gale's face has turned serious. "When I fall in love, it will be forever."

There's that intensity again, and it makes me a little nervous. I try to lighten the mood by humming the song with the same lyrics. "Didn't Natalie Cole do a cover of her father's rendition of that?"

"Possibly. Certainly the sentiment is worth singing about." Gale finishes the wine in his glass. "I'm looking for the real thing. Are you, Henry?"

"Of course."

"Really?"

I laugh. "Gale, I have spent more than a year now searching for Mr. Right. I have driven my friends—and myself—crazy with the pursuit. I am very tired of being alone."

"So am I."

He lifts the wine bottle to pour me some more, but I put my hand over the glass. I'm not even halfway finished with what I al-ready have. So he refills his own glass and takes a long sip.

"I am absolutely ready to fall in love," he tells me. "But the per-son I fall in love with has to really fall in love with me, too. It has to be on the same level, with exactly the same kind of feeling."

"That's what we all want," I tell him. "But truthfully, you can't really control that."

"Oh, yes, you can." Gale is looking at me fiercely. "You can control whatever you want in this life, so long as you set your mind to it."

"That's a pretty sweeping statement."

"It's what I believe."

I look over at him. Even with his aggressive, confident posturing, there's something about Gale that's terribly vulnerable, and I immediately feel for him. What heartache has he experienced that would make him so desperate now for control? What has driven him to sculpt his body so hard and taut, to mouth such fierce platitudes about life and love?

"You haven't been out for very long," I say, remembering his comment from our last date.

"No, not really." He seems to reconsider the statement. "Well, it's been long enough to figure a few things out. Men are not like women. Having relationships with men is far more difficult, both of us fighting for our instinctive place at the top."

I smile. "I sometimes think gay life is overrun with bottoms."

Gale shakes his head, not sharing—or perhaps not getting—my humor. "I don't mean just sexually," he says. "I mean the fact that men have been acclimated to feel they are the superior sex, and so when two men come together, it's like two rams butting horns, or two tomcats fighting for their territory. One eventually needs to be sublimated to the other."

I make a face. "I don't think it always has to be such a struggle."

"So why haven't you found a lasting boyfriend, Henry?"

Gale stands and begins clearing the plates off the table. I take a sip of my wine as I ponder his question. Could that be it? Is that the reason I'm still single? Because I've been unwilling to surrender my alpha male status to another man, or because none of my boyfriends were willing to give up theirs for me?

"I don't know," I say when Gale comes back into the room to scrape the crumbs off the tablecloth. "I'm not sure there's as much difference between the sexes as you make out. Did you have a lot of relationships with women?"

"No," Gale says.

"Then how would you know about the difference?"

"Because I do." He disappears into the kitchen with the last of our dirty plates.

I have to laugh. Jeff and Lloyd say that *I'm* an absolutist—that too often I see the world in just blacks and whites without any grays. Gale makes me seem like a real moderate in comparison. This is a guy who's set in his opinions, and no amount of discussion is going to move him.

Still, I'm drawn to him. Maybe it's the fear that's so obviously behind his rigidity. *He's been hurt,* I tell myself. *He's just as scared to trust and to hope as I am. Maybe together we can find our way back . . .*

I stand up, waiting for Gale to return to the room. When he does, I block his passage, taking him by surprise and kissing him. At first he's hard, defensive—but then he melts in my arms and starts kissing me back.

I run my hands down his firm lats to his hard round butt. "I think we left a few things unfinished last time," I purr into his ear.

His lips find mine again. Damn, he's a good kisser. I let my hands explore his body, from his butt to his shoulders to his thick silky hair.

"No whisker burn with you," I say approvingly, breaking our kiss and running my hands over his smooth cheeks.

He pulls away gently. "Let's go slow," he says.

"Fine. So long as we don't stop."

I try to smile at him but Gale avoids my eyes. He's nervous, I realize. And suddenly I wonder: *Has Gale never had sex?*

Is that the source of his fear?

"We'll go as slow as you want," I tell him, tracing the outlines of his eyes and his nose as we stand no more than an inch apart.

Gale leads me by the hand over to his mattress on the floor. This time the place is more orderly. The books that had been scattered around on my last visit are now neatly stacked against the wall. But the titles on their bindings are still visible: *The Male Couple. Gay Men and Sex. What Gay Men Really Want. How to Make Love Like You Mean It.*

We begin kissing again, sitting up. I unbutton Gale's short-sleeved plaid shirt, reaching inside to run my hands over the most beautifully shaped pecs I have ever seen. And the most exquisite nipples: as big as quarters with beautiful, lace-like areolas. I reach down and lick them each in turn. Gale shudders against me. I'm pleased. I like finding other nipple-sensitive men.

With trembling fingers, Gale undoes the buttons on my own shirt, and, almost in imitation, runs his hands along my chest. He moves his face close to kiss my nipples. Reveling in the electric sensations, I drop my own face down into his hair, inhaling his sweet, clean fragrance.

We resume kissing. My hands are wandering now, up and down Gale's smooth, hard back. I'm anxious to get his pants off, but whenever I start to move around to his crotch he stiffens, shifts, and redirects me elsewhere. *He's scared,* I tell myself. *I need to go slow.*

But it's difficult. The longer we sit here kissing like this, the more urgent my lust becomes. I want him naked. I wrap my arms around him tightly and knock him over onto his side, so we're lying down on the mattress, facing each other. We continue kissing. I move my hands back to his butt, and once more attempt to bring them around to his front.

"Don't," Gale whispers.

"It will be okay," I tell him. "Trust me."

"No," Gale says, and sits up.

"What's wrong?" I sit up beside him, my arm around his shoulders. "I like you, Gale. I like you a lot. We're looking for the same thing, you and I. This wouldn't be just a one-night stand."

"I can't," he says in a small voice.

"Why not?"

He turns to face me. "Because I've never done it before."

I cup his face in his hands. "I suspected as much. That's okay, man. I don't expect anything from you. I'd be honored to be your first."

Gale stands up, moving across the room away from me. "I just can't. Not yet."

I let out a sigh.

"Believe me, Henry," Gale says. "I'd like nothing more for you to be my first. And when that time comes, maybe, if you're still interested—"

"But how do you know when that time has come?" I ask, looking up at him. "How do you know it's not now?"

"This is only our second date," he tells me.

I laugh. "So what's the magic number? Five? Six? Twenty?"

I see his face become hard. "You don't understand."

"Of course I do." I get to my feet and approach him, taking his hands in mine. "Let's just sit together then. Talk. Kiss a little."

Gale's silent.

I reach in and kiss him lightly on the lips. "If I went too fast, I'm sorry."

"We haven't even done anything together yet," he says. "Like go on a hike, or go to a movie. How can we have sex before any of that?"

"Okay. So let's plan to do something."

He looks at me as if he's testing me. "Like what?"

"Like . . ." I consider our options. "We said we were going to go see Maggie Cassella, the lesbian comic. We could do that and have dinner."

"I'm not sure I like lesbian comics."

"I know, you said that. But you'll like Maggie. She's very funny. And we've only got a short time left, because most of the shows end this week."

"All right."

"Good." I take his hands again. "So let's kiss a little more."

"No." Gale maneuvers away from me, blowing out the candle that had been burning in the middle of the table. "I think I need to be alone now."

"Gale," I say. "This is what happened last time. If we're going to get to know each other . . ."

"Then we need to respect each other," he says, facing me. "And right now, Henry, I'm asking that you respect the fact that I'd like to be alone."

What else is there to say? "Okay," I tell him. "Thanks for dinner."

I turn to leave, but Gale stops me.

"I like you, too, Henry. Very much."

I give him a wan smile. "So if we're going to respect each other, I hope you'll understand that I don't do well with these abrupt dismissals."

"I'm sorry, Henry." His face suddenly softens, and his eyes are moist with tears. "I'm really sorry."

We embrace. I think Gale might cry, but he doesn't. He just

clings to me. Again I'm left to wonder just what heartache this poor guy has been through.

"I'll call you," I say into his ear, taking the power this time. "In fact, I'll call you tomorrow and we'll make a date."

Gale pulls back to look me in the eyes. He's composed himself. "Great," he says. "I look forward to it."

We exchange one last, brief kiss and I head out down his stairs.

Outside, the crickets are keeping a loud and lively chorus. I look up at the sky, dark purple, scattered with stars.

I head back toward Commercial Street, where the tranquility is broken by garish orange lights and the loud laughter of tourists on one last summer fling. I can't believe that my date with Gale has turned out exactly like the last one—with me left sexually frustrated in a town filled with horny gay men. I make sure I stay far away from the dick dock.

I take a look at my cell phone, which I'd silenced while at Gale's. I'm hoping to see that Shane called, but no. No new messages. I consider calling him. He's here in town somewhere. I'm certain that if I went out dancing tonight, to the A House or maybe Purgatory, I'd find him. I decide I should try. No one is more fun on a dance floor than Shane. I wonder if he's brought along any of his toys, like water pistols or light wands.

I'm smiling as I think of Shane, heading through the crowds on Commercial Street. No one ever understood us being together. "You went out with *him?*" Joey had asked arrogantly when I showed him a picture, clearly looking down on Shane for not having ripped abs and defined pecs. I admit that when Joey asked, I was a little embarrassed—Shane was also wearing a tiara in the photo. It was from some circuit party several years ago; who can even remember which one anymore? But now, thinking back, I'm ashamed of my embarrassment. I should have responded proudly, "Yes, I went out with him! And Shane loved me! Unlike you, you self-centered, lying bastard!"

I almost laugh out loud. It's not Joey's picture I should keep taped up at work. I should have *Shane* up there, reminding me of the one relationship in my life where I was always sure of how the other guy felt about me.

"Henry."

I stop. Someone in the crowd has just called my name.

It's impossible to spot who it is. There are hundreds of people on the street now, in that busy block between Spiritus Pizza and Masonic Place. Could it have been Shane? I crane my neck looking around.

"Henry!"

The voice is behind me. I turn.

"Shane?"

But it's Martin.

"Oh," I say. "Hey."

He smiles. "What's up?"

"Oh, I just had dinner with"—I pause—"a friend."

"Going out dancing?"

I'm not sure I should tell him my plans, because I don't want Martin tagging along. I know that's mean, but it's how I feel.

"Maybe," I tell him. "I'm . . . I'm looking for a friend who's in town."

He nods. "Well, there sure are a lot of people here. But they say next week is going to be a whole other story."

We step out of the street and up onto the sidewalk. "Yes," I agree. "After Labor Day it's like a pall settles over the Cape."

"I'm looking forward to it."

I smile. "I am and I'm not. Sure, the relative quiet in September is a nice change after the frenzy of August. But it gradually gets more and more quiet. Pretty soon stores and restaurants start shutting down. For me, every change is just a reminder that February and March are not far away."

"Is it really that bad in the deep of the winter?" Martin asks.

"Well, you'll find out." I laugh. "It can be wonderful, if you've got a project and a boyfriend. But for single guys . . ."

"Like us," Martin says.

Suddenly I feel uncomfortable. I just smile and start looking through the crowd again for Shane.

"So I found a place to live," Martin tells me. "I move in this week."

I look at him with some surprise. "Well, you sure beat the odds."

"I don't know why I was so sure I could, but I did." He gives me a wide grin, and I notice that he has beautiful teeth, white and straight and even. "This whole move to Provincetown has been one leap of faith."

I can't help but give him a genuine smile in return. "Well, I admire you for it. Not everyone has the courage to just give it all up and make a change like that, especially in . . ."

My words trail off.

Martin laughs. "Especially in middle age, you were going to say?"

"No," I lie. Indeed, that was *exactly* what I was about to say.

"It's okay," Martin tells me. "I suppose forty-five *is* middle age."

"Actually," I say, trying to undo my embarrassment, "if the life expectancy is about seventy-two, middle age is technically thirty-six." I smirk. "Which means I only have three years to go."

"Oh, Henry, you have nothing to worry about in that department."

"Sure I do," I tell him. "In gay life, middle-age arrives even earlier." I explain to him my "shoulder season" theory. Martin just smiles and shakes his head.

"Henry," he tells me, "age is merely a construct. It's all in our heads."

"Maybe so," I say. "But try telling that to all those guys out there." I nod toward the street, where a steady parade of hot shirtless boys files past, arms interlinked, laughing among themselves.

"I don't try," Martin says. "Why tell something to someone who's not ready to listen?"

I give him a canny look. "But you think I *am* ready to listen?"

"You brought the subject up."

I'm feeling generous all of a sudden. "You want to grab some coffee?"

"Aren't you looking for a friend?"

I shrug. "I'll see him on the dance floor, I'm sure. And it's too early yet to go dancing."

"Okay," Martin agrees.

This is good, I tell myself. I can make up for being such a shmuck when I turned him down for a date. I'll buy the coffee. That'll even things out.

We head back to Spiritus and order a couple of cups of joe. We both take them black. "Helps me stay awake if I'm going out," I tell Martin. We find places on the stoop out front and position ourselves to watch the street theater pass by. There goes Miss Richfield on her bike, all mouth and hair ribbon, hawking her show. A couple of straight tourists stop as she passes, the wife shouting at the husband to get the camera: "Quick, before she's gone!" It's like they're on a safari, and they've just spotted a giraffe.

"So," I begin. "You must have left behind a lot of friends in Pittsburgh."

"Oh, yes," Martin says. "My whole life was back there. But those who really love me encouraged me in my decision."

I smile kindly. "And those who didn't really love you?"

He smiles in return. "Well, those would be the ones who really thought they loved me the most. And they were dead set against my making the move, saying I was running off half-cocked in a midlife crisis." He takes a sip of his coffee. "Chief among them was my ex-boyfriend, who thinks I'm crazy as a loon for doing this."

"I guess that's why he's your ex."

"Precisely."

"How long were you together?"

"Twenty-one years."

I almost drop my coffee into my lap. "Twenty-one years? God *damn!* And you ended it?"

Martin gives me a confused look. "I thought you would understand why. He just couldn't grow with me, just couldn't understand what I needed to do with my life."

"But still," I say. "Twenty-one years . . ."

"Paul's a kind and good man," Martin says. "But he's still just as emotionally insecure as he was when I met him."

I'm still trying to understand what he's telling me. "So you gave up a *twenty-one-year* relationship so you could move to Provincetown and be a carpenter?"

"Yup. I sure did."

I smile ruefully. "Look, I can understand you wanting to make a change. But after all that time together, wasn't there a way of working it out? Coming to some mutually agreed-upon solution? Maybe he could have come with you."

Martin is looking off into the crowd in the street. "We tried very hard to make the relationship work for a very long time. But for the last eight or nine years I knew it was coming to an end. It took me that long to work up the courage to get out of it." He smiles. "That's when my friend Bert convinced me to get away for a weekend and come to P-town. The moment I got here, I knew this was the answer I had been looking for."

I want to be happy for Martin. Really, I do. He's following his dream, just as I did. He's taking a chance, which I admire. But I can't help but think about his lover back in Pittsburgh, who for twenty-one years had believed he'd found the One, that he wouldn't have to grow old alone. I can't help but think about that poor, brokenhearted man, left in despair by Martin's sudden decision to leave him and move away.

"Of course, Paul had Barry to console him," Martin tells me, as if he can intuit my displaced sympathy.

"Your dog?"

"Oh, no," Martin tells us, a crooked smile playing with his lips. "Barry is a hot little college kid we took in and with whom Paul began a hot-and-heavy affair about a year ago. I doubt he's missing me all that much."

"So you had an open relationship," I say.

Martin nods.

I sigh. "Maybe that's why the passion between you faded out."

"Who knows? All I know is that eventually we were strangers to each other emotionally." He looks at me intently. "I *needed* to make this move, Henry. It was time."

I'm still feeling sad for Paul. "My hunch is," I say, "that even with Barry around, no matter how hot he is, Paul is brokenhearted."

Martin shrugs. "He probably is. And there are times I miss him too. For twenty-one years, we did everything together. We met when we were both twenty-four. For two decades, Paul made a wonderful home for me. He's a great cook. I can hardly boil water."

"Maybe I'm a romantic," I say, then start to laugh. "Hell, there are no maybes about it! I *am* a romantic. And I just wish there had been a way for you to do what you needed to do while still keeping Paul in your life."

Martin is shaking his head. "The most important relationship you have in life is the one you have with yourself," he tells me. "And by being faithful to Paul, I was being *un*faithful to myself."

I have no answer to that. It sounds like something Lloyd would say.

"So what about you, Henry?" Martin asks. "Why is such a handsome, friendly, smart, sensitive, well-built guy like you still single?"

I suppress the urge to protest his choice of adjectives. Instead I just shrug. "The hundred-thousand-dollar question," I say. "I ask myself the same thing all the time."

"And what kind of answer do you come up with?"

"I don't know. I really don't." Suddenly I think I see Shane in the crowd—a tall blond guy in a funny jester hat waddling head and shoulders above the rest—so I stand up, ready to wave him down. But I'm mistaken—it's some other tall blond guy in a funny jester hat—so I sit back down and face Martin again. "I think the best answer is that I'm just unlucky."

Even as I say it, I'm hearing Lloyd's counsel in my head: "There's no such thing as luck. We create our own destinies." So I'm not surprised by Martin's response.

"I think when people say they're either lucky or unlucky, it's just a cop-out," he tells me. "There's usually something else going on besides just luck, whether it's for good or for bad."

"I bet you don't believe in coincidences either."

He smiles. "And to which coincidence are you referring?"

I smile back. "Believe it not, that was my first time at the dick dock."

"Mine too."

We both laugh.

How odd this is. Here we are, having a deep conversation about life and love, despite the fact that Martin once sucked me off under a dock. Yet I'm no longer embarrassed by the memory. Martin clearly isn't. It seems it was just part of life's adventure in his view. No luck, no coincidence. That blow job was meant to happen in order for us to be sitting here, having this talk.

I look over at him. Luke was right: Martin *does* have amazing eyes, surprising orbs of brightness set deep into his face. So much life inside there, so much experience. In his eyes I see evidence of his entire life, plain and obvious. It's like counting concentric rings in a tree trunk.

"Aren't you afraid of being lonely?" I ask, surprised that I actually articulate the question. But it's out of my lips before I can stop it.

"Sure," Martin replies, finishing the last of his coffee. "But I'm more afraid of wasting time. We're not getting any younger, my friend."

No, we're not. And though Martin has got more than a decade on me, I understand what he means.

Suddenly I can't wait to find Shane. Suddenly I seem to understand something that had eluded me before. I ended the relationship with Shane because he didn't fit the fantasy image of Mr. Right. And ever since, I've been wasting my time—spinning my wheels, treading water so I don't drown. Shane had *loved* me. Shane had wanted to spend his *life* with me. Happiness had been right there in my clutches, and I threw it away. All because Shane didn't fit the physical ideal I'd imagined for my lover.

I stand, looking down at Martin.

"Time to go dancing, eh?" he asks.

"Yes." I take his hand in mine. "Thanks for this talk, Martin. Really. It's helped me clarify some things."

He gives me a small smile. "Well," he says, "I'm glad I was good for something."

"You know," I tell him, "just the other day I was wishing for a wise older gay uncle. And I got him. Thanks."

Somehow Martin doesn't seem flattered. He lets go of my hand and smiles wanly. "You have fun out there tonight, Henry," he says.

"I intend to," I promise.

I give him a thumbs up and head back out into the throngs on the street. I make my way to the A House, where a line snakes down the street from the entrance. I keep turning around, expecting to see Shane behind me, head and shoulders above the crowd, in a funny hat or eye makeup. What will I do when I see him? An embrace, a kiss, and then I'll pull him out onto the dance floor. No one is more fun to dance with than Shane.

But he's not behind me in line, and he's not inside either,

when I finally get in. I take four laps around the place just to make sure. Could he be at Paramount, the other big dance club in town? I leave the A House and head across the street to check. But he's not at Paramount either. Maybe the Vault? Or Purgatory? But Shane's not into leather. Still, I pop into both places to check. Still no sight of him.

Where the hell could he be? It's Sunday night of Labor Day weekend. He's got to be out here somewhere!

I decide to call him on his cell. But I immediately get his voicemail. He's got his phone turned off.

I wait for the clubs to all let out, hoping to catch him in front of Spiritus. But no Shane. I just stand there, eyes searching the crowd. A couple of guys try to cruise me, but I avoid making any contact.

Where the hell is Shane?

I never find him. I trudge back to my apartment. Flopping down onto the couch, I flick on the TV, wishing I'd replenished the ice cream in the freezer. I content myself with watching Lucy Ricardo try to get a loving cup off of her head. I've never understood this episode. If she got herself *in* there, why the hell can't she get herself *out?*

It feels like the question of my life.

14

COMMERCIAL STREET

A perfect day has dawned. The sun, in primary yellow, blazes in an unbroken expanse of blue. Not a wisp of humidity, just warm dry air, with temperatures edging ninety and a light, salty sea breeze blowing in off the bay. The streets are already filling up with tourists at eight o'clock in the morning. Riding my bike, I'm threading my way through them as quickly as I can without hitting anyone. I don't want to be late.

I finally spoke with Shane this morning. He called a little after seven, knowing I'd be awake, tending to the guests. I was thrilled to hear his voice. We plan to meet at Tips for Tops'n at eight fifteen.

"By the way," I asked him, "where the hell *were* you?"

"When?"

"Last night! I tried calling you. I looked everywhere for you."

"Oh, I didn't go out. A bunch of us stayed in and watched a movie. Almodovar's *Law of Desire*. Ever see it?"

I had to laugh. Shane staying in on the Sunday night of Labor Day weekend to watch a movie. I couldn't imagine it.

But I can imagine him. All six lanky blond feet of him. I wonder if he'll have any sparkles on his face when I see him. Or maybe he'll come into the restaurant wearing a funny T-shirt, with fake boobs drawn on it or something. I'm already smiling thinking about what craziness Shane might—

"Watch out!"

Ahead of me a young mother in bright pink shorts is frantically attempting to push her two little kids out of the path of my bike. I swerve abruptly to avoid them, and before I can stop, I crash into the wooden fence in front of the Unitarian Meeting House. Over the handlebars I fly, landing hard on the grassy lawn.

For a second I black out. The next thing I'm aware of is the pain in my right shoulder and hip, which seem to have taken the brunt of the impact, and the crowd of people gathering around me.

"Hey, man, you okay?" some guy is asking me.

"Yeah," I say, with some difficulty. "I think so."

"Do you want me to call an ambulance?" some woman asks, hovering.

"No, no, I'm fine," I insist, trying to stand. But I'm dizzy. My feet collapse under me, and I'm back on the grass.

"He almost hit my kids," I hear the mother in the pink shorts saying. "He wasn't looking where he was going."

"I think you should go over to the clinic," someone else is cautioning me. "Make sure nothing's broken."

"I'm fine," I insist once more. "Just a little dizzy."

But when I try to stand again, I realize I'm shaking. My whole body is shuddering uncontrollably.

"Here," comes another voice, one I recognize. "Let me help him."

I look up. And there, suddenly looming against the bright blue of the sky, is Shane, pushing his way through the ring of people surrounding me.

"Come on, Grandpa," he says, extending his hand. "If you don't watch out, they're going to take away your license."

I grasp his hand. I find I'm able to stand, and some of the shaking subsides. Though the pain still throbs, I can tell nothing is broken. I'll have some pretty big bruises, but the soft grass cushioned my fall and prevented any major damage. I look over at Shane and he gives me a wry little smile.

"You didn't tell me you'd joined the Flying Wallendas," he quips. "What—was the guesthouse biz getting a bit boring?"

How good it is to see him. He's not dressed as I expected. Nothing outrageous. Just a plain white tee and a pair of khaki shorts. His blond hair is short, with no special colors. Dressed so conservatively, he could be any old tourist, his long, gangly arms and legs pale from lack of suntanning. I suspect this may be his first trip to Provincetown all summer. How unlike Shane.

Still, it's him—I'd recognize that look in his eyes anywhere. It's the look he'd often give me when I was being cranky or unreasonable, a look that said, *You are a crazy fool but I love you anyway.*

I take hold of his arm and he helps me around the fence. I spot the mother I almost hit, and offer her an apology. She's not very gracious. She just yells at me to watch where I'm going in the future and hustles her children into the Whaler's Wharf mall. I'm glad I didn't hit the kids, but in that moment I wouldn't have minded leaving some tread across *her* pink ass.

My bike is pretty banged up, but it's walkable. "Henry, Henry," Shane is saying, pushing my bike for me down the street. "Always causing a commotion."

I grin. "Well, nobody can ever say I didn't fall for you."

"Oh, yes, they can, sweetheart," he says. "They can definitely say it."

My grin stretches wider. "Shane, it is *so* good to see you."

He gives me one eye. "You should just be glad you're not seeing Dr. Lenny over at the clinic. You sure nothing's broken?

"I'm pretty sore," I say, "but I'm walking."

Shane stops, steadies the bike on its kickstand, and begins feeling my arms and shoulders. "Bend at the elbow," he says.

I obey. He runs his hands down the length of my arm, from shoulder to wrist.

"Any pain at all when you bend?" he asks.

"No," I reply. "It's just sore."

He stoops down in front of me so that his face his level with my crotch. He runs his hands up and down my thighs. I can't help but smile as I notice the glances of passersby. We are, after all, in the middle of the street.

"Lift up your leg," Shane commands. "Bend at the knee."

I do as he says. He's feeling my calf now.

"Doesn't hurt to bend your ankle?" he asks.

"Nope. It's just my butt and my right hip that are really killing me."

He moves around behind me. He begins to knead my butt. I get it. Shane was always hot for my body. He was the first to actually suggest I could make money by selling it. So he's getting his jollies feeling me up. In public, yet. It's so Shane. Always doing something outrageous.

"Well," he says, standing up, "I think we can rule out any broken bones. But you're going to be pretty black and blue."

"Told you so," I say.

"Can't be too certain about these things," he tells me, returning to the bike and resuming our walk. "Did you hit your jaw? Your hand?"

"No, Nurse Betty. I'm fine. Nothing a little Motrin won't take care of tonight."

He shakes his head. "I think you need a full-time bodyguard, Henry."

I grin. "You applying for the position?"

"Been there, pal, and done that."

I look over at him. It's obvious to me now that I really hurt Shane by ending our relationship. I've always liked to believe it was a mutual decision, and certainly Shane was far more even-tempered and mature than I was when Joey broke it off with me. But Shane was in love with me. And likely still is, the way he felt me up back there. His little quip about me needing a full-time bodyguard was his way of saying he'd like to get back together.

"Ow," I say suddenly, as a jolt of pain sears my thigh.

"Ah," Shane says, "the shock is wearing off and the pain is setting in."

"Oh, man." I groan. "Yeah, all of a sudden . . ."

"There's no way you can sit in a restaurant like this," Shane says.

"You want me to walk you back to the guesthouse?"

"No," I insist. "I'm going to be fine."

Shane makes a face. "Then let's go down to the beach where you can stretch out on the sand. I'll call my friend to bring us down some food and coffee."

I can't help but smile again. Shane doesn't want to share me with the public. He wants some quiet, intimate time alone with me. Just the two of us on the beach.

We head down the alleyway across from Spiritus as Shane flips open his cell phone. "Eddie? Would you be a love and pick up two egg-and-cheese bagels from the Connie's, and two large Columbian coffees? Henry's hurt himself, so we're just going to sit on the beach." There's a pause. "Yes, a bit of a bike accident." Another pause. "The beach across from Spiritus. You will? Great. Thanks love."

It's low tide, with tangles of seaweed delineating the high-water mark. Gulls make wide swaths through the blue sky. Plopping himself down on an overturned red rowboat, Shane watches me carefully as I ease myself down on the sand.

"I'm not sure I'll get back up again," I tell him, as the muscles in my thigh and butt burn in pain.

"That's what I'm here for, sweetheart," Shane says. "To pull you up."

I smile. Over the course of our relationship, Shane certainly pulled me up many times. I'd get depressed or antsy about something—Lloyd, the guesthouse, my mother—and Shane would always be there, with a funny story or a carton of Chunky Monkey ice cream. In fact, it was probably Shane who got me started on my ice-cream binges. No matter how much weight I gained from them, I can't help but remember those nights with Shane with a certain glow of nostalgia, the two of us shoulder to shoulder watching a movie, eating ice cream and popcorn.

Of course, at the time, I was always vaguely discontent, my mind only half present, and Shane sensed it. I was always wondering what was going on outside, beyond the four walls of our settled existence. Shane would see how I'd look at other guys when we were on the street, the way my eyes would wander away from conversations with him and follow some hot number who'd just walked past. I was still in tip-top shape then and I got cruised a lot, and Shane would see how I'd respond. I'd pretend not to notice guys looking at me, but when I thought Shane wasn't aware, I'd sneak a peek back, maybe even offer a smile. Shane never said a word. It's as if he accepted it as part of the territory of being in a relationship with me.

I was a schmuck. I was so unfair to him. I took for granted the one man who actually loved me—loved me enough to want to commit to a long-term relationship with me. I was forever on the lookout for something better, someone hotter. And because of it, I've ended up alone.

I look up at Shane, who's staring down at me with concern.

Might it not be too late?

The very thought sends me reeling. *Me, back with Shane?* Could I really make it work this time?

"So," he's saying to me, "what else besides a bruised butt is new with you?"

"Not a hell of a lot," I admit. "Same old same old."

"I hear Nirvana is doing a thriving business."

I nod. "It's been a great summer."

"And Lloyd and Jeff?"

I look off at the water. "They're getting married."

"How *nice.*"

Shane was never all that keen on Jeff and Lloyd. Early on, he spotted my obsession with Jeff, and later he understood all too well my crush on Lloyd. Once during the course of our relationship he complained that our bed was getting crowded, with both Jeff and Lloyd—figuratively, of course—in there with us.

"It *is* nice," I say about my friends' wedding plans. "I was surprised at first, but I'm getting used to the idea. They've asked me to be their best man."

He snorts. "Don't know why you'd be surprised. When you're in love, you get married. And no matter how annoying Jeff and Lloyd can be, it's always been clear that they're in love."

I cock my head to look up at him. "Have you suddenly become a romantic, Shane?"

"I've always been a romantic," he tells me. "You just never noticed, Henry."

"Maybe not," I admit. "And I'm sorry if that's the case."

"Apology accepted." He smiles down at me. "So what about you, babycakes? Any boyfriend since Joey?"

I shake my head. "Still single after one year and almost five months. Not that I'm counting."

"Not a date in that whole time?" Shane looks aghast. "I find that hard to believe."

"Not many," I say, patting my belly. "Mostly I stay in and watch old sitcoms and eat ice cream."

"Yes, I can see you've put on a bit of weight."

Leave it to Shane to state the truth. No beating around the bush or playing nice from him.

"Lately, though," I say, "I've had a series of encounters, all of which have left me more confused than ever."

Shane folds his arms over his chest. "Talk to Mama."

"Well, for starters, there was this twentysomething kid Luke, who I tricked with and who's now a houseboy at Nirvana."

"I thought fraternizing with the staff was a no-no."

I nod. "It happened before he was hired. And the reason he maneuvered himself into working there is so he could be near Jeff. He's an obsessed fan."

Shane smirks. "If we're lucky, he'll turn out to be Kathy Bates."

"Stop it. That's *exactly* what worries me."

"No, it's not," Shane says. "You're worried that Jeff will have him, and then you'll be cut out of the picture."

"I don't *want* to be in the picture with Luke," I insist. "Okay. So maybe that's part of it. I admit Luke is very, very hot, and I definitely was very attracted to him. Maybe my ego was hurt. Lloyd thinks Luke tapped some of my own shit, and that's why I'm so suspicious of him."

"Pray tell, what shit did he tap?" Shane shudders. "Really, that's a terribly unpleasant metaphor, Henry."

"Well, he tapped my insecurity, I guess." I laugh. "I'm not feeling as confident about myself these days, in case you haven't noticed. Hank the studly escort has left the building."

Shane narrows his eyes at me. "Henry, you've *never* been confident about yourself. Even when you were one hundred and seventy-five pounds of rock-solid muscle, you were not confident about yourself. I always needed to boost you up."

I smile up at him. "I know. And I miss that, Shane."

He tightens his lips. "Go on. Tell me more about this confused love life of yours."

"Well, the experience with Luke left me feeling kind of down on myself. So then this really hot guy Gale asks me out. Short, but perfect body. Like sculpted out of clay. We've had two dates. We kiss but that's all. He wants a relationship. Not a one-night stand."

Shane makes a face. "I can see where you have *nothing* in common."

"Stop being so sarcastic. The problem is Gale's very extreme. He wants to make sure I'm exactly the right one, exactly Mr. Right, before we have sex. It's because when he commits to someone, he expects it to be total. Not just sexual monogamy but emotional monogamy too."

"Have you called him on it? Maybe he can be reasoned with."

"I've tried. But I can't really get very far, so I'm just staying kind of guarded around him."

Shane stretches, removing his T-shirt, revealing his long narrow torso marked by pointy pecs that are starting to sag ever so slightly. He leans back, his face toward the sun.

"Seems to me," he says, "you've been confronted with some rather obvious extremes."

"Yeah, and it only gets more confusing." I tell him about Evan and Curt. "Finally, a guy who seems to fit all the criteria, and he's married."

"Damn that Supreme Court for giving us the right," Shane says, his eyes closed against the sun.

"Can you ever respond without a wisecrack?" I toss a pebble at him but he doesn't react. "The fact is, Evan came the closest anyone has come in a long time to being my vision of Mr. Right. Okay, so I only had a couple of hours with him, but he was sweet, and gorgeous, and built, and smart, and sensitive, and reasonable—"

"You could always poison the husband."

"But I learned something, Shane. Last night, when I was talking with this guy Martin—"

"Martin? Which one is this?"

I smirk. "Some guy who gave me a blow job at the dick dock."

Shane opens one eye and peers over at me. "You *have* been getting around."

I laugh. "It's so crazy. I still can't believe I let it happen. But I got to talking with him later. He's a nice guy." I hesitate. "He asked me out, in fact."

"And?"

"He's *forty-five*, Shane," I tell him.

"And that tells me what?"

"Why I couldn't go out with him. I'm not into daddies."

Shane sits up. "Why is a forty-five-year-old automatically a daddy?"

"Okay, okay. I just mean—well, I'm thirty-three."

"That still tells me nothing. What does Martin look like?"

"Well, he's quite handsome."

"For an older guy, you mean," Shane says sarcastically.

"Shane, there is a huge difference in our ages!" But even as the words come out, I'm remembering that it's basically the same difference between Luke and me, just in the other direction. "It just wouldn't work," I say. "I mean, we'd have nothing in common. He's probably into disco music and Barbra Streisand."

"Oh, Henry Henry Henry." Shane gives me a weary look, then lays back down across the rowboat. "Whatever."

"Look, I felt bad about saying no to Martin. Anyway, the point is, Martin said he realized that he'd been wasting time living in Pittsburgh, when he wanted to be living here. That's how I feel now. That I'm wasting time."

"So this Martin moved to Provincetown in order to *stop* wasting his time?"

I nod.

"Then what, pray tell," Shane asks, eyes still closed, "are you planning to do?"

I'm quiet a moment. A decision is slowly forming in my mind. "I'm going to make right something I did wrong," I say in a low voice.

Shane opens his eyes and rolls his head to his side to look at me. He doesn't say anything.

"I'm lonely, Shane," I say. "The last few months I've gotten to the point where I realize that I'm growing old alone."

"Right," Shane says quietly. "You're thirty-three. *Ancient.*"

"Hey, thirty-three turns into thirty-four, and then you're forty and then fifty."

"Oh, is that how it goes?"

I move closer to him, resting my chin on the side of the boat so that our faces are no more than a few inches apart. "Yes," I tell him. "That's how it goes."

Behind us a wave crashes up onshore courtesy of a speedboat out in the harbor. We remain quiet, looking at each other.

"Do you want to be alone forever, Shane? Wasn't it better when we were together? It might not have always been fabulous be-tween us, but we had each other. We weren't alone."

"No," he says, rather dreamily. "We weren't alone."

"I was wrong to always be on the lookout for the next best thing, Shane. If I hurt you, I'm sorry. What I was looking for, I don't know anymore. I had *you*. And I didn't appreciate what I had."

Shane says nothing. He just keeps looking at me.

"What I'm trying to say, Shane—"

"Don't," he whispers.

"I can't help it. It's just come over me. I realize now that—"

He sits up. "I said, *don't*, Henry."

"But I want to—"

Just then I'm aware of someone approaching us. I turn. A dark-haired guy with olive skin, shirtless in cutoff jeans. He's carrying a brown paper bag and two large coffee cups. He seems vaguely familiar but I can't place him.

"Shane?" the guy calls.

"Eddie," Shane says, standing.

I watch as the newcomer approaches. His face breaks into a wide grin, and his lips pucker for a kiss from Shane. I sit on the sand speechless.

Shane has his arm around the guy now. "Henry," he says, as the two of them turn to look down at me. "I want you to meet Eddie." He pauses. "My boyfriend."

Eddie—cute, about my age, lean and tight—reaches his hand down to shake my hand. With difficulty I stand to face him.

Shane's boyfriend.

Is there no end to making a fool of myself?

"Hey," Eddie says. His brown eyes shine in the sunlight. He looks to be Italian or Portuguese. Lean and hard with a strong handshake. Absolutely fucking adorable.

And he's Shane's boyfriend.

"Hey," I say in return.

Eddie smiles. "I knew your friend Jeff years ago."

That's it. That's where I've seen him. In photographs in Jeff's album. Except then Eddie was younger. And Jeff knew him as Eduardo.

"I recognize you," I manage to say. "Jeff has mentioned you." *He carried a fairly large torch for you for a long time, too,* I might add. But I don't.

"Tell Jeff I said hello, will you?" Eddie asks.

"Sure," I say.

I can't say much else. I'm struck by colliding emotions. The first is embarrassment: I had come dangerously close to suggesting to Shane that we get back together. The second is envy: Eddie is *hot*. Envy is followed very quickly by disbelief: this hottie is with *Shane*? Shane of the squishy body and average looks? And then I feel chagrined: how can I reduce Shane to such descriptions, this man who once loved me?

Finally, it is embarrassment to which I return: not so much for setting myself up for rejection, but for having allowed myself to imagine a reconciliation with Shane. It was an act borne of desperation—not because Shane is unworthy of me, but because I had thought him an easy catch, a quick fix to my loneliness. If I can't have whom I want, I was reasoning, I'll take Shane; having someone is better than having no one. Embarrassment mingles with shame. In truth, it is I who am unworthy of him.

Eddie is handing us our food and coffee.

"You are such a doll to do this," Shane is telling his boyfriend.

"You okay?" Eddie asks me. "You had a bike accident?"

"I'll live," I assure him.

It's what I told Joey, too, that day at the coffee shop when he said good-bye. I didn't believe it then, and I don't believe it now.

I watch as Eddie kisses Shane once more on the lips. "Well, I'll leave you two to catch up. I'm up at the house with the guys. Remember we're doing the bike trails in an hour."

"I remember, sweetums," Shane says.

"Good to meet you, Henry," Eddie says. "Don't forget to say hi to Jeff."

"Good to meet you too," I manage to say.

We both watch as he heads back up the beach toward the street.

"So," I say, turning to Shane, who's already sitting back down on the overturned boat unwrapping his breakfast. "How long have you two been together?"

"We just had our one-year anniversary."

It's like a knife jab. "Why did you never tell me?" I ask.

Shane smiles just before taking his first bite. He chews and swallows his food before answering. "Because you never asked," he says.

I sit beside him on the boat. The pain is still quite sharp, but I want to be even with him so I can look him in the eye.

"So you love him," I say.

"We're getting married," Shane tells me.

"Of course you are." I laugh a little. "That's what the gays are doing these days, isn't it?"

"*Some* of the gays." Shane looks kindly at me. "Eat your breakfast, Henry."

I'm not hungry. I take a sip of my coffee instead.

"Sorry for being such an idiot earlier," I say.

"To be quite frank, Henry, I'm used to you being an idiot."

"Gee, thanks."

He cocks his head as he looks at me. "I was with you for a long time, remember. I know how you can be."

I make a face. "It wasn't that bad. We had some good times."

Shane grins. "Henry, I have a feeling that your memory of our time together is a bit muddled."

"It is not. I remember it all very well."

He scowls. "So why did we break up?"

"Because we realized we weren't meant to be lovers."

Shane gestures with his hands as if to say his point is proven. "No, Henry. We broke up because *you* realized you weren't meant to be *my* lover."

"It was mutual."

He wipes his mouth with a napkin. "I accepted the inevitability of it. It was graceful. It was amicable." He leans in close. "It was *not* mutual."

I look at him. "So you wanted to keep trying with me?"

He smiles. "I would have kept trying with you until I was ninety." He takes a quick sip of his coffee. "I may have given up at ninety-one, but until ninety, I was willing to stick it out."

"But now?"

He shrugs. "You haven't commented on my ring."

I look down at his hand. Why hadn't I noticed it before? A gold band set with a small diamond flashes on his right ring finger.

"An engagement ring," he says, his voice thick. "Eddie gave it to me a few weeks ago. Can you imagine? A man like him giving an engagement ring to *me*?"

"Congratulations," I say.

"I never imagined the possibility. A man like Eddie—with whom once even the great almighty Jeff O'Brien was besotted—asking me to marry him."

"I said congratulations."

Shane looks at me. "Certainly, after you, I couldn't have imagined it." For the first time, there's some bitterness in his voice. "You haven't changed, Henry. I can't believe you still thought you could come traipsing back to me when everyone else failed you. How often did I feel that way? I was your port of last call, even when we were supposedly a couple."

"I said I was sorry, Shane."

"But then you tried to do the same thing today." He laughs. "Not for a second did you ask me what was new in my life. It was all about you. You presumed I was right where you left me. You gave no consideration to the idea that I might have gone on with my life."

I can't reply. He's right.

"From where I sit, Henry," Shane is saying, taking another bite of his bagel, "you've had three hot guys in a matter of weeks pick you up, and a fourth has tried. God forbid, he was a decrepit forty-five! And I'm supposed to feel sorry for you? Henry, if you think you were an idiot out here with me, I'd suggest you look at the rest of your life as well."

"Okay, Shane. I really don't feel like being called names."

"Sweetie, how can I take you seriously? How can I feel for you, sympathize with your loneliness, when you tell tales of all these men throwing themselves at you? Do you know how many guys would trade places with you?"

"But none of these guys are available for relationships!"

Shane makes a sour face. "How the fuck do you know? You don't give them a chance! The way I see it, you've prejudged that poor little Luke boy. You've never been honest with Gale. And you've ruled out Evan and Martin for your own idiosyncratic reasons."

"I am not getting involved with a married man!"

Shane shrugs again. "Lots of guys have successful three-way relationships."

"Not me," I insist.

"Then give me one good reason for rejecting Martin out of hand. And don't you dare say he's too old!"

"If you don't want me to be honest, Shane, then there's no point in talking." I'm holding my ground. "I'm just being who I am."

"Which is small-minded and selfish." He finishes his bagel, crumbles up the wrapper and stuffs into the bag. "Sorry to be blunt, but you are. You say Evan fit all the criteria for your Mr. Right. Apparently I didn't come close. And I'd bet my engagement ring here that the main disparity between Evan and me is the thickness and hardness of our pectorals and biceps."

My eyes involuntarily drop to Shane's saggy man-tits. I return my gaze to his face as quickly as I can reassert control.

"No, Shane," I say, "it's not like that . . ." But it's futile to protest.

"You say it wasn't always fabulous between us," Shane continues. "You're right. It wasn't. But it *is* always fabulous with Eddie."

"Well," I say, "I'm glad for you."

"No, you're not." His voice has softened. "And that's okay, Henry."

I make a move to stand, but the pain twists through my thigh again. I groan a bit and sit back down.

"You poor baby," Shane says, and begins kneading my leg.

Without even realizing it, I start to cry.

Shane seems to pay no attention to my tears, but of course he's aware. "You know that a part of me will always love you, Henry. Underneath all your frustrating outer layers, you're actually a loveable guy."

"Maybe you can write me a reference I can pass out to guys that I date."

He laughs. "Stop being so afraid of what you want, Henry. I have a sense you may be making it all a lot more difficult than it really is."

I don't reply. I just close my eyes and allow myself to feel the sensations of Shane's hands on my leg.

"I've got to run," he whispers at last. "We're all going on a bike ride . . ."

I open my eyes. Shane and his lover and his friends. He's moved on, found his own world.

"I really am happy for you," I tell him.

He stands, reaching down to kiss me on the forehead like the Good Witch of the North. "Take care of yourself, Henry," he says. "Promise?"

I nod.

"Come on," he says. "Let me help you back up to the street."

"I'll be fine. I want to sit here for a while longer."

He crosses his arms over his chest. "You haven't eaten your breakfast."

I nod. "I'll save it for later. Can I give you some money?"

"It's on me. Or rather, it's on Eddie."

"Thanks."

Shane cocks his head looking down at me. "You sure you're all right?"

"No," I admit honestly. "But I want to give it a try on my own."

He smiles. He gathers up his trash and turns to face me one last time. He blows me a kiss. I smile.

Then he heads up the beach and is gone.

I sit on the overturned boat and watch the waves for probably close to an hour. Guys with their dogs pass. A mother and father with a toddler running after them slosh barefoot through the surf. Finally I stand. The pain is still there, but I manage to trudge across the beach without falling.

I take it as a sign that I'm going to be okay.

15

AN APARTMENT IN THE WEST END

Three days have passed since I saw Shane, and I am a man transformed.

"Well," I say to Gale, "what is it going to be?"

Our eyes hold. I do not back down.

Gone is the passive Henry Weiner who's allowed himself to be lured into pseudo-relationship for too long. This time, I will not endure being asked once again to leave his apartment just as things start to get heated.

It took some effort to get to this new mindset. When I realized that—due to my Labor Day focus on Shane—I'd forgotten to call Gale as I'd promised, I quickly punched in his number and left a message on his voice-mail. "This is Henry," I said, summoning all the authority I could muster. "Call me. We are having dinner on Thursday night and then we are seeing Maggie Cassella's show before it's over. I'll be at your house at seven."

Well, he didn't call back right away. For a day and a half I waited, suddenly doubting the wisdom of my newfound aggressiveness. I think Gale's hesitation suggested he was struggling with the idea of someone else taking control. I was just about to steel myself and call him again—Shane's words "Stop being so afraid of what you want" echoing in my mind—when my cell rang. It was Gale. "Can we make it seven thirty?" he asked.

"No," I said, refusing to give an inch. "It won't allow us enough time for dinner before Maggie's show."

He grunted, but agreed. I'd won that round.

Now, I faced the greater challenge. Dinner had been fine, some laughs, some good discussion, and then, much to his surprise, Gale had adored Maggie, proclaiming, "She's not like most lesbians." In my head, I filed away his apparent dyke-phobia, vowing to confront him on it in the future.

So many layers of protection seemed wrapped around this guy. If I want him—and I've come to believe that I do, that he may be the One—I'm going to need to peel them away one at a time.

"So," I repeat, looking over at him, "what is it going to be?"

"I think you're being unfair, Henry," Gale says.

"Unfair? I'm not the one who keeps pulling away when things start getting good."

We've come back to his apartment, as usual, and in his doorway we shared a kiss. Once again my hands were all over his hard back and round butt. But, true to form, Gale extricated himself, excusing himself so he could take a pee. When he came out of the bathroom, I lowered the boom.

"Gale," I said, "if you're going to ask me to leave before we have a chance to make love, I'd like you to tell me now, so that certain, er, *expectations* don't get raised."

I can tell he isn't used to such directness. This new, assertive Henry Weiner is making him nervous.

He assumes a typical defensive posture, his arms crossed over his chest. "How can I know if I'm ready until I'm there, in the moment?" Gale asks me. "How can I predict how I'll feel at any given time?"

"All I'm saying is, if you're still not ready to go there with me, I just want to know. I'm not going to try to force myself on you. I'd just like to leave here on my own accord for a change. I'm tired of being *asked* to leave."

"You have no idea what you're asking me, Henry."

"Yes, I do. I am asking you to overcome your fear."

Gale's face goes white. He looks away.

I try a softer approach. "What was it, Gale? You say your family was never all that religious, but you have some fierce antagonism against religion. Did someone foist upon you the idea that sex was bad? Is that why are you still a virgin after all these years?"

"I'm not a virgin," he says in a small voice.

"But you said—"

"I said I'd never done it with a guy before."

I sigh. "So you've had sex with women."

"One woman."

"Okay. And now you feel weird being a man who's having sex with another man."

He gives me a strange smile. "You could say that."

I approach him and touch his cheek with the back of my hand. "Is this okay?"

Gale closes his eyes. "Yes."

"How long were you with this woman?"

"Six years."

"Did you love her?"

"I thought so. At first."

"Did she take it hard when you told her you were gay?"

He opens his eyes and looks at me. "That's not how it happened, Henry."

"Tell me then."

He moves away. "You know, Henry, you have a lot of nerve. You think I can just come back here after eating tofu burgers with you and spill my guts? That I can open up to you about my whole life and the way I feel about things just because we shared a few laughs at a comedy show?"

"Yes," I say. "I was actually hoping for exactly that."

"Why?"

"Because I like you."

He flashes those intense eyes at me. "Do you? Or are you just lonely, Henry? And am I merely convenient?"

I shake my head. "Gale, you are *far* from convenient."

He's fired up. "What's the most important thing—the most basic, underlying element—that you need from a lover? Tell me, Henry. What is it?"

I'm at a loss for a moment. Gale's tendency to ask such absolute questions can be jarring. "Honesty," I finally utter.

"Be more basic than that," he challenges me.

"What's more basic than honesty?"

He smirks. "Henry, we are talking right past each other."

"Well, if we are, I don't know what more to do about it."

Gale turns away. "I like you, too, Henry. But I can't be what you want."

"You don't even *know* what I want!"

He gives me an eye over his shoulder. "Do *you*?"

"I thought so when I walked in here. I thought I wanted you."

Gale lets out a long sigh. "I know I'm risking never seeing you again by saying this, Henry," he says. "But I'm saying it anyway. *Good night.*"

I feel the blood rise in my face. Now I'm angry. "So once again," I say, "keeping your control over a situation is more important to you than pursuing a relationship. You'd rather throw me out again than talk to me."

"Hey, you're the one who set the terms."

"Fine." I turn to leave. "I'm not sure what you had in your last relationship, Gale, but I think you'll find absolutes just don't fly in the real world."

"Thank you for dinner, Henry," he says coldly. "I had a lovely time."

I don't even respond. I just head out his door and back down the stairs to the street.

"Henry."

I look up. Gale stands at the top of the stairs.

"Let me know if you ever figure out what's the most important thing you need in a lover," he says. "I'd be curious to know."

He heads back inside.

Why did I ever think I could make a relationship with Gale work? One more of Henry Weiner's delusions. I don't think I've ever met a greater control queen. I'm fuming, literally hot under my collar. And my anger stems less from the fact that Gale has kicked me out of his house once again, but because he remains so stubborn in his refusal to yield, even just a little bit.

Okay, so maybe I bungled it by being too assertive. Maybe I should have handled the whole thing more gingerly. Maybe I shouldn't have set the terms quite so severely, and let the night just unfold. But I wasn't getting anywhere with him by going slow and easy either.

I head back down Commercial Street. With Labor Day having come and gone, the crowd on the street is thinner. The whole pace of the village has slowed down, as if the entire population had just exhaled a collective sigh.

I suppose that's going to be the end of Gale and me. I can't see how we could pick up and try it again. It's over, before it ever really began.

And it's a shame, really. I liked Gale. I didn't like the arrogant stubborn prick he could be, but occasionally I glimpsed another Gale: smart, vulnerable, sensitive. And one of the best kissers I'd ever encountered.

I suddenly feel overwhelmingly sad. All at once, my body becomes heavy, and moving my legs to walk takes considerable effort. Part of it is the lingering pain of my bike accident; my whole right side is black and blue, and working out at the gym has proven impossible these past few days. But I know it is much more than that. My body, like my mind, simply seems to be shutting down. I am tired—so fucking tired—of the emotional rollercoaster of dating, of searching for love. I need to get off. I need to stop.

"Hi, Henry."

I've paused to regain my equilibrium and I notice, sitting on the steps of the post office, is Martin.

"Hi," I manage to say.

He rises and approaches me. "You okay?"

"I'm just a little"—how to put it?—"bruised." Yeah, that says it all. Bruised in body, mind, and spirit.

"How did that happen?"

I laugh. "Life." I see he doesn't get the joke. "And a bike accident," I tell him. "I took a flying leap over the handlebars a few days ago."

"No broken bones?"

I shake my head. "Just stiff muscles."

"Maybe a massage would help."

I nod. "Yeah. Good idea. I should go see Will," Will being our local masseur.

Martin's smiling. "I was making the offer myself."

Oh, man. Is he hitting on me? I can't deal with this right now.

"Um, look, I need to get back to the guesthouse," I say, forcing my legs to move again. "Take it easy, Martin."

He nods as I push past him back down the street. I hate to be so abrupt, but I've got to let him know that I'm just not interested. Martin's a nice guy but—

Give me one good reason for rejecting Martin out of hand. And don't you dare say he's too old!

Shane's voice.

But he *is* too old! What the hell would we have to talk about? When I was twelve, he was twenty-four. I didn't even yet know I was gay, and he was already out there disco dancing to the Village People. Growing up, we didn't watch the same TV shows, listen to the same music, or learn the same things in school. If we tried a relationship, we'd have no cultural references in common. It would be a disaster!

Of course I know there are many intergenerational relationships that seem to work just fine. But it simply would not work for me. I want a lover who will get my jokes, understand my points. I want to be able to say, "That is so Alice in Chains" and have him understand exactly what I mean. Because if he's lived the same experiences I have, then he knows me. Or at least, he's got the tools to know me.

By the time I get back to Nirvana, I am ready to drop. I could fall asleep standing up. All I want to do is crawl into my bed and lose consciousness. I am so tired of thinking about relationships and men men men.

But my night is not yet over.

Coming in through the backdoor, I run nearly headfirst into Luke, who's just emerged from the basement steps carrying a milk crate full of papers. As usual, he's only wearing a thong.

"Hi, Henry," he says. But his voice is glum.

"Hello," I say. "Cleaning out your room?"

"Exactly. Tossing out all this trash that I once considered my great American novel."

Despite how tired I am, I look over at him. He's clearly upset—or at least, he's pretending to be upset.

"Why the loss of confidence?" I ask, against my better judgment.

"Jeff didn't like it," he says. "So why bother going on?"

Luke pushes out the back door. I watch him from the window. Heading into the small fenced-off area where we keep our dumpster, he upends the crate and dumps its contents inside. Then he comes back out onto the terrace and sits down hard on a bench. He lights up a cigarette.

I shouldn't go out there. But something compels me to do so. This kid is a sneak, but somehow the sight of him, sitting in his thong smoking a cigarette, breaks my heart just a little.

"Luke," I say.

"What?"

"I thought you were trying to quit."

"What do you care?" He doesn't look up at me.

"Look, the point is, why are you giving up after one critique?" I'm standing over him, resisting the urge to sit beside him. "It seems to me a critique is meant to help you get better, not quit."

"Jeff said he thought my whole premise was flawed," Luke says, taking another puff and exhaling the smoke over his head. "How do I fix that? I can't. So I'm tossing it."

"Well, that's your choice," I say.

He stubs the cigarette out on the ground and stands up. "But thanks for asking, Henry." He heads back inside, the screen door slamming behind him.

Behind me I hear the low growl of the cat from next door. The damn thing is in the dumpster again, and will probably leave a whole trail of trash after it's picked through our scraps. I head inside the enclosed area and clap my hands, prompting the cat to leap back over the fence into its own yard. But as I turn to leave, I spot something on the ground.

A binder of paper. Part of what Luke was throwing away.

I stoop down to retrieve it, intending to toss it into the dumpster. But somehow I just can't do it. The title grabs me: DARRYL'S STORY.

I stare down at it.

A man screams in the middle of the night, reads the first line.

Looking around to make sure Luke isn't watching, I take it

back inside. What makes me want to read this? It's not right, I know, but I can't help myself. Luke's been a mystery to me ever since I met him, and I suppose Lloyd is right: I do have a fixation on him. So if his words can tell me anything about who he is, who he *really* is . . .

Inside my apartment, I flop down on my bed and begin to read.

A man screams in the middle of the night.

I am dreaming. Mostly I dream in black and white—mostly black. I am dreaming of my father, who's talking to me, intense and focused, his face filling the screen of my dreamscape. He's talking faster and faster and higher and higher until he suddenly leans his head back and screams, his face turning into Elsa Lanchester as the Bride of Franken-stein.

"Whoa," I say, pulling back for a second before resuming.

I wake up, sweat in my armpits, sweat on my face, sweat dampening my sheets. The screaming continues. I think for a moment that I'm back in my childhood bedroom, and the screams are coming from my TV set, where a grainy black-and-white horror film casts flickering silver shadows in the darkness. But the screaming is real, coming from a man outside on the street.

I peer between my blinds. A few lights go on in an uneasy pattern down the block of rowhouses. A man in a terrycloth robe runs down his front steps. I keep still in the dark, tightening my muscles, my body sticking to my sheets.

New York at night is a swarm of insects. Giant cockroaches crawl out of the sewers. I know; I've seen them. Men scream and sirens sing. Heli-copters fly low overhead, their spotlights searching for assassins. I've seen them too.

Silence slaps my room. The screaming has abruptly stopped.

I peer outside again. The man in the terrycloth robe sees me. I let my blinds snap and retreat to my covers.

It is film noir here tonight. Peter Lorre is hunched in the shadows of my room. My father told me once, near the end, that life is not like the movies.

He said there are no happy endings. It's not Shirley Temple tap dancing backwards up the stairs with Bojangles Robinson. No, it's a different Robinson—Edward G.—wandering the streets, forever mad, hearing Joan Bennett—the woman he killed—saying over and over and over: "Jeepers, Johnny, I love ya." Film noir. Black film. Black life.

I'm dreaming again. My father is angry. I wouldn't kiss him good-night. "I'll go away if you want me to," he says. He points out the win-dow, a long arm and long finger like the Ghost of Christmas Yet to Come. Outside, the sun is setting without any color. Leaves are falling from our maple tree, gray leaves, and they blow across the grass haphazardly, out into the street. I'm crying, begging my father not to go. But he refuses to kiss me goodnight once I finally offer up my lips.

The sirens start and I'm awake. They get louder and louder, coming for the man who screamed. I get out of bed and walk barefoot through the still apartment. The dry darkness sucks at me. I fumble for the switch and find it, but the harsh white light that descends frightens me more than the darkness. The walls seem so close. I shut my eyes and then open them. The walls seem even closer, inching inward toward me like some hideous tor-ture conceived by Poe.

"I'm sorry, Dad," I whisper. I can't do it anymore. I'm sorry.

I suddenly feel very foolish, very alone, standing here in the middle of the living room in the dark, in my underwear, hugging myself with my eyes closed. I drag a metal folding chair into the kitchen and reach up, pulling the cord for the overhead bulb. As it comes to life, the glow burns into the blackness around the bulb, creating a shaky tension between light and dark. It shines directly over me, and I cast no shadow.

I pull open a drawer. I take out notebook paper and a felt-tip pen. I sit down on the chair beneath the light and start to write. There should be a note. The great George Sanders left a note. "Dear World," he had written. "I am leaving you with your worries in this sweet cesspool."

I write, "Dear Dad," but after several minutes of indecision I crumble the notebook paper and toss it into the sink. They'll call him eventually. A call to Mr. Brower's office with the grim news from New York. He'll take the call and listen silently, hanging up the phone without saying a word.

I stand up and pull the cord, feeling rather than seeing the darkness settle back upon me, feeling the dry suck at my naked body. I sit in the dark and think about Fredric March's walk into the sea at the end of A

Star is Born. *I think about Marilyn, her sweet sad eyes staring into eternity. I think about Lupe Vélez, her head stuck in the loo.*

For one moment, I rebel. My cowardice pushes me up, off the chair, over to the window where I press my hands to the glass and feel the cold night outside. It's quiet out there now. They've taken the screaming man away, to where I don't know. I watch as leaves dance down the street, swirling together, evoking strange, sad memories. A streetlight hunched in grief cries its light onto the asphalt. It's quiet now. But for how long? How long before the cockroaches crawl up out of their cesspools and come scratching at my door?

I feel for the chair in the dark. I sit, breathing heavily. I watch the wall over the stove, where shadows from the trees outside dance against the gray light of the moon. They begin to take shapes, images, flickering images of the silver screen. I will sit here and watch them, over and over, just sit here and watch my movies like I've always wanted to do.

My headache pounds now, overpowering my eyes. I can't recognize the movie. There's no sound. A silent film. Like those funny, grainy movies Dad used to show in his den with the drapes pulled closed. The ones with the ladies with the big bosoms and the little boys on their laps.

But this is my movie, I realize. I'm the star. At last, I'm the star, and I'm about to play the final, classic scene.

I turn on the gas and sit facing the yawning mouth of the oven.

I watch myself on the wall, sensuously descending a staircase.

"You see, this is my life," I hear a voice whisper from somewhere. "It always will be. Just me, and the cameras, and all you wonderful people out there in the dark." I pause, hands imploring. "All right, Daddy, I'm ready for my close-up."

As the camera moves in, I'm sitting here alone in the dark, smelling the sweet fragrance of the gas.

There's more—another story—but I can't read anymore. This has creeped me out. I don't know what the hell to make of it.

Is it any good? I can't tell. It's certainly over the top, but evocative nonetheless, giving me the goddamn chills. But I'm not so sure it's really "Darryl's Story," the lover Luke said died of AIDS. Sure, there's the hint that the narrator has AIDS—the night sweats—but his repeated references to the movies makes me wonder if the character is really based on Luke himself. And if he *is* Luke, there's something pretty nasty in that boy's background, with all those pervasive references to an overpowering father and the creepy suggestion of being made to watch porno films featuring naked women and little boys.

I wish I hadn't read the thing. It feels dirty. I push it off my bed, sending it sliding across the floor. I worry that Luke's story will keep me awake, but my fears are unfounded. My mind and body just want to shut down, and thankfully I enjoy a deep, restful sleep.

So deeply do I slumber, in fact, that I almost don't hear my alarm. When I finally come to, I hurry out of bed and shower as fast as I can. No muffins this morning. The guests will have to make do with frozen bagels.

We're only half full, so it's not a big problem. Everyone's in a great mood, eager to get out and enjoy the morning. We've got another day of glorious weather predicted, with warm temperatures and plenty of sun. Luke bustles around, changing linens, uncharacteristically quiet. I don't tell him, of course, that I read his story. But I find myself looking oddly at him, remembering his strange and disturbing words.

After the breakfast rush is over, I head over to Jeff and Lloyd's house. I haven't really had the chance to talk with them in a couple of days, and it would be helpful to get their perspective on this whole thing with Gale. I find Jeff on his deck lying in a chaise lounge, soaking up the sun in a blue and white Speedo while talking on his cell.

"Of course, Connie, you'll have the best room at the guesthouse," he's saying. "It's all taken care of. All we need you to do is sing."

I sit down beside him.

"And of course you will totally have top billing over Kimberley. It would be absurd to think otherwise."

I shake my head. Is this a wedding he's planning, or a concert?

"Okay, sweetheart. We'll see you in a couple of weeks."

He snaps his phone closed and looks over at me.

"Henry, will you pick Connie Francis up at the Provincetown

airport the night before the wedding? And Kimberley Locke is arriving the morning of. Can I put you in charge of the divas?"

I smile. "What makes you think I'm temperamentally suited to take care of divas?"

He gives me one of his lopsided grins. "You take care of me."

I laugh. "Of course I'll pick them up. How are the rest of the plans coming for the wedding? What else can I do to help?"

"Ah!" Jeff's blue eyes twinkle. "Does this mean you are now excited for us at last?"

"Jeff, I was always excited for you guys. I've just been going through—"

But before I have the chance to tell him about Gale, I notice Luke across the way, standing in the gate that leads to the guesthouse. And he's staring at Jeff in his Speedo.

"Hey," I whisper, leaning in toward Jeff. "You really did a number on Luke's head, telling him his writing was no good."

Jeff looks at me oddly. "I said no such thing. In fact, I told him he showed a lot of promise, and encouraged him to keep going."

I shake my head. "That's not the way he heard it."

Luke's approaching us now, and I notice how he keeps his eyes glued to Jeff's Speedo bulge.

"Henry," Luke says, finally lifting his gaze to me. "I've finished all the rooms. I was thinking of going to the beach for the afternoon. Do you need me for anything else?"

"No," I tell him. "You can go."

He nods and heads back over to the guesthouse. Not a word to Jeff. No gushing as he usually does.

"I'm sorry if he can't take criticism," Jeff says, standing up. "I really did tell him he had talent, but there were a few areas where I thought he was a bit too . . . intense. I suggested he rethink some of that."

I agree, but I don't reveal that I've sneaked a peek at Luke's work. I'm not very proud of myself for doing so.

Jeff peels off his Speedo, his dick flopping free. Even though I've seen Jeff's cock a million times, I divert my eyes automatically. We're sisters, after all. He drops the bathing suit back on the chaise and then steps carefully into the hot tub. "Join me?" he asks.

"Sure," I say, doffing my clothes in a hurry and immersing my-self into the tub's steaming hot waters. I let out a long sigh. It's just what my aching body needs.

"You know," I tell Jeff, "I met an old friend of yours the other day."

"Who's that?"

"Eduardo."

It takes a moment for the name to register for Jeff. "Eduardo?" he asks. "My Eduardo?"

I give him a face. "Jeff, he's not yours anymore. And hasn't been for a while."

"Where did you see him?"

"Brace yourself."

"Okay. Braced."

"He's dating Shane."

It takes a good half-minute before any emotion shows on Jeff's face. But then he smiles, settling back against the side of the tub. "I never would have predicted that particular twosome." He seems to think about it, imagining the two of them in his mind. "Ed-uardo was always good at seeing beyond superficiality. He clearly sees something in Shane others may have missed."

I smile. "Like me."

"Well, I hope he's happy."

"You mean that?"

Jeff smiles. "I do. Everyone deserves to be happy."

I shrug. "Well, he seemed to be. And so did Shane."

"Well, then, good for both of them."

"I guess."

Jeff makes a face as if he doesn't understand my hesitancy on the subject.

"It's strange," I tell him. "Part of me always felt a little better imagining that Shane was still out there somewhere, pining for me."

He smiles kindly. "I suppose I once felt that way about Ed-uardo."

"But no you want him to be happy, even if that's apart from you."

Jeff nods.

"I hope Shane is happy, too," I say.

"It's okay to feel a little bad, Henry."

"No," I tell him. "I'm tired of feeling sorry for myself. I want to feel happy for Shane, and so I'm going to make sure I do."

We sit in silence for a few minutes.

"How are your bruised legs from the bike accident?" Jeff asks.

I smile. "Better now. This spa works wonders."

"Yes, it does."

"Wish it could soothe all the rest of my ailments."

"You mean the heart-and-soul kind."

I nod.

Jeff looks over at me with concern. "Lloyd are I are worried about you, buddy."

But I meant it when I said I was tired of feeling sorry for myself. Suddenly I don't want to talk about my problems ever again. My problems bore me. Bore bore bore!

So, instead, I just smile. "Look," I tell Jeff. "These next couple of weeks should be about *you*. I really want to do whatever I can to make your wedding a great success."

Jeff smiles back at me. "I'm glad you feel that way, buddy."

"As the best man, I get to make a speech, don't I?"

"You sure do."

"I'll write a good one."

"You'd better." Jeff winks at me. "But remember, my mother's going to be there. Nothing too salacious."

I laugh. "You mean I can't talk about the six-way you and Lloyd had in this very tub?"

"You mean the one where that guy was chewing gum and lost it up Lloyd's ass while rimming him?"

I laugh even harder. "You mean there have been *other* six-ways in here?" I look down at the water and wrinkle up my nose. "Christ, I hope you use a lot of chlorine!"

We both laugh.

And then Jeff's cell is ringing. He leaps out of the tub to answer it. "Yeah yeah yeah," he's saying, motioning to me that he's sorry, that he has to take this call. He mouths the words *Kimberley Locke*. I signal for him that it's okay to go. I watch him wrap a towel around himself and go inside.

I don't stay in the tub much longer. I'm feeling edgy, like I need to be doing something more productive than just sitting here. As I'm drying off, I look over at the guesthouse. Luke is standing at one of the upper windows. I immediately feel creeped out. Was he watching us? *Spying* on us? I thought he said he was heading to the beach. I get dressed quickly, leaving my wet towel on the chaise next to Jeff's Speedo.

I think about calling Gale, but I reject the idea almost as soon as it enters my mind. That relationship is over. Done. Kaput. It's no use going anywhere near there again. But Gale's words do come back to me: *Let me know if you ever figure out what's the most important thing you need in a lover.* What the hell did he mean?

I spend the day by myself. Something draws me back to Luke's writing, which I pick up from the floor. I hold the binder in my hands, staring down at it.

"Darryl's Story."

Gale seemed to think my answer to his question wasn't enough. But honesty *is* what I want. *Truth.* That's what obsesses me about Luke. I want to know who he is. Why the truth of his story matters so much, I'm not sure. But I want to know.

I read the second story in the binder.

This is how my dream begins: the sound of shovels, the stabbing of earth.

A dark blue night. The moon as odd voyeur, its light glinting off the blades of the silver shovels. It is the eye of the sky, a hole into the heavens, perchance the passageway from which he might return.

I have had the same dream over and over ever since he died: I peel away my sweat drenched sheets, placing my feet against the cold of the wooden floor, feeling my soles stick. I push myself to stand and pull on a pair of jeans, plunging head first into the blue of the night. And once there, embraced by a sweet, damp, blue fog that cools my skin, I dig up his grave, and pull him out of his coffin. He is dressed in a blue jacket and white shirt and red tie, the clothes we buried him in, clothes that smell only a trifle musty now, like the old hand-me-downs my mother would keep in her hope chest, in our basement that flooded every spring. I shake him as if he might wake, and I am not surprised that he has not decomposed: he is perfect, in death as in life.

Finally his eyelids begin to flutter, like little moths.

When I awake, which I always do precisely at that moment, I feel nei-ther disappointment nor relief. It is just the endless rush of nothing that I feel, and I am always conscious of how wet my sheets are.

Was this how they found Marilyn? Nude? Drenched in her own sweat? I lie here, like Sebastian Venable, my flesh eaten from my bones.

I feel sick. I can't read anymore.

Is he writing about Darryl—or himself?

I hide Luke's manuscript under a pile of papers. I need to get it out of my head. All those disturbing images. Cockroaches, peo-ple screaming, suicide attempts, dead bodies, digging up graves.

What lives inside that boy's head?

Suddenly all I want to do is wrap my arms around him. I want to tell him everything's okay, that the pain doesn't have too be so bad, that I can make it go away for him, if only he'd let me. I ache to feel his body next to mine, my lips pressed against his ear as I whisper soft reassurances and promises of love. I want to taste his sweet skin, inhale deeply the fragrance of his hair. I want to make everything right for him, and in the process, make everything right for myself.

But how crazy is that? Why should I be feeling this way about Luke? Why has he so gripped hold of my emotions?

Because I was scared and confused like him once.

I remember another young boy, trying to find his way in the world. I remember another scared kid who tried to make his way in the world of adults. It was little Henry Weiner, crying in some stranger's Trans Am after his first night at a gay bar. Little Henry Weiner from West Springfield, unsure of who he was or where he was supposed to be.

But if Luke's writing is any indication, what he went through was far more traumatic than anything I ever experienced.

I go about my day trying not to think about what I've read. In the early afternoon, Jeff and Lloyd drive up to Boston to meet with their friend Naomi, who's going to be marrying them. They're planning to go over their vows and the order of the cere-mony. As their best man, I offer to go with them, trying to stick to my promise of being supportive. But we have a new guest checking in this evening, so I need to stay behind.

Of course, the other reason I need to stay here is that Ann Marie doesn't get back until six, and we can't leave J. R. alone, no matter how adamant he gets that he's old enough to look after himself. We're all still worried about the kid, in fact, who remains sullen and withdrawn. No matter how often we try to cheer him up, he resists our efforts. School has started again, and on his first two papers he brought home Ds. Lloyd worries that the boy may be clinically depressed, and there's been talk of J. R. seeing a family counselor. Poor kid. I wish I knew what to say or do to get through to him.

Since the day is so beautiful, I wait outside for our new guest, who arrives around four, a dithery redheaded woman with six large suitcases and a very prominent Bronx accent. I check her in, give her some maps and restaurant guides, and decide then, free at last, to get the hell out of the house. With Ann Marie home, I'm suddenly at liberty—and in that moment, a walk along the beach at sunset with my Walkman playing some classic nineties grunge seems mighty appealing. What better way to crowd out all my confusion of the past few days?

"Yeah," I murmur to myself. "Smells like teen spirit to me."

I grin, gathering up my CDs. A walk on the beach listening to Nirvana. *Perfect.* It'll be like I'm back in college, when my whole path was still in front of me, when I still believed I'd be happily partnered and settled down by twenty-five with a man named Jack.

But if the Walkman is going to play, I need batteries. I find none in the drawer in the kitchen, so I head into the basement, where I notice a light is on in Luke's room. His door is ajar; usually he keeps it closed. I've told him many times to turn the lights off when he leaves; the electric bill is already too high. I approach, intending to shut it off.

But what I see inside stops me in the doorway.

Luke is on his bed, lying on his stomach. He's humping a pillow.

And he's wearing Jeff's blue and white Speedo.

In that instant, all my sympathy for him vanishes.

"You perv," I say, before I even have a chance to think.

Luke sits up at once. He glares at me.

"Why am I a perv for jacking off?" He's angry, belligerent. "Don't *you* jack off, Henry?"

My lips are curling in disgust. "Not in Jeff's bathing suit, I don't."

"This isn't Jeff's," he insists, acting outraged at the suggestion. "It's *mine.*"

I glare at him. "I saw Jeff wearing it today. He left it outside. That's *his.*"

"It is not!"

"You are one fucked-up kid," I say, turning to leave. Suddenly all those weird images from his writing repulse me. No longer do I want to comfort him, tell him everything will be okay. I want to get as far away from him and his warped mind as possible.

But Luke is on me from behind. His arms snake around my chest and he pulls me into him. His lips are on the back of my neck.

"Don't go, Henry," he whispers urgently. "Make love to me again. You don't know how much I want you, how much I've wanted you ever since I first laid eyes on you."

"Fuck you, you liar," I say, but I make no effort to extricate myself from his grip.

"It's true, Henry," he's whispering in my ear. "It's *you* I want. Fuck this job. I'll give it up if it means I can have you again."

I turn around. I'm intending to tell him to fuck off, to push him away from me, hard and fast.

But instead, I kiss him.

Gripping his waist, I force Luke back down on the bed. Into the air I roughly lift his legs, yanking off Jeff's Speedo in the process, tossing it onto the floor. Meanwhile Luke's undoing my shirt, and with my free hand I'm dropping my pants. Naked, I crush down onto Luke's body, forcefully bringing his head up to meet my chest, where he sucks on my nipples. "That's it," I tell him fiercely. "Get me rock hard."

I assume he has condoms and lube in the drawer of the table on the side of his bed, and I'm right. For the briefest of seconds I imagine who else Luke's had down here, but thoughts don't last long in my mind. Except this one: *I want to fuck Luke.* If I can fuck him, some crazy part of me believes, everything will be better.

And so I do. It's the first real sex, I realize, that I've had since the last time I was with him. Gale has always stopped me before our pants were off, I never orgasmed with Evan and his crew, and I just can't count Martin's blow job at the dick dock. So once again: it's Luke.

Luke—who I flip over onto his stomach and whose legs I spread apart roughly, who gets no foreplay, no tender affection, and inside whom I finally climax, my semen filling up the condom. The sheer sensation of my orgasm seems enough to make Luke shoot as well, as suddenly the sheets beneath us are covered with his own slimy goo.

I remain on top of him, silent, immobile, for several seconds.

"Don't leave, Henry," Luke suddenly whispers, our hearts beating in unison.

I look down at this boy beneath me. I *should* leave. I should get out of here right now, as fast as I can. This is wrong—on so many levels—wrong, wrong, wrong. But something in Luke's voice compels me to stay.

I do what I imagined earlier. I wrap my arms around him. In his ear I whisper, "Everything's going to be okay."

He says nothing, so I repeat the words.

He simply folds himself into my embrace, and I pull him as close to me as possible.

I'll protect you, I'm thinking. *I'll protect you from the screams in the night, from the dark shadows that creep through your life, from the memories of that horrible father who hurt you so badly.*

But no further words are exchanged. I am left with only my thoughts, and the sweet scent of Luke's hair in my nostrils.

Not until the next morning do I finally leave his bed.

And by that time, my whole word has been turned upside down.

16

THE BREAKWATER

We're sitting here, Luke and I, on a rock halfway out across the harbor, part of this majestic bridge of granite that keeps the waters of the Atlantic from destroying the fragile final finger of Cape Cod. The sky threatens rain, and out here in the middle of the harbor the breeze is a good ten degrees chillier than on shore. Luke and I huddle close to keep warm.

"I'm glad we're friends again, Henry," he says, close to my ear.

I smile, kissing his cheek. I suppose hard, intense sex, followed by a dreamy, sticky night in each other's arms, would tend to smooth over whatever hostilities had existed between us. As soon as the sun was up, I'd slipped upstairs, not wanting to be discovered in Luke's room by Lloyd. But not before we made love again, this time going more slowly, savoring every moment. I kissed his neck, he licked my nipples. He buried his face in my armpits, I made slurping noises on his tight, flat stomach. And I fucked him again, gentler this time, but with just as shattering a climax.

Once more I close my eyes and rest my face in his sweet, sweet hair.

I'm not sure what I'm going to tell Lloyd. What makes it even more difficult is that I'm not sure what's going on between Luke and me. We've had wonderful sex—but exchanged precious few words. So I'm left wondering how he really feels about me. He called us "friends." Is that what we are? Friends who have sex? Or might it be more? Might he share these feelings I'm having, this rush of emotion that makes he want to sit here all day, just holding him in my arms? Have I imagined all of Luke's manipulation, exaggerated his obsession with Jeff? All I know for sure right now is that it feels awfully good sitting so close to him.

"So," Luke says, "you said we needed to talk."

"Yeah," I agree, but I voice nothing more.

He turns his face so he can look me straight in the eyes. "I meant it when I said I'll quit the job," he tells me, "if that's what will allow us to continue seeing each other."

I try to see the truth of his feelings in his eyes. "Is that what you really want? To see me on a regular basis?"

Luke smiles. "Why is that so hard for you to believe?"

"Luke, it's been obvious that your interest is in Jeff."

He stiffens. "That was *not* his Speedo, Henry! We just have the same suit. That's why I was staring at him yesterday. I thought I had an original." He looks at me as if I don't believe him. "Go over and look on his deck and you'll see. I was over there this morning, and his Speedo is sitting there. Mine is put away in my drawer."

I sigh. Of course, Luke could have gone next door and replaced the bathing suit on the chaise lounge this morning just to cover his tracks. But maybe he's telling the truth. I just don't know anymore.

But I do know the sex with him was awesome. And I just can't seem to keep from kissing him. Never has a boy tasted quite this sweet.

I pull back gently to look into his eyes, keeping my arms tightly around him.

"Luke," I say, "I have a confession to make."

"Oh?"

"I read some of your writing." I wait for him to react, but he doesn't. He just keeps looking at me with those mysterious eyes of his. "The stuff you threw in the dumpster. One binder had fallen on the ground and I picked it up, intending to throw it away, but I . . ."

"But you took it back into the house," he says. "You read my work without my permission."

I feel terrible. "I'm sorry."

Luke only smiles. "It's okay, Henry. What part did you read?"

"I'm not sure. Seemed like it was a short story, or maybe two short stories . . ."

"Well, what was it about?"

I look at him. "Well, you titled it 'Darryl's Story.'"

"Oh, that. What did you think?"

I'm not sure what to say. "Well, it was disturbing."

"Good. I wanted it to be."

"You succeeded."

He smiles. "But did you think the writing was good?"

"I can't judge," I tell him.

He pouts. "You hated it. Just like Jeff."

"No, no, no. It fascinated me. It . . ." My voice trails off until I can find what I want to say. "It made me want to know who you really are."

"So you *did* like it."

I shrug. "Like it? I'm not sure. All I know is that I haven't been able to stop thinking about it." I look intently at him. "Or you."

Several seagulls screech in their amazingly human-like voices. They land not far from us in the water, batting their wings angrily.

"Well, I'm glad I got you hooked, Henry," Luke says, suddenly energized. "That's what a writer hopes to be able to do."

I shake my head. "But is it true, Luke?"

He smirks. "Jeff usually answers that question with a line about his work being emotionally true, if not always literally true."

"But much of what Jeff writes *is* literally true."

He nods. "Exactly."

I sigh. "You're a mystery, Luke."

He makes a little laugh sound in his throat. "I don't know why you think that. I've told you far more stories of my life than you've ever told me about yours."

"Well, that's just it, Luke. They all *sound* like stories. What you write, what you say . . . I'm never sure what's the truth. What's real. What isn't."

He grunts. "So you're saying you don't believe what I've told you about my life?"

"I'm saying what you've shared so far doesn't always seem to add up." I sigh. "Your stories read as if they're about this person you say was your lover, this Darryl, but part of me thinks they're really about you." I look at him and raise my eyebrows. "Maybe I'm just suspicious by nature."

"Well, answer me this, Henry," he says. "Do you at least believe that I like you?"

I start to reply, but find I don't have the words. Why is it so hard for me to believe that this attractive young guy wants to be with me?

Maybe because I grew up never believing *anyone* would ever want to be with me. "Henry," my mother would say. "You need to be more manly. You should be out playing baseball. No girl wants to date a sissy boy."

And then, in high school and college, I was always the pencil-necked geek, my yearbook pictures still embarrassing to look at. No wonder Jack never looked at me that way. My shirt never fit quite right; my hair was always too long or too short.

Then, when I came out as gay and started trying to find my way in the gay world, I immediately felt out of place in the world of the Body Beautiful at the clubs. Only when I met Jeff did I start to improve my body and my wardrobe—but then I always had my mentor to compete with, and when one competes with Jeff O'Brien, the outcome is always predetermined.

Except maybe this time it's different. Maybe—just maybe—Luke is telling me the truth. It really is *me* he likes. Not Jeff.

"Okay," Luke says, almost as if he's psychic, "I'll admit to you that I've been very attentive to Jeff. Maybe even ass-kissing a bit. But it wasn't because I wanted him, Henry. It was because I hoped he'd help me with my novel."

"Well, that's been very obvious. Even to him." I narrow my eyes. "But I suspect it was a bit more as well . . ."

"No! It was all about Jeff reading my work." He pouts. "Well, that was a big mistake. He just cut me right down."

"I think you might be over-reacting . . ."

Luke leans his head on my shoulder, not listening. "But *you* think I have talent, don't you, Henry?"

"Sure . . ."

"So do you think maybe Jeff's afraid of a little competition?"

Luke laughs, and the sound unnerves me a little. "Especially from someone younger, with more years ahead of him?"

I look over at the top of Luke's dark blond head. "Why don't you tell me exactly what Jeff said about your work?"

"It wasn't *what* he said, but *how* he said it." Luke sits up, immediately assuming an impression of Jeff, all chin and attitude. "'You've got a ways to go,'" he says, mimicking Jeff quite well. "'Don't be arrogant and think your first draft is all it will take.'" The kid sniffs in indignation. "Arrogant! Who's he calling arrogant? Maybe he ought to look in the mirror!"

I'm amazed at how quickly Luke has turned on his idol. It's a little chilling, in fact. From soft and warm he's suddenly hard and defensive. I feel myself tense. I actually pull back a bit from him.

"Well," I offer, "criticism is supposed to be tough or it isn't helpful. You didn't just want him to say 'Great job' and not mean it, did you?"

Luke is indignant. "My writing professor thought it was brilliant! She thought it was publishable just as it was!"

I make a face. "But has *she* published anything? Jeff *has*, remember."

Luke scowls. How dark his face seems now. Gone is the light that had drawn me just moments earlier.

"I'm *glad* you read my work, Henry," he says. "Because it shows *some* people appreciate what I'm trying to do. I'm not writing bland, boring commercial shit like Jeff."

"But I thought you said Jeff's work was—"

"Authors like Jeff are afraid of the new generation," Luke says loudly, cutting me off. "We see things differently than they do. We say it a new, fresh, exciting way. We've had a different experience of being gay and they're afraid we're going to put them out of business."

"Luke, I don't think Jeff feels—"

"But *you* found my work fascinating. You said you can't stop thinking about it." He beams. "That proves I'm on the right track. So I'm going ahead with it! Full speed ahead!"

I sigh. "Well, I'm glad you're not discouraged any more." I give him a small smile. "But you threw all your work away."

He tosses a hand at me. "That was just my hard copies. All my work is still on my computer. Did you really think I'd be that stupid? Maybe Jeff has no faith in me, but I know *you* do, Henry."

Do I? I say nothing.

Luke doesn't appear to notice. "Just watch. My novel is going to be *huge*. I'll show Mr. Jeffrey Fucking Arrogant O'Brien."

I don't like the sound of that. I don't like the way this conversation has gone at all, in fact. "Really, Luke," I tell him, "I don't think Jeff meant to discourage you."

"Oh, yes, he did. He wants to wipe out all the competition. But he'll see. I'm not going to give up!"

Suddenly sitting so close to him doesn't feel so good anymore. Luke seems edgy, even dangerous, where just moments ago he was soft and comforting.

But he seems unaware of my change in feelings. "If *you* believe in me, Henry," he says, "that's enough." He kisses me, lots of tongue. I try to kiss him back, but he just doesn't taste as sweet as before. When he pulls back, he looks directly into my eyes and asks, "Shall I go back now and give Lloyd my resignation?"

"No." I need to think this through. This is all happening very fast, and now I'm very confused. "Let me talk to Lloyd," I say. "He should hear what happened between us from me."

"Okay," Luke says, slipping his arm back around me and returning his head to my shoulder.

We sit there for a few minutes in silence, watching the gulls circle overhead and listening as the water trickles between the rocks. The tide is moving inexorably back in toward shore. In the distance there's the low steady foghorn, warning ships not to come too close to this place.

"Hey, Luke," I say, my mouth in his hair.

"What?"

"Do you ever listen to Alice in Chains?"

"Alice in what?"

"Never mind."

My bruised thigh is starting to ache from sitting in one position. I suggest we head back to the guesthouse. I assure Luke that I'll handle things with Lloyd. We walk back through town holding hands. But when we get to the guesthouse, I can't find Lloyd anywhere, though Jeff is once again pruning the rosebushes. I send Luke inside and head out to talk with Jeff.

"Where's Lloyd?" I ask.

Jeff lowers the shears. I can see he's concerned. "He went on a drive with J. R. and Ann Marie. I don't know when they'll be back."

"Is everything okay?"

"No, actually, it's not." Jeff resumes deadheading the faded blossoms. "Ann Marie's very worried about J. R. Whatever is bothering that kid, Lloyd is hoping to get to the bottom of it."

"Why didn't you go with them?"

Jeff turns to look at me. He's near tears. "Because for whatever reason, I seem to be the root of J. R.'s discontent. He's distant to Lloyd, too, but it's me with whom he seems to have the real issue."

"Why you?"

"Who knows? Because I make him do his homework? Because I won't let him go into Internet chat rooms?"

I sigh. My problems are going to have to wait. This conversation is long overdue.

"No," I tell Jeff. "It's not because of any of those things. It's because you're gay."

Jeff looks at me as if I'm crazy. "What?"

My self-absorption these past couple of weeks embarrasses me all of a sudden. "You know, I've been wanting to talk with you about all this, but so many other things keep getting in the way."

"So tell me now."

I pause, glancing up at the window above us. Sure enough, I sense movement behind the curtains. Is Luke there, eavesdropping? "Come on," I say to Jeff, taking his arm. "Let's go over to your house."

Inside Jeff's living room, where privacy is assured, I sit him down on the couch and position myself in the chair opposite him. Mr. Tompkins, Jeff's big old fat cat, jumps up to cuddle in his lap.

"What's going on, Henry?" Jeff asks.

I take a deep breath. "About a week ago, I had a chat with J. R.

It was short, but I think I got some insight into what's bugging him."

"And you didn't immediately tell me?"

"I'm sorry, Jeff. I admit I've been too self-obsessed lately."

He sighs. "Just tell me."

"Well, it's hard to put it in words. J. R. was very worried about the newspaper taking a picture of the wedding and him being in it."

"That makes no sense at all."

"It kind of does. You see, I think the reason he doesn't want to play basketball this year is because kids on other teams call the Provincetown players—"

"Faggots," Jeff says, finishing my thought. "Yes, I know. Ann Marie finally told us. And I've called the principal of that other school and told him that I expect a full investigation—"

"See, Jeff, I think that's what J. R. worries about. That somehow he's going to be thrust into the spotlight about some gay issue, and consequently everyone is going to think *he's* gay."

"For God's sake, he's nine years old!"

"And that's how a nine-year-old thinks."

Jeff shakes his head. "Why is he suddenly thinking being gay is something he has to defend against? We raised him to understand diversity, and the Provincetown school system has lots of kids who have gay and lesbian parents!"

"Yes, but they still run up against the real world from time to time, and it can be tough on a kid."

Jeff runs his hands over his face. "I know this is part of it, but it's not the whole thing. Something else is going on with J. R., something that goes even deeper than this. That's what Lloyd is trying to find out. He thinks J. R. needs to talk with a counselor, but he wants to try to understand the situation better himself first so we know what we're dealing with."

"I know this is hard on you, Jeff."

He shakes his head. "The hell with me. It's hard on *J. R.* Whatever it is."

I nod in agreement. "So you don't know when they will be back?"

"No. They took a drive down to Chatham and might take the boat out to Monomoy if they can get J. R.'s spirits up."

"J. R. loves going out on the boat."

"Well, he used to."

I reach over and touch Jeff's knee. "You'll get to the bottom of this. I know you will."

"What makes you so sure? What problems have *you* gotten to the bottom of lately, Henry?"

I frown. "That's not fair."

"I'm sorry."

Suddenly all I want is to be alone in my room. "Look, would you have Lloyd call me when he gets back? I need to talk with him about something."

Jeff raises his eyebrows. "What's the problem?"

"Nothing . . . I just need to talk with Lloyd."

"Henry, I'm sorry if I snapped at you." It's his turn now to touch my knee the way I'd just touched his. "What's going on?"

I hesitate, but then I let it out. "I slept with Luke again."

Jeff grins, and I can tell he's grateful for the opportunity to lighten his mood. "You sly dog, you," he teases.

"Jeff—" My tongue seems tied. My thoughts and feelings are doing somersaults in my head, and I can't seem to keep them straight. "He's—I mean, what do you—I just don't know what to think about Luke."

Jeff leans forward on the couch to look at me. "What's gotten your panties in such a twist, Henry?"

"Well, for one, he's very angry with you, and that makes me a little worried."

"At me? Why?"

"Because he thinks you were trying to discourage him in his writing. He thinks you view him as competition."

"Oh, yeah, I'm really worried," Jeff says sarcastically. "Henry, you should have read some of his stuff—"

I decide not to reveal that I already have. "Just think back to the conversation you had with him. Could you have possibly come across as too critical, too hard?"

Jeff shakes him head adamantly. "Not at all. I told him it

needed work, but that he should keep going, that I thought he had talent somewhere inside him. It was very mild criticism."

I sigh. "I think for someone like Luke, hearing that he has talent 'somewhere inside him' instead of being told that he is the next John Updike is always going to be translated into, 'You suck.'"

"Well," Jeff says, "his anger at me may stem from more than that."

I look over at him. "What do you mean?"

He closes his eyes, then opens them again after a few moments. "After I gave him his criticism yesterday morning, Luke seemed pretty quiet, but he *did* say he appreciated my honesty. I thought that was that. So I came back here to the house, and I was at my computer when I heard somebody enter through the door behind me. And it's Luke. Naked."

"Naked? As in thong naked?"

"As in naked naked." Jeff laughs. "He says he wants to 'thank' me for reading his manuscript, and since he couldn't pay for such professional criticism, he wanted to find another way."

I can feel my body going numb.

"Man, he looked very sexy standing there." Jeff grins. "Like I have to tell *you* that, Henry. You've obviously been unable to resist him. The kid's adorable."

"And so you—"

"Turned him down." Jeff smiles wanly. "I just couldn't do it with him. Remember, Lloyd and I were off to plan our wedding later that day. I just couldn't fuck this kid and then go off to talk about wedding vows." He shakes his head, glancing toward the window. "I tell you, Henry, planning for this wedding has put me in such a different place. The weirdest thing is: it actually wasn't all that difficult to turn Luke down."

He laughs. I say nothing.

"Okay, so it was a *little bit* difficult," Jeff continues, "especially when he turned around and showed me his ass. What a bubble butt. But in the end, I just said no, and sent him back across the way."

The image of Luke showing Jeff his ass—the same ass I would fuck later that night—sears my brain.

"I've got to go," I say, standing.

Jeff looks up at me strangely. "What's the matter?"

I boil over. "You just don't get it, Jeff. Do you *mean* to be insensitive, or are you just so insensitive that you don't know *when* you're being insensitive?"

"*What?*" Jeff stands to face me. The cat jumps off the couch. "Henry, what did I say?"

I snort. "Then I guess it's the latter."

Understanding seems to cross Jeff's face, and his hand reaches out grip my forearm. He wants to keep me from leaving.

"Okay, okay, you're right," he says. "I wasn't thinking. I'm sorry if I was insensitive. But Luke coming on to me didn't mean anything . . ."

"Oh, no, nothing at all. Except that, when he couldn't get you, he turned to me as a consolation prize. *Story of my fucking life!*"

Jeff's shaking his head. "That's not the way it was, Henry."

"That's the way it always is!"

"Not this time. Luke had an ulterior motive going after me, Henry. If he couldn't get me to champion his work on its own merits, he'd try to become my 'mistress' and maybe get me to help him because of *that*." Jeff looks me straight in the eye. "But he came on to *you*, Henry, not because he wanted anything from you, but because he *liked* you."

"It doesn't wash, Jeff. It just doesn't wash."

He lets my arm go. There's really nothing else that can be said.

"Just have Lloyd call me when he gets back, okay? I'd appreciate you not saying about Luke. I should be the one to tell him what happened with our employee."

"I'm sorry, buddy," Jeff says again as I head out.

I wave him away. "Just forget it. That's what I'm going to try to do."

I head back across the way. I can't bear to see Luke right now. Knowing that he came on to Jeff earlier in the day makes me feel like sloppy seconds—and damn it, it hurts.

And now try telling me that wasn't Jeff's Speedo, you freaking perv!

I suspect he's watching me from the window as I hop into my Jeep with the top down and tear out of the driveway. I'm not sure where I'm headed. I just cruise down Route 6, cranking up Pearl

Jam as loud as my ears will permit. And at the moment, that's very loud indeed.

It all makes perfect sense. Jeff's story explains Luke's seething anger at him. He was rejected by his idol not once but twice, and I just blundered into the middle of it. Yet again, Henry Weiner proves his stupidity by allowing himself to think, even if just for a night, that Luke—that anyone—might really like him. *I am such a fool. Such a big old idiotic—*

My cell rings. A local P-town number I don't recognize.

"Hello!" I shout.

"Henry?"

The wind and the music combine to make hearing difficult.

"Who's this?" I ask. "Speak up!"

"Henry, it's Evan."

"Evan?"

"Yeah, you remember, the other night you—"

"Yeah, I remember. Hold on."

I glance quickly in the rearview mirror to see if anyone's behind me. No one is, so I swerve over to the side of the road and ram the Jeep into park. I switch off Pearl Jam.

"Henry, you there?"

"Yeah, I'm here."

"So how the hell are you, dude?"

"I'm just ducky, dude, how are you?"

My voice is hard, but Evan laughs. "I'm just great," he says. "Listen, Curt and I were hoping you could join us for dinner tomorrow night."

"Dinner?" I'm feeling belligerent. "And then maybe a dip in the hot tub?"

I hear Evan chuckle. "That could be arranged."

"I'm sure it could. I'm sure it's *often* arranged."

Evan laughs again, but I can tell he's starting to become wary of me. "So can you come?"

"Oh, yes, I can come, although I gave no evidence of it the other night."

It takes Evan a few seconds to get the joke, and then he doesn't seem to find it all that funny. "It's hard getting a straight answer out of you, Henry."

"Maybe that's because I'm not straight. Instead, I'm gay, a big flaming homo—trapped in a culture that prizes sexual romps and game-playing more than anything real and lasting."

Evan doesn't respond.

"How many others are you inviting, Evan?" I ask. "Is it one for you and one for Curt, or will this be an all-out orgy?"

Evan's voice is tight. "We were just inviting you."

"Why would you want to see me again?" I ask. "Has there been a little bed death since tying the knot during that fabulous ceremony on the Maui volcano? Is that what it is? Curt just doesn't get you hot and bothered anymore, so you need to bring in outsiders to spice things up?"

"Henry," Evan says, "if you don't want to come to dinner, all you have to do is say no, thank you."

Suddenly I feel like a shit. Evan doesn't deserve this.

"I'm sorry," I tell him, the air rushing out of my puffed-up chest like a balloon. "Really, I am. I was totally out of line."

"I'll say."

"I've just had a really bad day so far."

"Sorry to hear it." He doesn't sound sincere. Who can blame him? I just bit his head off for extending me a dinner invitation.

"Look," I say, "it's just that I really liked you, Evan. I allowed myself to imagine maybe there might be something more between us."

"Oh," he says. "I see."

"But it was my fault. I made some presumptions, but they were wrong."

Somehow I can tell he's smiling. "I'm sorry we never got to take our walk on the beach."

"You know what? You can't say that to me."

"Why not? Henry, we really liked you."

I fall silent.

"I should have explained to you more clearly that Curt and I were lovers," Evan says. "I should have explained to you that we're not just players, that we really like getting to know the people we have sex with."

"But see, here's the deal," I tell him. "I'm looking for more than just sex . . ."

"So are we." Evan pauses. "In fact, we've been talking about the possibility of developing an ongoing relationship with someone."

"A three-way relationship, you mean?"

"Yeah. I know it's crazy to be talking about this right now. We hardly know each other. But I just want you to know, Henry, that we're not just looking for sex."

For a brief moment, sitting here on the side of the road, I almost tell Evan sure—I'd love to come to dinner. I'd love to consider everything you—and Curt—might have to offer. And it's not just the memory of Evan's hot body that's making me feel this way. Even more, it's the memory of how much he loved Provincetown, how in tune he seemed to be with my own sensibility. He came so close to fitting my dream of Mr. Right—

Except for one thing.

He has a husband already.

"I just can't," I say finally. "Thanks for the invitation. But I can't allow my heart to get ripped out from the inside of my rib cage."

"Henry, we wouldn't do anything to hurt you—"

I laugh. "Of course you wouldn't. It would *me*. I know how to hurt myself very well on my own."

"It doesn't have to be about getting hurt."

"Look," I tell him. "I'm sure you're great guys. But I think I'm going to become a monk. It's the only safe path for me."

Evan laughs. "If you do, you'd be the sexiest monk out there. I'd hate to think of a hottie like you being taken out of circulation."

I smile. "I appreciate you saying that."

"It's true."

Is it? I just don't know anymore. I flip the rearview mirror down so I can stare up into my reflection. I look tired. I look old. Yet Evan just called me a hottie. Which is true?

"Well," Evan's saying, "if tomorrow night doesn't work, then would you at least keep our number on your phone? And call us if you're ever inclined to do so?"

"Yeah," I tell him. "I can do that."

"Hope your day gets better, Henry. I really do."

I sit there for a long time after hanging up the phone, just staring down the road ahead of me. To think that I was so desperate

for a boyfriend that for a moment there I was actually considering dating a married couple . . .

Lots of guys have successful three-way relationships.

Shane's voice.

And he's right: lots of guys do. So is it possible that I turned
Evan down too soon?

Maybe, in fact, I ought to heed Shane's point: I rejected Evan
and Curt out of my own fear-based idiosyncrasies. Maybe I *could*,
in fact, have a wonderfully fulfilling relationship with the two of
them. Some multi-partner relationships seem to work out just
great. For so long I've lamented not having a boyfriend. Now I'd
get two for the price of one.

I laugh a little to myself. Is this really me, Henry Weiner, thinking this way?

All of a sudden I'm worried that some cop is going to come up
behind me flashing his lights, so I start the Jeep again and pull a
wide U-turn in the middle of Route 6. I'm heading back toward
Provincetown. But the call from Evan has certainly gotten me
thinking.

The joy of being gay, Jeff and Lloyd have taught me, is that we
can create relationships however we choose, that we don't need
to fit proscribed patterns. We can build families based on what
matters to us, on whatever our own individual tastes and needs
might be. Monogamy too restricting? Toss it out! One lover too
limiting? Get two! Or three!

Jeff and Lloyd have certainly lived that way at times. There
have been other lovers for both of them, even while the two of
them have been together. They've always made room for change,
for experimentation, for challenge. And look at them today. All
that nonconformity didn't make them weaker. In fact, it made
them strong enough and committed enough to want to get *married*.

So why am I still playing Cinderella, believing that the only way
to find my Prince Charming is to go the ball and get him to notice me above all the other girls?

Rounding the hill in Truro, I observe the panorama of Provincetown that lies ahead: the narrow arc of sand that cuts through the
bright turquoise water, the row of storybook cottages on one side,

the rolling dunes on the other, the exclamation point of the Monument completing the picture at the far west. This is my home. For better or for worse, this is where I've cast my lot, and this is where I've got to find my heart.

Oh, I could move. I could quit my job and go back to Boston, where the pool of potential mates is a thousand times larger. But so is the potential for heartbreak. I realize, as I drive back into town, that no matter where I go, my questions and turmoil will follow. This is about me: it's not about where I live, or who I see, or what kind of games other people are playing. All that matters is what I allow to matter.

And here, everything matters. *No one passes through Provincetown.* Here, there is purpose. Even without a plan, I remind myself, there is purpose.

Still, I hesitate going back to the guesthouse. I still don't know how I feel about Luke. Maybe Jeff's right. Maybe Luke did turn to me on the rebound, but he wouldn't have done so if he didn't like me in the first place. Why shouldn't I believe that? He's a scared kid, after all, and he felt rejected by someone he admired. I've been in his shoes many times. Maybe I shouldn't be so quick to judge him.

Passing Clem and Ursie's restaurant on Shank Painter Road, I resist the urge to stop for a frozen custard cone—that is, until I spot Ann Marie and J. R. out front. I quickly swing the Jeep into the parking lot.

"Hey!" Ann Marie sings out, seeming thrilled to see me.

"Hey you two," I say, hopping out of the Jeep and taking note of their cones. "I was being so good in passing by here until I saw you guys. What flavors did you get?"

"I have a swirl," Ann Marie says. "J. R. got chocolate."

"It's the best, huh, buddy?" I ask the boy.

He just shrugs as he licks his cone.

I look over at Ann Marie. She shakes her head as if to say she and Lloyd were unable to get through to him.

"Did you guys take the boat out?" I ask.

"No," Ann Marie tells me. "J. R. just wanted to come home."

I look down at J. R., who's intent on his cone.

"Can I have a lick?" I ask.

He just frowns, avoiding eye contact.

I stoop down in front of him. "Can I just have one lick so I don't have to buy a whole one for myself? Pretty please?"

He finally eyes me. "That would be *gross*."

"Come on," I say, teasing him, my tongue hanging out. "Let me lick."

I'm like a big old dog trying to lap his cone out of his hands. I succeed in getting a small hint of a smile. "Uncle Henry!" J. R. says, holding his cone over his head. "Get away!"

"Lick, lick, lick!" I cry, pretending to jump.

And the kid's frozen custard promptly falls from his cone onto the dusty asphalt.

"Fuck!" J. R. shouts. "Now look what you did!"

"J. R.," his mother scolds. "Watch your language!"

"I'm sorry, buddy," I say. "I was just horsing around. Here, let me buy you another one."

"Well, you gotta make it *two* scoops now since you ruined that one," J. R. tells me.

"Absolutely," I say, approaching the window.

"With rainbow shots on it too," the boy adds. Then he pauses. "No, just make it chocolate shots. No rainbow."

I smile tightly. Rainbow shots, rainbow flag. Wouldn't want to get a frozen custard cone that looked too gay.

I order double-scoop chocolate cones with chocolate shots for both of us. The three of us sit down on a bench and lick away, looking up at the late afternoon sky.

"So if you didn't go out on the boat," I ask, "where did Uncle Lloyd take you today?"

J. R. doesn't answer, so his mother chimes in. "We went shopping in Chatham—"

"Boring," J. R. intones.

"Then went swimming at the Wellfleet pond," Ann Marie finishes.

"That must have been more fun," I say, looking over at J. R.

Ann Marie is beaming. "Yeah, we saw one of those huge turtles—"

"What's so great about seeing a turtle?" J. R. asks.

"Was it fun to be with Uncle Lloyd?" I ask.

The kid shrugs.

"Did you guys have a good talk?"

Ann Marie leans in. "J. R. wasn't really in a talkative mood."

I look down at the boy. "Seems like you haven't been in a talkative mood for a while." I take a long lick of my cone. "I can relate, you know. I've been feeling pretty shitty myself lately. And you know what? When you feel like that, nothing feels quite so good as feeling sorry for yourself."

I notice a small flicker of the boy's eyelashes, but he doesn't look up from his frozen custard.

"Yep," I continue, "wallowing in a puddle of self-pity is like being a pig in shit. You're just rolling around in all your own bullshit and that's all you want to do—no matter what anyone else tries to tell you."

"Henry," Ann Marie whispers, "the *language* . . ."

I ignore her. "But finally, you know what happens, J. R.? You realize shit *stinks*. Phew! Oh my God, it *reeks!* And you find you've got it smeared all over yourself."

Finally the kid looks up at me. Despite himself, he's smiling. The sure-fire way to get a nine-year-old boy to smile is to talk about stinky shit.

"So you know what I'm going to do?" I ask him. "I'm going home after I eat this delicious frozen custard and I'm taking the hottest shower I can. I think it's time I cleaned myself up, don't you?"

"You're weird, Uncle Henry," J. R. says, but he's still smiling.

"Yes, I am weird," I agree. "It's both a blessing and a curse."

I finish my cone and bid the two of them good-bye. I hop back into the Jeep, honking the horn as I pull out of the lot.

I'm not sure this is the best time to talk to Lloyd about what happened with Luke, given that he's probably disappointed he didn't have much success with J. R. today. But I can't put it off any longer. I'm determined to move on, to stop wallowing in my own shit, just as I told the boy. I need to own up to what happened, and then try to figure out where—if anywhere—Luke and I might be heading.

Yet when I walk in, the guesthouse has an odd stillness hanging over it. I can't quite figure out what it is that I feel when I step inside. No one's at the front desk—but since all our guests are already checked in, and we're notexpecting any others, no one needs to be. Still, Lloyd is usually somewhere nearby. There's usually some sound, some stir of activity somewhere.

"Lloyd?" I call.

No answer. I flip open my phone and call over to his house next door. I get the machine. Maybe he and Jeff have gone out.

Then I notice the light on in the basement. I take a deep breath. If Lloyd's not around, I do have one other task to attend to.

I need to talk with Luke.

It's time for him to be honest with me.

Who *are* you?

And who am I *to* you?

I want to know.

Heading down the stairs, my heart is beating fast. I'm not sure why I'm so nervous. Nothing's really changed since our talk this morning on the breakwater. All that's happened is that I found out that he put the moves on Jeff. So what? Who cares? I just need to clarify that what happened between us was real, and figure out if he's really someone I might want to—

I hear a sound.

A groan.

I step up my pace. Once again, Luke's door is ajar. I hurry into the doorway.

And inside, on the bed, Luke is in the arms of Lloyd.

17

NIRVANA GUESTHOUSE

It's Luke who notices me first. Once again, he doesn't seem surprised to see me. His eyes seem to dance over Lloyd's shoulder, almost as if—could it be possible?—he's *glad* that I've caught him.

Lloyd, however, is a different story.

"Oh, man," he says, rolling off the bed and staggering to his feet, fastening the buttons on his pants.

"Sorry to interrupt," I spit, turning on my heel and hurrying back through the basement toward the stairs.

Lloyd is quickly behind me. "Henry, wait!"

"Why? Looks like you weren't quite finished in there. Carry on!"

I rush up the stairs. Only at the top do I turn around. Lloyd is following, pulling his shirt on over his head.

"Henry," he's calling. "Listen to me, please!"

"Why?" I shout back at him, standing at the top of the stairs arms akimbo. I'm sure I look and sound like some old fishwife. "Why should I listen to you? So you can spout all your feel-good wisdom? Your stupid mumbo-jumbo? Goddamn you, Lloyd! Of everyone, you're the one I always thought I could trust!"

He's reached the top of the stairs. He grabs me by my arms and directs me into the room behind the front desk, where he shuts the door and locks it. "Henry," he implores. "Please sit down."

"I prefer to stand."

He sighs. "I'm sorry, my friend. I know we agreed not to fool around with the staff. I don't know what came over me—"

"I know what came over you! That fucking little temptress and his big sad eyes and cute little stomach!"

"Henry, please—"

If I'd been a bitch to Evan earlier, I'm a raging harpy with Lloyd.

"*Jeff* turned him down!" I shout. "*Jeff* was able to keep control! Goddamn you, Lloyd! You're getting married in a couple of weeks! *Married*! You fucking asshole!"

Lloyd looks at me as if I'm making no sense. "Henry, this has nothing to do with Jeff—"

"Yes it does! Do you know how he's been feeling lately? He's been so inspired by the idea of marrying you that he's not wanted to even *look* at another guy! When that little tramp downstairs threw himself at him yesterday, Jeff turned him down!"

Lloyd sighs, not saying anything. I can tell he didn't know about Luke's attempt to seduce Jeff.

I approach him, my voice still just as shrill. "Do you have any idea how special it is that you and Jeff are getting married?" I poke him in the chest. He moves his eyes to look at me. "Do you? Any idea? Standing up in front of the world and saying, 'We love each other and we're committing to each other for the rest of our lives'?"

"Of course I know how special that is," Lloyd says softly.

"And still you went and did—*that*." I can't even say it. "With that fucking little tramp, who we should have kicked out of here weeks ago."

Lloyd maintains his calmness in the face of my venom. "Henry," he says, "I know you had feelings for Luke. I didn't realize they were still so intense."

I laugh. So there's something else about which Lloyd is still in the dark.

"Luke didn't tell you, did he?" I ask.

"Tell me what?"

I just laugh harder. There's no point now in telling Lloyd about my night with Luke. The sooner I forget it, the better.

"Henry, please," Lloyd says. "I know I shouldn't have done it. He was just upset, and he was near tears, and I was comforting him, and . . . and things got carried away."

I look at him hard. "Did you ask him what he was upset *about*?"

"I tried, but he wasn't saying much. He started to cry and I put my arms around him."

"Oh, man." I cover my face with my hands and move as far away from Lloyd as I can.

"Henry," he implores. "What did I say?"

I face him. "That's what happened with me, wasn't it? When you and I made love all those years ago. Do you remember?"

"Of course I remember."

I look at him. "I was upset that night, too. Near tears. Maybe I even shed a few. And you took me in your arms and we made love." I laugh, bitterly. "So once again Dr. Lloyd to the rescue. Do you enjoy playing the savior to lost boys?"

"Henry, you and I were *friends*. I cared about you. That's why it happened between us." He gestures toward the door. "I care about Luke, but not the way I cared about you then, or certainly not the way I care about you now."

I can't bear to hear any of this. "You know, nothing matters at the moment. I just need some time away from this place." I bend over, typing in a few keys on the computer. I find the information I'm looking for. "There are no reservations until next weekend. I'm going to take a couple of days off. Is that okay?"

"Yes," Lloyd says calmly.

I turn and face him bitterly. "You're free to go back downstairs now and finish your ministrations."

He's looking at me without any emotion. "That's it? You just want to cut this discussion off like that?"

"Actually I do."

He's angry at me for shutting down, for closing him off. "You don't want to talk about this anymore? You just want to leave without telling me what's really going on for you?"

I won't budge. "That about sums it up."

"Fine." He turns to leave, pausing at the door. "Have it your way then, Henry. Enjoy your days off." He closes the door behind him.

Whether Lloyd goes back downstairs to Luke, I don't know. I doubt it—but who's to say? Maybe he just can't help succumbing to the crafty little Lolita. Either way, I really don't care.

I pack quickly, not wanting to run into anyone. I have no idea where I'm going, just that I want to get out of Provincetown. I want as much distance between myself and all of these people— Luke, Lloyd, Jeff—as possible.

It's not until I cross the Sagamore Bridge that I realize where I'm going.

It takes three hours, and three repetitions of Pearl Jam's *No Code*, to get to my parents' home in West Springfield. As always, it looks the same. A two-story colonial with a front façade of white brick, carefully trimmed hedges along the driveway, a rusty old basketball hoop over the two-car garage. My father's green Buick LeSabre sits outside.

Why did I come here?

Maybe because, at this moment, I have nowhere else to go.

"Henry?"

My mother's on the front step, making a great show of surprise to see my Jeep pulling into her driveway.

"If that's my son, I'm not sure I'd recognize him," she's saying to no one in particular. "We might have to fingerprint him just to be sure."

"Hello, Mom."

I give her my cheek. She kisses me on the lips instead and grips me by the shoulders.

"Oh, it's him all right! It's my Henry!"

She pulls me into her embrace. She smells of talcum powder. For a fleeting moment, I'm glad I'm home. I'm glad my mother is hugging me.

"Herbert!" She's calling into the house as we enter. "Your son is home!"

My father, no doubt holed up in the basement watching TV, makes no reply. My mother's gesturing for me to sit as we walk into the kitchen. There's a pot of chicken soup bubbling on the stove. The place reeks of boiled chicken. How perfect is that? I come home, feeling lost and adrift, and my mother's got a pot of chicken soup waiting for me.

"That soup's not for you," she says, apparently observing the flare of my nostrils. "It's for Mrs. Pilarski down the street. Her husband just dropped dead. Sixty-two. *Sixty-two*! That's not old anymore! They found him out in the backyard. He'd been cutting back his tomato plants. And poof. He was gone."

She shakes her head and walks over to the stove, where she gives the soup a stir. I notice how thick her hips have gotten, and the hint of hunched shoulders. Her hair is almost all gray now, which only a few strands of her once vibrant auburn.

"How long can you stay, Henry?"

"Well, I'm heading into New York," I lie, "and thought I'd just stop and say hi . . ."

"So a few days then?"

"Well, I don't know . . ."

"Herbert! Come upstairs! Your son has deigned us with his presence for the next few days."

One of the big events of my childhood was the refinishing of our basement. Carpeting was rolled in over the concrete floors. Paneling went up along the walls; a drop ceiling was put in. A toilet with a very loud and powerful pump was installed in a closet-sized bathroom. Once the thirty-six-inch television was built into the wall, my father was all set. He could practically live in the basement, coming up only for meals. He sometimes even slept down there on the couch.

I hear no sign of him stirring, and for a moment I have a flash of old Mr. Pilarski dead among his tomato plants. But if Dad's watching television—probably some History Channel documentary on the Great War —then he's not going to stir no matter who's just arrived upstairs.

"Why are you going to New York?" my mother asks.

I think fast. "To see some friends." I can't tell her the real reason I left Provincetown, that I'm a lonely miserable slob who feels he can't trust anyone. But she probably already guesses that anyway. "I have a couple days off, so I'm on no set schedule."

My mother makes that clicking sound in her throat. "After the summer, you *need* some time off, Henry," she tells me. "I know how hard you work running that guesthouse. Lloyd should make you part owner of the place, if you ask me."

"I don't *want* to be an owner," I tell her, for the hundredth time.

"Henry, will you *ever* own your own house? You're thirty-*three*."

"Mom, what do you have to drink in the fridge?"

She's immediately opening the refrigerator door, peering inside and ticking off the contents. "I've got tomato juice, seltzer, whole milk—sorry, Henry, I refuse to buy that skim—ginger ale, and cranberry juice."

"Would you pour me some ginger ale?"

"Of course, baby. Do you want a sandwich? I've got some turkey."

"Sure, Mom."

She pours me a tall glass of ginger ale and busies herself making the sandwich. "Did you see the new pictures of Rachel and Rebecca when you walked through the living room?"

Rachel and Rebecca are my sister Susan's twin daughters. "No, I didn't," I tell her.

"Well, go back in there now and look."

"I'll look in a minute."

"They are adorable! They're twelve now. When was the last time you saw Rachel and Rebecca, Henry?"

I sigh. "Last spring."

"Well, they've grown even since then. They are beautiful girls. Beautiful!"

"I know they are," I say. "I wish I could see them more often. But Susan lives so far up in the Berkshires—"

"Yes, I know she does, but she gets down to see us, and she's nearly as far away as you," Mom says, employing her usually exaggeration. "Go in and look at the twin's pictures!"

"Can I eat my sandwich first?" I ask as she places it in front of me.

Her tone quickly changes. "Of course, darling. Are you hungry? Why didn't you say so?"

The phone rings. I take my first bite as my mother rushes to answer it. The caller appears to be some neighbor, for she immediately launches into the account of poor old Mr. Pilarski dropping dead amid his tomato plants. "I know! Right there in the backyard! And Evelyn found him! She'd been calling and when he didn't come in, she went out to look and there he was . . ."

I decide to take my sandwich and my ginger ale downstairs. My father, no surprise, is in his recliner, feet up. He's watching TV as I imagined, but instead of World War II, it appears to be a feature on the Loch Ness monster.

"Hey Dad," I say.

"Henry."

I look at the screen. "So do you believe in Nessie?"

He shrugs. "I believe she's made quite a bit of money for some obscure village in Scotland we otherwise wouldn't know a damn thing about."

"This is true." I sit down just as the show turns to a commercial. "How've you been, Dad?"

For forty years, Dad was a claims adjustor for an insurance company. It's why I went into insurance myself. Every day Dad tied his tie and put on his sports jacket and drove to his office in downtown Springfield, arriving at eight thirty sharp. He did his work, ate his lunch, and was home by five forty-five. About ten months ago, he accepted an early retirement package. Now he's here in the basement stretched out in his recliner nearly round the clock. Mom usually brings his meals down to him.

"Can't complain," Dad says. "Things aren't bad."

I notice a stack of DVDs on the table next to his chair. Old *Honeymooners* reruns. The TV miniseries *The Winds of War*. And the complete Benny Hill collection.

I smile. "Looks like you won't run out of viewing choices."

"Your sister is always bringing me something new. She worries about me down here. Thinks I'm just going to rot away and get Alzheimer's if I'm not engaging the brain."

I look around the room. My hideous high school picture sits in a frame on a bookshelf. "You pretty much keep to yourself, huh?"

"Well, your mother comes down with supper and once in a while she'll sit here with me if there's something good on the tube." He shrugs. "But she's got the upstairs and I've got this rec room here. So it works out."

I sit back in the chair looking over at him. When did the tall, distinguished man who was my father become this old, overweight, gray-haired codger in a recliner? It's not that his life was ever very broad, but Dad had his friends. He liked a game of cards once in a while with his buddies. Now, according to my mother, ever since his retirement he's content just to sit down here watching television. Yet he doesn't seem unhappy.

"Look, you see there," he says, pointing at the TV screen. The Loch Ness monster documentary has resumed, and it's showing the famous image of Nessie's long neck sticking out of the water like a brontosaurus. "They've done some kind of, what do you call it, digital enhancement of that picture, and they can see it's a fake. Some guy cooked it up fifty years ago, and they're still showing the damn thing."

I nod, looking from the screen back at him. "Are you happy, Dad?" I ask.

I don't know where the question comes from. It's an echo of the question Mom asked me not so long ago, the one that sent me scrambling for an answer. My father looks over at me strangely.

"Happy?" he asks. "What the hell kind of question is that?"

"You're right. I'm sorry."

"Don't start lecturing me like your sister does," he tells me, returning his gaze to the TV set. "I'm doing just fine."

"I wasn't really asking about you," I admit. "I guess I was thinking about me. You know, what's ahead for me."

My father gives me one eye, but keeps the other on Nessie. "Well, I suppose you're luckier than I was. You don't have a job that you'll need to retire from."

I lift my eyebrows in surprise. "You used to say that was *un*lucky. That by quitting my job at the insurance firm I was giving up my pension."

"That's true." He's quiet a moment, apparently engrossed in something the narrator is saying about Nessie. "But on the other hand," he continues, "whatever you seem to be doing with that guesthouse, you seem to be enjoying it. And doing work that you enjoy, being employed by none but yourself, means you can keep on working right until the day you drop. You might not have any benefits, but you don't have any boss kicking you out either."

I nod. "I do enjoy my work," I say, as much to myself as to him. "But work's not all there is."

"What else is there?"

"Well, you had a family by the time you were my age."

He nods. "Yes, I did." He turns to face me. "You thinking of adopting a kid, Henry? They had a special on CNN the other night about all these gays adopting kids."

"No no no," I say. "I don't even have a partner."

"A lot of these gays didn't either. I don't think you need two to raise a kid, to be perfectly honest. Your mother did it all on her own."

"What do you mean? She had you."

He shakes his head. "I was never around. I was either at the office, or down here watching TV, or at Charlie's playing poker on a Sunday afternoon. Am I not right?"

I shrug. "Mom was always the disciplinarian."

"And the cook, and the chauffeur, and the bedtime story-teller."

"You were the breadwinner."

"Okay. So I did that. My point is, Henry, if you want a kid and you don't have a special someone in your life, you should still get the kid."

"I don't want a kid." I pause. "I want a special someone."

My father looks over at me. With a deep breath he lifts the remote control from the table beside him and snaps off the television set. The sudden quiet startles me, as it always does.

"You ever had a special someone, Henry?" my father asks. "Not sure I've ever heard you speak of one."

"You met Joey briefly last year," I remind him. "But, looking back, I suppose he doesn't really qualify as a special someone. I used to think he did, but not anymore."

Dad sighs. "They're hard to find."

"You found Mom."

"Yes, I did," he agrees. "And do you have any idea how much I loved your mother when I first met her?"

I shake my head.

"I thought about her day and night," he tells me. "I couldn't wait to be in her presence. When she agreed to marry me, I got down on my knees—literally—and thanked God."

It's an odd image. My parents have never been affectionate. In my memories, they're mostly apart. Mom at the stove, Dad down here. In the few family photos that include all of us, Mom and

Dad are always at opposite ends of the picture, their kids between them. They've never really argued, at least not that I ever saw, but they've never really joked either, or shared a kiss or a squeeze. But still. *Forty-one years together.*

"So that's why it's lasted," I say. "You were deeply in love."

"No." He shakes his head forcefully. "The key to a successful marriage is to fall *out* of love."

"What?"

He winks at me. "When I was twenty, I couldn't leave your mother alone for an instant. Now it's forty years later, and sometimes we go days without seeing each other. She'll call down and ask if I want a sandwich and I'll tell her I can make one down here." He gestures to a small refrigerator on the far wall. "So long as she keeps that stocked with turkey, cheese, and strawberry ice cream, I'm fine."

I laugh. "All the creature comforts."

"Absolutely. So sometimes it's literally days that we don't see each other. And that's okay. She's got her interests, I've got mine. She talks on that phone nonstop with all her old lady friends. She goes into town to get her hair done. She goes out to play canasta. I stay here and watch my shows. So we're both happy."

"No offense, Dad," I tell him, "but I don't think that's how I want it to go with my special someone."

"That's the way it goes with *all* special someones, Henry. Gay, straight, in-between."

I fold my arms across my chest. "I don't want to become that cynical, Dad."

"It's not being cynical. It's being practical. I've seen some husbands and wives who are always bitching at each other. She's telling him to turn off the TV set and he's yelling at her to stop her nagging. Your mother and I never have a cross word. We live here in perfect harmony."

Almost as if on cue, my mother is calling down the stairs. "Herbert, send Henry up. I want to show him the pictures of the twins."

"Yes, dear," my father calls back, gesturing for me to do as she bids.

I stand. Above us, I can hear the sound of my mother's footsteps crossing the linoleum kitchen floor. I look down at my father in his chair.

"But tell me one thing, Dad." I point up at the ceiling with my thumb. "That's a good sound, isn't it? Sitting down here, knowing she's upstairs, knowing you're not alone."

He shrugs.

"You'd miss those footsteps if they suddenly stopped," I tell him.

He sighs. "I suppose I would."

"Deep down, you love her as much as you did when you were twenty."

He flicks the television back on. "More," he says.

I smile. I head up the stairs with my dishes to look at pictures of my sister's girls.

That night, I lie awake a long time in my childhood bed. On the bureau against the wall stands the trophy I won in third grade for the school science fair. On the wall, a poster of Kurt Cobain, frayed at the edges, still hangs, affixed by red thumbtacks. How many hours did I sit in this room, my headphones clamped over my ears, listening to my music and trying to imagine what my future outside this house would be like? How many dreams did I have in this bed, dreams of a life I could barely imagine but wanted so much to someday make real?

I knew I was gay at a young age. I'd lie here, staring at this very same ceiling, and imagine myself as an adult, living openly as a gay man, walking with my lover, refusing to hide—the way my old friend Jack had done. Jack—who had gone off as a teenager to find a life as a gay man, something I'd have to wait many years to find.

But still, I knew it was out there, waiting for me. I'd read the accounts in *Time* and *Newsweek* about gays "coming out of their closets." I also read about men who would marry and have children and live a lie. I knew I could never live a lie. I was determined to fall in love, to find my Prince Charming and live happily ever after. I'd scrunch my pillow to my face, the way I'm doing now, visualizing my soulmate beside me. In my mind, he was a handsome man with a cleft chin who looked something like Richard

Gere, except that I still always called him "Jack." I'd fall asleep with Jack breathing in my ear beside me.

Lying here now, the sounds of my childhood both comfort and unsettle me. There's the familiar sound of the clock on my bureau, the sound of the dehumidifier clicking on every fifteen minutes in the hallway. Outside my window a certain night bird hoots, a sound I've never heard anywhere else but in West Springfield.

I don't belong here anymore, if I ever really did. Right now I miss Lloyd and Jeff and Ann Marie and J. R. something fierce. I miss Provincetown, where the only sounds at night are the faraway calls of the foghorn—except on summer nights, when horny gay boys are always on the street. That's my home. That's where I belong. That's where I should be, not here in my bed of childhood dreams, which only makes me feel as if I've come full circle, without having gotten anywhere at all.

But still, I think I needed to come here tonight. I needed to come back to this place. It's been a reminder that I *do* have a family—and as much as I love Mom and Dad, it's not them. My family—my real family—are not the people in this house. I might not have a lover, but I do have a family that loves me.

I know Lloyd would never have let himself be seduced by Luke if he'd realized I'd slept with the kid the night before. He'd have gently turned Luke down out of consideration to me. Not that he would have been obligated to do so, but I know Lloyd well enough to know he would never knowingly hurt my feelings. Neither would Jeff, not really, for all his occasional insensitivity.

So maybe it's time Henry Weiner stopped being quite so sensitive himself.

I think of my father down in the basement. Apparently, my sister worries about him; I'm not so sure I do. Certainly he's content with his lot, and really, it's not such a bad life. He's at the stage when he doesn't need another person to wrap up his happiness and hand it to him like a birthday present. He's learned how to make himself happy, with his TV programs and private refrigerator stocked with ice cream. I smile. The more I think about it, the more I realize how much my Dad and I are alike.

Lloyd's voice is in my head: *You should be complete by yourself.* And then Shane: *You won't be able to really love anyone until you learn to love yourself.*

My smile broadens as I imagine Shane in drag, doing Whitney Houston, warbling about "The Greatest Love of All."

That's when I hear a light tap at my door.

"Henry?"

It's my mother.

"What is it?" I call.

She opens the door a crack. "Just making sure you're comfortable."

"I'm fine, Mom."

"Well, I'm going to bed now, darling," she says. "You sure you don't need anything?"

I sigh. "Thanks, Mom. I'm really fine."

She makes that sound in her throat. Tiptoeing over to the bed, she plants a kiss on my forehead.

"Henry," she asks, "are you happy?"

For once, I don't hear the question as an accusation.

"I'm getting there, Mom," I assure her. "I'm getting there."

18

DREAMLAND, AGAIN

Here is what I dream this night in my childhood bed.
I'm sitting in a graveyard watching Luke dig up a grave.

No, I don't like this. I need to change the channel. I'm good at doing that in dreams. I'm usually conscious enough to change my dreams, to turn them around, to change direction if I don't like the way they're heading.

If only I could do that awake, too. But only asleep do I seem to have that power.

Slowly I make Luke, his shovel and the graveyard disappear. But I sense the kid is still following me. I'm hurrying, rushing somewhere. Behind me I hear Luke's footsteps, and they're gaining on me.

We're running across the breakwater, which doesn't seem to end. Instead of terminating on the sandy shores of Long Point, the rocks continue out across the water, leading into infinity. I'm running faster and faster, jumping from rock to rock, terrified of falling in between, getting stuck—because then Luke would catch up with me. He'd be on me. He'd get me. And I'd be—

I'd be what?

Why am I so frightened of Luke?

He's just a kid.

I stop running. I turn to look behind me. Luke is some distance away but he's approaching fast. I stand my ground. I wait for him. But as he nears, I see it's not Luke at all. It's someone I don't know, a haggard looking man, wasted from illness. He runs right past me, not even stopping to look.

"That was Darryl," comes a voice behind me.

Luke has magically appeared at my side. I don't question how it happened. It's a dream after all.

"Why is he running?" I ask.

"Because you don't think he's real."

I look at him closely. "Is he?"

Luke laughs. "Henry, you just *saw* him!"

"No, I only *read* about him."

"You think I'm a brilliant writer, don't you?"

"I think you're a messed-up kid," I tell him. "But I want to help you."

"You do? Really? Even after all that's happened?"

I grip him by the shoulders.

"I think you're Darryl," I tell him. "I think Darryl is you."

All at once Luke's soft features begin to dissolve. They seem to melt, as if all the flesh behind his skin dries up. Suddenly, instead of a beautiful young boy, there's a wasted cadaver standing in front of me. I pull back, letting out a sharp cry.

"You don't want to help me," says this hideous version of Luke. It runs away from me, down across the rocks of the breakwater.

I sit up in bed in a cold sweat.

Is that it? Is it *Luke* who has AIDS?

I used a condom when I fucked him, I reassure myself, trying to get back to sleep. But it's difficult to find a comfortable position. My sheets are sticky. I suddenly remember his description of himself, stuck to sweaty sheets, his flesh picked from his bones.

I wish I were home. I mean my *real* home. My *real* bed, in my own apartment. Right now I want nothing more to be back in Provincetown, the foghorn calling outside my window, Jeff and Lloyd and Ann Marie and J. R. just across the way.

In the hallway my parents' dehumidifier clicks on, and finally its low hum lulls me back to sleep.

When I dream again, it is Gale who waits for me. "The thing is,

Henry," he's saying, standing at the top of the stairs outside his apartment, looking down at me below, "you don't know who any of us are."

"That's right," I agree, "because you won't tell me."

He shakes his head, smirking. "You don't ask the right questions."

"Don't go blaming me!" I shout. "I'm not the one who throws you out every time you get too close."

I'm suddenly aware Gale is wearing a long black raincoat belted around his waist. He throws his head back and laughs.

"What is it you want from me, Henry? *This?*"

And suddenly he throws open his raincoat, revealing his naked body. His dick must be a foot long with an enormous mushroom head. I gasp out loud.

He runs into his apartment.

"No, not this time," I shout. "Not this time are you going to get away!"

I hurry up the stairs in pursuit. But when I get inside his place it's not Gale's apartment at all. It's Evan and Curt's condo, and I spot them in the hot tub. But they're not alone. They're submerged up to their shoulders with Jeff and Lloyd—as well as a fifth person I can't make out right away.

"Do you have Luke in there with you?" I ask.

"No," replies the fifth person, hidden in shadows. "Luke's not here."

I peer in close so I can make him out.

It's Martin.

"Come on in, Henry," Martin says. "The water's fine."

"No, thanks," I say. I'm angry that he's in there with them. It feels wrong somehow. I feel betrayed by him in some crazy sort of way.

"You sure you won't give it a try, Henry?" Martin asks.

"No. I've got to find Luke."

"Suit yourself," Martin says.

I head outside into a very bright day. The sunlight nearly blinds me, in fact. I realize that I'm working my way through a crowd. I'm at Tea Dance. Boys everywhere, shirtless and delicious, and a majestic blue sky dropping into the green sea beyond. There's one thing wrong, however. There's no music. The soundtrack of my dream has gone silent. Utterly, eerily silent.

I spot Luke leaning against the railing, in the spot where I first met him. He's drinking a bottle of water. He looks good. Real good. Sexy, dreamy, unattainable. Backlit by the sun, he seems to glow. His eyes flicker over to me when he realizes I've seen him.

"Hi," he says, "I'm Luke."

We shake hands.

"You'll protect me, won't you, Henry?" he asks, holding my gaze and refusing to let go of my hand.

"Of course," I promise him. "But protect you from whom?"

"My father," he says. "You know what he did to me."

"From your writing, I have some clue," I tell him. "Let me make it all better for you."

"Yes, Henry, please."

I take him in my arms.

"We don't have to live with hurt and fear all our lives," I tell him. "Let me make you happy, Luke. I know I can make you happy. Make you forget all the pain."

We kiss. My heart swells with a sense of happiness at last. This is what I have searched for . . .

But when I pull away from the kiss, Luke is the wasted cadaver he was earlier. He starts to laugh, revealing skeleton teeth.

"You said you'd protect me," he says between laughter.

"Then tell me the truth!" I demand. "Be real! Tell me who you are!"

He just keeps laughing, his body decaying right here in my arms.

No, I don't like this.

Time to change the channel.

By sheer force of will, I cause Luke to change back to his beautiful self.

"There," I say. "That's better. You'll tell me now? Who you really are?"

"Yes," Luke says, contrite. "I will."

Of course, at that very moment, I wake up.

And he was just about to tell me who he was! He was just about to be honest with me for the first time!

I fall back to sleep, determined that, come morning, I'll retain that skill to change things if I don't like them. It will no longer be a power that works only in dreams.

19

BACK BAY, BOSTON

It feels good being back in Boston, with all its hustle and bustle. I've stopped here on my way back to Provincetown, figuring an infusion of city life is just what I need.

"And maybe a new look, too," I say to myself as I walk along Newbury Street, my gaze bouncing from boy to boy, each and every one them *stylin'*, as they say. Good hair, hip clothes, accessorized with BlackBerries and iPods. I determine that some new clothes and accessories are the order of the day.

I pop in to see the stylist who used to cut my hair when I lived in the city. "Sweetie," Pierre says, taking a good look at me up and down. "You still look like you did when you left Boston. How many years ago was that now?"

"Never mind counting. Just work your magic."

Pierre gives me one of those new faux-hawks, kind of like a Mohawk without the buzzcut. He cuts my hair closer on the sides while gelling and pushing the top into a raised line across the center of my scalp.

"Whaddya think?" he asks, turning the chair so I can face the mirror.

I'm not quite sure, but lots of the guys on Newbury Street were sporting this do. I give Pierre the thumbs up.

After that, I hit a couple of shops, buying myself some new clothes. I stop in at all my favorites at the Copley Place Mall. It's just what every lonely hearted girl needs as a pick-me-up: a fresh wardrobe for fall. I buy whatever I see on the mannequins. At Abercrombie, I snatch up a bunch of T-shirts with numbers on the chest (I've heard "9" subliminally draws attention). At Banana Republic, I choose a couple of those new striped, collared, short-sleeved shirts that I've seen guys wearing, half-tucked into their jeans and collar up. I pick out a lime green and a powder blue.

"Great choices," says the clerk as he rings me up. He's a very young, pimply faced boy wearing a similar shirt, except his is pink.

"Thanks," I say, quite certain that he's flirting with me. I practically dance out of the shop.

I ignore the obvious: that everyone else looking at the same shirts is a good ten years younger than I am.

Stuffing my bundles into the back of my Jeep, I look around at the city. Once, this was my life. This was home. This is where I came when I was young and naïve. This is where I came of age, where I finally found the life I'd dreamed about in my childhood bed.

But Boston is no longer home. I start the ignition. It's time to head back to Provincetown.

I've been gone three days. Both Jeff and Lloyd have left a couple of messages on my cell, telling me whenever I want to come home, they'll be ready to talk. I feel like a selfish brat running out like this, especially with their wedding coming up in less than two weeks. They shouldn't be worrying about me; they should be gearing up for their big day.

When I pull into the driveway of the guesthouse, there's a Land Rover parked in my usual spot. I glance up at the porch and spot a couple of guys heading back down the steps.

I'm quite surprised to see that it's Evan and Curt.

"Hey," I call out the window.

"Hey," they each call back.

I park the Jeep on the side of the Land Rover and hop out. "What's up?" I ask.

Evan smiles. "We were dropping off our number in New York."

Curt's eyes twinkle. "In case you ever want to come to visit us."

I'm actually touched. "Thanks," I say. "You heading back to the city?"

They nod. "I wish we didn't have to," Evan says. "You are very lucky to live here full-time, Henry, you know that?"

"I suppose I am." I smile. "Thanks for reminding me."

"Hey," Evan says, his eyes finding mine. "You have time for a quick walk? We were thinking of taking a stroll on the beach before we get on the road."

"Sure," I say, feeling far more generous toward him than I did a few days before. "But it's not raining," I add, a small smile on my face.

Evan smiles back at me. "We'll have to do that another time."

We cross the street and trudge through some straggly sea grass to reach the east end beach. Except for a flock of gulls, we're the only ones out here.

"It never fails to amaze me how fast the town empties out after Labor Day," I say.

"There are many rhythms of life in Provincetown," Evan observes, "and it is the collective dance that makes this place what it is."

I laugh. "That's rather poetic."

"Evan's a poet," Curt says, "and doesn't know it."

We all laugh. "My first six years in Provincetown were spent as the classic summer gay resident," Evan says. "Friends and I would rent a house from Memorial Day to Labor Day. We managed to spend most weekends here, and usually a couple of solid weeks in August. They were heady, boisterous days. I was in my early twenties and full of spunk."

I look off at the water. "Well, I was a kind of Johnny-come-lately to the party, but I had a few years of spunk myself."

"I bet you did," Curt says, winking.

Evan seems lost in a world of his own. "Back in those days, we didn't give much thought as to what the winter must be like here. After all, didn't Tea Dance shut down in September?"

We all laugh again, then I look rather seriously at Evan. "And now you'd like to experience life here year-round."

He nods. "I'd like to quit my job like you did, Henry, and find a way to make a living here."

"A romantic dream," Curt says. "But if we could do it, we would."

"Maybe I'm just caught up in the memory of those glorious summer days when I was just a young kid full of dreams," Evan says. "I look back on that time with a great deal of warmth and nostalgia. I know it seems frivolous, but those days were very special."

"Of course they were," I tell him.

Evan seems buoyed by my affirmation. "You know, I had a show at my gallery not long ago featuring the work of some of the great artists of Provincetown. We did a whole history of the vibrant arts scene here from the 1940s through the 1960s. But you know what I realized?"

"Tell me."

"That my experience was every bit as genuine and valuable as the heyday of the Abstract Expressionists or the counter-culture days of Andy Warhol. I really believe this. It was the early 90s, and gay culture was just starting to step out loudly and proudly, and I was part of that fresh new energy."

"Yeah," I say, "Jeff writes about that period in *The Boys of Summer . . .*"

Evan shakes his head. "Yeah, but unlike your friend Jeff, I wasn't interested in anything beyond just having a good time. I wasn't part of any literary or intellectual crowd back then. My friends were just a bunch of partiers. I remember once feeling a bit hedonistic and superficial, and I expressed some embarrassment when I ran into an older guy I admired a great deal. He'd just spent his evening among painters and poets having lots of fascinating cultural conversation. Meanwhile, I was still slightly buzzed from a Foam Party at the Crown and Anchor with a bunch of house boys and rowdy tourists."

"Hey," I tell him. "That was who you were then."

"Exactly! And this is what my older friend told me. He said, 'Dawling'—he was from the Bronx and always pronounced 'darling' as 'dawling'—'what you experienced tonight was every bit as much of a Provincetown experience as mine was. Be glad you're a part of it.'"

"It's true," I say. "I remember those Foam Parties myself, and sleeping in until noon, stirring to life gradually as the sun pushed through my shades, and the heat in the room became unbearable."

Curt is smiling. "There was a certain lazy, glorious rhythm to those days, wasn't there? Dragging our sleepy heads to the beach, where we'd bake until it was time for Tea. Then came After Tea, remember that?"

I'm grinning ear to ear. "Yeah, I loved After Tea. It just kept the party going."

"Then, of course," Evan adds, "that was followed by dinner and a nap before sprucing up for the bar. Summer Camp at the Crown—remember that? And the Love Shack!"

"And finally, pizza among the throngs on the steps of Spiritus," I say.

"Some things, thankfully, never change," Curt says.

"But *we* do." Evan has stopped walking. He looks from me to Curt, then back to me again. "We're older now, and other things matter more now. Tricking, dancing, sleeping late—there's more to Provincetown than all that, as wonderful as it was."

"I agree," I tell him.

"Now it's about relationships. It's about finding a sense of home and family." He looks out over the water. "It's about being who you are in a place that allows you unlimited possibilities."

I smile. "Sometimes I've worried that Provincetown limits my possibilities. Thanks for reminding me how wrong that is."

Evan smiles. "Will you see us again, Henry?"

I look from him to Curt, not sure what to say.

Evan fills in the silence. "I've felt badly ever since our phone conversation," he tells me. "I don't want you to think I was just playing you."

"It means a lot to hear you say that," I reply. "I've been losing faith with people lately. Maybe I've been a little premature in my judgments."

"Give us a chance," Evan says, drawing close.

He kisses me. Deep, full. Our lips part and I taste his tongue. Curt is beside me now, and I kiss him, too.

"When can you come to New York?" Evan asks.

"I . . . I don't know."

"We'd like you to visit us," Curt offers.

"I . . . I like you guys. I just don't know what I want our friendship to be."

Evan nods. "That's okay. We can just see what happens."

"At the very least," I say, "I'd like to get to know you both better.'

"Well," Evan says, "we'll be back at Halloween. It's so much fun here on Halloween. We'd love to see you again then."

I nod. "I'm open to the possibility."

Evan smiles. "That's all we can ask."

We head back up to the guesthouse. We kiss again, all three of us. Then they get into their car and drive out of town.

For a moment I miss them terribly.

I take a deep breath, collecting my things out of my Jeep. Did I really mean what I just said? That I was "open to the possibility"? What the hell does that mean? The possibility of exactly *what*? Having sex with them again? Moving into a three-way dating situation with them? Could I do that? Would I *want* it?

Inside the guesthouse, Lloyd is at the front desk. He says nothing when I enter. He just walks over to me and gives me a tight bear hug. I hug him back. Over his shoulder I notice a young guy with a mop of black curls hauling a basket of laundry down into the basement.

"Who's he?" I ask.

Lloyd smiles wryly. "Our new houseboy."

"Lloyd, you didn't need to fire Luke over me."

He shakes his head. "I didn't fire him. He quit."

I sigh. "It's probably for the best."

Lloyd nods. "Henry, I want you to know, if I'd been aware of what happened, I would never have done anything with—"

I hold my hand up to stop him. "I know." I make sure the new houseboy, whatever his name, is safely down the stairs and out of earshot. "Does Jeff know what happened with you and Luke?"

Lloyd nods. "Of course. I told him."

"And what did he say?"

"Nothing."

"Nothing at all?"

He sighs. Suddenly I see the heaviness in his eyes, the slump of his shoulders. "He didn't need to say anything. I saw the hurt quite plain. He told me he wanted a few days to think." He closes his eyes. "I haven't seen him since."

"Holy fuck," I say, sitting down hard in a chair.

Lloyd sits opposite me. "I don't understand it fully. I mean, we have an open relationship. We both, from time to time, have outside connections . . ."

"This is hardly outside, Lloyd," I say, anger starting to tighten my throat again. "This was right here in the guesthouse."

Lloyd stands up, agitated. "I know! It was wrong! It was stupid and inappropriate!" He paces over to the desk then turns and walks back toward me. "But I don't get Jeff's reaction. It's far more intense than I would have expected."

I stand up and face him. "And you have no clue why?"

"If you have some idea," he says to me, "I'd like to hear it."

"For a bright man, you can be incredible dense," I say, stunned that I can use such a word to describe Lloyd Griffith, my hero, my inspiration. "In less than two weeks you're going to be getting married. You can't appreciate how hearing about you and Luke made Jeff feel?"

"I didn't realize it would be so . . ."

"Come on, Lloyd. Jeff has been wanting to make your wedding really, really special, and so he's been refraining from any—what did you call them?—'outside *connections.*' It hasn't been easy for him. He turned down Luke himself!"

Lloyd looks at me with interest. It's clear he didn't know that little detail.

"It's true," I say. "Luke came on to him. But Jeff said no. Can you believe it? Jeff O'Brien! Mr. I-Can't-Help-Myself-Around-Cute-Boys. He turned him down! I have to tell you, I have gained a whole new measure of respect for Jeff because of this attitude."

"I didn't know he was feeling that way," Lloyd says, his hand on his forehead. "He never shared this with me."

"He didn't want to say anything to you. He didn't want you to feel pressured to act the same."

Lloyd gives me a dry little laugh. "Then if that's the case, then isn't he being a little hypocritical to walk out?"

"Since when has Jeff ever been rational when it came to affairs of the heart?" I sigh. "Still, hypocritical or not, he's hurt." I look at Lloyd intently. "Where is he, any idea?"

"I suspect he's in Boston. Maybe with Melissa and Rose. I've been trying to honor his privacy and not call around looking for him. I know he's been talking with Ann Marie, because I got word from her that he's okay—but she hasn't shared where he is."

"Oh, man." I run my hands through my new faux-hawk, and realize Lloyd hasn't said a word about it. I suppose there hasn't been a moment for any small talk. "What does this mean for the wedding? It's not far off."

Lloyd looks suddenly as if he might cry. "I don't know. We were supposed to be making final plans with the caterer today . . ." He covers his face with his hands. "I just wish he'd come back so we could talk."

My heart breaks. Suddenly making sure Lloyd and Jeff's wedding happens is the most important priority of my life.

I put my arm around my friend's shoulders. "Jeff will be back," I say. "I'll find him and *bring* him back if I have to. Your wedding must happen! You guys must say 'I do.'"

Lloyd removes his hands to look at me, offering me a small smile. "You've become rather the determined advocate, I must say."

I look him deep in the eyes. "You can't let this slip away from you. You've got to make sure this wedding takes place."

His gaze moves off into the middle of the room, staring at nothing. "Maybe," Lloyd says, "I succumbed to Luke because I wasn't ready to settle down into marriage."

I take a step back. "*What?*"

"You know me, Henry," Lloyd says, looking at me, speaking dully. "I'm a freebird. And marriage . . . Maybe I'm not ready. Maybe . . ." His voice cracks a little. "Maybe I don't want the commitment that marriage brings."

"Oh, fuck," I say. "Lloyd, this is *not* how you feel!"

He looks at me sharply. "How do you know I feel?"

"Because I do! I know you guys love each other and you want to spend the rest of your lives together! You want to stand up in front of the world and announce that you have each found the One—"

"Henry," Lloyd says, "I suspect your sudden enthusiasm to see us married is more about *you* than it is about us."

I say nothing.

"Listen," Lloyd says. "I just need some time to think. Jeff needs his space, I need mine." He gestures toward the front desk. "Now that you're back, will you take over? We've got a guest coming in around eight. I just need to go home and be alone for a while and think."

I nod. "Yeah, I can watch the desk. But Lloyd . . ."

He holds up his hand. "No more arguing the case for marriage. Jeff's reaction—well, it's given me pause. Maybe in fact he's not ready to settle down either."

I watch him head out the door. I want to scream after him: *Don't give up! Nothing is too difficult that it can't be worked out! Don't you realize how important this is? Don't give up!*

But I say nothing more. Lloyd's right. My sudden enthusiasm for their wedding does indeed have more to do with me than it does with them. I had come to see their marriage as an ideal—something to which I might aspire. Jeff and Lloyd offered—even with all their idiosyncrasies—*inspiration.* But now, if their union crumbles, what hope does that leave me?

Alone. That's where it leaves me.

I begin going through the mail that has piled up while I've been gone. But my mind can't seem to focus. I can't believe how heartbroken I feel about what's happened between my friends. And all because of that little conniving Luke . . .

I hear a door creak. I look up.

The new houseboy has come up from the basement. We make eye contact.

"Are you Henry?" he asks.

"Yes."

"Lloyd told me you were the manager." He extends his hand. "I'm David."

Yes, you are, I think, shaking his hand. Michelangelo's David. The boy is exquisite. Those black curls. Olive skin. Big brown eyes. Pug nose. Full, red, pouting lips. He could be a Caravaggio painting brought to life.

And . . . is he looking at me?

Are his eyes twinkling?

Oh, no. I will not go *there* again.

I immediately look back down at my paperwork. "Good to meet you, David," I say. "Has Lloyd showed you all the basics?"

"I think so," he tells me.

"Excellent. Then I won't need to repeat anything." I resist the temptation to look back at him. If I do, I fear, all is lost. "Have a good night, David."

I sense him standing there, waiting for me to look at him again, but I keep my eyes on the desk. It's rude, I know, but at the moment I can't do anything else.

Eventually David disappears back down into the basement, and I breathe a sigh of relief. But my heart is still so heavy that I know I won't be able to sleep tonight.

I pick up my phone and start punching in numbers.

I've got to find Jeff. *Their wedding has to take place!*

And yes, not only for them.

For *me.*

20

COMMERCIAL STREET

I'm back on my bike—actually, a new bike—for the first time since
the accident. I'm a little shaky for the first couple of blocks, but
then I start once again gliding easily and confidently. It helps that
there are far fewer people on the street now, fewer irate soccer
moms to run down.

I have no specific destination. I just needed to take a bike ride
and clear my head. I didn't sleep well. My heart aches whenever I
think about Jeff and Lloyd. I left a zillion messages for Jeff with
every friend I could think of, in case he had turned up there. Ann
Marie was coy, not wanting to divulge where Jeff was, or even
whether she knew for sure. On his cell phone voice mail, I left three
long messages, the gist being the same in all of them: "Don't give
up. You guys love each other. Anything—and I mean *anything*—
can be worked out."

Is that why I keep looking from side to side as I cruise down the
street? Am I hoping I'll run into Luke? Maybe. Maybe I really do
believe that anything—*anything*—can be worked out.

But instead of Luke, I run into two other players in my supporting cast on the steps of Spiritus.

Martin and Gale.

They're sitting on one of the benches. On either side stand a
couple of early twentysomething boys. I notice one of them is
wearing a shirt like mine, except he's passed a white belt through

the loops of his jeans. I like the look, so I make a mental note to pick up one just like it.

I approach. I'm very curious to know the connection between Martin and Gale. I hadn't been aware that they knew each other. "Hey," I say.

Martin, no surprise, speaks first. "Well, hello, Henry. How are you?"

"I'm great," I tell him, standing in front of the bench. With my new clothes and new hair, I feel oddly confident. Even a touch cocky.

"Good to hear it," Martin says. "Do you know Gale?"

"Oh, yes," Gale says, nodding at me, holding his emotion in check. "We've made each other's acquaintance."

I smile. "How you doing, Gale?"

"Enjoying this lovely day," he tells me. "Who knows how many more we have left now that summer is over?"

"And these are," Martin says, gesturing to the group of boys standing around the bench. "I'm sorry, boys, I've forgotten all your names."

"I'm Justin," says one. "And this is Kyle, and Zach, and Troy."

I shake hands with each of them in turn.

"They're from Albany," Martin tells me. "We all just met. I happened upon them when I stopped by for a cup of coffee, and we got to chatting about what to see and do in Provincetown." His eyes twinkle. "But just as they were about to wander off and leave me alone, this exquisite young man came by and sat down." He nods over at Gale. "That seems to have made them decide to stay a bit longer."

A couple of the twinks from Albany giggle. I notice all eyes are glued to Gale, who just smirks as he sits there in his tank top and formfitting jeans.

"Is this your first time to P-town?" I ask the boys, not to any one of them in particular but instead to the entire group. After all, they seem to be one monolithic creature, with eyes moving in unison and names that are instantly interchangeable.

"Yep," says one of them—Zach, I think. But none of them look at me for very long. Their gaze remains trained on Gale.

And why not? He's gorgeous. No wonder he had such a hold

on me. Those round biceps and muscled thighs. That smooth skin and eternally youthful face.

Suddenly I'm jealous. Not so much that Gale might take one of these boys home with him—or that one of them might get *him*—but because none of them seem to notice me. Even in my new clothes and my fashionable new hair, I feel invisible. I hate the feeling. But I hate even worse that I'm trying to compete. Instead of just sitting back and observing the situation, as Martin seems to be doing, I'm positioning myself shoulder-to-shoulder with these boys, ten years younger than I am.

"So," I say to the boy nearest me. "What's Albany like?"

"It's good," he says blandly. "You ever been?"

"Twice. When I was a kid. I grew up in West Springfield, so it was only a couple of hours—"

He's ignoring me. Even before the words are out of my mouth he turns and whispers something to the boy next to him. They smile to each other. They seem to be looking at my shirt. Or is it my hair?

Fuck. Are they *laughing* at me?

"So," says another of the boys as he leans in toward Gale. "Do you work here?"

"Odd jobs," Gale tells him, clearly adoring the attention but determined to play hard to get. He's fully aware that just by sitting there doing nothing, he's stimulating all sorts of pheromones in these four youngsters. "Thankfully Martin here has found me some work to do."

I look over at Martin. He nods. "I hired Gale to help me do some carpentry jobs in town," he tells me. "He's very skilled with a hammer."

"I bet he has lots of skills," one of the Albany boys quips.

"That he does," Martin agrees, and I notice that he and Gale exchange a small smile.

Fuck. Have they hooked up? Has Gale gone with—*Martin?*

If my preoccupation with Luke these last few days has pushed Gale off the center stage of my mind, suddenly I'm focused once more on my dark muscled friend. Why is it that we want someone even more when we see others wanting him?

Yet I realize as I stand here in my trendy new clothes that no one except Martin has initiated conversation with me. The Albany boys continue to pepper Gale with inane attempts to start a dialogue, while my presence is utterly irrelevant to any of them, except maybe Martin.

Hey! I want to shout. *Do you know once upon a time guys paid good money just to touch my abs? Do you know I once made two thousand dollars a week just for taking off my clothes?*

"Henry."

I look down. Martin is talking to me. Of all of them, he's the only one aware that another human being stands in front of them.

"Have you been out of town?" he asks. "I haven't seen you around."

"Yeah," I tell him, resentfully withdrawing my attention from Gale, even if temporarily. "I went to see my parents for a few days."

"Ah, being the good son."

"Well, I'm not sure my mother would agree. She was already asking when I was coming back, and complaining when I said I wasn't sure."

"You're a good son regardless," Martin tells me. "I can just tell."

My attention is drawn back to Gale, who has suddenly stood, stretching, showing off his small, lean body. The boys almost all fall down on top of one other.

"Gotta pee," Gale announces, and turns to walk inside the pizza shop. I suspect he did it partly just to show off his butt to these boys.

"You know," I say, not caring how obvious it appears, "so do I."

I follow Gale inside, where a line has formed outside the one restroom.

"So you've been good?" I ask Gale as I come up behind him.

"Just fine," he replies. He makes a point, again, of not asking me.

"Gale," I say, "I'd like to give us another shot."

Even as I say the words, I'm wishing I could take them back. Do I really want to dive into that morass again? Gale's not for me, not with all his rules and expectations. And I still haven't even figured out how I feel about Luke. But I can't deny that seeing Gale out there, the way those boys were all over him, has reignited my interest.

"Really?" Gale turns around to face me. "Okay, Henry. Come by tomorrow night. Say six o'clock?"

"Okay." Part of me wants to say no, forget it, I don't really mean it. But part of me is thrilled, too. "Okay, tomorrow at six o'clock."

The restroom is now free, so Gale heads in. I resist an urge to follow him, to attempt a little make-out session in the bathroom. Gale's pee shy, I remember. He'd no doubt bar the door.

Since I don't really have to pee, I head back outside, where Martin is now bidding good-bye to Justin-Kyle-Zach-Troy.

"Heading home?" I ask him.

He nods. "Enough goofing off. I'm building some cabinets for a customer."

"Hang on, I'll walk with you," I tell him. But first I turn to the boys. "Tell Gale I'll see him tomorrow night," I say, in a deliberately provocative voice. They don't respond.

"A date?" Martin asks me as we walk off down the street.

"Maybe. Kinda sorta." I laugh. "With Gale, it's never all that clear."

"I see."

We walk a few minutes in silence.

"Do you like him?" Martin asks finally.

"Well, I guess I do . . . I think so."

He laughs. "Henry, why are you going out with him if you don't really know why you're doing it?"

I stop walking, so Martin does too. I laugh at myself. Martin's question sums up the absurdity of my life. "Because I'm a fool," I admit. "Because when I saw him sitting there, all of what I'd felt for him in the past came rushing back and I just—" I look over into Martin's eyes. "Because I'm a fool."

"You're not a fool, Henry," he tells me. "Not any more than any man who has ever searched for true love is a fool."

It's the first time I've really appreciated how beautiful Martin's eyes are. Oh, sure, Luke has said so, and I've acknowledged before that Martin was a handsome man. But only now, in the late afternoon sunlight, do I fully appreciate the beauty of his eyes.

They're not just blue. They're iridescent, like a Siberian husky's. Set into his craggy, unshaven face, Martin's eyes *glow*.

"I've been having some...romance confusion," I admit. "There was this other guy..." I decide not to use Luke's name. "And for a moment I thought there might be something happening between us, but I think I was wrong."

"You just think you were wrong?"

I shrug. "How do you ever know for sure?"

"Oh, you'll know," Martin says. "That's the easy part. When you find the right guy, you'll know it."

We're walking again. "Well, if I'm not a fool, I'm a masochist. Always returning for more punishment."

Martin smirks. "Some men in this town would be happy to accommodate."

I laugh. "I don't mean that kind. Though maybe what I do need is a good session with a belt across my butt to wake me up to some common sense."

"Stop, you're getting me all excited."

We both laugh. "I keep going for all the wrong guys," I tell Martin. "Even now, when I know Gale isn't right for me, I still go after him. I don't get it."

"Sometimes you've got to just make absolutely sure," Martin says. "But if you're still not sure after the third or fourth time, then I suspect you're barking up the wrong pair of legs."

"Gale sure does have a nice pair," I say.

"That he does." Martin hesitates, as if he's trying to decide whether to say something. "Look," he says finally, "I've gotten to know Gale in the past week since we've been working together. He's a great guy. But I'm not sure he's ready for a relationship."

"He *thinks* he is," I say. "He thinks he's *more* than ready, in fact, and it's everybody else who's not."

Martin shrugs. "I think the question is, are *you* ready, Henry?"

Once again I stop walking. "No," I say definitively. "I'm getting there, but I'm not quite ready."

Martin beams. "By admitting that, my friend, you've just taken one giant step toward actually *being* ready."

"It's funny, because for so long, I was like Gale, assuming it was always the other guy's fault, that I had all the answers, that if I could just find the right guy, I'd be all set." I shake my head. "So when I kept falling down and failing, I couldn't understand it."

"You may have been falling down, Henry, but you weren't failing."

"Well, it sure felt that way."

Martin shakes his head. "You were simply gaining the experience and the skills and the knowledge you were going to need for when you actually do find the right guy."

I narrow my eyes at him. "So you didn't have all those things? Experience and skill and knowledge? Is that why your relationship ended?"

Martin considers this. "I suppose I didn't have all of those things when Paul and I got together. But I gained them as we went along."

"So why didn't they keep you together?"

He smiles as we resume walking. "Sometimes those same skills help you *out* of a relationship as well as into one."

I think of Jeff and Lloyd but push the thought away. I will not allow myself to think that their wedding might not happen. Instead I ask Martin, "Are you saying you're perfectly content being single now?"

"*Perfectly* content? No, not perfectly. But content. Yes, I'm quite content. I love my life. These past couple of weeks here in Provincetown have made me see the world in a whole new way." He looks off toward the water as we pass between two houses. "For the first time in a very long time, I like being alone with Martin again. He's quite fun to have around."

I smirk. "Do you make it a habit to talk about yourself in the third person?"

"Well, I'm still learning to welcome him back. For a very long time, he was out in the cold." Martin has stopped walking again. He points up a flight of stairs alongside a house. "My apartment," he says.

"Wow, what a great water view."

"And you predicted I couldn't find something," he chides.

I smile. "I'm glad I was wrong."

He looks out toward the harbor. "Waking up to that view every morning, I am so happy to get out of bed. That's quite the novel experience for me. It's been a very long time since I've felt that way."

"I felt that way once, too," I tell him, "when I first moved here."

He looks at me kindly. "But no more?"

I give him a smile. "Tomorrow morning, I'm not sleeping in. I'm getting up the way I used to do, and going running on the beach. I need to remember why I love living here."

"Good for you, Henry," Martin says.

I pause before saying what's on the tip of my tongue. I'm not sure why, but I do. Still, I make sure I say it.

"It is always good talking with you, Martin. Thank you."

He blushes slightly. "Anytime, Henry." Again he gestures up the stairs. "You know where I live."

"I do," I tell him. And before I'm even fully aware of what I'm doing, I lean forward and kiss him on the lips. Not a long kiss— but definitely more than a peck.

We don't speak after that, just wave good-bye with our hands. Martin heads up the stairs and I turn back to walk the way we came. When I pass Spiritus, they're all gone, Gale and his gang of boys. I hop back on my bike, which I'd locked on a nearby fence, and pedal back to the guesthouse.

And—praise be to God—I see Jeff's car parked in the driveway nextdoor.

I hurry over to the house. I tap on the screendoor. I can see Jeff and Lloyd sitting facing each other on opposite couches inside, Mr. Tompkins in Lloyd's lap.

"Am I interrupting?" I ask.

"Come on in, Henry," Jeff calls.

He gets up to embrace me. "Got yourself a new do, eh, Henry?" Jeff drapes his arm around my shoulder as he leads me inside.

I run my hand over my new hair. It feels spiky and hard. "Yeah. You like? I bought a whole new wardrobe in Boston, too."

Jeff cocks an eyebrow. "Watch out world, Henry Weiner is loose."

"How about if we go out and sit in the yard?" Lloyd suggests.

"Good idea," Jeff replies.

Thank God they're speaking to each other.

Only after we've all settled into Adirondack chairs do I realize that Jeff didn't say whether or not he likes my faux-hawk. But no matter. Pierre said I looked ten years younger.

We sit for a few seconds in silence. The sun feels warm on my face. The smell of salt in the air revives my senses.

"So Lloyd was telling me when you walked in how Luke quit," Jeff says. "How did it happen?"

Lloyd sighs. "He said he was rethinking staying on in Province-town for the winter. And I didn't try to persuade him to stay."

I look over at Jeff. "Did he come to say good-bye to you?"

"No," Jeff replies. "I think his attempt to conquer Lloyd was his final word to me."

"Look, I can't sit here making small talk," I say, looking between them. "I have to know that you guys have worked this out."

Jeff begins to speak then stops himself. He and Lloyd exchange looks that I don't like.

"Come on, you guys! Please! You can work this out! Please tell me you can. You can't let this one stupid thing run—"

"Henry." Jeff's voice silences me. "There's nothing to work out."

I sit forward in my chair. "What the fuck does that mean? You guys can't give up on each other! You can't just toss aside—"

"Henry." Now it's Lloyd's voice that cuts me off. "We aren't giving up on each other."

"Or tossing anything aside," Jeff says.

I look at them. I can almost feel my eyes pleading with them.

"So," I ask, "will you please assure me that the wedding is still on?"

Jeff looks at me with eyes I almost don't recognize. "Henry," he asks in a quiet voice, "why has that become so important to you?"

"Because it *is*! Please tell me. Are you still getting married?"

Jeff looks over at Lloyd in the chair next to him. For a second neither says anything. My heart skips a beat.

Then Lloyd reaches over and takes Jeff's hand.

"Of course we're still getting married," he tells me, though he keeps his eyes locked with Jeff's.

"Oh, thank God," I breathe.

"Henry," Jeff says, "I really am touched by how concerned you were about this."

I've actually begun to cry a little. "I couldn't bear it if you guys had decided against getting married all on account of . . ." I look over at Lloyd. "Of what happened."

"You can say it," Jeff says, a small smile on his face. "Lloyd slept with Luke."

"I will *never* say it," I reply, shuddering.

Lloyd is shaking his head. "I am human. I have a libido. I plead guilty to both those charges. And Luke was upset. I didn't plan my response. It seemed to come from the situation."

"We've been over this," Jeff tells me. "We've moved on."

"No," Lloyd says. "I want Henry to understand." He sighs again, seeming to clutch Jeff's hand even tighter. "I don't know if seducing me was a ruse on Luke's part to get back at Jeff. Maybe that was some of his motivation."

"And maybe he just thought you were hot," Jeff says.

Lloyd manages a small smile. "Well, I'd hope that was at least *part* of it. But I really think there was something else going on. He was genuinely upset, and he was even more upset when he quit and walked out that door." He looks over at me sincerely. "I think he was upset because he was worried he had lost you, Henry."

"Oh, I doubt that very much," I say.

"It's what I feel quite strongly."

"Look," I tell both of them, "what matters right now is not Luke or me. It is the two of you. I want to make sure that you are both going to be able to move past this and really celebrate this important ritual that's coming up. The most important ritual of your lives most likely."

"Like I said," Jeff tells me, "there is nothing to work out."

"I find that hard to believe, Jeff."

"Henry, look." He leans forward in his chair. "Lloyd and I did not make any agreement to be monogamous in the weeks before the wedding. That was my own choice. This is what I realized while I was away, that it had been *my* decision, made completely on my own, with no input from Lloyd. And so I was wrong to be angry with him over something we'd never discussed."

"But it was a natural reaction," I say.

"No." Jeff is adamant about this. "It was an *immature* reaction. All along, I never felt it was necessary for Lloyd to feel the same way that I did. What happened with Luke was not a comment on Lloyd's love for me." He looks back over at Lloyd. "Sitting there feeling sorry for myself in Melissa's spare bedroom in Boston, I saw how hysterical I was being. I *know* how Lloyd feels about me. And it is more—*much* more—than enough."

"Thank you, Cat," Lloyd says, rather emotionally.

I look over at Jeff trying to recognize something familiar in his words. This is not the Jeff I once knew. The old Jeff would never have gotten over this so easily. He would have carried on, fretted and stewed. He'd have been terribly threatened by Luke, completely distraught.

"So," I ask, challenging him, "you didn't feel any pang—*anything*—when you found out Lloyd had been fooling around with Luke?"

Jeff smiles. "Well, obviously I felt some pang if I retreated to Boston to sulk." He laughs. "But even as I was doing it, part of me knew I was on automatic pilot. That I was just reacting out of habit. Sitting there at Melissa's, by myself, suddenly it all just became very clear." He looks over at me directly. "Henry, nothing would ever make me doubt Lloyd's love for me. *Nothing.*"

Lloyd stands and squats beside Jeff's chair. They share a brief kiss.

"This is the man I love," Lloyd says, talking to me but looking at Jeff. "No one—no matter how cute his ass might look in a thong—could ever make me feel otherwise."

"In fact," Jeff says, looking from Lloyd back to me, "what really worried us about this whole situation was *you*, Henry. That's what we were talking about when you walked in—about the possibility that Luke may have been manipulating you, and that your feelings were hurt."

Now Lloyd's approaching me, stooping in front of me the way he'd just done with Jeff. He places his hands on my knees and looks up at me. As ever, his green eyes seem to peer into my soul.

"Henry," he says, "I really don't believe Luke was being entirely manipulative. I think you should seek him out. No matter which way this goes, I think you'll want some closure with him."

I don't know what to say. Certainly I'm not at all eager to see Luke again. But Lloyd is probably right. A few answers might help me put the experience behind me. But I also know this has been a summer of very few answers, so I'm not sure I can expect any more this time.

"We'll see about Luke," I say, standing up. "But listen, you guys. Thank you. Thank you for not giving up on each other." I pause. "And thanks for being my friends."

"We love you, Henry," Lloyd says.

"I know."

We embrace again. Jeff joins us for a group hug. It feels a little silly, but also—I can't deny it—pretty nice.

Their words have a huge impact on me. Even as we all move back to our daily lives, the sentiments of my two best friends linger in my mind. What resonates is not just their expressions of love and support for me, but also their declarations of love for each other. What's most impressive is the way Lloyd and Jeff seem to have gotten past trivialities—which, in this case, is exactly what Luke is. They've based their love and commitment on something so profound that not even a player like Luke could disturb it.

It's called *trust*.

I smile to myself as I return to the front desk. Maybe the world has far more shades of gray than I've ever allowed myself to accept.

And maybe, just maybe, I should consider what Lloyd said about Luke's feelings for me.

But not right now. I just can't bear to think about any of that right now. Not Luke, not Gale. I need a mindless task to occupy my mind, so I settle on sorting through the mail that arrived while I was away. I just need to get back to my routine, to fall back into the groove of my life.

Still, there's one thing I do without even thinking too much about it. I feel no great emotion in doing so, just a simple recognition that it's time.

I take down Joey's photograph from my in-box and throw it away.

When I'm finished sorting the mail, I have a stack of promotional flyers I think Lloyd ought to look at. One is from a company that builds glassed-in sunrooms, something we've been thinking of adding. Another is from a sauna installer. We'd like to add a sauna out back this fall. I decide to carry the flyers over to Lloyd so he can check them out at his convenience.

When I get to the house, everyone seems to have gone out. I'm thinking of just leaving the flyers on the kitchen table when I hear a sound. I step into the backyard and spot Jeff and Lloyd emerging from the hot tub, wrapping white terrycloth towels around their waists. My hand is on the screen door as I start to head outside—but then I notice Lloyd come up behind Jeff and put his arms around him. He presses his lips to Jeff's shoulder. It's such a tender gesture, such a delicate moment of intimacy that I pause, not wanting to intrude. I watch as Jeff's arm reaches behind him, coming to rest on Lloyd's butt. They stand that way for several moments, leaning against the glass windows of the house, unaware that I'm watching them.

In that moment, in that embrace, I see all the love that lives between them—all the history, all the joy, all the grief, all the struggle, all the triumph. I step back away from the door quietly. This is their time. I leave the flyers on the table and quietly return to the guesthouse.

The image of the two of them, holding each other in that way, is one that I know I will treasure all of my life. There's no envy—a refreshing change. All I feel is happiness.

I've said I'd never want a relationship like Jeff and Lloyd's, with its all amorphous boundaries and definitions. Yet, in so many ways, what they have is *exactly* what I want. A relationship so strong and so devoted that nothing can possibly shake it. A relationship defined by who they are, and how they love. A relationship that fits. That *works*. That will endure.

I know it wasn't always easy for Jeff and Lloyd as they made their way to this point. A great deal of heartache and confusion and just plain hard *work* has transpired along the passage from there to here. But they *made it*. And in two weeks' time, they'll stand up and declare to the *entire world* that they made it.

I feel like crying. I know it sounds corny, but my heart is just ready to explode with happiness for my two friends.

Maybe I'm not yet so over the hill that I need to give up all hope that someday that might be me, as well.

But with who?

I think about heading back into town, yet for some reason, I feel the need to be by myself—kind of like my father in his basement room. But I'm not depressed. Far from it, in fact. I'm just in the mood to hang out with Henry. I'd forgotten he could actually be fun to have around.

So I pop a big bowl of popcorn—no butter—and stretch out on the couch in front of the TV. *The Facts of Life* is in its last five minutes. It's one of the later episodes, after Cloris Leachman had replaced Charlotte Rae, and Jo is trying to save somebody from jumping off a building. I'm completely befuddled by the plot, but it doesn't matter. Natalie makes one of her typical wisecracks and the laughtrack responds, cuing the end credits. I settle in for a night of great old TV, happy as a bedbug. Up next, I'm told, is *Growing Pains*. And after that is *The Golden Girls*.

"The answers to every problem in life." I tell the TV in between handfuls of popcorn, "can be found by watching Dorothy, Rose, Blanche and Sophia."

But first: *Growing Pains*. It's one of the Leonardo DiCaprio ones. I always enjoy spotting movie stars in supporting TV roles before their careers took off. I remember Leo on the show. He was one of my first crushes, in fact. My sister Susan used to have a poster of him on her wall, except she always referred to him by his TV character's name, Luke—

My hand stops its delivery of popcorn to my mouth.

I sit up, staring at the TV.

As the episode opens, DiCaprio's character is calling his stepbrother, played by Kirk Cameron, "Mike."

Holy fuck.

I stand up, knocking some of the popcorn out of the bowl. What did Luke say his stepbrother's name was? The one he supposedly had sex with? *Mike!* I'm sure of it!

A stepbrother who became a born-again Christian.

Just like Kirk Cameron.

I look back at the screen. Leo is teasing Kirk. They're rough-housing in the bedroom. How many gay guys of a certain age used to fantasize about those two hotties getting it on?

It's just the way Luke described it.

And what did he say about the guy who adopted him? He was a lawyer! Just like the father on the show! And where was *Growing Pains* set? Long Island! Where Luke claims to come from!

I'm immediately at my computer, Googling *Growing Pains*. Yes, here it is: character profiles. I click on the one for "Luke."

"Holy shit," I say to myself as I read what's written there.

In his last appearance, "Luke" was depicted as going off with his real father to run a truckstop in Tucson. Exactly what our Luke claims for himself! And the cincher is the character's last name, *Brower*. Though we've known him as West, he's admitted it was a made-up name—and somehow Brower is ringing a bell for me. I dig out Luke's binder of short stories from under a pile of papers. Sure enough, in that piece, the narrator's last name is Brower.

Can it be possible?

He's taken on the identity of a character from an old TV show!

But he's also given him considerably more backstory—with all that talk about an uncle who looked like the Penguin and the lecherous guys who gave him rides when he was hitchhiking.

I sit there at my desk staring out the window. The sun is setting in a dazzling display of reds and golds and greens. What was in this kid's head to imagine himself as a television character?

Sometimes, he once told me about the people he saw on the screen, *it seems like they're your best friends.*

In that one instance, at least, I believe he was speaking the truth.

21

ON THE PIER

"**I** wasn't sure you'd call," Luke says to me.

We're sitting on the pier, in the same place we sat several weeks ago, not long after we met. It seems a lifetime ago. Luke looks smaller today, younger, huddled in a dark blue hooded sweatshirt. It's cold out here on the pier. The wind whips in off the harbor with a chilling force. Summer is definitely over. Winter is whistling down the road.

"I wasn't sure I would either," I tell him.

But I did. I called and asked him to meet me here. Lloyd was right. I needed some kind of closure. I don't know what to expect—even if I should be expecting anything at all. Still, I've made love to this young man. I've read his words, glimpsed into his soul. Might there still be a chance to find out who he really is?

Sitting on the bench beside Luke, I stuff my hands deep down into my pockets. I don't say anything else for the moment. I want him to take the lead. I want to see where he goes.

"Well," Luke says, possibly a bit unnerved by my silence. "I'm *glad* you called, Henry. I hated thinking that I had totally fucked it up with you."

"Gee," I say, a small smile cracking the edges of my lips, "whatever would make you think *that?*"

Luke gives me a very earnest face. "Henry, you've *got* to believe me. I was upset because I was sure Jeff had told you what happened, about how I tried to . . ." His voice trails off. "How I humiliated myself in front of him. But I didn't care about that. What I cared about was the possibility that I might have lost you forever."

"Is that so?"

"Yes, it is. So, you see, I was quite upset, and it was all about *you,* Henry, and that's when Lloyd tried to comfort me and—"

"I know the rest," I tell him.

He looks at me with those imploring eyes of his. "All along, my real feelings have always been for *you,* Henry."

I look at him kindly. "I'm not sure you know what your real feelings are, Luke. Or if they're even yours."

He looks at me oddly.

"Maybe they're Becky Sharp's," I say. "Or some other character from a movie or a television show."

He stiffens. "I'm being honest with you about how I feel."

I shrug. "Maybe you are. But still, that doesn't tell me what I want to know."

He makes a face. "What do you want to know then?"

"Let's start with your real name. You've admitted you made up 'West.' Did you make up 'Luke' too?"

He laughs. "What are you driving at, Henry?"

"I want to know who you are. Who you *really* are."

"Why?"

"I'm not entirely sure," I admit. "Maybe because I'm tired of living with dreams and fantasies. I'm tired of not knowing who people are, or how they feel, or why they're in my life."

He gives me an arrogant smile. "Maybe you're tired of not knowing who *you* are, Henry, or how *you* feel."

"That too." I'm nodding my head in agreement. "Definitely that too." I narrow my eyes at him. "But at least I haven't pretended to be a character from some Eighties sitcom."

He looks at me sharply. "How did you—?" Then a small smile creeps across his face. "I see you've been watching TV Land."

I smirk. "It's one of my favorite things to do, though I don't claim to have the encyclopedic knowledge of television classics that you do."

His smile grows. "Okay then. How about if I told you my name was George Burnett? Or David Healy? Or Joey Russo?"

I shake my head. "I wouldn't buy it. I'm not sure exactly who played them or where, but I'd wager, if I searched hard enough, I'd find all of them on the Internet Movie and TV Database."

Luke laughs. "That you would." He laughs again, harder. "And every one of them, I can assure you, is far, far more interesting than Frank Hall of Lewiston, Maine."

"Ah," I say, extending my hand. "At last. Hello, Frank. My name is Henry."

We shake.

"And I suspect," I add, still shaking his hand, "that Frank Hall's life is far more interesting than you think."

He drops my hand. "And what makes you suspect that?"

"I've read your work, Frank. I know the hurt you carry around with you."

"Oh," he says, eyeing me. "You do?"

"Yes. And if you'd allow it, I'd like to know more."

He's still looking at me strangely. "Know more about what?"

"Your health, for one." I reach for his hand, but he moves it to his face, deftly avoiding contact with me. "You write about Darryl being sick, but I think it may be you."

He says nothing. He just keeps staring at me.

"And your father," I say. "That was perhaps the most disturbing suggestion of all in your work . . ."

"Henry," Frank Hall says to me.

I look at him, listening.

"I made all that shit up."

It's my turn to remain silent.

"Really," he says, smiling again. "I did. I figured this was the kind of shit the sells. Pain and death and parental abuse." He lets out a whoop of a laugh, one that frightens me, causes me to sit back on the bench. "It's what they call 'literary fiction.' Not like that commercial puke Jeff puts out."

"Don't start degrading Jeff's work again," I tell him.

"Look, Henry, all you need to know about me is that I'm in love with you. Isn't that enough?"

I look at him for a long time. How long I've wanted to hear those words from someone. *I'm in love with you, Henry.*

But I look over at him and say, "No. It's not enough."

"Why not?" Luke—or Frank—seems exasperated. "I'd have thought you'd say that was the most important thing to know about someone."

I shake my head. "Maybe a week ago I'd have said that. Not anymore."

"I don't understand you, Henry."

"You know, Frank," I say, "there was a time when I called myself a different name, too." I lift my chin, puff out my chest. "Frank, meet Hank. Remember I told you I was an escort for a while?"

"Sure."

I look off over the water. "I thought Henry Weiner wasn't good enough, or interesting enough, or sexy enough. So I invented this character named Hank. He didn't last very long. But still, there was always this belief way down deep that Henry just didn't cut it. Henry was just not good enough."

"Not good enough for what?" he asks.

"For everything!" I gesture around me. "For anything!"

Finally—a bit of understanding, a trace of honest emotion on the face of the young man sitting next to me. The cocky smile slowly fades from his face as he joins me in looking out over the sea.

"There's not much to write about in Lewiston, Maine," he tells me. "So I had this brilliant idea. I'd create a character and I'd live his life. I'd test stories out on people, and if I got a response, if people believed me, I'd know they'd work in my novel."

I'm nodding. "That's why your stories always sounded like memorized passages from a book"

"You always saw through me," Luke says.

"Not always," I admit. "Because sometimes—sometimes I think you were telling us the truth, even when you were, in fact, not."

He narrows his eyes at me. "What do you mean?"

"You've really been as lonely as that boy you described meeting Darryl at a bookstore. You really did want to get out of your hometown as much as that kid with that cat-murdering uncle."

Frank looks back out over the water. "Even more . . ."

"Lloyd is perhaps the best judge of character I know," I tell him. "The fact that he always held out some hope for you says something." I look into Frank's eyes. "We're not so different, you and me. We've both been telling the world stories about ourselves in order to distract attention away from who we really are."

"So who *are* we?"

I shrug. "A couple of lonely guys, just looking for someone to wake up with every morning."

"Then don't give up on me, Henry. If you believe the under-lying truth of my stories, believe me when I say I really like you. And always have. That day when we first had sex, I treasure it."

Does he? I look at him. Maybe he does. Maybe, in this moment, he really believes what he is saying to me. Maybe, in fact, he really does like me.

But then I have what Lloyd calls a "psychic moment." I can't ex-plain it. It's just there, a bit of knowledge in my head that I know to be irrefutably true.

"Your name isn't even Frank Hall, is it?" I ask.

"Names don't mean anything," he tells me.

"They do to me."

I stand up.

"You don't believe that I love you?" he asks, almost in a panic.

"Actually, I do believe that," I say.

"Then goddamn it! It's not enough?"

"No," I tell him. "It's not enough."

"Henry," the kid says, and there's real panic in his eyes. "Don't walk away from me! Please!"

"I want a relationship, it's true," I tell him. "I've spent the last year of my life spinning my wheels as I looked for one. I was run-ning after this one and that one, transferring my emotions as often as I changed my socks. I was willing to chase down anyone— *anyone*—if I thought maybe they might like me. But now . . ."

The kid on the bench—whatever his name is—looks up at me, waiting for me to finish.

"Now, I want something more than that."

"Like what?"

"Something that's real. Something that seems to be impossible for you, my friend."

The young man on the bench turns his face away from me.

"Good luck to you," I tell him. "I hope you realize that there's plenty to write about in Lewiston—or wherever it is you really come from. More than you ever believed possible."

I leave him sitting there staring out over the harbor. I walk off the pier, heading into town, where I spot Ellie, the miniskirted transvestite street singer. Once, in another life, she was a fire-breathing Baptist preacher. Now she's dragging her wagon, tottering on her high heels, and warbling: *The record shows, I took the blows, and did it my way!*

Up and down this street, character after character passes, each one a brand-new creation. The middle-aged woman who dares hold her girlfriend's hand in public for the first time. The leather-man who walks proudly, his enormous codpiece preceding him. The painter standing on the side of the road at his easel, who was told in art school he had no talent, but who flourishes here, liberated from the tyranny of rules and tradition. In this place that celebrates reinvention, our previous lives are immaterial. Here, we become who we want to be.

If only the boy I'd just left could understand that. And trust it.

Did he really make it all up? All those stories that haunted me? Those nightmarish images and dark scenarios?

I realize all at once that it doesn't matter anymore. It is a liberating feeling. I can't stop the smile from pushing across my face.

Walking past Ellie, I give her a hearty salute. She waves back in solidarity. We are new creatures, she and I. We have been reborn.

I have not felt this good, this solid, since—well, I can't even remember. I feel alive. I feel inspired. I feel—dare I say it?—*complete.*

"Henry!"

I turn. On his bike, heading toward me, is Jeff. He slows as he approaches and comes to a stop in front of me.

"Lloyd said you were meeting Luke," he says. There's concern on his face. "Everything go okay?"

"Just fine." I smile at him. "It went far, far better than I could ever have imagined."

Jeff gets off his bike, pushing it as we walk the street. "So are you two friends again?"

I smile. "Jeff, he and I were never friends."

He sighs, not really following my meaning. "You sure you're okay?"

"Actually, never better." I zip up my jacket. "What great air, don't you think? I love the first brisk winds of fall. People wish they could bottle the air here, you know. They want to take it back with them to wherever they call home. Do you know how lucky we are to live here, Jeff?"

He smiles. "I've got a pretty good idea."

"I'm seeing Gale tonight," I tell him. "I wasn't sure I should go through with it, but now I think I should."

"And why's that?"

"I need to tell him I was wrong."

Jeff gives me a puzzled look. "Wrong about what?"

"I was pushing him to go faster than he was ready for. And in truth, I wasn't ready myself." I laugh, spreading my arms wide as we walk down the street. "Do you know how wonderful it is to be single?"

"Henry," Jeff says, leaning in. "Are you sure you're okay?"

"I told you. Never better!"

Jeff smirks. "So Henry Weiner is happy to be a single man?"

"Ecstatic." I turn to him. "If I had gotten into a relationship with any one of these guys—or, in the case of Evan and Curt, any two—well, it would have come undone just as fast as my relationships with Joey or Daniel or Shane did. Don't you see, Jeff? I was caught in a vicious pattern, but now I have the luxury of getting to know myself on my own! To get myself ready for Mr. Right, whenever he might come along."

"Uh, excuse me," Jeff says, crossing his arms over his chest and stopping in the road in front of me, "but isn't this what Lloyd and I have been telling you all along?"

I smile. "Yes, it is. But only now can I really see things clearly."

"Oh, yeah?" Jeff looks me up and down. "If that's the case, then how come you're still wearing those clothes?"

My exuberance comes to a sudden stop. "What's wrong with my clothes?"

Jeff just grins and gestures to my outfit. I look down at myself. I'm wearing my number 9 T-shirt under a black jacket with ABER-

CROMBIE ATHLETIC DEPT stenciled on the back. I'm also wearing the new white belt I bought for myself this morning. I think I look pretty *stylin'*.

"Henry," Jeff says, putting his arm around me and pulling me close, "I'm all for you revamping yourself. But let me give you a bit of advice. The fastest way to looking old and tired is trying too hard to look young."

"*What?*"

He smiles. "It hit me the other day when I was in Boston trying on a pair of sunglasses." He looks around to make sure no one can overhear him. "I looked at the label. They were these huge goofy things I see a lot of the kids wearing—and they were from the Mary-Kate and Ashley line."

"You mean, the Olsen twins?"

"Yes," Jeff says, cringing. "Do you know how absurd I felt in that moment, that I actually was considering *buying* them? Worse, *wearing* them!"

"Well, I'm not wearing anything by Mary-Kate and—"

"Henry." Jeff looks at me. "Buddy. The only people wearing Abercrombie anymore are guys in their thirties and forties trying to blend in with teenagers—which ain't *never* gonna work, and not only because the kids aren't wearing that stuff anymore."

"So you're saying this jacket . . . this shirt . . ."

"And the *hair*." He tousles my faux-hawk. "Ten years from now, we're going to look back on this do the way we look at the *mullet* today."

I catch a glimpse of myself in a shop window. Suddenly my haircut seems very silly indeed.

"But who are *you* to talk, Jeff?" I'm suddenly annoyed that he's spoiled my good feeling about myself. "Mr. *Botox?*"

He deliberately lifts his eyebrows as high as he can, exposing the natural wrinkles of the skin.

"I'm clean, buddy," he says. "I'm off the stuff."

I can't help but laugh.

"It was the same day I had the revelation about the sunglasses," Jeff tells me. "I was in Boston to get my regular forehead fix. I wanted to be smooth and tight for the wedding. And suddenly it all seemed so crazy. Who was I smoothing myself out for? Lloyd doesn't love me any less for having a few wrinkles in my forehead."

"But see?" I poke Jeff gently in the chest with my finger. "You *have* someone. I *don't.* Therein lies the difference. You don't need to try to attract someone in quite the same way that I want to."

He takes my finger and brings it to his lips, kissing it. "You're not going to attract them in that haircut. Trust me on this, Henry."

"Okay, okay." I roll my eyes. "I get your point."

"I'm glad you're in a better of frame of mind," Jeff says, mounting his bike again. "And I tell you this stuff only because I love you."

"I know."

"I'm not sure what you and Luke talked about," Jeff says, "but whatever it is, I like it. Don't lose this new attitude."

"I won't," I promise. "But first I've got to get out of these clothes."

He laughs. "I've got to run, buddy. We're meeting the caterer to go over some last-minute stuff."

"Okay. I'll see you back at the house."

He shakes a finger at me. "You better be writing a good speech, Mr. Best Man. I don't want a dry eye on the beach."

I smile and pucker him a kiss. I watch him pedal off.

Then I head over to the salon to have my hair evened out.

Of course, if I had really liked the look, I would have kept it. But Jeff only spoke what I already knew to be true. This attempt to keep up with the kiddies was just my latest attempt to hide from who I really am. Henry Weiner is thirty-three years old. Mr. Right is just going to have to deal with it.

Back in my apartment I stand in front of the full-length mirror and really look at myself. Without the silly disguise, I don't look so bad. Pretty damn *good*, in fact. Why is it that I always see in this mirror someone old, out of shape, and unappealing? Why is it that I never see a good-looking, broad-shouldered, upstanding, decent guy? He hasn't been hiding. He's been right there all along.

I think about Luke—or Frank or whoever he is. What did he see when he looked in the mirror? Did he see the cute body, the adorable face? Maybe that's all he saw. Maybe he saw nothing else—no mind, no heart, no soul. Maybe that's why he made up so much about himself, to fill in what he perceived as gaps. For whatever it was that his mirror reflected, he didn't like it very much.

I was being honest when I told him we really weren't so different.

What did all those terrifying, unsettling things I'd read in his manuscript conceal? Were the truths of that kid's life even *more* painful? I suspect I'll never know the answer to that question. At the end of *The Boys of Summer*, Jeff wrote that people sometimes come into your life and leave without ever revealing their truths. We're left only with ambiguity. But it's the peace we must eventually make with that ambiguity that finally sets us free. We come to accept that there are some things we'll never understand, some people whose blanks will never be entirely filled in. In a way, it's not so different from how I never knew what happened to my childhood friend Jack when he took off in pursuit of his dream. Did he find it? Did he make it? All that I carry of him now is his name—and what the memory of him has come to mean for me.

But while so much about the boy I left sitting on the pier will remain a mystery to me, I do know this much: the bitter dissatisfaction he carries around about who he really is and where he really comes from is something I want no part of.

I think about my mother and my father. They weren't perfect. But they loved me. Even on this last visit, they offered small gestures as proof of their love. My father shutting off the TV set when he thought I needed to talk. My mother kissing me on the forehead. It is true that, away from them, I have found a more sustaining family. But my parents loved me the best way they knew how. Though I needed to find my way out of West Springfield—a feat for which I perhaps do not give myself enough credit— my childhood and my family and my hometown experience remain vital parts of who I am: A pencil-necked kid who worked at Roy Rogers and snuck out of gym class and into gay bars. A soft-hearted romantic who fell in love too many times in his life. A guy who's sometimes been selfish and sometimes been naïve. But for all that, Henry Weiner isn't so bad.

Getting dressed for my—what do I call it? Date? Farewell?—with Gale, I can't help but think of the way I tried to compete with those boys surrounding him at Spiritus yesterday. Boys who weren't even born when I had my first orgasm, humping my mattress while looking at pictures of a shirtless Tom Selleck in *TV Guide.* There I stood, in my Abercrombie jacket and ridiculous haircut, desperately trying to get Gale's attention away from those children—an apple trying to compete with four very juicy, fresh-from-the-tree oranges. And throughout that sorry spectacle, Martin had sat there indifferent to the whole game, solid and real.

This is what I need to tell Gale: that I was trying to be someone that I wasn't—specifically, someone who was grounded enough and secure enough to be ready for a relationship. Quite unfairly, I was pushing him and making demands when I had no business doing so. He was right to resist.

Yet even as I knock on Gale's door there's a pang of something that I can't quite name. I remember coming here the first time, and the hope I felt that maybe, just maybe, he was the One for me. Of course, there had been warning signs all along that Gale was equally as unprepared as I was to enter into a relationship. Like Luke, he held back from ever revealing his true self—the soft, vulnerable, frightened part of him I sense lurks somewhere within. Yet *unlike* Luke, Gale never lied about who he is, never wove strange fictions about himself. He just erected a fortress around himself so high that it's proven impossible for me to scale.

Maybe, without even knowing it, that's what I've been doing as well.

"Hello, Henry," Gale says as he opens the door.

Something in his very manner is different: the way he holds the doorknob, the way he says my name. He's softer, less forward. With a florid sweep of his hand, he invites me in.

He's wearing jeans and a long, loose-fitting white T-shirt. Even so, I can make out the hard definition of his pecs and the roundness of his shoulders. He smiles at me as he shuts the door.

"Can I offer you some tea? A cup of coffee?"

"No thanks," I say. "I don't think I'll be staying that long."

He arches an eyebrow at me. "No? Just in and out?"

I nod. "I just came to say . . . that I'm sorry."

Gale looks at me without fully comprehending. "Please," he says, gesturing for me to sit at his small kitchen table. "Have a cup of tea at least."

I agree, taking a seat and watching as he pours two cups of steaming hot water into two cups. I marvel at the muscles in his back, the way they move underneath his shirt. He drops a tea bag into each cup and then carries them over to the table.

"I'm not sure why you feel the need to apologize, Henry," Gale says. "At least, if there are apologies to be made, they should come from both sides."

"All right," I say. "Fair enough." I remove the tea bag with a spoon, setting it down on the saucer under the cup.

"You were right about something," Gale says, sitting opposite me. "Far more important to me than finding a relationship— which, as you know, I consider my holy grail—was keeping control." He smiles as he sips his tea. "Thank you for pointing that out to me."

"Maybe we aren't so different," I tell him. "My need to push you—make demands—that was my own way to control."

"It's not easy, is it?" Gale asks. "Just letting things happen as they're meant to?"

"Not at all," I agree. "But I'm getting better at it."

Gale smiles. "I'd like to say I am, too, but I'm not sure I'm quite ready to let down all my defenses."

"That's your decision," I tell him. "But I really think behind your very controlled exterior, we're not so different. The secret parts of ourselves . . . I suspect they're pretty similar."

He smiles mysteriously. "Oh, I doubt that very much."

I'm surprised by his comment. "Why would you doubt it?" I ask. "Look, we've both put up fronts to hide the real person underneath. A real person who's strong enough and good enough to be let out into the open, if only we could learn to trust that."

Gale stands. He walks across the kitchen to the sink, then turns and faces me again. He seems anxious all of a sudden, as if this is the part of the conversation he's been dreading.

"This is where you're wrong, Henry," he tells me. "What you

see out here in front is the real Gale." He taps his chest. "The Gale inside—the person underneath—is the *old* Gale, who was weak and confused. The strong, resilient, *manly* Gale is quite new."

I frown. "Why do you dislike that other part of yourself so much? Why do you call that part of yourself weak and confused?"

Gale shrugs. "Because that part of myself wasn't a man."

"Gale," I say, trying to sound as kind and compassionate as possible. "Just because you have some softness to you doesn't make you less of a man."

He walks back to the table, picks up his teacup, and paces, holding the cup in his hands. "Would you like to hear about my last relationship?"

"Yes," I say. "The one with the woman?"

"That's right. We were together for six years." Gale walks across the small kitchen floor, anxiously taking sips of his tea. "She was the strong one, you see. She made all the decisions. She told me when to sit, when to stand, when to go to bed. And I *hated* it. The relationship didn't fit me. It was *wrong*. And as the years went on, it only felt more wrong."

He pauses before going on.

"I'd met her when I was quite young," he continues. "What did I know? I thought this was the way these kinds of relationships worked. But as each year passed, I felt more and more uncomfortable. I was living a lie."

I'm nodding. "That's when you realized you were gay?"

Galee smiles, walking over to me standing directly in front of me.

"Silly boy, I was always gay." He runs his fingers through my hair. "You just can't see, can you?"

He places his hand on my shoulder, urging me to stand. As I do, he sets down his teacup and wraps his arms around me. He pulls me into him for a kiss. My arms reach around the delicious hardness of his body. We're locked that way for several minutes, kissing deeply. I breathe in Gale's exquisite masculine scent, a fragrance quite unlike anything I've ever experienced with a man before. My cock rages in my jeans.

Gale's lips are on my ear. "And this is the part where I usually say stop," he whispers. "Isn't that right?"

I kiss his neck. "Yeah. That's usually how it goes."

"Not this time," he purrs. "This time, *you'll* be the one to end it."

I pull back and look into his eyes. "Why would I do that, Gale?"

He gives me a rueful smile. "You really don't know, do you, Henry?"

I hold his gaze, his beautiful round brown eyes searing my soul. And then, in an instant, another psychic moment.

I understand everything.

I move my hand around from his butt to his crotch.

There's nothing there.

At least, nothing that I expected.

No erection.

No penis, in fact, at all.

"You understand my modesty a little better now, I think," Gale says quietly.

For several seconds I'm struck mute. The bulge in his pants I'd once admired . . . *not real.* All of this . . . all of what I've thought of Gale . . . is an *illusion.* His firm round pecs—so round and so full. But in fact they were the breasts of a small-bosomed woman, hardened by testosterone.

"Why did you never tell me?" I finally ask, still close enough that I'm practically whispering in Gale's ear.

He smiles as if I'm being absurd. "Would you have come back? Honestly, Henry. Would you have come back?"

I take a step away from him. I don't know what to say.

"If you can't answer that question, Henry," Gale asks, "then might you finally be able to answer the other one I posed?"

My eyes flicker up to his face.

"What is the most basic thing you want in a lover?" Gale asks again. "You said honesty. Well, I'm being honest with you now, aren't I?"

"Yes," I say, barely audible.

Gale smiles. "It *is* more basic than that, isn't it, Henry? The most fundamental thing you need from a lover is that he be a man."

I cannot speak.

"It's okay, Henry. I didn't expect you to respond any differently."

"I—I'm sorry."

Gale walks back over to the sink, staring out the window at the harbor beyond. "I'll say it again, Henry. I'll accept your apology only if you'll accept mine as well."

I'm too stunned to move. I just stand there looking at the back of his head for several seconds. But then I force myself over to him, and place my my hand on his shoulder. His muscles are still hard, still solid.

"If I had known all along . . ." I say.

Gale turns to look at me. "Oh, so if when I asked you out the first time, I'd added, 'By the way, Henry, I'm a female-to-male transsexual without a penis,' you'd still have gone out with me?"

"I . . . I'd like to think so."

Gale smiles. "I'd like to think so, too. And well you might have. You're a good man, Henry. But that's a lot to spring on a person."

I look past him out the window. How can I lie? How can I be so sure that I would have gone out with him? Even if I had, would I have been so eager to make love? So urgent to press for a relationship?

How can I pretend that, had Gale been truthful with me from the start, I would even be standing here at this moment? The truth is, I probably would not be. It would have ended way before this point. I'm not proud of myself. In fact, at this very moment, I despise my pettiness, my small-mindedness. But I can't lie and pretend otherwise.

Gale lets out a breath and continues his story. "I finally came to the conclusion in my relationship with Cathy that I was uncomfortable with being a woman. But that's not all I realized, Henry. I came to understand that I wasn't meant to be *with* women either." He laughs ironically. "It might have been easier if I'd really been a lesbian right from the beginning. Women don't seem to have the same hang-ups around genitalia that men do. But I can't deny my orientation any more than I can deny my gender identity."

"I'm sorry," I say again.

Gale sighs. "Stop saying that. In the end, there's nothing to be sorry for. It will take a while to find a man for whom genitalia doesn't matter. Do you see now why I'm so picky, so cautious—so *controlling?*"

I grip him by the shoulders. "But by *being* so controlling, Gale, you're going to push people away from you before you even know what's possible with them."

He laughs, and the bitterness isn't completely disguised. "Oh? Given *your* reaction, Henry, I'm certainly not encouraged that openness would be a better strategy."

"Point taken." I take a deep breath. "But your softness isn't something you should be ashamed of. It's not something you should try to hide. In fact, I suspect there's some parts of the old Gale you really shouldn't toss."

He smiles wryly. "All I really remember about her is that she spelled her name with a 'y.'"

I'm not sure what he means.

"Gayle," he tells me. "She spelled it with a 'y.'"

I look down at him. "Just because you changed the spelling—just because you've changed the body—doesn't mean the same soul isn't inside."

Gale says nothing, just holds my gaze.

"I've been going through my own little awakening lately," I tell him. "And there are two things that stand out really clearly. First, I've got to like what I see in my mirror if Mr. Right is going to like me back." I pull him close to me, looking into those soulful eyes of his. "And second, whoever turns out to *be* Mr. Right must like what he sees in *his* mirror as well." I press my forehead against his. "Does that honestly describe you, my friend?"

Gale closes his eyes and does a remarkable thing. He cries.

"There," I say. "I knew somewhere under all that hard muscle shell was a real human being."

"I never look at myself in the mirror," Gale says, gently moving out of my arms to wipe his eyes with a paper towel. "At least, not without something to hide the last vestiges of Gayle." He smiles wanly. "With a 'y'."

"Well, maybe you ought to *start* looking," I advise him. "Today I looked at myself and saw a few other things beside my love han-

dles, which usually dominate the whole picture. It was quite a revelation."

Gale looks at me severely. "You are a gorgeous man, Henry
Weiner. How could you ever think otherwise?"

"It was easy," I tell him. "As easy as it's been for you to look in
your mirror and see only what you didn't want to see." I take his
hand in mine. "You're a gorgeous, sexy man as well, Gale."

"You really think so?"

"I do." I smile. "Maybe someday things might be different for
us. And maybe not. I can't stand here right now and honestly say
how I might feel. But the truth is, right now, I don't think either
one of us is ready for a relationship."

Gale looks away. "I thought if I found the perfect man . . ."

"You already are the perfect man," I tell him.

He looks back at me. "Thank you, Henry."

"Once we each believe that about ourselves, well, then maybe
we can start looking for Mr. Right."

Gale laughs. "You know, this isn't how I expected this would go.
I thought you'd run out of here in horror." He looks at me with
real happiness on his face, maybe the first time I've ever seen it in
his eyes. "It's been a very pleasant surprise."

"For me, too, actually," I say. "Hey, how about taking a walk
with me? It looks like the sky is getting dark. It might rain." I smile.
"And I love walking on the beach in the rain."

And so we walk. We break the pattern of my leaving Gale's
apartment alone once things reach an emotional peak. This time,
he comes with me.

It does indeed rain, the raindrops stirring up a rich fragrance
of salt and sand on the beach. We don't talk a lot, just point out
crabs moving slowly in the surf and watch fishermen tying up
their boats. At one point I slip and nearly fall into the water, but
Gale catches me. By the time we reach the pier we're soaked, but
we're laughing. It feels good to laugh.

Climbing up onto the pier, we spot an adorable sight. On the
same bench where Luke and I sat earlier, a little boy is sitting with
a girl, holding an umbrella over both their heads. "Isn't that
sweet?" Gale asks, grabbing my coat.

I nod. In that moment, I think about Luke—I think about how

different my two meetings today have turned out, the one with him and the one Gale. Luke remains a mask for me, with no real evidence that anything at all exists behind it. But where Gale, too, has lived behind a façade, his whole journey has been about reaching the real person inside—a glimpse of which he allowed me to see today. I feel terribly sad for Luke, but my sadness is counteracted by the sense of honest friendship I've discovered with Gale.

As we approach, we're considering the children ahead of us on the bench. "If only things could stay that simple," I observe. "Why are adults so good at making things difficult?"

"Let them always be as happy as they are right now," Gale says, as if breathing a little prayer.

The children are sitting rather far apart, as if they're on a date but too nervous to come to close. They're quite young, nine or ten maybe. It's hard to make out much at this distance and in the rain. But it's clear they aren't saying anything to each other. They're just sitting there, the boy shakily holding the umbrella over the two of them as the rain grows heavier.

That's when I recognize him.

"Hey, that's Jeff's nephew." I take a few steps forward. "J. R.! Hey, dude!"

The boy looks up at me with some degree of surprise, even panic.

I've reached the bench, Gale following quickly behind. "What are you doing, sitting here in the rain?" I ask.

"Nothing!" J. R. shouts, standing up and, in the process, moving the umbrella away from the little girl, a pretty brunette in a yellow raincoat.

"Hey," I tell him. "Now your friend's getting wet."

"It's okay," the girl says. "I don't mind."

"I know you," Gale says, looking at her. "You're Tony Silva's daughter, aren't you? I've been over at your house with Martin, building some cabinets."

"Yes," the girl says, smiling. "I'm Lynette."

I look from her over to J. R. "So I'll ask again, buddy. What are you guys doing out here on the pier in the middle of a rain-storm?"

"Nothing!" J. R. yells. "I told you, *nothing!*"

I look at him oddly. "Easy, buddy. It's okay. What's up with you?"

"I gotta go," he tells Lynette. "See you later."

"Okay, bye, J. R.," she says.

"Wait a minute, kiddo," I say, nabbing J. R.'s shoulder as he tries to pass. "What's gotten you so riled up?"

"I gotta go home," he tells me.

"Actually, I think we should all get moving," Gale says. "It's really starting to pour." His eyes find me. "Thanks for everything, Henry."

I smile. "Thanks for the walk."

"I hope we have more of them," he says.

"I do, too," I reply.

Gale turns to looking down at J. R.'s friend. "Now I'll walk you home, Lynette."

The little girl turns once more to J. R. "I'll see you at school," she tells him. The boy just grunts.

We watch as Gale and Lynette hurry off the pier. Once Gale was a little girl like Lynette. Except not really. He was always different, always living behind a mask. Now, finally, he's free. I'm not sure how I feel about all that I've just learned about him. I don't know where another walk with him might possibly lead. But I'm glad he didn't throw me out once again. I'm glad we at least moved past that point. I'm glad we're friends.

Then I turn to J. R.

"So," I say, looking down at him. "You going tell me what's gotten you so anxious?"

"Can we just go home?"

I sigh. "Okay, buddy. Whatever you say."

We head off down Commercial Street. J. R. tries to offer me some of his umbrella but he can't reach that high. "Doesn't matter, buddy," I tell him. "I like the rain."

We walk a few yards in silence. On the horizon I hear a rumble of thunder.

"So, J. R.," I say.

"What?"

"There's really no need to be embarrassed about sitting with a girl."

He stops walking, two big blue eyes glaring up at me from under his umbrella. "Just don't tell Uncle Jeff."

"Why? You weren't doing anything wrong."

"Just don't tell him!"

I'm mystified. "J. R., talk to me. What's gotten you so upset?"

"I don't want Uncle Jeff to know I like Lynette."

We've resumed walking. "Are you afraid that Lynette's going to think you're gay or something? Is that what this is all about?"

"No," he says decisively.

"Then what is it?"

"Just don't tell Uncle Jeff, *okay*?"

"Fine." I stop walking. I stoop down and grip the boy by the shoulders, finding, for a moment, a little shelter from the rain under his umbrella. I look him in the eyes. "But listen to me for a minute, dude. I've been doing a lot of thinking lately. I've been thinking about how sometimes I try to be something that I'm not. How sometimes I don't tell the truth about how I feel, even to myself. Do you think sometimes you do that too, buddy?"

"I don't know," J. R. says.

"I think maybe you do. And it's okay. We all do it. But once in a while, it's a good thing to check in with yourself and see what's going on."

The boy is silent as we hold each other's gaze.

"When I've been the most confused about myself," I tell him, "do you know who have always been my best friends? Who've always been able to help me figure stuff out? Your Uncle Jeff and Uncle Lloyd. I think if you tried talking to them, they could help you out, too."

He shakes his head. "They wouldn't like what I told them."

"Listen to me, buddy. No matter *what* you told them, they will *always* like you. They *love* you, dude. You've got to trust that."

His eyes flicker away as the first crackle of lightning cuts through the gray sky.

"Come on," I say, standing up. "Let's go home."

We hurry through the street as it fills up with rain.

22

HERRING COVE BEACH

So here we are. Jeff and Lloyd's wedding day. The rains lasted nearly all week, only to have the clouds suddenly clear out this morning, to everyone's relief and surprise. The sun seems to be burning away any lingering haze. For the first time in several days, we can all see more clearly.

Actually, for me, it's the first time in more than a *year*.

Straightening my tie at the mirror, I like how I look. Not in a very long time have I been able to say that. Staring back at me, Henry Weiner looks pretty dapper—pretty *stylin'*—in his blue suit and checkered bowtie. That studly escort Hank, I tell myself, has nothing on Henry.

Out at the beach, I help Lloyd's mother from her car. She arrived on Thursday with two of Lloyd's brothers, and has been staying at the guesthouse. She's a delightful woman, small and white haired. Completely no-nonsense, she's thrilled that her son is "finally settling down," as she put it, and it doesn't matter if it's "with a man or a woman or a goldfish." She's just happy, she told me, that her baby has a "home."

That he does. And I'm part of that home, I realize, as he's part of mine. I take Mrs. Griffith's arm and help her onto the wooden ramp we've installed from the parking lot onto the beach. She walks with a cane, but she's pretty agile on her own. I can see where Lloyd's resiliency comes from.

The next car to arrive is Ann Marie's. She's got J. R. and her mother with her. Far more tightly coiled than Lloyd's mother, Mrs. O'Brien, I've been quick to learn, is not one to smile without great cause. She seems overly solicitous of J. R., and frequently leans down to talk to him. He's her talisman, I realize, her steady compass through a world she doesn't know very well. With her dyed red hair and too bright lipstick, she wears her fear quite plainly on her face. Jeff being gay has always been difficult for her to accept. But she's here. That's what matters. She's here.

"Now don't leave Grandma alone," she's saying to J. R., who takes her arm. "Stay with Grandma now, Jeffy."

"Don't call me Jeffy," the boy says, looking distinctly uncomfortable in his gray suit, his collar open without a tie.

"Hey, buddy," I say as he passes. "How are things back at the house?"

He just shrugs. Sad to say, my little pep talk to him last week didn't produce much in the way of tangible results. He's remained just as distant as before, and when Jeff and Lloyd asked him one last time if he'd be their ring bearer, he again said no.

"Are Jeff and Lloyd on their way?" I ask Ann Marie, who looks fabulous in a bright yellow dress.

"I think so," she tells me. "They were tying each other's ties last I saw them. Is the singer here yet?"

At the last minute, Jeff had canceled the divas. Or maybe they backed out, I don't know. All I know is, earlier in the week, one of them, I'm not sure which, was balking about flying in on Cape Air, and wanted to be picked up at the airport in Boston. There was also the question of somebody's fee being higher than what Jeff had originally been quoted—and all of a sudden, instead of Connie Francis and Kimberley Locke, we've got some local singer, a waitress from the Mews, one of our favorite restaurants. "Who was I trying to impress by bringing in divas?" Jeff asked rhetorically, shaking his head. Like the Botox, I suppose, a high-profile wedding suddenly seemed unnecessary.

"Yes, the singer is here," I tell Ann Marie, nodding out toward the beach, where the waitress has begun to tune her guitar. "I think everybody's here but the grooms."

I glance around at the gathering crowd. Over there, old friends

Melissa and Rose are chatting with Jeff's brother and his daughters. Closer to the water stand our buddies from our days on the circuit, Billy and Oscar and Elliot, as well as Elliot's hunky new boyfriend Cesar. Elliot confided to me that he's giving Cesar an engagement ring tonight. Seems everybody's getting married.

Except me. Yet I can honestly say that, standing here watching the guests arrive, everybody kissing each other and exclaiming over the glorious day, I feel quite content with my own single-hood. I think about Luke—Frank Hall or whatever his name is—sitting on the pier, all alone. I think about Gale, who was once Gayle, trying to find a new way to be in the world, not knowing whom he can trust. In so many ways, I'm no different than they are. But I have something they don't.

I have a family.

"All right, everyone," comes the voice of the officiator, Lloyd's old friend Naomi. A tall, dark-haired woman, she wears a flowing flower-print muumuu and a wreath of daisies around her head. "Gather around me, please," she says, waving to the guests to come together. "Our ceremony is about to begin."

That's when I hear the car door behind me. I turn. Jeff and Lloyd have arrived, both of them looking magnificent in their tuxedos with red roses pinned to satin lapels. As they approach me, they're holding hands and beaming.

"What a day, huh?" I ask them.

Jeff can't contain his exhuberance. "It's like a dream."

"Henry," Lloyd says, reaching inside his jacket and withdrawing a small box, "you'll have to bring these over when Naomi gives the signal." I take the box from him. Opening its lid, I see two shining titanium rings inside.

Jeff's smile turns tight as I look over at him. "You'll have to be our ring bearer as well as our best man," he tells me, "since J. R. won't do it."

"Yes, I will."

We turn. The boy must have been watching for his uncles to arrive. He's left his grandmother's side and now stands before us in his too-big suit, pulling at his shirt collar with his finger. "I'll be your ring bearer," he announces.

Jeff's face turns into a beacon of light. "J. R.—you mean it?"

The kid nods.

Jeff reaches down to embrace him. "J. R., thank you, so much!"

Lloyd places his hand on the boy's shoulders. "You have made us very, very happy."

I hand the ring box to J. R. "Guard these carefully, buddy," I tell him.

J. R. nods, accepting the box.

Out on the beach, Shirl, the singer, begins her song.

When I fall in love, it will be forever . . .

I smile. Gale once said that those sentiments were worth singing about. Indeed they are, I think, walking behind Jeff and Lloyd onto the beach. Will it ever be me in their place? Will these people who have gathered here ever come to a ceremony for me?

In a restless world like this is, love is ended before it's begun . . .

I look around. Jeff's mother is crying. He stops as he passes her, taking her hand and bringing it to his lips. I note that Ann Marie's mascara is running as she sheds her own tears.

And the moment I can feel that you feel that way too . . .

I watch as Jeff and Lloyd take their place in front of Naomi, their hands still linked, their eyes only on each other.

. . . is when I fall in love with you.

Shirl finishes her song. Naomi steps forward.

"We are here today," she says, "to witness the joining together of two souls, Jeff and Lloyd."

The group murmurs appreciatively. Beyond, the surf crashes on the beach, and a gathering of gulls chitters loudly.

My mind flashes back to a night in Boston, many years ago. It was during that period where Jeff and Lloyd were living apart, neither of them sure of what lay ahead for the two of them. Jeff was stretched out on his couch, staring at the ceiling. I knew he was scared, depressed, worried. I asked him if he could imagine a life without Lloyd.

"Of course I can," he replied. "Life would go on. I suppose I might even find someone else, someday. But there would always be a chunk missing, like one of those mosaics you see where a couple of tiles have fallen out. It's still beautiful, but not complete." I remember smiling then. The writer in Jeff was coming out. I appreciated the image.

Yet today, the mosaic around us is complete. The sun, the waves, the sand, the people. I admit that I'm in my own world as Naomi speaks, offering her blessing on Jeff and Lloyd. There's a poem from Rumi, a Native American prayer, a parable about the Buddha. I can tell Lloyd wrote most of the ceremony. It's the spirit of the event I absorb more than any of the actual words. I'm kind of hovering above the ceremony, in fact, and I discover that, right beside me, is a man that I can't quite see, a man whose face is unknown to me but whose presence is very, very familiar. With him beside me, I, too, feel complete.

Jack, is that you?

He doesn't answer, but I feel quite certain it's him. The man from my childhood bed, with whom I'd fall asleep every night during my teenage years. The man I'd named for a childhood hero, and who I believed so strongly I'd one day find.

And now he's here.

Not in physical form. Not yet. But if I'm real, he's real. I once called him Mr. Right, or the One—but that's reductive. That describes him only from my perspective. He's so much more than that. He's full of life and contradictions, flaws as well as virtues, and he will not be enough, on his own, to meet every single one of my needs. Nor will I meet all of his. But he will make me complete, just as I complete him.

"And now," Naomi is saying, "a word from our best man."

I look up. I'm on. I clear my throat, and turn to face the gathered crowd.

For a moment I can't speak. I have no idea what I should say. Then the words find their way.

"When Lloyd and Jeff asked me to say something," I tell the crowd, "I was at a loss. 'Give a good speech!' they instructed." I laugh. "Talk about pressure."

The crowd laughs in return.

"I tried writing down a few things. I'd get two or three sentences down, then crumble up the paper. It all sounded too earnest, too trite. Jeff would probably say earnest and trite describes me to a T"—more laughter from the crowd—"but I just couldn't subject you all to that. Besides, I wanted to say something that no one else would say."

I look at my two friends.

"So I decided to wing it. I decided I wouldn't write anything, that when the time came, I'd just speak from the heart. I decided I would just tell you what I was thinking at the moment, how I felt standing here as your best man. And how I feel right now is . . . *inspired.*"

Overhead a very loud gull sweeps through the sky, as if punctuating my words. We all look up briefly at it, then I begin to speak once more.

"I am inspired by you, Jeff and Lloyd," I tell them. "I haven't always understood your relationship. I have often envied you it. But you have taught me something very special about men who love men. You have taught me that there is no way to contain that love. It spills out, big enough to encompass everyone here. Certainly you have included me in your love, and for that I am grateful. I am a different person for having known you, for having been loved by you, for having loved you."

"Here, here," someone calls out from the crowd.

"You give us hope," I continue. "You give us hope that the kind of love you have found with each other—and cultivated so beautifully—might be possible for us. Might, in fact, be possible for everyone. You have taught me so much about love and commitment. Each time I think I have the answer, you challenge me to think again. Indeed, you inspire us *all* to defy definition, to upend our expectations. You challenge us to live creatively, mindfully, and most of all, authentically. Thank you for that."

I realize I've made them both cry. I can't help but smile.

"Earnest enough for you?" I ask.

"Yeah," Jeff says, tears in his eyes. "But definitely not trite."

Everyone laughs.

Naomi is opening her arms to the crowd. "May we now take a moment to summon to our hearts those who are not here today," Naomi says. "Jeff's father and Lloyd's father."

The crowd falls silent, bowing their heads. I look over at the mothers of the groom. Mrs. Griffith is holding her chin high, her eyes staring off at the water, a solemn memory of her husband surely coming to her mind. Mrs. O'Brien, by contrast, is smiling—the first smile I've seen on her all week. Her lips move in a silent greeting to the beloved husband who now fills her vision. Jeff and Lloyd have their mothers in their sight, and no doubt their fathers in their hearts.

"And also," Naomi intones, "let us remember our wonderful friend, David Javitz, who you know is looking down on these two right now and saying, 'What the hell took you so long?'"

Laughter once again from the crowd.

Naomi looks over at J. R. "The rings?"

The boy steps forward. His small hand is trembling as he hands the box to her. She smiles, taking the box and opening it for Jeff and Lloyd. The two rings sparkle in the sunlight.

Lloyd takes the first ring and slips it onto Jeff's finger. "With this ring," he says, "I thee wed." He steps back and looks at the man he loves. "With you, Jeff, I have found home. This is the great promise of life. That we find our soulmate, that we come together and find our sense of wholeness. Thank you for making me whole. Thank you for loving me. To you, I pledge my love and my life."

Jeff takes the second ring from the box and slips it on Lloyd's finger. "With this ring," he echoes, "I thee wed." He smiles, his eyes sparkling in the sun. "When I was a little boy," he tells Lloyd, "I used to talk to you. I knew you were out there waiting for me. I didn't know your name, I wasn't sure exactly how you'd look, but I knew you were there. Thank you for making me complete. Thank you for loving me. To you, I pledge my love and my life."

They stand there their hands clasped between them.

"And now," Naomi says, raising her arms, "with the authority vested in me by the Commonwealth of Massachusetts—"

Cheers ring out.

"—and by God," Naomi continues, "I now pronounce you legally and spiritually married."

Such a simple, yet radically profound statement. I shed my own tears of joy for my friends.

I'm the first one they embrace after their own kiss. "I love you, buddy," Jeff says.

"And I love you," I tell this man who changed my life.

"You are a great gift," Lloyd says as he wraps his arms around me. "I love you with all my soul."

And finally, I realize, that's exactly what I've always wanted from him.

Then it's J. R. they embrace.

"Thank you for being our ring bearer," Jeff says emotionally, holding the boy close to him.

"Uncle Jeff," J. R. says, fighting tears. "I promise I'll try to be gay, too."

We all look down at the boy. "*What?*" Jeff asks. "J. R., what do you mean you'll try to be gay?"

His little face is torn with anguish. "I know you want me to be happy like this, too," he says. "I know you want me to get married to a man someday, to be gay like everybody else, and I promise I'll try."

Suddenly I understand the boy's dilemma all these weeks. He sees all of us celebrating who we are, talking about the joys and opportunities of being gay—and he's felt left out, especially with his budding feelings for little Lynette Silva. I stoop down alongside Jeff and Lloyd to look into J. R.'s eyes.

"Buddy," Jeff is saying, "I don't want you to be gay if that's not what you are."

Lloyd puts his hand on the side of J. R.'s face. "And neither do I. We just want you to be you, the *real* you."

"But it's like Uncle Henry said," J. R. replies. "Men who love men are special."

I smile. "That we are, buddy. But not all men who love men are gay."

Jeff cups the boy's chin in his hand. "We love you, and you love us," he tells his nephew. "That's all that matters. Like Henry said, there's no way to contain that. Everybody gets some. Gay, straight, man, woman. Hey, we love your mom, don't we? And she's not gay. And she's not a man."

"Well, honorary on both counts," Ann Marie says, hovering above us, privy to this whole little conversation.

"Is that what you've been struggling with, J. R.?" Jeff asks. "Were you worried I'd love you less if you didn't turn out to be gay?"

The boy shrugs, then nods, falling into his uncle's arms.

"Dude." Jeff holds the boy close. "If you like babes, that is *so* okay with me."

"He already has a babe," I say.

"Oh, yeah?" Jeff asks. J. R. nods. "What's her name?"

"Lynette," the boy says. "And she's hot."

"You go call her," Lloyd says. "See if her parents will let her come to the reception."

"Really?" J. R. asks, his eyes lighting up.

"Really," Lloyd replies.

"Excellent!" J. R. rushes off, pulling his cell phone from his pocket.

Ann Marie makes a face. "I think nine years old is a little young to have a *babe*," she says.

"He's my nephew," Jeff says, standing up. "He can't help his sexual magnetism."

"Hey, Mr. Magnetism," I say. "I noticed the creak in your joints as you stood up. Need a hand back to the car?"

Jeff looks from me over to Lloyd. "Can you divorce a best man?"

Lloyd shakes his head. "I think we're stuck with him."

"Let's go," I say, grinning. With one arm around Jeff and one arm around Lloyd, I walk with them back to the car.

23

MARTIN'S PLACE

"Well," he says, "I didn't expect to see you tonight, what with the wedding and all."

"Do you mind?" I ask.

"Come on in," Martin says.

Back at the guesthouse, Jeff and Lloyd's reception is winding down. Most of the guests have left, the cake has been eaten, and last I saw, Jeff was falling asleep on the couch, his head in Lloyd's lap. I decided to go for a walk, to watch the sun set over the trees. This is why I live here after all. The beauty exists to be savored at any moment.

Somehow, I ended up at Martin's apartment. Walking inside, I see he was right about the view. An amazing perspective of Province-town harbor greets me from his living room. Enough afterglow remains to dapple the water with light, as a couple of boats rock lazily nearby, secured by their anchors. From Long Point, the light-house sounds its low, resonant horn every few minutes. A more peaceful setting I couldn't imagine.

But suddenly the tranquility is shattered by the frantic yapping of a dog.

"Peggy!" Martin claps his hands. "No need to go spastic. This is Henry."

I look down at my feet. Martin has gotten a pug.

"When did you—?" I stoop down to nuzzle the dog's face. "Oh, man, she's adorable!"

Martin stands over us beaming. "I got her a couple of days ago. As much as I like being on my own, a little company is always nice."

I'm close to tears as I let Peggy lick my hand. "I had a pug once," I tell Martin.

"Really? What happened?"

I sigh, looking into the dog's apoplectic eyes. "I had a boyfriend who made me give her away." I stand. "It was another life. I can't imagine that ever happening again."

"Good man, Henry." Martin smiles over at me. "Can I get you something to drink?"

"Oh, I've had plenty of champagne, thanks."

"Coffee then?"

I nod. "That would be lovely."

He sets about brewing a pot. "So to what do I owe this unannounced visit? Had enough of the wedding festivities?"

"It's been a wonderful, beautiful day," I tell him, gazing out once again over the water. The little furball named Peggy trots into the living room, following me. "I just decided I needed to take a walk."

I look down at myself. My tie is gone, but I'm still wearing my blue suit with the red rose Lloyd pinned on the lapel.

"Needed some time to yourself, eh?" Martin asks.

"I suppose I did. Just some quiet time to reflect." I turn around and give him a smile. "And then when I found myself passing your place, I thought . . . why not?"

"Why not indeed?" Martin returns my smile. I see he has dimples in his cheeks, something I'd never noticed before. "Sit down, Henry," he tells me. "Make yourself comfortable. The coffee will be ready in a minute."

I take a seat on his sofa. Peggy jumps up with me, eager for more face time. I oblige, rubbing noses. She immediately settles down into my lap, almost like a cat.

The sofa squeaks and smells a bit musty. My hunch is that the apartment came furnished, though the many boxes stacked around the place bearing Pittsburgh postmarks suggest Martin is making it his own. Box by box, he's begun putting his books and CDs on the shelves, and on his walls he's hung photographs of himself with friends.

I turn my eyes to watch Martin as he goes about making the coffee. Unshaven, he's the very image of a carpenter, of a man who makes his living with his hands. His shoulders are strong and wide, his forearms thick and hairy. His jeans are scuffed, with a hole in one knee, encasing strong thighs.

He seems to feel me looking at him, and lifts his eyes to meet mine. "The wedding was nice, you say?"

I smile. "It couldn't have been better. It was far more affirming than I could possibly have ever imagined. I just feel so happy—so really happy—for my friends."

Martin looks at me through slightly hooded eyes. "No envy at all? No wistful wishing that you were in their place?"

I consider the question. "No envy," I tell him. "But yes, maybe some wistfulness."

"Wistfulness isn't bad," Martin says. "It's actually quite a lovely emotion." He smiles at me. "And only lovely people are ever wistful."

I laugh. "It helps that I've concluded I'm not yet ready for a relationship. I've realized I've got to devote more time to Henry before I can consider someone else in my life." I look out at the harbor again, the light fading rapidly. "It's quite the liberating idea. Takes the pressure off. Gets rid of the longing."

Martin nods. Behind us I can smell the coffee brewing. "I know the feeling," he tells me as he opens a cabinet looking for cups. "Being here by myself has been a wonderful, eye-opening experience. I'd forgotten things that I used to like to do, like cook for myself."

"I thought you said you couldn't cook," I say over my shoulder.

He laughs. "That's what I always thought. But I'd forgotten I knew some of the basics—like how to grill a hamburger or flip an omelette."

He returns with two mugs of steaming coffee. He's remembered I take mine black; there's no sugar or cream. I notice his hands as he sets the coffee down in front of me. They're large, with rough skin and several scars.

"Thank you," I say.

We let the coffee cool for a moment before drinking. Martin sits opposite me in a chair. "Peggy likes you," he observes.

I smile. "If I didn't know better, I'd swear she was Clara." I stroke her fur. The dog makes a rumble of contentment.

The light is nearly gone now outside the window, but the moon is making itself apparent, a tiny fingernail of white sliced into the violet sky. I decide to give Martin my news.

"So," I tell him, "you know how the wedding couple traditionally gives their best man a gift?"

Martin nods. "What did you get? Jewelry? A pewter cup?"

"No." I take in a long breath. "They gave me a partnership in Nirvana."

"No way! Wow!"

I smile wanly. "I never thought I'd want to be a partner in the guesthouse. But they made the offer. I'm stunned."

"Will you accept?"

"I think I will," I say, taking a sip of the coffee. "I'll finally own the place where I live. My apartment will really be mine."

"It's a sign of their high esteem for you," Martin says.

I laugh. "Yes, absolutely, but it isn't completely altruistic on their parts. Lloyd and Jeff have decided they want to spend their winters in Palm Springs. They're buying a house there."

"Oh, I see." Martin sits back in his chair, his hands behind his head. "So that means you'll have to run the guesthouse on your own during the off-season."

I nod. "Which means I need to make a real commitment to being here."

"I thought you already had," Martin says, sitting forward now and snapping on a lamp as the darkness creeps into the room. "You speak of this place with such love."

I smile. "True. But every once in a while I've imagined leaving . . . going some place where the pool of available men is deeper and wider." I take another sip of my coffee. Damn, Martin makes a good cup. "But I guess that's not on the forefront of my agenda anymore."

"Well," Martin says, "I'm glad you'll be sticking around."

"I am, too." I look over at him. "It will be difficult without Jeff and Lloyd here for the winter. They're my family. But I think maybe it's time I learned to spend a few months of the year without them."

"You mean, learn to stand on your own?"

I nod. "And to expand my family to new people." I look over at Martin and we exchange a small smile.

"Expanding one's family is always a good thing," Martin says. "It keeps the lifeblood alive. It's why I moved here myself."

I think about the idea of expanding my family, of making room for new friends and new love. Is that why all these new people have come into my life?

We sit silently for a few minutes. I look over at Martin as I continue to stroke Peggy the Pug.

"So you know about Gale," Martin says finally.

I'm surprised by his comment. It's not where I was expecting the conversation to go.

Martin observes my surprise and smiles. "He told me about himself very soon after we met. It's hard to work beside someone all day and not learn some things about them." He raises his eyebrows. "He also told me about the conversation he had with you."

I look at him over the rim of my coffee cup. "He trusted you far more quickly than he did me."

Martin smiles again. "He was looking at you very differently than he was me, Henry. For you, he had romantic feelings. I, on the other hand, was father confessor." He sighs. "Of course, that's how most of the boys see me here in Provincetown."

"You don't like the role?" I ask.

"Oh, I don't mind. But sometimes . . . well, it would be nice occasionally if someone actually thought of me in a different sort of way."

I look over at him. In the amber light cast from the lamp, Martin looks softer, not so much the tough-skinned craftsman or the wise older man with all the answers. He looks like a very young man, in fact. How unfair I had been in characterizing him as the older gay uncle I'd always wanted. How limiting are such roles, the narrow viewpoints we persist in seeing each other and ourselves.

"And yet," I say, trying to understand, "I thought you weren't looking for a relationship."

"Not looking is one thing." Martin smiles. "But it would be nice to think the possibility still existed, someday, out there."

I don't say anything. I return my gaze to the window, where the moonlight is now upon the water. In the distance the lighthouse keeps up its steady wail.

"Well," I finally offer, "Gale isn't ready for a relationship. You were right about that. I think when we both owned up to that fact about ourselves, we saw the way clear to being friends."

Martin smiles. "More of that new family you talk about."

"Hopefully."

"But I'll tell you one thing, Henry," Martin says. "Gale might have a ways to go before being ready for a relationship, but it seems to me you're getting closer all the time."

"Do you think so?" I ask, looking intently over at him.

"I do."

We smile at each other. Peggy seems to detect some energy in the room. She raises her head, gives a little yip, and jumps off my lap, scampering over to Martin.

"Who's my good girl?" he asks, rubbing noses with her as she jumps onto his lap.

I stand, walking around the room, examining Martin's things. You can learn so much about someone just from looking at his books or his music.

"Hey." I'm running my finger along Martin's CDs, stacked neatly on a shelf. "Quite an eclectic collection."

"Yeah, I love all kinds of music."

"Everything from disco to rock to—" My finger stops on one particular CD. I smile. "Alice in Chains."

"The best grunge band, I think, *ever*," he tells me.

I look over at him. But before I can say anything else—think anything else—one of the photographs on the wall behind him catches my eye. I approach. It's Martin, several years younger, but still recognizably him. Handsome, solid, with those amazing blue eyes. He's posing with another man on the edge of some rocks.

Martin has come up behind me. "That's Paul and me at the Grand Canyon," he says.

"But the inscription says . . ." I look closer. "Paul and *Jack*."

Martin smiles. "Yeah. That's what my really good friends call me. You know, from my last name, Jackman."

I move my eyes from the picture to his face.

"Your good friends call you . . . *Jack?*"

"Yes." He smiles again. "Would you like to call me that, too, Henry?"

I look up into his eyes.

"Yes," I tell him. "I'd like to call you Jack."